WHEN
WE WERE
BRAVE

BOOKS BY SUZANNE KELMAN

A View Across the Rooftops

WHEN WE WERE BRAVE

SUZANNE KELMAN

bookouture

Published by Bookouture in 2020

An imprint of Storyfire Ltd.
Carmelite House
50 Victoria Embankment
London EC4Y 0DZ

www.bookouture.com

ISBN: 978-1-83888-252-5
eBook ISBN: 978-1-83888-251-8

Dedicated to all eighty spies who lost their lives in the Prosper Network, and the many other men and women of the Resistance, some we shall never know.
Thank you for your courage, daring and willingness to go without hesitation to fight for what you believed in.
You are the best of all of us and undoubtedly embody the words of the poem by Cecil Spring-Rice:

The love that never falters, the love that pays the price,
The love that makes undaunted the final sacrifice.

May we endeavour to truly appreciate the remarkable gift of freedom you provided for us.

Prologue

France, June 1945

Vivi rushed through the streets of Paris, sweat trickling down behind her ears and gathering under the collar of her German uniform. At every turn, she was aware of heightened energy. On what seemed like every corner, the people of Paris were whispering in huddled groups. She hoped it was the news she and Marcus had been waiting to hear, but feared the enemy might still gain the upper hand.

Vivi barely had time to check over her shoulder as she raced down the darkened alley, her footsteps beating out an echoed rhythm that fought against a cracked water pipe that gushed out a beat of its own. Arriving at the door of the address she had memorised, Vivi stopped to catch her breath and wipe at the beads of perspiration that had collected under her cap. Gulping back hot sticky air that burned her lungs, she gathered herself, trying to clear her mind and remember everything she had been taught; it felt like an eternity since her training.

Her racing heart began to return to normal as Vivi momentarily considered her life and the man she loved. She had to do this. For him and for the cause they both believed in. Tears brimmed in her eyes as Vivi remembered the night before when they'd lain in one another's arms, a full moon streaming through the window, casting its shadow across their bed, when she'd thought, just for that moment, even amidst all the madness, that somehow her life was perfect.

But in the last twelve hours, all of that had been put in jeopardy. Now Vivi had to focus on what was right. But would she be strong enough to do what she had to do? The betrayal was so hard, but the one thing that kept her alive every day was the knowledge that she was doing all this for love, the noblest reason of all.

So there was one last thing she had to do. One thing that could make the difference between who won this war, and who lost.

Summoning up the courage she needed, Vivi knocked on the door.

Chapter 1

Sophie Hamilton paced the steps of the Imperial War Museum and glared at her phone again. Already twenty minutes late, Matt hadn't even bothered to return her texts. Acknowledging the time, she sighed deeply and, unable to wait any longer, knew she would have to go in without him.

Rushing through the glass doors because she was late, Sophie's feet echoed across the white marble foyer and she cursed herself for wearing stilettos, particularly this new pair that were chafing the back of her heels. Racing towards the lift, she barely had time to notice the splendid exhibition of military history all around her, only briefly glancing at the V2 rocket that dominated the hallway and the Spitfire, with its polished silver propeller glinting under its spotlight as it dangled from the windowed ceiling above her head. She hustled because she knew Jonathan, her supervisor, was probably having a panic attack about now and she pictured him anxiously pacing the exhibition halls upstairs as he waited for her.

Arriving at the lift, Sophie wedged her hand in the door just in time to stop it closing. The only other occupant, a young man staring at his phone, pretended not to see her as she panted inside.

Getting the first glance at herself as the lift door slid into place, Sophie felt even more frustration building towards her boyfriend as she tried desperately to comb her hand through the blonde bobbed hairstyle she'd had cut and blow-dried for the occasion. But even in the hazy reflection of the door she could see that it was now lank and stringy because she'd spent nearly twenty minutes outside in the drizzle.

Drawing in a deep breath, Sophie attempted to calm herself. She wasn't going to let Matt spoil this for her. She'd been looking forward to it all week.

The lift door opened on the next floor and a mother and child entered. The scrubbed, pink-cheeked girl, with red-ribboned pigtails that bounced with a life of their own, squeezed her mother's hand with excited anticipation. Sophie caught her breath and quickly averted her gaze to the floor, the sight of this happy family picture still too raw and painful for her to even observe.

As the lift climbed again, Sophie dragged her thoughts back from the heartache she'd been through in the last year and instead focused on how relieved she'd been to get this job, how she'd needed it for her sanity.

Taking six months off from the intensity of her legal career had been her grandmother's idea.

'You just need a break, Sophie. Give yourself the chance to catch your breath,' she'd stated, stroking her granddaughter's hair.

Gran, of course, had been right. Being a high-flying corporate solicitor had definitely had its perks, but one of them hadn't been having time to grieve her personal loss. And when she had been found by her secretary sobbing at her desk one morning four months after losing Emily and her mother, it had been a relief to let go and accept that she couldn't just go on as normal.

At first, she had told herself it would just be a sabbatical, but as time had gone on it had been harder and harder to even contemplate going back to that hectic pace of life. For now, she was working part-time for a small charity that specialised in archiving historical materials. Sophie had always loved visiting old houses. Her job was to categorise all the treasures that went back centuries, some from houses that the charity had been working in for years. There were no time pressures and no client counting on her to be at her best.

And even though she didn't know what the future held, this job was perfect for her, right now.

The lift door slid open and, carefully, without looking in her direction, Sophie sidestepped the young girl even as the presence of her once again tugged at her heartstrings. Swallowing down her pain Sophie moved at a clip towards the event.

The museum had created an atmospheric experience to support the exhibition and as she raced toward it the sounds of London during the Blitz stretched out down the hallway to greet her. The high-pitched screech of air-raid sirens followed by the ominous rolling thunder of bombs dropping on London boomed from the wall speakers. Interspersed with the sinister sounds of war were the best of Winston Churchill's speeches and an uplifting recording of Vera Lynn singing 'We'll Meet Again', supplied by the BBC Home Service. With this evocative backdrop, plus the dim lighting and retro signage, Sophie felt as if she was stepping straight back into the 1940s.

As her eyes adjusted, she marvelled that this new exhibition had been possible at all and was excited to finally see the photos that the museum had asked Jonathan to provide as part of it, and which he had gushed about, blown up to life size.

All at once her boss was in front of her.

'There you are, Sophie,' declared Jonathan, unable to hide the desperation in his tone as he strode towards her. 'I've been looking for you everywhere.' He glanced at his wristwatch.

'I'm so sorry. Matt said he'd meet me here, and I was waiting for him.'

He shook his head, barely acknowledging what she was saying, the worry furrowing his brow. 'We really need to get going,' he continued, anxiously. 'I am expecting the mayor at any moment. Do you have my notes?'

'I sent them to you yesterday,' responded Sophie.

Her boss was often scatty and was endlessly losing things, and he stared at her with a look of abject panic.

She had backed up the notes on her phone just in case. 'I have a copy.'

Jonathan teased out the breath he was holding. 'Thank goodness,' he spluttered. Glancing over her shoulder, he noticed the arrival of the mayor's party and rushed off to greet them.

The event started on time and Jonathan delivered his speech perfectly, reading it from Sophie's phone. In it he gave the crowd a flavour of London during the 1940s, and described to them how the photos had been found when the charity had been moving an ancient desk to be sold at Sotheby's. The negatives of the photographs now being displayed in the museum had been in an envelope with the date March 1944 scribbled on the front. They had somehow slid down behind a drawer and wedged themselves at the back of the desk.

Sophie listened to Jonathan and wondered what it would have been like to be alive during that time and how brave people had to have been. Sophie didn't feel brave. She didn't think she would have been able to survive through all that trauma.

What a miracle it had been that the negatives had not only been found but had been in such good condition after so many decades. Once it was obvious the photos could be saved, Sophie's job had been to research the history of them. Relying on her legal background of piecing together evidence, she had established that during wartime, the photographer Karen Johnson had been a family friend of the lord of Hawthorne Manor, the latest home Jonathan and Sophie had been working on. In the 1940s, a London newspaper had commissioned Karen to take pictures of the ever-changing city and to capture the tenacious spirit of the people of the capital, determined to rebuild at any cost, especially from the damage done from the relentless bombing campaign of the Blitz in 1940–41, when London had been bombed for fifty-six out of fifty-seven days. Although many photos of the devastation of London had been taken during the war, Sophie knew these would be something special – captured as they were through the lens of one of the most prominent photographers of that period.

Karen Johnson's untimely death in March 1944 caused Sophie to speculate that she had been staying at the manor with her friends at the time and the envelope had been with her belongings, then somehow, in the grief of her death, been misplaced.

After Jonathan's flawless speech, much to Sophie's relief, she then accompanied the group of World War Two enthusiasts as they toured the gallery, listening to him talk about the significance of each piece and how the reconstruction of London had been so intensive.

Congratulating their charity on the work that had not only uncovered the photographs, but also the treasure trove of World War Two artefacts on display, the mayor left just as Jonathan's partner, Grant, arrived, and Sophie knew he would be able to take over babysitting her boss so she could grab a glass of champagne and relax a little.

Deciding to excuse herself from the group, just as Grant and Jonathan started enthusing about their new puppy, Sophie started to look around the gallery on her own. As she studied each photo in more detail, her thoughts returned to her relationship with Matt. It wasn't just that he was busy, or even that it felt like they'd hardly seen each other in the last few months. Something was nagging at her, something she couldn't quite put her finger on. Something that was more than just their mutual grief.

Sophie sipped her champagne as she scanned the photograph of the bombing of the Woolworth Building in 1942 and its reconstruction. It had been taken by Karen earlier than the rest of the collection, but borrowed to add more content. Sophie tried to imagine what it'd be like to be part of such a horror, and to come back to work the next day and find you no longer had a job or a place of work. She drifted to the next print. A group of women were bent over wearing headscarves and trousers, smiling with that

British 'can do' attitude as they removed rubble from what would've been somebody's home. The next picture was of the Baker Street bombing. It revealed the randomness of the bombing patterns. In the photo, two buildings stand, almost unscathed, either side of an empty space where another has been completely demolished. On the pile of rubble sat a young boy who was the focus of the photograph. He was dirty-faced, in a grey school uniform and sweater, holding a tattered Union Jack.

As Sophie studied the image, something caught her eye, someone a little out of focus and off to the side she hadn't noticed the first time she'd seen the photograph, when it was so much smaller. She drew closer and realised that what had caught her attention for a second had been a thought that a woman she could see in the photo was her mother. All at once, the weight of grief slammed into her again, starting in the pit of her stomach, searing up her body until it culminated in her throat, coming out as a strangled gasp.

Sophie hated how her loss and pain did this to her every time. She knew she would feel gutted, utterly devastated, after the tragedy, but she hadn't been prepared for the waves of sorrow that could appear for months afterwards and literally threaten to take her legs from under her. As Sophie stared at the picture, she shook the thought from her mind, recognising how ridiculous it had been. The woman in this picture couldn't possibly be her mother. This photograph had been taken during the war, more than a decade before her mother was even born. It was just one of those odd phenomena that happen when someone dies and in your desperation to claw them back from death you project them everywhere. Someone with the same haircut across the room makes your heart skip a beat, or a person crossing the street with the same stride stops you in your tracks and, for one tiny moment, your heart leaps with the connection. For that one sliver of a second you think there's been a mistake and that the person you miss more than life itself is still alive. Then the cruel pain and weight of your mistake brings back the anguish in such a staggering way it threatens to engulf you and it is as if it all just happened yesterday.

Catching her breath, Sophie drew closer to the picture. It wasn't just projection. It was uncanny. The woman's stance, height and trim figure, with the elegant swan neck, was so familiar to her. Her head was turned to the side so that Sophie couldn't see her face, just her head in profile, but this person could, very easily, be a member of her family.

Then something else struck her. The woman was wearing a tight A-line skirt and a jumper that Sophie could see under her unbuttoned coat, and on the lapel of the jacket was a piece of jewellery that also felt familiar to her. It looked a lot like her family crest. Sophie had always thought the brooch an ugly thing, with a stag's head and gangly antlers. But it was very distinguishable and this was a very similar, if not the same, piece she had seen many times on her great-grandmother's lapel in photographs.

Sophie looked at the woman again, the way her chin was cocked to one side, just as her mother would do when she would ask a question. Was it possible it could be her great-aunt Caroline? Sophie took stock of the Hamilton females. On her grandfather's side, there had been three children alive during the war. Her great-uncle Tom, her great-aunt Caroline and her grandfather, John. The boys had been young but Auntie Caroline had been in her mid-twenties during the war, so this could be her. Sophie's grandmother and John's wife, Bessy, would know for sure. Maybe she should call her and ask. How excited would she be to know there was a photograph of her late sister-in-law in the museum?

All at once, someone grabbed Sophie from behind and she jumped, so lost in her thoughts. She spun around, and Matt was in front of her, grinning. 'You wouldn't believe how many exhibitions I've been in,' he spluttered, out of breath. 'So sorry I'm late, Soph. Did I miss anything exciting? Did Jonathan make it through the speech without you holding his hand?'

He was being light and playful, which was his way of avoiding the fact that he was over an hour late. Sophie didn't respond to his lively banter, hoping her coolness would alert him to the fact she was angry.

He noticed the chill straight away. 'I'm sorry, Soph, seriously I am,' he continued. 'Don't be angry with me. You wouldn't believe how busy it's been at work. The US exchange dropped like a stone this afternoon, and everyone in the office was panicking. You know how we are affected with Brexit and all these international concerns.'

'I imagine that for some reason the problems with the stock market meant that somehow your fingers were unable to text me, then?' The hurt was evident behind her tone, but her response colder than she'd wanted to sound.

He held up his phone. 'Battery's dead,' he stated, sounding sheepish. 'I meant to charge it before I left the house this morning and I completely forgot. It ran out about three hours ago and I haven't got my charger with me, so I've been winging it, which is why I couldn't find you in here. Though, I have to tell you, there's a wonderful exhibition about Anne Frank down the hall that I think you'd love.'

She shook her head. This pattern was becoming familiar to her. When they had first got together, he'd always been so dependable, almost too dependable, wanting to see her as much as possible; now he was always late, with some excuse for why he couldn't make it on time. Sophie was in her late thirties and Matt hadn't been her first relationship, but she had been very focused on her career up until they'd met, and their shared desire for success had made it a very companionable one. But everything had changed for them when she had unexpectedly become pregnant with Emily. She had been surprised but overjoyed, Matt had been shocked at first. But his precious daughter had won him over from the very moment he had held her in his arms and her tiny hand had hooked itself around his little finger.

She looked over at Matt, trying to read him as he continued to accompany her around the gallery, asking her questions about the pictures, but seeming distracted.

Before she left the museum, Sophie returned to the photo that had intrigued her so much and took a quick picture of the woman in it. She wondered if her grandmother would recognise her.

Making her way out into the damp streets that were now aglow with blue twilight, she walked beside Matt in silence.

'Would you like to get some dinner?' she asked, just to make conversation.

He grimaced. 'You know, normally I would, Soph. I really do need to get back to work.'

'In the evening? Aren't most of the markets closed now?'

'Yeah, they are, but I do need to check in on a few things. I ran out and left them all in the middle of something. Let's have a rain check on that.'

He kissed her on the cheek as he hailed a taxi. Sophie sighed. Maybe her gran would be up for a visit after all. She called her and heard the familiar voice of the sweetest woman in the world.

'Hey, Gran, it's me. I was wondering if you were up for a visit?'

Bessy sounded delighted at the idea, and Sophie hung up and made her way to the Tube. It was about thirty minutes from the Imperial War Museum to Hackney, where her gran lived, which gave her plenty of time to contemplate how remarkable this photo was as she stared at it on her phone. Once again, Sophie felt the familiar waves of nostalgia and grief wash over her. If it hadn't been the 1940s it could be a photo of her mother, Alice, or maybe even a future picture of her daughter, if Emily'd had the chance to live longer.

Chapter 2

Arriving at Bessy's comfortable apartment in Hackney, Sophie was once again amazed to see how the area had evolved over the last few years. Once a little run-down and known for its violence and crime, the East End was undoubtedly making its way up in the world.

'Hello, love.' Her gran's beaming face greeted her at the door, and the smell of something wonderful cooking embraced her as she stepped inside. Her grandmother hugged her as tightly as she always did until Sophie had to remind her she couldn't breathe. Bessy chuckled. 'It's because you're so skinny. If you weren't so thin, you'd be capable of being hugged.' She shuffled down the hall as she continued to chat to Sophie over her shoulder. 'No man wants a woman too skinny.'

'I already have a boyfriend, Gran. Matt, remember?' Sophie responded defensively.

Her gran eyed her questioningly as she entered the kitchen. 'Isn't it about time you two settled down?'

This was a conversation she frequently had with her grandmother in one form or another. A woman who'd been married just after her eighteenth birthday found it hard to understand why her granddaughter was still unwed, especially considering Sophie and Matt had had a child together.

Sophie hastily changed the subject. 'Something smells amazing.'

Gran nodded, moving to the stove and retrieving her oven gloves. 'I've got a bit of dinner warming for you, in case you were hungry.'

'Oh, I'm fine, Gran, you shouldn't have gone to any trouble.' Sophie was about to continue to protest when the older woman put her hand in the air, signifying the conversation was over and Sophie would be eating a plate of shepherd's pie, the source of the delectable aroma that permeated the whole kitchen, whether she liked it or not.

Sophie made her way to the table and into one of her gran's 1970s' chrome and yellow faux-leather dining chairs, which featured in so many great memories from growing up. It felt like her heart sighed with a feeling of being home. Sophie had often visited the estate in Cornwall that her extended family still owned. But, much to the chagrin of her grandfather's family, when he had died, her grandma had moved back to the place she grew up, and Sophie's mum, a single mother, had come back too, bringing Sophie with her.

'Hackney's my home, love,' Bessy would declare to her granddaughter. 'Cornwall's charming, and it was your grandfather's home, but this is where my friends are.'

Sophie's great-uncle Tom now lived in the manor in Cornwall, along with his family.

'It wasn't really my cup of tea,' Bessy would say when Sophie asked her about her move from the West Country.

Bessy placed in front of Sophie a plate of steaming creamy mashed potato, browned under the grill, that covered minced lamb with onions and vegetables, then bustled off to her cooker to put the kettle on.

'Always good to see you, Sophie,' her gran continued in a singsong way.

Pudding, Gran's rather large tabby cat, hopped up onto Sophie's lap and kneaded her thigh as Sophie considered Gran's words. She wished she came to see her more often. She loved it. But the sadness of the last year had crippled her; it had taken all of her focus just to dress and get to work in the morning.

'Well, obviously I wanted to see you. But I also have a mystery I'm hoping you can help me solve,' Sophie stated, unable to resist heaping a large forkful of the delicious shepherd's pie into her mouth, suddenly feeling ravenous.

'A mystery?' Gran said, raising her eyebrows under her permed blonde hair.

'I have a photograph I need to show you.'

Her grandmother retrieved her reading glasses and settled on a chair at the table next to Sophie to look at her phone. She peered at it. 'How am I supposed to be able to see that?' she asked. 'It's tiny.'

Sophie laughed and pinched and stretched the image on the screen to enlarge the picture for her grandmother to see.

'Well, that's fancy,' Bessy chuckled, as if Sophie had just performed magic. She stared at the photograph in her granddaughter's hand as Sophie explained the museum exhibition.

'The photographer took this shot in Baker Street during World War Two. But look at this woman coming out of the building next door to the rubble, Gran.'

Bessy drew her chair in, and lifted the camera even closer to her eyes. 'Why, that's uncanny,' she mumbled. 'It looks like one of the Hamiltons, doesn't it?'

'I know, I thought the same,' Sophie responded. 'And look at the brooch.'

Her grandmother stared again at the phone. 'Well, blow me down. If that isn't that awful ugly thing that's the Hamilton coat of arms.' She shook her head. 'I detested that brooch. Your grandfather tried to give it to me. I respectfully refused. This is a mystery though, you're right. Your great-grandfather had business interests in London, but the whole family was down in Cornwall, particularly during the bombings. Nobody wanted to be in London. All of them evacuated down there. What year was this taken, love?'

'It was a picture of the bomb destruction taken in early forty-four.'

'Oh, well, that narrows it down. It can't have been your great-aunt Caroline. She moved to Canada in 1943, and I always remember because John says she left just before his seventh birthday. That means—' She stopped and sucked in a breath. 'It can only be one person...' Her voice petered out to a whisper.

Sophie waited, but there was a long pause where her gran appeared thoughtful. Then she stood up abruptly, responding to the whistling kettle, saying offhand, 'Let's see about that cup of tea, then.'

'Gran?'

'I think you should leave things in the past, love. I mean, this looks a little like one of the Hamiltons and it could be similar jewellery, but I don't think it's anything more.'

Bessy poured hot water into the teapot and brought it back to the table, then moved to get her biscuit barrel, placing chocolate biscuits on a plate and putting them in front of Sophie.

'Tuck in, love. We won't get any meat on those hips unless you eat something.'

'Gran, why are you avoiding the conversation? Who is this?'

Her grandmother took off her glasses, rubbed her eyes, and blew out a long, slow breath. Then, after a long pause, continued in a serious tone, staring at a spot on the table. 'It's a family story nobody ever talked about, dear. If it's not your great-aunt Caroline, it could only be one other person, Villainous Vivienne.'

'Villainous Vivienne?' Sophie echoed, her eyes growing wide, a smile creeping across her face. 'She sounds like a criminal in a 1930s' detective novel. Who the heck is Villainous Vivienne?'

'That was the nickname the locals gave her, love. She was your grandfather's other sister.'

'Grandad had another sister as well as Caroline? Nobody has ever even mentioned another sister.'

'We all tried to forget the stories about Vivienne. It was an extremely painful time, that should have been left behind in the past. No one wanted to talk about it.'

Savouring the tea that her grandma had poured for her, she said, 'You're going to have to finish the story, Gran. Why was she villainous?'

'It was harrowing in those years after the war,' continued Bessy, staring out of the window as though she were lost in some distant memory. 'Your grandad talked about it a bit when I met him. The whole family was scarred by what she did. I never met her and I can only tell you of what I know. I have a letter that I could look for that may help piece together more of the story, but the upshot of it is that, yes, there was another sister. She was reckless, not like the rest of them. At the beginning of the war, she ran away from home and somehow ended up out in France, though no one knew what she was doing for certain – giving away all the British secrets and sleeping with Nazis for all they knew. Your grandad told me she was always a bad 'un. Impulsive, you know, thought she could take on the world. After a few months in France she arrived back home overnight with her tail between her legs, and it was rumoured she did something terrible over there, a mistake that cost people their lives. But she wouldn't talk about it. Your grandad always believed the Nazis corrupted her during that time.'

Sophie sat back. This sounded like a movie. 'What do you mean, corrupted?'

'When she got back in 1943 she worked as a nurse on the family estate in Cornwall. As you know, it became a hospital during the war.'

Sophie nodded. She'd heard many stories about the time that the entire manor had been converted into a hospital. Her grandfather and great-uncle Tom had lived there during that time.

Bessy continued, 'Because she spoke German, Vivienne ended up taking care of a Nazi POW who came down in a plane. Very little was known about him. Not only did she fall in love with him, but she also helped him escape back to Germany to do his work for Hitler. Vivienne converted to Nazism and joined the party. It was an extremely sordid tale, and it practically killed your great-grandfather. He was heartbroken that his daughter had done such a despicable thing. And no one really understood why. She had a beautiful life, everything ahead of her. Why would she do such an abominable thing as to betray her country?

'After she left, the family suffered terribly, and after the war, they were stigmatised. It took decades for people to cease talking about it. I suppose she didn't think about that when she changed sides and ran off with a Nazi. How it would affect the family. It was a dreadful time, your grandad said. He still felt fearful about sending our children, your mum, to school. Always fearful of retaliation. But Cornwall was where the Hamilton family home was located. It's not like they could just get up and leave. When men came back from the war, and they found out stories like this, traitors were victimised, especially in a small village in a place like Cornwall. You can only imagine what that was like.'

Bessy covered her granddaughter's hand. 'Thank goodness it's all behind us now. You don't need to be raking it up, Sophie. This is not a story you want to dwell on.'

Sophie sat back in her chair and returned to sipping her tea as Bessy rose to start the washing up. She always liked to be busy when she was troubled or worried, Sophie had noticed.

'What happened to her?' Sophie asked.

'Nobody knew,' Gran whispered, wistfully, staring out of the window. 'She died in Europe with her Nazi as far as we all knew.'

'Do you have a death certificate or anything?'

Bessy pursed her lips and shook her head, placed the dishes in the drying rack and shuffled off to get a tea towel. 'I believe Tom tried, years after the war, just to put the whole thing to rest, but they couldn't find anything. They were all so ashamed, it was a terrible time.'

Sophie realised she'd seen surprisingly few pictures of the Hamilton family. 'Do you have any other photographs, Gran? Of Vivienne, I mean.'

Her grandmother thought for a second. 'I might have one. I only kept it because it was a wedding photograph of your grandfather's cousin and I didn't like to throw that away. I think I know where it is.'

Sophie followed her into her front room. Pudding jumped down and padded behind them then stretched out in front of the electric fire, flicking his tail. Bessy reached into a cabinet that was piled full of bills, pamphlets, old family records and, finally, a box of photographs. Pulling it out, she placed it on the table and combed through it until she found what she was looking for. Holding it, Sophie looked at her great-auntie for the first time, a relative she never knew she had.

As the eyes of the woman stared back at her from the black-and-white photograph, it was like looking into a mirror. The same eyes, maybe even the same shade of green as her own, elfish smile and light-coloured hair. She didn't look like a traitor, she looked like Sophie or her mother, Alice. It was hard to see anything evil in a woman who looked so like one of their own. In that moment, as she locked eyes with Vivienne for the first time, Sophie knew she wouldn't be able to let this go.

Chapter 3

As she travelled home that evening, Sophie downloaded a couple of books about the war during the time her great-aunt had been alive. The last words her grandmother had said as she'd hugged her on the way out the door had been, 'Please let sleeping dogs lie, Sophie. Don't be digging up the past. It could upset your great-uncle Tom. That was a dreadful time for them all.'

And even though she wanted to heed her grandmother's warning, something about this fascinated her. One thing she knew from her time as a lawyer was that there was always more than one way to view a story.

First, she couldn't believe that no one in her family had ever spoken about Vivienne. It was as though she'd never existed, as if the minute she'd left British soil, she'd vanished. Also, if they didn't know what had happened to her, with no information about where she had gone or even how she had died, how could they be so sure she was a traitor?

Arriving home, Sophie poured a glass of wine and periodically checked her phone for any messages. With a sinking feeling she noted Matt still hadn't texted her and she missed him. Once she had got pregnant they had tried to live together. But it was never easy. It turned out they were compatible on expensive dates and weekend breaks, but living together showed both of them how different they were. After Emily's death, Matt had wasted no time moving out. He'd said he had found it difficult to be around Emily's things, in the house where they had become a family and where her young presence had coloured their world. They had dealt with the grief so differently: he wanted to avoid it, whereas Sophie needed to be immersed in it.

Every night after Emily's death, Matt would walk into the house and head straight out into the garden gasping for air, suffocated by his sadness and the memories of the joyous baby laughter that no longer filled their rooms. They had talked about moving, but Sophie wasn't ready because for her being in the house had the opposite effect it had on Matt; sitting in the Winnie-the-Pooh-themed nursery had been her only comfort and a way of moving through her sadness, and the thought of leaving her home overwhelmed her. With their ongoing anguish it had seemed a natural progression for him to stay over at his old flat that had recently become unoccupied. He was away more and more days a week, though he had assured her it was just till he felt better and when one of them could move forward. Once he had left with his last case of clothes, Sophie had known in her heart that he would never sleep in their bed again.

But even with their ongoing pain, until the last few months he had messaged her at least three times a day, with a goodnight text before he went to bed. But the last text she had received had been from the day before. Surely he had charged his phone by now?

Sophie sighed and settled down in her tiny cosy living room with a cocoa and a stack of books. In a pinch she would read on her phone, but she'd found since she had started this new job she enjoyed the experience of physical books more, searching through pictures and descriptions of buildings, and their histories that stretched back through the years. It gave her great satisfaction to meander through the streets of London of the past through the books' pages, and Sophie loved being able to recognise a particular building and know its story. They were becoming familiar to her now, feeling like old friends, regal and dignified, guarding over the city for centuries.

Sophie gathered the books about World War Two she had recently purchased to prepare for the exhibition and opened a chapter about the buildings along Baker Street. Where the picture had been taken had no firm address, so figuring out exactly where Vivienne was standing took some time but with some delving and investigation on her computer, and with the knowledge of the buildings around it, she pulled together the pieces of the puzzle.

The young boy perched on the rubble was at the top of Baker Street, and the building next to the bomb site, with its white stone steps and Grecian pillars, was very recognisable. An online article stated the building with the pillars housed a lot of civil servants and the government had used it during the war, with one of the offices even being SOE – Special Operations Executive – an independent spy network set up by Churchill during the war to work alongside MI5 and MI6. Sophie sat back and thought about that. It was interesting. If Vivienne had been such a wild child, what business did she have in a bureaucratic building in London so far from her home in Cornwall? Especially one involved in war work. Is that what Vivienne had been doing on her visit to France? The passage didn't go into any further detail about the organisation, but it confirmed Sophie's suspicions. The woman stepping out of that building in the photograph, who could've been a reflection of herself or her mother, was a mystery to be solved.

Sophie decided to email her cousin Jean, who lived with her great-uncle Tom, with a crop of the photograph, asking if she could shed any light on the person who was in it, and also if it was possible for Sophie to come down to the manor sometime for a visit. It had been so long since she had been there and the thought of getting out of London for a break sounded good.

Jean, who was invariably up late, messaged her straight back, saying she remembered talk of a mystery sister years before, but that until Sophie's email she had completely forgotten about it, as no one mentioned her. But Jean had no idea if the woman in the photograph was the mystery sister. Though she had some hazy recollection from when she was a child, of her dad talking about a Vivienne in hushed tones with her mother, she had never been told anything about the woman in question. Her email went on to say that her dad's memory was extremely fragile now, and that Sophie might not get much help from him. *Though I am sure he would welcome a visit from his favourite grand-niece*, she had added with a smiley emoji.

Sophie closed her laptop. Her gran was being too pessimistic. And though Jean had sounded a little concerned about how Sophie's great-uncle would react, she seemed to share Sophie's interest in finding out more about Vivienne.

Making herself a cup of tea, Sophie settled down to review her work calendar. She had been pretty busy over the last few weeks, but the exhibition was now open, and there was a bank holiday coming up soon. She couldn't see why she couldn't travel down for a week or so to see her great-uncle and cousin Jean – who she really viewed more as an aunt. She would ask Jonathan in the morning. Then, against her better judgement, she flipped open her phone and typed a text to Matt.

Sophie kept it light, even though she desperately wanted to know what was really going on between them. She was finding it hard to understand how, after they had been through so much together, they appeared to have quickly drifted apart. She weighed everything she said now.

Hey there, great to see you at the gallery today. Sorry you've been so busy. I am considering going to Cornwall for a short break. If I decide to, let's try to get together when I get back. Love you.

She studied the message before she sent it and acknowledged that she hesitated. Recently, even asking to get together with him had made her feel as if she were asking too much. Sophie decided to send the message just as it was, and not second-guess herself. Pressing *send*, she watched it go and noted that it indicated that he'd read it, but he didn't respond. She felt her stomach tighten again with this further rejection. She wasn't mistaken to be feeling his distance; that just confirmed it.

Making her way to her bed, she passed Emily's room and, without turning on the light, pushed open the door and whispered into the darkness, 'Goodnight, sweet girl.' It was a ritual Sophie did every night and if she didn't put on the light and see the raw emptiness of the room and the bed, for just a moment, just one small moment, she could pretend her darling girl was still with them, curled up deep in sleep.

Climbing into her own bed, William, her intensely affectionate cat, crawled under the covers next to her from the warm bed he'd made for himself on a chair under the table. Cuddling up close to her, his loud purr comforted Sophie as she fell asleep wondering about her mysterious great-aunt Vivienne and what Bessy had told her about Vivienne going to France at the beginning of the war. Had it been on war work?

Chapter 4

Spring 1943

Vivienne Hamilton, Vivi to all her friends, played nervously with the catch of the heavy brown suitcase, inside which was hidden the standard-issue B2 wireless, and contemplated the task ahead of her assigned by the British Spy Organisation. When SOE had briefed her before leaving, they'd made everything sound like a matter of routine. However, now that she was on a fishing boat in the middle of the night after many hours of travel heading towards the Brittany coast of northern France, she suddenly felt apprehensive.

The captain of the small vessel, Mr John Thompson, whom Vivi had known since childhood, must have sensed his passenger's nervousness, because he came to check on her as she sat bundled up below deck.

'We will be there in the next hour,' he stated, looking at her with concern. Then he added as he tapped her hand in a fatherly way, 'Your mother would be proud, Vivienne, if she were still alive.'

Vivi nodded, grateful to soon be off the water, but her stomach churned with fear as she readjusted her skirt. The French clothes she had to wear felt unfamiliar to her and were undeniably of a style she would not customarily choose. Staring at herself in the mirror before she'd left home that evening had made her realise that she was really going to do this.

It had all seemed more of a lark when she'd started. A friend had dared her to do it when they had seen the advertisement in the paper, and she was always up for a little adventure. Having escaped from a finishing school that her father had wanted her to attend, Vivi had been hiding out in London with a group of friends where they had been enjoying as much alcohol as they could manage before Hitler came to town and seized it all. When one of them had seen the advertisement in the newspaper appealing for individuals who had knowledge of France, Vivi had been very interested. Her funds had been running low and unlike a prodigal daughter, knowing she wouldn't be received with open arms back home, she had found the advert enticing. Maybe it was a courier job, something entertaining, something that would offer her lots of money and a little excitement.

When she had got to the office to apply it hadn't been what she had expected – it'd felt more like it might be some dry civil-service affair. But when Vivi had told the secretary that she spoke fluent German and French, the woman's eyebrows had risen slightly above her reading glasses. Vivi had gone on to add all the places she'd travelled, which had been considerable before the war. She didn't add how many hearts she had broken, just the fact she had lived in France for a while as a travel companion for her mother. At that time her brothers were away at school and her sister Caroline helped her father run the estate, as she got ready to move to Canada with her new fiancé. Her mother, a bohemian at heart, had loved her father dearly but not the drudgery of running the estate, so had escaped frequently to enjoy the European lifestyle with her daughter before the war and before she had become ill and had succumbed to cancer the year before.

All at once, the boat Vivi was travelling in hit a considerably large wave, and an arc of cold foamy spray reached right down into the cabin, covering her shoes and soaking her stockings, reminding her she was on her way to work for the British underground in France. Because *that* had been the real reason for the notice in the newspaper. It was a recruiting campaign that vetted individuals who could be advantageous to the Allies' undercover military operations in Europe.

With not much else on her horizon and with the exciting talk of learning how to parachute and handle live ammunition, Vivi had been willing to give it a shot, if for nothing else than to have a great after-dinner story to regale her friends with on returning. But there had been no glamour when she'd got there, the basic training had been extremely demanding, with SOE – a branch of the secret service – putting her through many rigorous tests of endurance and physical training to see if she would break under pressure. It had been her sheer obstinance and stubbornness that had kept her in the game, and every time they lost another recruit who buckled under the strain, Vivi had set her sights on the prize, determined not to fail. They had put her through her paces for months, first in the south of England and later in the north of Scotland, where she'd been trained in every kind of necessary skill, from how to operate her wireless to how to perform hand-to-hand combat. But nothing could prepare her for the tremendous fear Vivi felt right now. She swallowed it down. She could do this.

As the little fishing boat bobbed towards the sunrise and the land she could now see coming into view, Mr Thompson eyed her again with concern. Vivi remembered with fondness him selling fish right out of his boat on the beach when she was a child.

'Would you like something to drink?' He offered her tea from a canteen he had above deck.

She eyed it distrustfully. 'Do you have anything stronger?' she enquired, quirking her eyebrow.

He chuckled and offered her a swig of a flask he had in a breast pocket. 'You'll do well, Vivienne,' he stated with assurance. 'You always were bold as brass. I can remember chasing you away from my boat more than once when you tried to steal my fish.'

Vivi enjoyed the memory. She'd completely forgotten about the days when her older sister Caroline would dare her to do such things.

'I got away with one once,' she reminded him, with a smirk. 'This is a little different than stealing fish,' she added, passing him back his flask.

'Ah, but there's that brave streak that's inside you, Vivi. Not everybody has it, and you'll find it when you most need it.'

Vivi smiled. His words of reassurance helped her a little, though her stomach was in knots.

As the sun came up, fingers of pink and red sunlight illuminated the rugged rolling rose-coloured granite of the coastline, the jagged stone rounded smooth by the constant buffeting of a relentless and dangerous sea. Dotted along the shoreline were stone cottages, still darkened in sleep, where a mixture of welcome and fear greeted her as Vivi contemplated her next step. She was glad to finally be back on solid ground, but what waited for her ahead?

The captain cut his motor and glided to a desolate rocky cove where, overhead, seagulls screamed and swooped, dropping mussels and oysters onto the rocks below for their breakfast. Usually, SOE preferred to parachute in their operatives, and they had trained Vivi to do that. But with the inclement weather they had been experiencing and Vivi's thorough knowledge of the coastline, her superior officer had been convinced to allow her to travel in this unorthodox way.

As they drifted to the cove the French fishing fleet always used, their boat disguised to blend in, it astounded Vivi how ordinary everything seemed – a sweet little beach, a perfect spot for a family holiday. Except for the barbed wire, of course, and the ominous swastika billowing in the breeze on top of a bluff. Not having been in France since before the war, she hadn't known what to expect with the occupation – soldiers waiting with weapons drawn, or gun turrets? But not this.

Hunched out of sight, a black figure emerged from the rocks and moved swiftly towards them. Mr Thompson threw out his rope to the sleepy-looking Frenchman, who caught it and helped guide the boat in. His eyes widened a little when he saw the beautiful woman getting to her feet from the seat she'd been squatting on for hours. She knew that her blonde hair, that she'd had coiffed into the latest Parisian bob, and her emerald green eyes drew attention. An experience she normally welcomed to help her get what she wanted. But now it was different. Her life depended on her *not* being noticed. So she lowered her head as she took his hand to allow him to help her out of the boat. He wished her good morning in French, and she answered him with a nod before moving swiftly onto the beach. She waved her thanks to the captain, who prepared his craft for the return journey.

It was chilly and her guide led her through the rocks and along a winding path, thick with sea grass that twirled itself into twisted spirals buffeted by the bracing morning wind. When she arrived in the village of Le Diben, the Frenchman – who was wearing a black skullcap and had a day's worth of growth on his face – nodded at her and pointed in the direction of what was the only sign of life, before disappearing down a side street. Nervously, Vivi clicked along the cobbled pavements as a harsh north wind swept down the street and chilled her to the bone. She was conscious of how quiet it was; just the sound of her echoing footsteps. She wondered if she looked a little odd walking through the streets so early in the morning with a suitcase and a modest bag of personal items she'd been allowed to bring.

In her mind, Vivi repeated the code words she'd been told to remember as she approached the only coffee shop there. Café Liaison seemed appropriate for what she was about to undertake.

Arriving, Vivi was disappointed to see the café was still closed. So she sat at one of the little metal tables outside with her case carrying the wireless at her feet, hoping that it wouldn't draw too much scrutiny.

As Vivi lit a cigarette and drew in the smoke to calm herself, two Nazis marched by and nodded to her. 'Fräulein.'

Vivi answered in French, as she had been taught, and nodded her head. This was the first time she'd seen someone in the enemy's uniform, and her task suddenly felt extremely real. It had seemed a little like a game while she'd been training, and now that she knew what was expected of her, she felt her heart start to pound.

Behind her, a rattling clatter made her jump as the owner of the café rolled up a metal door to open the coffee shop. Turning, she caught sight of a man who eyed her with slight apprehension as she waited there, obviously an odd sight so early in the morning. Knowing this was her contact, Vivi was surprised. She wasn't sure what she'd been expecting, but it wasn't this older, balding man with a cigarette dangling from the corner of his lips, droopy eyes and a less than clean apron, behind which hairy shoulders hinted at just a vest underneath even though it was cold.

'Mademoiselle?' he acknowledged in a sleepy drawl. Then he informed her he would have nothing for her to drink or eat for another half an hour while he set up his café. She nodded, responding to him in French that it was fine and she was enjoying the view. But honestly, she just sat staring out into the water, wishing the minutes away.

When finally he was ready for customers, Vivi went to the counter, and he watched her, a little bemused, as she looked through the glass at the pastries he had to offer.

A petite woman by his side with tight brown curls also eyed her with curiosity. Vivi pretended to be deciding on breakfast and waited until the woman went back into the kitchen. Then she leaned forward and whispered the words SOE had given her.

'I am wondering, sir,' Vivi enquired in French, 'if perhaps you have swordfish on the menu for dinner?'

The man looked taken aback and raised his eyebrows then studied her up and down before repeating, 'Swordfish? *You* want swordfish?'

That was not the response she was expecting. Nervously she wondered if she'd got the wrong place.

'I'm sorry. Maybe I made a mistake,' she blurted out. 'I was looking for a café that maybe sold that to eat.'

'No, you're in the correct place, mademoiselle. But the swordfish only comes on Tuesdays,' he stated, now replying to her with the response that she had been expecting to hear. He then added with a hint of sarcasm, 'I'm just not used to a woman desiring to eat such a delicacy. The flesh can be very tough.'

Vivi knew he was doubting her abilities and wanted to tackle him right there and then. She pictured placing him in a chokehold she had been very accomplished in to prove her salt. But instead she pinched her mouth into a smile.

The ash from the end of his cigarette dropped down his apron, and he screwed up his left eye as the smoke spiralled its way there, too. Eventually, he shrugged his shoulders, nodded his head, and shuffled into the kitchen. A young boy came out and, mounting his bicycle, pedalled off down the street.

If Jepson was correct, once she'd had this conversation, the man would alert someone who would take her to the next part of her mission. She also knew the name of the operative, an agent called the Terrier, allegedly named that in response to his ability to get in and out of challenging situations with ease.

The café owner arrived back at the counter and nodded his head.

'I am looking into your swordfish,' he informed her in a dull monotone. 'Would you like some breakfast, instead?'

She wasn't hungry. In fact, her stomach was churning, but she realised that sitting there without a drink or anything in front of her would look suspicious. So she scanned another tray of pastries that his wife had just carried out from the kitchen as she continued to stare at Vivi with wariness. The plate of croissants smelled delectable. Vivi pointed at one and ordered it along with a café au lait. Then, passing across her fake French ration card, Vivi positioned herself back at her table, keeping her wireless at her feet.

It was more than two hours, just past nine, before the Terrier eventually came to meet her. By this time the café had filled up and all around her people were making conversation as they started their day. Vivi didn't notice him straight away. It was uncanny the way he blended in until he sat down at her table. He had an energetic charm, appearing a couple of years younger than herself, with thick, dark hair, and soft brown eyes that assessed Vivi.

At first, she assumed he was someone making a nuisance of himself, and she told him in French in no uncertain terms that the chair was taken. But the Terrier ignored her, continuing to occupy the table, and pushing back the beret on his forehead, he smiled.

'You are not what I was expecting,' he said, revealing his identity to her. 'But, of course, if the seat is taken and you prefer to sit here for the rest of your life, I'm happy to go back to my bed. I'm not used to taking care of customers with your taste in seafood so early in the morning.'

This handsome Frenchman was her agent; once again she'd expected someone more professional-looking. The man who sat in front of her seemed like he'd be good for an eventful evening with a glass of beer and a game of poker, but not for serious espionage. Vivi nodded, hastily picking up her suitcase. He stopped her by lifting his hand.

'I need a cup of coffee, mademoiselle. If I am to be up so early, I need some help to stay awake.' He signalled to the café owner, who brought him what was plainly his regular drink, and he sipped it slowly as he watched Vivi with interest.

Chapter 5

After Terrier was revived by his second cup of coffee, Vivi quickly understood where he'd picked up his nickname. He took off down the road, and even with the weight of her wireless under his arm, Vivi found it hard to keep up with him. He scurried down alleys, snaking across town in a manner that made her feel dizzy, finally arriving at a dark doorway, which she guessed was his home, where two rusting bicycles stood leaning against a fence. He handed one to her.

'We have to cycle to Morlaix, which is the closest town with a train station, to get you to Paris,' he whispered, cramming her case with the radio into a basket on the front of his bike and covering it with old sacking. She did the same, buckling her small suitcase into a basket with its white paint peeling off.

'We cannot take the direct route, just in case someone is watching us,' he continued as she mounted her bike, him cycling off down the dark passageway before her.

Vivi looked over her shoulder. She realised, suddenly, that she needed to be consciously aware, as they had taught her during her training. This sleepy little town had momentarily lulled her into complacency. With relief she noted that the alley behind them was empty.

Terrier led her down a back road and out along a farm path, which was muddied, grooved and difficult to navigate due to tractor tracks and horse manure. Vivi clung onto her handlebars, trying desperately to steer her way through. Along the way they passed whitewashed cottages with stone walls and slate roofs. They were acknowledged by the odd buxom housewife, hanging out lines of dripping grey washing, who stood and stared at them, or waved and shouted a greeting to the Terrier as he passed by on his bicycle. They stopped occasionally to rest and drink a little water before continuing and soon they were on level roads. Even though the weather was brisk it was invigorating to be cycling through the beautiful French countryside. Rolling hills and tiny farmhouses with a scattering of chickens and tired-looking cattle watched them as they sailed by.

It took them nearly three hours before they were finally on the outskirts of Morlaix. Even from a distance she could see the spectacular viaduct that towered over the city, transporting the people of Brittany to the rest of France via the railway. Morlaix, though bigger than Le Diben, still was a lovely quaint French town. The main road ran through the town square, framed on either side by shops. The rows of buildings, built in the traditional French style, housed a multitude of tiny mullion windows that peered out, wide-eyed, from their ornate stone window sills.

Terrier cycled off down a side street and, after winding down another alley, stopped and dismounted his bicycle. Vivi did the same, grabbing her case of clothes as Terrier bundled her radio, still wrapped in the sacking, under his arm. He approached a dark doorway then tapped a rhythm onto the door. When the door opened, Terrier ushered Vivi quickly inside. Once the door was locked behind them, even though he was sweating and exhausted by the ride, he lapsed back into his previous charm. With great affection, he greeted the woman who had opened the door. Although Vivi and he had barely spoken en route, and without even being informed, Vivi could tell that she was his sister. The same dark eyes and thick, black hair with a similar slender build, and she stood at about the same height as her brother as he greeted her, kissing her on both cheeks, and introducing her to Vivi.

'Anne-Marie, this is the Sparrow, or Claudette,' he stated, using Vivi's undercover names.

Anne-Marie glanced at Terrier in confusion. 'At this time of day? She did not arrive in the familiar way?'

Vivi surmised they were talking about the fact they'd expected her to parachute in, the usual way SOE operatives landed.

'Our newest little songbird sailed in this morning.'

Anne-Marie showed Vivi to a guest room, where she placed down the wireless and arranged it under the bed as SOE had directed her, just in case there was a raid. She stretched: the exertion of riding three hours across mostly rutted tracks, on virtually no sleep, was starting to have an effect on her body. She could feel it in her stiff shoulders and aching calves. However, Vivi had no desire to rest, with the anticipation of what lay ahead keeping her wide awake. And after taking a minute to freshen up, she found the siblings in the kitchen.

Terrier was sprawled across a chair, smoking a cigarette and chatting with his sister when Vivi walked in.

'We were discussing the next part of your trip,' he informed her. 'When operatives parachute in during the middle of the night, it is easier. Unfortunately, you shall have the pleasure of our company for a while longer. There is only one train that runs to Paris, and that leaves early in the morning. As you came in when you did, you've already missed it.'

Vivi felt apprehensive, knowing the longer she was anywhere, the greater chance there was of being exposed. Anne-Marie must have perceived her fear and placed a hand on her arm.

'You are secure here, Sparrow. No one knows of this place.'

'We only use it occasionally,' Terrier added. 'I live in Le Diben and I hate involving my sister in my adventures.' He stamped out his cigarette, waves of smoke coiling up from his lip. 'But it is the only way. There is nowhere appropriate here for a female operative to be overnight without raising suspicion. You and I will travel together in the morning,' he added.

That surprised Vivi. She'd expected to be making the journey alone but was grateful she would have his company.

As the day wore on, they settled into easy conversation. Terrier had a great sense of humour, and Anne-Marie was the perfect foil for his jokes and stories. She playfully punched him on the arm or shook her head in mock disbelief as he regaled Vivi with funny anecdotes of their childhood.

Anne-Marie cooked them a lovely late lunch, and after two glasses of wine, Vivi had to pinch herself to remember that she was undercover on her way to Paris to be a spy. She felt as if she was abroad visiting friends. They talked and laughed about all manner of things, avoiding conversations about their work in the war or the occupation as she had been trained to do.

Terrier appeared to have nothing else to do for the day, and as late morning moved into the afternoon, Anne-Marie brought out another bottle of good French wine and a gramophone record player, on which she started to play music. Terrier pulled Vivi to her feet before she had time to react. He laughed as he drew her in firmly, pinning her hands playfully behind her back.

'I hope your training is better than this,' he joked.

A playful smile moved across Vivi's lips, as quickly twisting her wrists she moved them into a different angle, so she was able to force him to release his grip and then pin him herself, her arm around his neck, as Anne-Marie roared with laughter.

Vivi whispered into his ear, 'Would you like to see where I keep my knife? You're in the perfect position for me to slash your throat.'

Terrier thrust his free hand into the air as he too roared with laughter. She spun him around, and gently took both of his hands and started a dance with him, as Anne-Marie sang along shouting out her encouragement.

'There may be a war on,' he rasped out through stilted breath as he tried to keep up with Vivi's impressive dance moves, 'but we can still enjoy ourselves, no?' he said, quirking an eyebrow.

Vivi felt the stress leaving her body. Everything leading up to her mission had been so intense, the warnings so dire, consequences so weighted. The last thing she'd expected to be doing in France was dancing with a good-looking man.

Later, Anne-Marie served them dinner. She had food that Vivi had not seen since before the war – there were eggs, butter and coffee, and she wondered if Terrier or Anne-Marie had connections to the black market.

As they laughed and talked late into the evening, the conversation drifted to what they all wanted to do once the war was over.

'I just want to go back to having a peaceful life,' Anne-Marie mused wistfully.

'You don't enjoy all this excitement, then?' Terrier's eyes flashed as he lit another cigarette.

Anne-Marie shook her head as she started to clear the dishes to the sink. 'No, I want to be very boring after the war. I want to get married and have three children, and grow fat and be happy.'

Vivi contemplated her words. She hadn't thought much about what she would do after the war. She tended to be an impulsive person, driven by whatever was calling to her at the time.

Terrier shook his head. 'Not me. I want to go out in a blaze of glory. I would rather live a short but exciting life than die of boredom in obscurity. I want to take out one hundred German soldiers before I die. Then they will create a great monument to me, the Terrier, and they shall put it right here, in the centre of your town, Anne-Marie.'

Anne-Marie shook her head, laughing. 'You're incorrigible,' she said, tapping her brother's cheeks with the palm of her hand.

Vivi watched this interaction with a sense of awe. They obviously loved each other deeply and weren't afraid to show it. Her British upbringing had not allowed her to be so free with her feelings, but suddenly she missed her family.

After they'd managed to work their way through another bottle of wine, Vivi realised she needed to get some sleep. After all, she was on her way to Paris the next day. But this had been exactly what she'd needed. As she made her way up to her room, Terrier escorted her with a candle through the dark, as the electricity was being rationed by the Nazis.

Standing in the doorway of her bedroom, he looked down at her suggestively, his dark eyes unable to hide the fact that he obviously found her attractive.

'You will be all right here, alone?' he asked, with a curl of his lip.

Vivi looked deeply into his eyes. She liked this person, he was a rogue, but a lovable one – a modern-day pirate with a heart of gold. She took the candle from him. 'I don't think complicating anything would be a good idea right now.' She leaned in and kissed him gently on the lips. Just a friendly kiss, to say she was grateful.

He looked at her expectantly, and she drew a hand across his cheek. 'Goodnight, dear friend, sleep well.'

Chapter 6

Vivi didn't sleep well that night, instead she tossed and turned, the heaviness of the wine and rich French food affecting her dreams. The faces of her family and images of home filtered their way into her thoughts, along with so many mixed emotions of what lay ahead.

When she was woken early by Anne-Marie, Vivi could hardly lift her head from the pillow and instantly regretted the night before. When she crawled slowly downstairs, Terrier was already awake and not showing any signs of being the worse for wear from the night before. He laughed at her as she eased herself into a chair.

'You will need to become more French, if you are to live in France,' he joked with her. 'Your Britishness is showing.'

Vivi shook her head, slowly, refusing breakfast when it was offered but drinking two cups of strong black coffee.

Once Terrier had eaten they started out for the train. Anne-Marie packed them a little food and, kissing her brother, she then turned to Vivi, kissing her too, warmly on both cheeks. Then looking directly into her eyes she whispered, 'Thank you for what you are doing for France, I know we can count on you to help end this war. My country will never forget your bravery.'

Vivi's emotions swelled up again, a mixture of excitement, but also fear. It was all well and good in basic training, but now she was meeting real people in real situations, the reality of what she was taking on had started to become much more meaningful to her.

They arrived ten minutes early for the train, and Terrier changed like a skilled performer. As he shifted into playing the part of being her boyfriend, he purchased the tickets for them and, taking her arm, propelled her swiftly to the train they would take to Paris, hauling her heavy case so they could cross at speed.

The station was swarming with Nazis. Vivi tried to keep her eyes down and not meet anyone's gaze. Terrier hustled her to the platform. Boarding the train, his eyes stayed intensely engaged, surveying all of his surroundings until he closed the door on their carriage.

He'd told her they would doubtlessly be checked two or three times. At the first checkpoint, Nazis got on board to check their papers, and Terrier slipped into another role, resting his head back on the seat and drawing his beret down over his eyes, pretending to be dozing. Vivi watched him with admiration, musing he could make a living as an actor after the war if he wanted.

The door slid open abruptly.

'Your papers,' demanded a stern voice as a Nazi commander strode into the carriage.

Vivi's heart was pounding in her ears and her mouth became dry. She had to remind herself not to speak to him in German but in French. Terrier didn't move or flinch as Vivi, hand shaking, sifted through her handbag to locate the papers he required. She was so nervous that she dropped them, and as she leaned forward to pick them up, she kicked over her suitcase and it fell to the floor with a thud. Its weight betraying it had more than clothes inside.

The Nazi stopped and peered down at it, a puzzled expression on his face. Vivi froze in fear. If he picked it up, he would unquestionably feel it was heavy and may wish to investigate. He leaned towards it, but suddenly Terrier was upon it, snatching it up and passing it back to her, smirking. Then picking up her papers, he thrust them at the guard.

'My girlfriend is so clumsy. If it isn't bad enough that she packed half her house, I'm the one who has to carry it.' He leaned forward to the guard, whispering, 'I think I will find a different girlfriend. This one is hopeless.'

The German, bewildered, studied the pair. Terrier began searching for his own papers, swaying, pretending he was intoxicated.

'I'm sorry,' he slurred, thrusting his beret back on his head. 'We had a little celebration last night.' He lurched on his feet, continuing to sway, and belched. Disgusted, the guard stepped backwards.

'Your papers, monsieur?' he growled, obviously annoyed. But he had already moved on from Vivi and her suitcase.

Terrier found his papers and handed them over, continuing his story just for good measure. 'At our party last night,' he said, brushing Vivi's face as he proceeded to participate in his performance, 'my woman, she had too much to drink.' Vivi tried not to reveal her surprise as he tapped her cheek. 'It has made her a little worse for wear this morning, you know,' he declared, taking hold of Vivi's hand, patting it between both of his.

She tried to smile meekly, realising how inept she was at this. The German officer nodded in response and, thrusting back their papers, exited the carriage, slamming the door. And he was gone.

The Terrier sat down in the seat and grinned broadly. Vivi was so overcome she worried she might actually *be* sick.

'You look so pale,' he remarked. 'Which, I suppose, for someone who also has a hangover is more plausible.'

'Is that why you suggested it?' she enquired in a whisper.

'You looked frightened to death. It concerned me he would suspect something. This way he would not demand any further questions.'

She nodded, grateful for his insight. Even though other guards checked them twice more before Paris, it went uneventfully. After Terrier had passed back her case, Vivi had secured it under her seat. She also kept her papers in her pocket so she wouldn't have a recurrence of what had taken place previously.

As they continued, she looked across at Terrier as he finished a sandwich Anne-Marie had packed, then lit a cigarette and sat staring out of the window watching the whole of France pass by.

Vivi's heart started to swell as she watched him, she was so grateful for his bravery and resourcefulness. She was trained and knew what to do in combat or as a courier, and how to decode a message in record time, but Vivi realised as she stared over at Terrier there were other skills she didn't possess: the ability to adapt to unexpected situations as they arose, and his unshakeable bravado. Though she hoped she wouldn't need them. In another time and place she knew they could be the best of friends and she wanted time to discover that. Vivi suddenly pictured a possible life for all of them after the war when she would come over to visit the siblings in France. They'd all laugh and maybe they would go on a picnic into the beautiful French countryside. They would eat French cheese and drink good, fine red wine and tell tales of the time when they had all been spies.

When they arrived at the Gare du Nord, nothing could prepare Vivi for what it would feel like. The platform was heaving with German officers in their sharp-edge grey uniforms and shiny black jackboots as they barked out orders. Many of them were accompanied by German shepherd dogs gnashing their teeth and straining on thick metal chains that snarled and snapped at the passengers hurrying along the platform, a very successful intimidation technique. The people cowered, with eyes cast down, some apparently refugees judging by the amount of baggage they carried, seeking to escape the horror, but they all scurried along as the German officers kept them moving. As the squeal of the brakes slammed the train to a stop and circles of hot white steam rose up from the tracks and filtered through the open window, the smell of soot and engine oil was suffocating and Vivi coughed. Staring out to the platform, she noted that the look on every face she could see was of apprehension and fear and they all reflected back her own feelings. Vivi sat paralysed for a moment, not wanting to get off, and it took Terrier tugging on her arm to break the spell she was under. Raising to her feet her legs started to shake uncontrollably and all she could think was, what on earth had she been thinking of, believing that she could do this? Suddenly, it all felt so real and so very dangerous. In the little villages on the coast the Germans had been there, but on the whole, the atmosphere in the rural towns had been tense but casual. Here in Paris, it was extremely different. She was grateful for Terrier's arm as he locked it in hers and hustled her off the train and along the platform. Once on the street he began his usual evasive walking course, taking them up and down streets and back alleys.

As they walked, she felt overwhelmed with the change to the city she had visited before the war. Remembering it as a lively town with a unique joie de vivre, now the streets were teeming with marching Nazis and angry-looking swastikas hung from every government building. And the fear on the street was palpable. Vivi repeated over and over to herself the address of the safe house she'd been given before she had left Britain as a way to calm her mind and quell the fear that was rising up from her stomach and tasting bitter in her mouth. Terrier had reminded her of it on the train, instructing her if there were any complications, anything at all, to go to the safe house.

'Do you understand? Fifty-three Boulogne Street. Ask for Madame Mazella; she will provide a room. You tell her that Terrier sent you. Do you follow me? Is that clear?'

Vivi had nodded, hoping that she would never need a safe house.

As they finally reached their destination he tapped on the door of the home she was to live at and Vivi was grateful to get away from the desperate atmosphere on the streets of Paris. The house was in Boulogne-Billancourt on the outskirts of the city – a simple, unpretentious place – and though she hadn't been completely sure of what to expect, this nondescript building hadn't been it.

The door opened. An older woman played her part.

'Ah, I'm overjoyed to see you. What a dear you are, to bring our sweet cousin Claudette all the way. Thank you so much. We have been anticipating her arrival.'

They headed inside, and the tiny woman with animated eyes and grey hair captured tidily in a tight bun shut the door behind them.

'Are you sure you weren't followed?' she enquired in a hushed voice.

He shook his head. 'No one ever follows me,' he responded playfully as he kissed her warmly on both cheeks.

She then glared at Vivi, and Vivi could tell she wasn't what she'd been expecting. Then making up her mind the woman shook her head. 'You are too pretty. They need to send us plain girls. She will attract every Nazi in this town.'

Vivi didn't know how to respond to that.

The Terrier laughed. 'Which is precisely why they won't suspect anything. They will be expecting the plain girls, but with the good-looking ones, they'll only be thinking about one thing,' he quipped with her, playfully, tapping her cheeks and continuing, using his nickname for her, 'Come on, Maman, you are not to fret so much. This war will be won soon, and young Claudette here will help you win it.'

They made their way into the house and Vivi shivered. It felt dark and gloomy compared to being outside. This was an old gentleman of a house with heavy brown mahogany-panelled walls and a high white ceiling. The room she was led into was dominated by floor-to-ceiling bookshelves and large pieces of older furniture. Vivi noticed everything was meticulously clean and polished but there were no frills. A solid oak dining table was at the other end of the room with a large blue-and-yellow ceramic bowl in the centre, which Vivi surmised had probably contained fruit in peacetime. A smooth veneered sideboard with family photo atop anchored the other wall. Around the dark-stone fireplace comfortable chairs were placed for optimum warmth with threadbare covers over the armrests and backs of the chairs. More books were stacked in a pile by the side of one of the chairs and the smell of strong coffee and pipe tobacco lingered about the room.

The SOE had instructed her that when she was placed, they would not advise the people of what she was specifically doing, but they knew to give her a room. The less they knew, the safer it was for all of them.

Maman led her upstairs and the room they had given her was sparsely furnished but clean and had a delightful view of the park across the street. When Maman left her Vivi took a minute to catch her breath and look out. Trees were alive with the abundance of new growth and spring flowers waved in the breeze, straining their heads towards the shafts of early-afternoon sun. As Vivienne took in the sight she mused how everything felt so eerily normal, plants and trees growing in their innocent way unaware of the madness of the world all around them.

Vivi placed her suitcase under the bed and went downstairs to meet the family.

'Maman', as the Terrier called her – her real name was Florence – was married to Pascal Renoir, a man half the size of her, a stooped, brittle-boned person with dark hair and tiny eyes that observed her through thick glasses. But he had a pleasant enough manner, kissing her on both cheeks with the lightness of a feather.

'Thank you, mademoiselle, for what you are doing for France,' he stated in a soft voice. His delicate hand barely touched her as he shook her own.

All at once, the door opened, and a young woman came in. A little younger than Vivi, maybe in her late teens or early twenties. She paused when she saw Vivi, and she grinned at her mother. 'Is she the one?' she enquired.

A stern look from her mother conveyed they should not be speaking about such things.

'You must get into the habit of discretion, Yvette. This is your relative, Claudette, from the south. Do not forget that. Treat her as though she is family.'

Yvette flushed with embarrassment, then kissed Vivi on both cheeks. 'Hello, cousin. It is good to see you. I'm glad you could remain with us for a time.' Yvette looked across at her mother to make sure that what she said was sufficient.

After Vivi had settled in, Madame Renoir disappeared into the kitchen and occupied herself preparing dinner, confirmed by the clatter of pots and pans coming from the little side room.

Monsieur Renoir asked Vivi how things were going in the outside world. 'We get very limited information. Paris is so locked down, even our newspapers have been censored. Please tell us about how the war effort is going.'

Vivi updated him on the highlights, and he shook his head, as if not wishing to take it in.

'So sad. The world has gone mad.'

Yvette, however, didn't seem so overwhelmed with their plight. 'I love your hair,' she said, running her fingers through it. 'Did you get it done in England this way? It's very chic right now.'

Vivi laughed. 'I'm glad you like it. I had to get it done in the French style.'

Yvette's mother shouted from the kitchen to her.

'Tomorrow, Yvette will take you on a trip around the city so you can see some of what is going on for yourself. We have a bicycle we've held onto for you, though everybody needs the rubber. But I think it will be the best way to get about.'

Yvette eagerly agreed.

After Vivi bid goodbye to Terrier, who disappeared that afternoon, underlining to her that he had war work to do, she settled down to enjoy a pleasant dinner with the new household. They were very welcoming. However, when Vivi got to her room she suddenly felt lonely for home. She'd been concentrating so much of her time preparing for the mission she hadn't realised how strange it would be and she desired what had been familiar to her growing up. She thought about her childhood. She wished she could wander into her father's study and sit with him as he read the newspaper to her, updating her in his low voice about all the things of considerable importance. Or be with her Aunt Beebe who had helped at the manor ever since Vivi was a child. She'd spent many a rainy afternoon perched on a stool in the kitchen listening to her tell tales as she baked bread or pastries, talked about books she had read, or gossiped about the comings and goings of the village.

On leaving, there had been rumours that their enormous house would be changed into a hospital, a development that her father had readily encouraged. She thought about her little brother Tom, his keen, inquisitive mind and how he'd follow her around the house asking her all manner of questions so he could be in her presence. She pondered how it had been hard to not write to her older sister Caroline, newly married, to tell her about what she was doing, as her superiors had demanded of her. They had always been close. Lastly she saw John, his ruddy face smiling up at her, demanding that Vivi read him yet another story.

Vivi hadn't thought about it before she left, but now, she realised, with the presence of the German army all around her, that her life was in jeopardy every moment of every day and there may be a chance that she wouldn't see any of her family again. She felt the tears creep into her eyes and quickly wiped them away. She had to be brave. Everyone did. Or they would never win the war.

Chapter 7

Present day

From then on Sophie couldn't seem to let go of the story of her mysterious great-aunt. The picture of Vivienne haunted her dreams and occupied her days. She wasn't sure if it was her innate curiosity or the fact she missed her mother so much, and here was another connection with a woman who could have been her mother's twin, and that alone made her want to know more. The lawyer in her also found it hard to rest without knowing Vivienne's definitive motives for leaving the country with a Nazi. Yes, it looked bad, but one thing she had learned in her former line of work was that you always need to keep an open mind, as things could often look bad on the surface.

A few days after visiting her gran, Sophie decided to visit the National Archives, which housed extensive military records as well as historical documents, in order to conduct a little research to see if she could find out if Vivienne had an early war record – the one that Gran had hinted at. Arriving there she moved swiftly inside, recognising a number of the staff, as she had been spending at least two days a week in there doing research ahead of the exhibition.

Peter, an amiable young archivist who happened to be a World War Two buff and had been very helpful to her, smiled when she approached his counter. 'Don't tell me,' he said, sitting back in his chair and locking his hands behind his head. 'You're searching for more information about the London bombings?'

'Not any more, we opened the exhibition already. Though I do still need information from that time period. But this time I'm actually interested in the history of buildings on Baker Street. I was reading that apparently SOE was located there and I am especially interested in any records of agents visiting there in forty-four. It is kind of a needle in a haystack, but I am trying to track down what someone might be doing visiting there during that time.'

'Intriguing,' responded Peter. 'This is easier now we have a lot more files from the war in the public record. Okay then, let me take you to that section.'

As they walked Peter filled her in on what he knew about SOE. 'The Special Operations Executive, which was established during the war by Winston Churchill, was a British spy network that sent agents into all of Europe to disrupt German activities during the war. Its purpose had been to conduct espionage, sabotage and reconnaissance in occupied Europe.' As they reached the correct section, Peter finished his history lesson. 'They had over thirteen thousand people working for them between 1940 to 1946, with at least five thousand working undercover as spies. They were mostly wireless operators, couriers, Resistance organisers and saboteurs.'

Once again Sophie wondered whether her aunt could have been one of them.

As Peter left her, Sophie started working her way through the files kept by SOE, looking for information about agents who had visited Baker Street in early March 1944 when the photograph had been taken. Eventually, she found a copy of a file that recorded all the agents who had visited the offices during that time but it only stated their code names and their initials to help protect their identity.

A letter inside the file informed the reader this log had been kept in a secret vault until after the war, locked to protect the spies and their whereabouts. Sophie ran a finger down this register that had been maintained meticulously by the officers who had overseen the spy network from London.

There were only five spies mentioned having visited the office in early March before Karen Johnson, the photographer, died.

And one of them had the initials 'V.H.' Next to them was the word 'Sparrow'.

Sophie sat back in her chair. V.H., Vivienne Hamilton. Her instinct had been correct. She felt like cheering. Up until now, it had just been a rumour from her grandmother, but now it said it here plainly. Vivienne Hamilton had been working for the British sometime during the war and her code name had been Sparrow. But if she had been working for the British, why on earth did she smuggle a Nazi out of the hospital and disappear to France?

Sophie felt momentarily satisfied with herself. That was until she searched through more of the records and came across something alarming. In Sparrow's file there was information about her assignment in Paris but on the next page there was an official letter thanking her for her work and discharging her from SOE. The stamp across the page stated she was no longer fit for duty. It was dated in 1943, the year before the photograph on Baker Street. So this part of the story was true. She had been working for the British in SOE early in the war but they then had dismissed her. What had she done? And why was she seen leaving the same building a year later if she no longer was an agent?

There was also a mention of the spy network Sparrow had been a member of in France. This spy cell was known by three names: F-section, which was short for French section, the Physician Network, and Prosper Network, the latter named after the man who headed it up. Something about its name rang a bell in Sophie's mind – she had read it before. Sophie had placed a lot of the research she had been doing at home in a Google document and now pulled it up on her phone. Yes, here it was, she noted as she scrolled down the screen. The archival records stated that Sparrow had been assigned to the Physician Network, which had been compromised during the war, resulting in a large number of agents from that French spy network being caught or killed in 1943. Many shortly before her aunt had been discharged. Vivienne had been lucky to make it home alive, or… Another thought ran like a chill through Sophie's body. Had her aunt helped with the deception? Had she compromised Physician?

Quickly, Sophie returned to her aunt's file for anything else that could help. There was only one other piece of paper in it. A photocopy of a document with columns of letters on it. Underneath the letters was a scrawled note.

> *Passed from another agent so unable to confirm the fist.*
> *Received June 1944 – Not creditable as spy is no longer in the*
> *network. Determined to be enemy using an outdated code.*

Sophie stared at the list of jumbled letters all in little blocks of five. What did they mean?

She moved back to the desk where Peter was sitting.

'Did you find any ghosts?' he asked with a smile.

'I did,' stated Sophie as she continued to stare at the sheet of paper. 'I think my aunt might have worked for SOE during the war.'

'Wow,' responded Peter looking impressed. 'Did you not know before?'

'There is a little controversy around it, but I think I have found her file for SOE and this was in it. Would you know anything about what this is?'

She handed the paper to Peter.

'This is a coded message,' he responded, nodding. 'Dated right before the Normandy Landings. Normally these were transmitted from wirelesses by SOE operatives in the field.'

'Do you know what it says?' enquired Sophie, getting excited.

Peter started to laugh. 'We have hundreds of these unknown messages on file; unfortunately, unless you know this particular agent's cipher, it is almost impossible to decode.'

'Cipher?'

'Each agent had their own cipher – usually they would memorise a poem – and from that they would pick a word to create their coded message. Then by a series of columns and rows using this code word they would send a message.'

'Well that doesn't sound too difficult to crack as long as you know their poem,' stated Sophie. 'How come you have so many that aren't decoded?'

Peter smiled. 'They never used just a single word. There are some great books you can download about how that was done. The important thing is to know the agent's cipher.'

Sophie nodded, feeling despondent. 'How would I find that out?'

'If I knew that, I would be a very popular archivist,' said Peter. 'What do you know about your great-aunt? Did she have a favourite poem? That might be a starting place. Otherwise, I'm afraid you may never know what this says.'

Sophie shook her head. 'I have only just found out about her recently. Also, do you know what this means?' she enquired further, pointing to the scrawled note.

Peter read it. 'Yes, this implies this was not sent by a real agent, but someone trying to lure real agents out of hiding in order to reveal themselves. They probably used her name signature.'

He pointed to the first few letters on the document. 'This is the code for this SOE operative's name, or her signature, this informed the receiver this was coming from your aunt, or, it appears by this note, someone pretending to be your aunt.'

Sophie stared at the first five letters, the name of her aunt, in code.

'And what does "unable to confirm the fist" mean? Is it a typo?'

Peter started to come alive, he obviously loved this part of history. 'Not at all. "Fist" is correct. All the messages were communicated by Morse code. The fist they talk about here relates to the way an agent typed their messages. Each agent had a particular style of tapping that could be read like a fingerprint. Heavy on a particular letter or longer on another. The receivers back here knew each agent in the field's tapping fingerprint, or as they called it their "fist". This helped them to be sure it was the actual agent and not someone pretending to be them.'

Sophie was amazed. She'd had no idea it had been quite so complicated.

'What section of SOE did your aunt work for?' Peter asked.

'From what I can tell, something called the Physician Network.'

Peter's eyebrows disappeared under his fringe. 'That is why there is this note then. This was sent in forty-four and that network was compromised in forty-three. So everything coming in from those agents was really scrutinised. Did your aunt survive?'

'From that period, yes. But she disappeared in 1944, very probably back to France. How were the agents compromised?'

'Well, one story is that in 1943 the Nazis managed to get hold of a wireless and seemingly knew one of the agents' codes. A lot of agents were uncovered. The fake radio operator sent Resistance fighters to locations for a drop or a pick-up only to find the Gestapo waiting for them. It took a while for England to figure out how the agents were being uncovered and in that time, sadly, many died – over eighty in all. The other very controversial story is that the British spy network back here knew the radio and agent were compromised and continued to send fake messages to sway the Germans from the intended route of the D-Day landings. That they were willing to sacrifice their agents to keep that up and running. But that has never been proven.'

Sophie was astonished and sensing her hopelessness, Peter added, 'Look, it may not be impossible to crack the code. You just need to find out everything about your aunt. Is there any opportunity to go through her things? Or talk to family members who knew her? You may get lucky.'

Sophie nodded and closed the records. She recognised that what she was missing was the human element. What had her great-aunt been like as a person? Did she truly seem the sort that would run off to Germany with a Nazi and work for the enemy?

Sophie went to the copy machine and had just finished copying all of Vivienne's records when her gaze drifted out of the window and something she saw made her heart stop.

The man strolling past the window was the same height as Matt, had the same wavy hair, and appeared to be wearing the jumper she'd bought him for Christmas. But it couldn't conceivably be Matt, because under his arm was a beautiful blonde woman who was beaming up at him and chatting to him with great enthusiasm, as he grinned down at her.

Sophie was frozen. At first she just stood there staring, watching them, an inky darkness hovering on the edges of her vision, threatening to consume her as her heart thundered in her ears. Her mind had to be playing tricks on her. As the couple started to disappear from view Sophie came to her senses, knowing she needed to confirm what she'd seen. Racing through the building, she ran towards the door to get a better view. Surely it couldn't be Matt. Stepping outside, Sophie watched him walk up the street. She knew for sure now. This was her boyfriend, or was he also someone else's? The realisation of the truth of those words struck her brutally. She had to confront him there and then, otherwise she would collapse. Racing after him, she ran up the street and called out his name.

He stopped sharply and pulled his arm away from the woman he was with, looking anxiously about him. He whispered something into the young woman's ear, and she stepped aside, as if they wanted to make it appear they were just walking side by side, but that only confirmed it for Sophie. If it had been something innocent, maybe a co-worker he'd just had his arm around for a second, why would they be responding like this?

All at once Matt spotted her. Years of being in a relationship with him had trained her to recognise guilt on his face. He strode towards her, speaking in a nervous jumble.

'Oh, Sophie, how wonderful to see you. I didn't think you'd be here today. Isn't your research done for the exhibition?'

'Matt?' she spluttered out, and she couldn't keep the heartbreak from her tone.

He stopped babbling and seemed to have been rendered momentarily speechless.

She forced out words. 'How long has this been going on?'

He stepped back, appearing not to be ready to have this conversation. 'What? Oh, you mean Mandy and me?' he said, acknowledging the young woman who had stayed up the street and had not ventured any closer. Maybe she was afraid of the confrontation. 'We're just friends. Friends from work,' he continued to babble again. 'She got transferred to my department recently, and she's been helping me with some of my accounts.'

'Helping you?' said Sophie coldly. 'It looks like she's doing more than helping you, Matthew, you had your arm around her.'

Mandy strode towards them. 'Matt, you need to tell her; you promised you would do that this week. It's time.'

He stared at Mandy then and appeared to decide there was no point continuing to lie.

'Sophie, I'm sorry.' He ran a hand through his hair. 'Things have been so difficult since, you know…'

He left his unfinished statement hanging in the air for her to fill in the blanks. 'Since we lost Emily,' were the words that went through her mind. This was his way of dealing with it – by moving on. Just as he had left their home, he was leaving her. Burying all that grief inside instead of dealing with it. They had been through the worst, the hardest of circumstances that any parents should face. What had happened had changed everything.

Matt continued, 'The truth is, this is just too hard. Whenever I look at you all I see is...' he swallowed down his tears, '... her.' His voice then cracked. 'And I can't do it any more.'

His words stabbed her in her heart as she knew exactly what he meant, he reminded her of all the sadness as well. Sophie looked up into his distraught face and she saw it clearly for the first time, though she now suspected the truth had been there for a while. Just as a book on grief she had read had stated that the loss of a child was often just too much pain for some couples to go through together. He wanted to escape into what was safe and familiar and for him, that wasn't with her. Sophie knew she should be angry, but there was also part of her, she suddenly realised, that in some ways was relieved.

He was still talking and as she tuned back in to what he was saying she heard, 'I don't know, Sophie. I don't know what to tell you but I don't want to have this conversation out here. Can we get together for a glass of wine later?'

She glanced over at Mandy, who was looking sheepish as she looked towards the pair of them with compassion while he talked about their mutual pain. None of this was easy. Slowly, Sophie nodded.

'I'll text you,' he stated, and couldn't get away fast enough. As he strode up the road, Mandy had to almost run to keep up with him and Sophie noticed that he didn't put his arm back around her or take her hand.

She stood there staring after them for what felt like an eternity, struggling, using that time to let the truth sink in. She and Matt were finished. He'd found someone else and the hardest thing to come to terms with was that as she had watched that woman swish away at his side, it could have been her four years ago. The old her, the high-flier, the one that got to work early and left late. And she acknowledged with the weight of realisation that that was what Matt had found attractive. They had both been people on the edge, barrelling through their life in a manically driven way. And to escape his pain Matt had quietly gone on and replaced her, with a younger hungrier version.

Chapter 8

Heading home on the train, Sophie sat despondently, looking around the carriage. And it hit her: she was single again. Well, not officially, but she knew it was simply a matter of hours. Did that mean she'd have to start dating again? Now, aged thirty-eight? The thought of it gave her anxiety. Staring at the motley crew of commuters, Sophie wondered if she'd find love again. She closed her eyes and leaned her head against the window, allowing the coolness of the glass and the rocking of the train to soothe the loneliness and grief that threatened to wash over her.

Sophie opened her eyes and looked out of the window. The city buildings had disappeared and the train had slipped into suburbia. Family homes flashed past her, almost like a slap in the face with her present thoughts.

When she got home, Sophie went straight into the flat and poured herself a large glass of wine. Not much of a drinker, normally just having a couple of glasses if she went out for dinner, she felt suddenly like she needed it. As she stared out of her kitchen window, tears slid down her cheeks again as she realised how much her life was about to change. She then sat there staring at the phone, like a ridiculous schoolgirl, wishing he would text her.

At six thirty her phone chimed.

Can we meet at Anthony's?

Sophie paused only a second before typing in the word, 'Okay'.

She didn't even bother putting any make-up on or doing much with her hair. One didn't need to get dressed up to be dumped. When she arrived at Anthony's, a favourite place of theirs, half an hour later, he was already sitting at a table, nervously fingering his glass, and she hated it. Because Sophie was still attracted to him, and deep down, she just wanted them to stay together. Who else understood? Or shared their memories? Was wanting that so wrong? He was her last connection with their daughter. Taking in a deep breath, Sophie pushed her way into the busy bar. The sound of eighties music pumped out through the speakers, and the Friday evening chatter as people prepared for the weekend was lively and raucous. As she made her way through the crowd, the room was stiflingly hot with the smell of alcohol and sweat mingled with aftershave. Matt greeted her with a nod of acknowledgement as Sophie made her way to the table where he was sitting. He'd chosen this place on purpose, she knew. Not some quiet restaurant where every word could be heard, but a place he could say what he needed to say and exit quickly.

At the table, Matt stood up. It felt awkward, she didn't know what to do. He took the initiative and hugged her. She noticed as he did she started shaking inwardly and her body felt limp, as if all her energy were draining out straight through her feet. Hurriedly, she sat down.

'Can I get you a drink?' he asked.

'White wine, the usual,' she shouted over strains of Culture Club.

He nodded and disappeared, and she swallowed down the tears that were about to get the better of her as she sat there. He arrived back with her glass of wine and placed it in front of her. He seemed nervous.

As he sat down, Sophie felt a sudden sense of icy calm, and decided she would take control. Up until now, he'd had the upper hand in this situation, but she was done with that.

'Listen, Matt, I don't want to draw this out. It's obvious that things between us are over. I know why it happened but now I want to know when, and for how long?'

He fingered the stem of his glass again and took a large swig of his red wine before he answered her.

'God, Sophie, I'm so sorry. I don't know where to begin.'

'Why don't you start with Mandy?' she demanded sharply, and his eyes flicked up to meet hers.

He nodded, looking down at his hands. 'We met about three months ago. She was new at the Exchange, and I helped her out navigating her way around our procedures. It can be challenging in a business with mainly men. But nothing was going on. I swear we were just friends. She had a boyfriend, and you and I were together. We had a passing acquaintance, but nothing serious, just friendship.'

His words tweaked at Sophie's heart. It sounded familiar, like the beginning of their own relationship.

He continued, 'Anyway, six weeks ago, while we were both still having such a hard time, she and her boyfriend split up, and though I didn't want to socialise, I just offered to take her out for a drink to cheer her up. We got talking. You know, we both do the same job, we have a lot in common. Anyway, I thought no more of it. I hugged her goodbye that night, but nothing more, I swear. But after that things… developed.'

'Oh, didn't they just?' said Sophie, hating herself for allowing the sarcasm to reveal her pain.

His shoulders slumped forward as he nodded his head.

'And?' Sophie continued, she needed to know it all.

'Well, the truth is I think I love her, Sophie. I honestly tried not to. I tried not to let those feelings happen.'

'How noble,' stated Sophie sarcastically. 'And you couldn't have come to me and talked before now?'

'I wanted to, trust me. You can't believe how many times I tried to tell you about it. But whenever I saw the pain you were still going through, that I was still going through, I just couldn't add any more. I kept thinking soon we will be over all of this grief and I can tell her…' His voice drifted off and he took a large swig of his drink.

Sophie wiped away the tears that had brimmed up. Angry at herself, she had wanted to look strong, didn't want to look like the one who'd been dumped. 'Well, that's that then, isn't it?' She forced out a strong tone. 'You've moved on, and now you've sorted out your problem with me as well.'

He looked up sharply, appearing to want to protest her harsh view of their situation. But gave up without saying a word to rebut her claim. He just stared at her, all the sadness and guilt of their situation in his expression.

Sophie knocked back the rest of her drink and stood up. He stood up too.

'Please, don't let us part like this. This is why I hadn't said anything yet. I wanted to find a way for us to still be friends. Could we still try to do that?'

Sophie swallowed down her anger and hurt. 'I don't think so, Matt. You may have been in love with someone else for weeks. I'm not sure I want someone in my life who spent any time in love with somebody else and didn't tell me, who can forget me and the family we… once had. Just like that.'

He flinched with the reality of her words, but said nothing, just nodded sadly.

Sophie grabbed her bag and made her way towards the door, turning briefly to see him standing there watching her, and she hated the hurt on his face. She could only imagine it reflected the same on hers.

That journey home Sophie was numb. She knew now. There was also something of a relief in that they were definitely over. She had wondered for a while. At least knowing, she could start to try to work out how to move on, on her own.

She held in her tears until she got home, then, exhausted, threw herself in bed, sobbing, not even bothering to undress. She curled into a ball as William rubbed his nose around her face, his purr loud and reassuring. Finally completely spent, her throat dry and raspy from crying, she passed out, though she didn't sleep for longer than a few hours at a time. The pain of her year of grief and now the end of her relationship made her desperate and edgy and every time she woke up, it was with a jolt, and she'd start sobbing again.

The final time she fell asleep, she had a dream that left her shaken when she woke. In it her mother had come to her, and running her fingers through her hair had whispered, 'Everything is going to be all right, Sophie, I promise you that.' And, sobbing, Sophie had hugged her so tightly it had felt real. But then when she pulled away from her to wipe her eyes she saw her mother had morphed into her great-aunt Vivienne and though she didn't say anything there had been this pleading look in her eyes, as though she needed Sophie to help her in some way. And even in her dream something had struck her. The feeling of the not-knowing was the worst part of it all. Not knowing for weeks about Matt's secret relationship; there was the same not knowing about her aunt. Everyone seemed to just accept she was a traitor and as she looked at her aunt's face in her dream, she felt this odd pull into the past. As though in finding out what really happened during the war would also help her find her own balance again. She needed everything in her life, including her history, to make sense. Or the future was just an impossible unknown.

Chapter 9

When Sophie finally opened her eyes in the morning, she caught her breath. The feeling of needing to put things right continued to haunt her while she was awake. This was one thing she could definitely do.

On some level she felt that it was no accident that the photograph had come into her life right now. Just when she needed something to distract her, to anchor her.

She shuffled into the kitchen to make a cup of coffee and examined the significance of all the things that had happened. If Sophie hadn't had her emotional breakdown, she wouldn't have been in this job. If she hadn't worked for the trust she wouldn't have been at the exhibition, and would probably have never seen the photograph. She wouldn't have taken the time to go to an exhibition when she had been working eighty hours a week, it was uncanny how it all had happened.

Resolving to not spend the whole day just feeling sorry for herself, Sophie threw herself into the research. Starting out from the legal stance that people were innocent until proven guilty, she asked herself what possible reasons anyone might have for leaving the country with a Nazi. To understand her aunt's motives, first Sophie recognised, once again, that she simply needed to know more about her, and what she was doing during that time. She knew from her gran that Vivienne had been in France, and then a nurse in Cornwall, but that didn't explain why she was all dressed up, wearing her family crest in London. That had to have been an important meeting.

Sophie continued to read the books she had downloaded about SOE. If she was working from the premise that her aunt was innocent then was it plausible that she somehow could have been working for the British again? That could change everything.

Sophie picked up her phone and looked at the picture of her aunt.

'What were you doing, Vivienne?' she asked out loud. 'Were you really a traitor?'

Sophie continued to bury herself in the research. Hardly eating or sleeping, she spent the whole weekend learning everything she could about SOE, burying her feelings of sadness whenever they came up with a determination to find out the truth. If nothing else she realised she wanted to find out how and where Vivienne had died. Sophie wasn't sure why this was so important to her, but it was all she could do and think about. And every time she saw the picture of Vivienne from her dream, the face so similar to her mother's, she felt compelled.

On Sunday night she made a decision. She would definitely take that time off and go down to Cornwall to where the story started. Back to the family estate where Vivienne had grown up, worked as a nurse and had ultimately met the German POW who she'd supposedly run off with.

When she called Jonathan he seemed unsurprised to hear from her. Both she and Matt had mutual friends in the trust, which was how she had known about the job in the first place, and it seemed that the gossip grapevine hadn't let her down, as news had clearly already spread of her and Matt's split.

When she asked him if she could take a week off, her boss responded sympathetically.

'Sorry, Soph, I heard what happened. Take all the time you need, and we'll see you back soon.'

She nodded at the receiver, her eyes brimming with tears again. 'I'm going to go down to Cornwall for a break, if you're sure that's okay.'

'Of course. It's quiet now the exhibition has started. All I'm going to be doing this week is paperwork. Take all the time you want.'

She turned off her phone and went to pack a bag. Sophie had read that boats used to transport agents to France, setting off not far from where Vivienne lived, which was something she wanted to investigate more. Also, there had to be more records down there of the Cornish war effort. Maybe if she looked around in the local museums, she'd find something. Sophie also hoped she might get a chance to go through the family attic. There was so much stuff up there, and what might have seemed unimportant to her relatives may lead to more information about Vivienne.

She left her cat, William, with her next-door neighbour, who adored him. Then Sophie packed her boot and filled her car with petrol, willing herself forward, fighting the terrible sinking feeling whenever she thought about Matt. Sometimes the gravity of the end of it would knot up her stomach and make her feel desperate. But she couldn't think of anything better to help clear her head than a trip down to Cornwall. The beaches and the open spaces would be the perfect remedies to forget about her life in the city. Sophie took a deep breath, and then, getting into her car, she knew, somehow, that when she came back she would not be the same person. She would be a new version of herself, braver and more together. As she set off, she thought of Vivienne before her life became so complicated, setting off on her mission in 1943, when she was working for SOE. Sophie reminded herself she had that same blood running in her veins and would focus on being as brave as her aunt. She hoped that in unravelling this part of her family history, she might just be able to gather up those loose threads and weave them back into her own life so it made sense again.

Chapter 10

1943

On her first full day in Paris, Vivi woke early but found Yvette already downstairs sitting at the kitchen table waiting for her. Maman's kitchen was alive with cooking smells and lively banter between a mother and daughter.

'I have such plans for us today. Maman has packed us a little picnic, and I will be your guide so you can see all the charms of my city.'

Yvette's mother scolded her with her gaze, hissing, 'This is not a sightseeing excursion, Yvette. Her desire is to identify what is going on here to do with the war. You need to be vigilant so that no one observes you paying too much attention. You understand this, of course?' She directed the last question to Vivi.

Vivi nodded. 'They have trained me in surveillance,' she informed her hostess.

After breakfast, the two young women, just a few years apart in age, took off touring the city and quickly fell into a pattern. When they came across German bases or activities, they both got off their bikes and pretended to inspect a wheel or be working to adjust the seat while Vivi looked through the spokes or surreptitiously glanced over the handlebars, attempting to take in as much information as she could in the manner they'd trained her. Familiarising herself with everything the Germans were doing in the city, and where they were based, was an essential part of her work. Vivi paid particular attention to the Renault factory that the Allies were interested in destroying. This had been identified as the location of where the enemy was producing vehicles for the German war effort.

Around lunchtime they discarded their bikes along the banks of the Seine, where Yvette unpacked the basket with cheese, bread and apples. As they gazed out across the water, they fell into easy conversation, where it didn't take Yvette long to relax into confessing all of her fears to Vivi.

'What if I never have a chance to meet a boy I could fall in love with? This crazy war is taking all the good men to work for the Germans. And anyway I could be dead tomorrow, and I will never experience what it is like to be kissed or ever be in love.'

She took a bite out of her apple, and Vivi sat back and turned her face to the spring sun that was defying the war and attempting to warm the cold season. She contemplated the same question for herself. She'd had a few brief relationships, but had never really been in love. Vivi had been so busy getting ready for this mission she had barely thought about it over the last few months, and the thought suddenly struck her, now she had chosen this dangerous path, real love might never be an option for her.

'Yvette, you've time for that. You've had to grow up quickly.'

'And there is no one around,' Yvette continued as she snatched at a clump of grass with frustration. 'Even if I had the chance, there's no one to have the chance *with*. I really hope it ends soon.'

Vivi nodded, lighting a cigarette and looking across the water. 'We all do.'

On returning home, Vivi ate dinner with the family and then excused herself to transmit back to headquarters in Britain.

Locking herself in her room, she closed the curtains, pulled out the wireless, and the crystal she needed to make the radio work. Vivi placed them both on a small dressing table in the corner. As she turned on the wireless, the signal was weak and she was unable to establish a link. Tentatively she opened the window and looked up and down the road, surreptitiously. All was quiet, so she snaked the antenna that came with her equipment outside. Vivi had been instructed to do this if the signal was weak. She noticed her hands were shaking. It was risky transmitting this way with German detector vans roaming the city to find wireless operators just like her and she would only have a limited amount of time to convey information to the signal centre for SOE in England.

Listening in on the device, she took a deep breath as she fitted her crystal and waited for it to warm up. Then, with great speed, she tapped out her code name and hastily transmitted the message that she'd arrived safely. Vivi waited with bated breath as information filtered back to her, confirming in code they had received her message and wishing her luck.

As Vivi listened, she kept her eye on the clock. She knew she could not transmit for more than fifteen minutes. If the Nazis that drove around the city spotted the antenna or encountered her transmission, not only would it place her in jeopardy, but the whole family in the house.

She finished her message and slid the wireless in its case back under the bed. Glancing in the mirror, Vivi noticed beads of sweat glistening on her forehead and felt her heart pounding through her ribcage.

*

The following evening Vivi slipped out of the house to connect with her circuit leader, Frank, for the first time at the Resistance meeting. Her job eventually would be to work for him as a courier between others in the circuit and transmit messages back and forth to London.

On the way, she used Terrier's zigzag pattern of moving through the streets, trying not to lose her way. When she finally arrived, she knocked on the door and gave a coded word, and a nonchalant young man nodded and brought her inside. He led her down a hall and into a darkened room.

Inside, the members of her cell, within the Physician Network, were huddled around discussing their plans. As her eyes started to adjust to the darkness, she was surprised by the sight of the different types of people. A motley cluster of very young men, some still boys, too young to fight, and also mature men, several with war wounds, probably from the First World War, she surmised. They stood huddled around a map talking about the nearby Renault factory that they were hoping to sabotage.

'The pianist is here,' declared the young man who had opened the door to her. 'The pianist' was the general code name for the women or the men who were working as wireless operators around the city to transport information back to British headquarters about anything the Resistance needed.

They all acknowledged her and the leader stepped forward and introduced himself as Frank, before quickly moving on to business, eventually turning to Vivi. 'We need explosives and more guns. Could you request an airdrop for the end of the week?'

Vivi nodded and only then did she realise how much she was a part of this. An active part of this war. Until now, everything had felt detached or overwhelming, even operating the wireless. But when she looked at the picture on the map of the Renault factory that she and Yvette had observed the day before, she suddenly felt emboldened. This was why she was doing this, to fight for France and for England.

After the meeting, she slipped back out of the house. As the curfew was already in place, she crept along the darkened streets, finding her way home. Moving in through the back door, Vivi was intercepted in the kitchen by Yvette.

'You're not supposed to be out after curfew,' she stated, her eyes huge, staring up from the book she was reading.

Vivi smiled. 'Yvette, I know. Sometimes there are no alternatives. This is when the meeting was planned.'

'Is there anything I can do?' she enquired enthusiastically. 'I want to be part of the war effort.'

Vivi looked down into the face of this young woman who seemed so keen to help out. 'You've already been a tremendous help, Yvette. Thank you.'

The next evening, Vivi communicated the information to headquarters, and by the end of the week, she had information to relay back to Frank and her cell. After the broadcast she made her way out of the house in the evening, to let them know all was set. Vivi reached the location of the underground meeting. Slipping inside, she saw the same group was there, and she informed them that the drop would happen at the end of the week at around 2 a.m., just outside the city, this time in a field of an obliging farmer, another Resistance sympathiser. They acknowledged and thanked her, but on leaving the house, Vivi sensed that someone was behind her. Her lessons in espionage and how to lose someone had been drilled into her, plus her short time with Terrier had sharpened her senses even further. She moved swiftly away, swung down an alley and then another one, and then slipped back onto the road. Turning another corner, she could still hear footsteps behind her. She stepped into a darkened doorway. The step sounded high-pitched, like a woman behind her in heels. She held her breath as the individual approached but was relieved to see who it was.

'Yvette, what are you doing here?' she hissed into the darkness.

Yvette's face was full of remorse but also pinked with slight excitement. 'I wished to see what you were doing. I want to be part of all of this.'

'Yvette, do you know how dangerous this is? The reason I do not tell you anything is that I'm trying to keep your family safe.'

'Were you meeting with the Resistance tonight?' she asked in a hushed tone.

Vivi looked around her, then moved rapidly off down the street. 'Say nothing more until we are at the house,' she whispered, glancing over her shoulder.

Yvette walked sheepishly beside her as they made their way for home.

Stepping inside the house, Vivi closed the door and drew the shades shut. She tried to control the fear mixed with anger she felt just below the surface.

'Please listen, Yvette, this is not a game. You put us all in danger: me, your parents, everyone. You cannot follow me again. Do you understand? This is highly dangerous. So many people's lives would be at risk if anything were to go wrong.'

Yvette's eyes grew wide, and Vivi could see tears brimming. 'I just wanted to help. I don't want to be the only person who's not doing something. I want to be a spy like you.'

Just then, her mother appeared at the kitchen door, and had obviously overheard the exchange between the pair of them.

'Yvette, I do not want to hear any more of this talk. You will go straight to your bedroom. Do you understand me?'

Yvette nodded and left the room.

Her mother shook her head, visibly shaken. 'She is such a foolish child, I cannot believe she put you in danger. I am so sorry.'

Vivi nodded, but it troubled her. This was undoubtedly a complication.

Chapter 11

In order to not create suspicion, Vivi had a job working under her alias 'Claudette', the Renoirs' cousin from the south. It had been agreed that she should have papers that described her as a tutor so she could easily travel from house to house, allowing her to conduct any business for her circuit. Part of her job was to visit the homes she had been directed to by Frank and pass on messages, fake ration cards and forged travel documents.

On her first day, she left the house. Nervously, she rode her bike to the first address, and arriving, she knocked on the door. An older woman opened it and glared at her curiously.

'Bonjour. My name is Claudette. I am here to instruct the children.' This was the code she was supposed to use on visiting each house.

The woman's eyes opened widely, acknowledging the real reason for her visit, and she called her inside, adding in a loud voice just in case anybody was listening, 'We are so glad you are coming to teach our children. We have been waiting for you.'

On closing the door, the woman looked Vivi over.

'You are very young.'

'I have been trained,' responded Vivi, defensively.

The woman nodded, even though she didn't seem reassured. 'Follow me,' she instructed, making her way into another room. 'The girl is here,' she hissed to her husband, who was reading a newspaper in a corner of an overly tidy room. A man with lively eyes, he was long and lean as he stood up to greet her. He was more affable than his wife. Stretching out his hand, he shook hers firmly.

'Thank you for what you are doing for France, mademoiselle.'

She smiled. 'My name is Claudette. My cell leader, Frank, sent me. He said you will give me my weekly courier tasks.'

'You can call me Pierre,' he responded, beckoning her. 'Come with me. We have considerable work to do to prepare you.'

He took her into a sitting room, then he pushed open a hidden door. Behind it was a room holding stacks of maps, charts and plans, on a large desk. Permits, ration cards and code books were also placed in neat piles. He locked the door behind them.

'We call this room the storehouse. As things are transported back and forth, occasionally we require a place to hold these things. So you and I, you see, will become well acquainted.'

Vivi glanced around the room and couldn't help feeling a thrill.

'You understand that you will also be a courier, as well as a wireless operator?' he enquired, searching her face intently.

Vivi nodded.

Pierre laid out a map on the table. 'So that we can protect all the members of your network, not everybody knows of each person's identity and location. There are only a few of you that will make the trips between them. But you understand that discretion is of the utmost importance.'

Vivi listened, nodding her head and feeling the weight of responsibility. Maybe his wife had been right when she had insinuated Vivi might not be ready for all this.

Pierre must have read something on her face, because he touched her hand. 'I'm confident you'll be fine. We will move you around. The people you are with, you like them?'

She nodded. 'They're very kind.'

'You will be there for about three to six weeks, then we'll move you to the next house. Sometimes you'll be in lodgings, sometimes with families, sometimes not even in central Paris.'

Vivi knew they moved the operatives around the city to keep them safe, in case they were being watched.

'Do you understand what you are required to do?' Pierre asked.

Vivi nodded. She had been prepared for all of this.

'Let me get you a cup of tea,' he said. 'Why don't you sit down and start to familiarise yourself with some of this information? You will need to know the whereabouts and memorise the first three addresses here.' He highlighted points on a map.

He stepped out of the room for a moment and called out to his wife, who returned a sharp reply, preparing tea she did not sound very thrilled about. It appeared to Vivi that she was very suspicious of her. He stepped back inside the hidden room as Vivi scoured the map he had given her.

'I need you to go to this address tomorrow morning.' He pointed to the map. 'There you ought to receive thirty travel permits. Wear something loose-fitting. While you are there for the hour, teaching their young children, the operatives will sew the travel permits into your clothing, so take something that you are happy having altered, a jacket or a coat. Have you taught children before?'

She nodded her head. 'I was a tutor for a while in the south of France, when I was travelling with my mother, which is why this is my cover story and why I was chosen for this particular mission.'

'So you have some experience?'

'Limited, but yes.'

'We have made sure that each operative is prepared for you to read books to their children, encouraging them in general studies. Then, if anyone asks the children, they will confirm you are their tutor. Do you understand? You will also have a short time to talk with the operatives in the house. They will give you any messages that need to be passed on.

'Once you have the travel permits tomorrow, we need you to take them here.' He pointed to another address. 'Arrive at the same time the following day, wearing the same jacket. They will know whatever you hand to them will have the travel permits in it. While you are instructing the children there, they will unpick the stitching, pull out what they need, and then return it to you in the same fashion.

'For this evening's wireless broadcast, we also need you to ask London to send us some more equipment. I have the exact list here. Can you memorise it?'

She nodded her head as he handed her a written note.

'You will do the same thing all over again with each house. Go to the address, pick up documents, go to the next and deliver them. They also may have messages for you. Are you all right with all of this?'

She must have been looking pale as her head was starting to swim, but she nodded. 'I understand.'

'You're going to do fine, Claudette,' he reassured her, placing his arm on her shoulder. 'Just remember to blend in. Be friendly and act normally. Your pronunciation is excellent. How long were you in France before this?'

'I lived here for a few years.'

'You have the accent of the south. Your papers reflect that?'

She nodded.

'This is good. Then hopefully you won't be stopped. And if you are, you can tell them what you did before the war. But say as little as possible.

'Once you have handed over the papers to the second house, you will need to come back here for more instructions. You will visit me here every Tuesday and Friday at ten in the morning. We have our grandchildren here on those days, and you and I will have a short time to talk while they have something to eat. My wife has books that you can read to them and studies you can teach them. I'm afraid some of your obligations won't be quite as heroic as you may have imagined.'

Pierre's wife brought in the tea, as he continued to give Vivi more information. After she left, her mind was buzzing with all she had to do. That evening she transmitted the list she'd memorised then, after winding up the broadcast, placed the wireless under the bed.

The next day, she set out first thing and found it a pleasant journey. Even though it was early spring, the weather was beautiful in Paris. Vivi made her way to the first house and knocked on the door. A young woman with lively eyes and a mane of blonde hair opened the door and beamed at her.

Vivi introduced herself. 'Bonjour. My name is Claudette. I am here to instruct the children.'

The woman nodded in response. 'We've been waiting for you, Claudette,' she said as two school-aged children appeared and peeked out from behind their mother's back while a younger child cried plaintively in the background. 'As you can see, the children are ready for some distraction.'

She drew the children into the house as one of them grabbed Vivi's hand and started to bounce up and down. 'Are you going to read to us?'

'I am,' she responded, smiling down at the tiny beaming face.

The woman's husband greeted her in the hallway.

'This is the tutor who has come for the children,' said the young woman, nodding at her husband.

'Excellent,' he said.

Vivi removed her coat, which she had carefully stuffed with rags to make it look bulky, just in case anyone had watched her arrive, and handed it over to the young man, who smiled then retreated with it.

Vivi made her way into the front room, which was alive with the presence of children, toys scattered about the place, and the general dishevelled feeling that went with the house of a young family. She quickly established herself and reviewed the books that the young mother handed to her.

'Would you like a story?' asked Vivi. 'You can call me Mademoiselle Claudette.'

The children eagerly nodded and settled down to listen at her feet. Vivi read to them, and then they painted a picture together. After an hour, she headed off into the study while the children took a break and had something to drink.

The young man, the woman's husband, introduced himself. 'I'm Michel.'

'Claudette,' she responded.

'I have completed the task,' he said, pointing to her jacket on a chair, its pockets now padded.

Nodding, she waved goodbye to the children and put her jacket back on. It was significantly heavier than before, and she wobbled down the road on her bicycle before finally finding her stride. As she rode on her way home, she noticed her calves were beginning to become much stronger with all the physical exercise she'd had since she arrived in France.

Vivi pondered her new work as she glided through the Parisian streets. It was harrowing: the constant fear of being discovered and the Germans everywhere in the city – there was no doubt about that – but it was also quite exhilarating. She was settling into it and enjoying the feeling of supporting the war effort. The thing she loved most was being with her current host family. They were so kind to her. As she cycled home that day, she looked forward to the meal, not knowing the danger that was waiting around the corner for them all.

Chapter 12

Present day

As Sophie made her way out of London, she realised it had been several years since she'd been back to Cornwall. She used to go far more often, before her work schedule had become so busy and she had been taking care of her daughter. As she passed through Exeter and on to Plymouth, the road started to open out, and she swore she could already smell the sea, even though she knew it was probably just in her mind.

Her mother, Alice, had not enjoyed coming back to Cornwall as much as Sophie. She had been more of a city girl, happy to remain close to her mum, Bessy. But to Sophie, there was always something about Cornwall that felt like she was coming home. She loved being close to the water, the stretches of open countryside, and the slower, more leisurely pace of life that appeared to expand through warmer days. It was also almost always a few degrees warmer than London at any given time.

Sophie pulled into Hamilton Manor's long tree-lined drive. The estate was set back with outstanding gardens. Jean's son, her second cousin Jamie, now oversaw the day-to-day running of the estate, and though her great-uncle Tom still lived there, his health had declined so much with a recent mild heart attack and ongoing dementia, that these days he did very little on the estate, being more of a guest in his own house. Though her auntie informed her he still appreciated walking about as lord of the manor.

On arriving at the wide oak doors, Sophie took a moment to consider the building. A beautiful example of British architecture with a Tudor wing that had been added in the Georgian era with a façade of smooth white stones that were almost pearl-like in the sunlight. The large steps up to the door were worn and crumbling in places, as were the cornices and corner pieces, but still, it was impressive.

Sophie knocked at the door and was astonished when her great-uncle Tom opened it. The look of confusion and surprise on his face mirrored her own.

'Alice, is that you? What on earth are you doing down here from London?' he enquired, mistaking her for her mother, a broad smile breaking over his face.

The pain of her loss pierced her heart but she didn't let it show. Deciding not to draw attention to his mistake, she slipped into his arms for an easy hug and noted he smelled the way she always remembered – a gentleman's aftershave mingled with pipe tobacco.

'Did Jean know you were coming?' he asked, beaming.

'She does,' responded Sophie. 'Is it a happy surprise, Uncle Tom?'

'Absolutely. Maybe I'll get some good cooking now that you're here. Jean seems to have me on some sort of bland diet of boiled vegetables and chicken. I'm afraid I'm going to start clucking,' he said, shuffling off towards the main room.

As Sophie followed, she reminded him, 'You do need to take care of your health, Uncle Tom.'

He poo-pooed her with a hand gesture. 'It was only a minor heart attack, scarcely a scratch of a heart attack. I expect my ticker just wanted a little rest. So much fuss, and now I have to eat boiled vegetables.' He grimaced.

Tom made his way to the back of the house and down a set of stairs that took them into the old servants' section. The main house, which was considerable and chilly, was kept in pristine archival condition, ready for the droves of summer tourists who liked to look around the place where it was rumoured Henry VIII had once stayed overnight on a stop in Cornwall. Opening up the estate was the only way that her family could pay the extortionate heating bills and upkeep of such an ancient building.

As they got to the bottom of the stairs, the warmth of the kitchen stretched out to meet her, and she heard her aunt Jean laughing inside.

'We have a visitor,' announced Uncle Tom as he opened the door. 'One of those escapees from the capital.'

'Ah, there you are, love,' said her auntie Jean, putting down a wooden spoon from something she was stirring on the stove and sauntering over to envelop Sophie in a huge hug.

The kitchen smelled of something spicy, like chilli con carne, it was warm and appealing. Her uncle wandered over to the stove and picked up the lid of a pan. 'Oh, this looks interesting,' he stated.

Quickly releasing Sophie, Jean hurried over to the stove, taking the lid from him and putting it back down. 'That's not for you. I've got a nice piece of haddock for you.'

'Why can't I have this?' enquired Tom, scrunching up his eyes like a petulant child.

'You know what the doctor said. Boiled fish and vegetables for you if we want to keep you around, Dad.'

'Sounds like you hate me,' he scoffed. 'What's the point of living if I have to eat food like that to last?'

He shuffled back out of the room mumbling to himself and Jean shook her head.

Sophie enquired after his health in a low voice. 'Is he doing okay?'

'He's having a good day today – he does better when he takes his pills,' Jean said, cocking an eyebrow. 'And we'll probably have him around for a while yet. Though the forgetfulness comes and goes, and some days are very hard. How was your journey down, love?'

'Very pleasant. I love coming here,' said Sophie, stretching, and sitting down in the chair at the broad pine farmhouse table.

'Let me get the kettle on, make a cup of tea, and you can tell me all about things in London.'

After a long chat with her auntie Jean, where Sophie somehow managed to glide past any mention of Matt, she caught her up to date on her gran's news and what she had been doing in her new job, then they got to the business at hand.

'So, tell me again, dear,' Jean said, covering her hand with her own, 'about where you found this photograph.'

Sophie told her all about the exhibition and the story that her grandmother had told her.

Jean shook her head. 'It's an absolute mystery to me, I'm afraid, no one has ever really talked about her. I didn't want to say anything to Dad. He goes to bed early now. Maybe over this week you can do some searching? There are boxes of photographs in the attic, and surely there must be something from this mystery sister. There must be a birth certificate or whatever somewhere. Maybe we could piece together this history for you.'

'I can't believe Uncle Tom would never have talked about his other sister.'

Jean's voice dropped to a whisper. 'All I can tell you is there was a lot of heartbreak for years after the war. I don't remember anything being told directly to me during my childhood. But I do remember stories of people being hostile towards Dad in the village. Who knows? This may help me put together the pieces of my own family puzzle.'

With her grandmother's stern warning about Uncle Tom's health still echoing in her mind Sophie sipped at the tea her auntie Jean had automatically placed in front of her. Sophie pondered Jean's words, seeing the encouragement in her eyes, and hoped that she wouldn't somehow uncover something that might make things worse.

Chapter 13

The next day Sophie woke up and, as she stretched, she could almost feel all the stress of London leaving her body. Cornwall was starting to work its magic on her. She loved the city and all its buzz, but when Sophie needed to find herself, collect all the fragments of herself, Cornwall was invariably the place to do it. Showering, she got dressed and went down for breakfast. The hub of the little kitchen was warm and alive with the buzz of morning conversation between Jean and her son and she settled herself at the farmhouse table to connect with her family. She looked forward to listening to all the local gossip, the regaling of family stories and all that needed to be done on the manor at this time of the year.

Her cousin Jamie was just on the way out the door when she'd arrived downstairs. He gave her a hug. 'Unfortunately, I'm afraid I can't stop and chat, Sophie, as the weather is mild and I have to inspect trees today. The wind we've had over the last few weeks has weakened some limbs. I need to get out and get those dealt with. We don't want them taking out a new bride in the spring, now do we?' he stated, grinning at her as he grabbed a piece of toast spread with his mother's home-made marmalade and headed out the door. 'Enjoy your day,' he sang out as he left.

As she watched him leave she tried to recall the boy she had often climbed trees and fished with in the lake on endless summer holidays. The scrawny teenager of her youth had filled out into a good-looking man with curious brown eyes and a close-cut beard. He looked a lot like his father, her uncle Philip, who had passed away when they'd both been young. Now, as he trudged out in his green wellies and green Barbour jacket, he looked every bit the country farmer.

Her auntie Jean was busy making breakfast. 'How would you like your eggs, Sophie?'

'Eggs? I actually don't really eat breakfast normally.'

'Well, you're in the country now, and the country air will make you hungry. You need to make sure you eat something.'

'If you're going to force me, then scrambled eggs would be wonderful.'

Jean nodded and started working at the stove as the sizzle and smell of butter filled the kitchen. 'What are you planning on doing today? Make sure you get plenty of relaxation while you're here.'

The words stabbed at her, reminding her of one of the reasons she was here – yes, to do the research, but also because of the break-up with Matt. She hastily pushed thoughts of him away from her mind.

'There's a lot going on in town today,' Jean continued. 'It's market day. And even though it's not outside at this time of year, the village hall has stalls if you wanted to pop in there,' she suggested, cracking eggs into a bowl, whisking, and pouring them into the hot buttered pan; where they spluttered and spat.

'I think I will continue doing the research about Vivienne, our phantom ancestor. I was wondering if that little museum is still in town.'

Her auntie stopped and stared out of the kitchen window for a second then realised what she meant and nodded. 'Oh, of course. Harold Westlake keeps that place spic and span. Probably because half of it's dedicated to his father's supposed heroics during the war. But yes, it's still there. Let me see. If you check in the paper, it should tell you what time it's open under the local section.'

Sophie opened the newspaper folded on the table as a full English breakfast was placed in front of her. 'Good grief, Auntie Jean. How do you expect me to eat all this?'

Her auntie smiled. 'At least it'll put something in your stomach, even if you can't manage it all. There are plenty of mouths around here to help you out.'

Sophie's attention was drawn under the table where she could hear the thudding, wagging tails of the family's two golden retrievers as they rapped on the floor, knowing their cue. She dived into the food, which somehow tasted so much better in the country. Free-range eggs, country sausage, stewed tomatoes, and her auntie's home-made marmalade and crusty bread.

Studying the newspaper, Sophie could see the museum would be open at midday. She glanced at her phone. Just after nine. Good. She'd have a little time to get ready and maybe do some further online war research.

'It is lovely being here,' she mused as she spread Jean's golden marmalade on another piece of toast.

'And we love having you,' Jean added, pouring her a cup of tea. 'Though you should know my dad is having one of his forgetful days today. You may find him rather different on these challenging days.'

Sophie nodded. She had been surprised the day before when he had been so chatty, after the stories of his dementia from her gran, and it made her sad that he had so many health concerns.

'I will pop in and say hello,' she answered.

'Just don't expect much,' Jean said.

After breakfast Sophie went upstairs to her uncle's room. He was sitting looking out of the window. She went over and kissed him gently on the head.

'Hello, Uncle Tom. How are you today?'

He looked at her with a vague expression, so different from the day before. Sophie could tell he didn't remember who she was, so she gently nudged him towards the truth.

'It's Sophie, remember? I'm Alice's daughter.'

He nodded then. 'Alice is dead, you know.'

The pain of those words struck her hard even though they were the truth. 'Yes, I know,' she replied, softly.

'A car accident, such a horrible thing,' he stated, reminding Sophie of how hard the last year had been.

She quickly changed the subject. 'What are you doing today, Uncle Tom?'

He looked at her and then looked down at an unopened newspaper in his lap that Jean had possibly put there. 'Looks like I'm reading,' he said – more of a statement, than an affirmation.

She nodded. 'Can I do anything for you?'

He stared back out the window, his silence answering her.

'I'm going into town if you'd like anything.'

He shook his head, and she made her way to the door. On the way out her eyes were drawn to a painting on a sideboard and she couldn't help but pick it up and look at it. It was an original; sparrows all sitting on a branch. Could it be anything to do with Vivienne? She caught her breath and turned it over. It was dated during the war.

Tom must've seen what she was looking at out of the corner of his eye and turned around. 'My sister gave me that. She painted it herself,' he said, almost matter-of-factly.

'Caroline?' enquired Sophie, her heart thumping.

'No, not Caroline…' he muttered but he didn't elaborate, just looked out of the window, numbly. But she knew. Something inside her told her this was from Vivienne.

Sophie rebuked herself for letting him see her pick it up. She hadn't wanted to bring up any memories of his lost sister to him after her gran's warning. But she wondered what the picture's significance was and if he was going to say anything more.

He nodded his head. 'Lovely green eyes. She had beautiful green eyes, my sister did, just like yours. I still remember the words she said to me like it was yesterday. "Don't forget who I am, Tom. Don't ever forget."'

He then stopped abruptly, as though his brain had just disconnected, and he said no more on the matter, though she waited for a couple of moments, just in case a thought returned. But instead he noticed the newspaper and picked it up and appeared to be reading the headlines. Then, he stated to her in an even tone, 'Liquorice allsorts. Could you pick me up some liquorice allsorts from town?'

Sophie nodded, placed the picture back down, left the room, and went back to her own to continue her research about nurses during the war in Cornwall.

Once the clock chimed eleven in her bedroom, she shut down her laptop, plugged it in to charge, and made her way into town. It wasn't very far, so she decided to leave her car behind, as it was a nice walk. She strode through the countryside, inhaling the fresh salty air. It was raw and chilly with a light frost still dusting the fields, even though it was late morning. Bracing, as her mother always used to say, and as the air rippled through her lungs like icy needles, she liked the way it felt, chilling her face and clearing her head.

Helford village was busier than usual because it was market day, and she made her way into the village hall where the scent of lemon wax polish and strong coffee greeted her. All around the room little stalls were set up on long trestle tables. Instantly, Sophie could tell she had walked into the bustling heart of the village. People stood in groups socialising with each other and getting out from the seasonal chill. The room echoed with the chatter of housewives and pensioners, and the aroma of home-baked goods was wonderful. Browsing each stall, she picked up some handmade watercolour cards and some herbal tea to say thank you to her auntie for having her, and there was a confectionary stall where she managed to get her uncle's liquorice allsorts.

With all her wares packed in a brown paper bag, Sophie made her way out and over to the museum. Ducking into the small doorway, a musty smell greeted her, the smell of aged documents and damp clothing. It was a little chilly inside, with whitewashed brick walls and tiny windows high up, but a warm electric fire pumped out just enough heat to keep the ice from the air.

An older woman with plump red cheeks rose to her feet with an expectant look when Sophie walked in.

'Welcome to the museum. Feel free to take a booklet,' she sang out, handing a pamphlet to Sophie. 'It'll help explain things to you, and if it's been of any value, we do appreciate a donation.' She pointed to a jar on the counter. 'We also have books you can buy in the gift shop, at the end, about Cornwall and the war. Let me know if there's anything I can help you with.'

Sophie nodded and, taking the booklet, started to move around the exhibition. So many pictures of the harbour through the years, including how it had looked during the war. Apparently, even though Cornwall was relatively far from France, the Cornish had taken quite an active part in the war. The Helford Estuary had been the base for a flotilla of fishing boats that had been used to transport agents and spies into France, which the sailors had managed by posing and mingling amongst the French fishing boats off the Brittany coast.

Also in the museum were a couple of old uniforms, a gas mask, and some stories that had been laminated onto the wall. As she read through all of them, nothing jumped out at her. The woman, obviously excited to have a customer and unable to stay behind her desk, found Sophie halfway around the exhibition.

'Is there anything particular you're looking for? Or are you just visiting?'

'There is,' said Sophie. 'I'm interested to know about anything to do with my family home. Hamilton Manor. It was converted to a military hospital during World War Two. I wonder if you have any information about it.'

The woman paused to think. 'No, I don't think we have anything about that on the walls, but we do have clippings from the newspaper. I'm sure they would've mentioned something about it in there. Let me go and look for you.' She bustled off and came back with a large sagging leather scrapbook.

Sophie thanked her and settled down at a table to look through it. The older woman seemed to feel an obligation to help explain everything in it as Sophie turned the pages. It documented the highlights of the war through the local paper, the *Helford Herald*. It showed stories about young men who had gone off to war and what their small town had done to prepare. Growing their own vegetables, collecting paper, rubber, metal and rags for the war effort and aluminium for the Spitfire Fund.

As Sophie turned to the third page, the woman said, 'Ah, here is something you might be interested in,' and pointed to a small piece on the right-hand side. 'This talks about all the different things that the big houses did during the war.'

Sophie read quickly through it, and her family's house was mentioned briefly as a military hospital but didn't elaborate on anything. As she continued to flick through the scrapbook, the woman bustled off, saying she might have something else in a different book. But as Sophie turned to the next page, there was a huge piece about Vivienne from the front page of the newspaper, and her heart stopped. There was a photograph of her great-aunt, standing in her nurse's uniform outside the manor with a row of other nurses. The headline read, 'Local Nurse Turns Traitor.'

Chapter 14

With her heart thumping, Sophie quickly started to read through the newspaper article. It was shocking and provocative, going into great detail about how Vivienne had executed her plan of taking a high-ranking Nazi POW out of the hospital, seemingly intending to smuggle him back to Germany. It was very sparse on what had happened to Vivienne thereafter, but it talked about a local fisherman who had transported her over in a boat and how he'd been held at gunpoint by the German officer.

Sophie was shocked, but there was nothing else in the paper. She continued to look through the folders. As the older woman came back with a book, she saw the story and swallowed.

'Of course, that awful woman would be a relative of yours. I hadn't put two and two together until now. Most unfortunate, most unfortunate indeed. But don't worry, it was a long time ago, and the rest of your family did great war work. They took care of a lot of people in that hospital. I think I've got something about it here.'

She handed Sophie another historical book, which documented all the hospitals converted from stately homes during the war and how they'd been transformed to take in prisoners and soldiers. Sophie read through it. It was indeed amazing to see the transformation the manor had gone through. There were about six pictures of the ballroom, which looked like a hospital ward. 'Can I buy a copy of this?' she asked.

'Of course,' responded the woman. 'That'll be £19.99.'

Armed with her book, Sophie was just about to leave when an older man she imagined might be the Harold Westlake her auntie had mentioned came in through the door.

'Well, hello there, did you enjoy the exhibition?' he enquired, eyeing her quizzically.

'Yes, thank you. I'm interested in the hospital at Hamilton Manor and the work that Cornwall was involved in during the war.'

The gentleman's eyes lit up. This was undoubtedly a subject he liked to talk about.

'Ah, we were very important,' he stated loudly. 'Our boats transported spies, you know.'

'Really. Out of Helford?' Sophie had wanted to leave, but he was now in the flow of his story and she didn't want to appear rude.

'Oh, yes,' he continued with obvious pride.

He drew her attention to a wall with pictures of boats lined up. Past sea captains were smoking cigarettes, and trussed in knitted sweaters, heavy trousers and boots, posing on their decks, including his father, he informed her.

'Can you imagine what it must've been like?' he said with great admiration. He led her over to a photo, and pointed out two or three boats and sea captains. 'This fellow, John Thompson, he made about thirty trips with different spies. They used a boat that was marked up like a French boat and he used to go over and mingle with the fishing boats in France, and then they would transport the spies to the shore. He did that early in the war. Even got into a near-lethal fight with an actual Nazi once.'

Sophie's eyes flashed up at him. Was this another avenue for her to get more information about Vivienne? 'Do you know much about that story?'

'Oh yes, it's well documented,' he said, going away and pulling out an account in another leather-bound book about the Helford fishermen.

'The Helford Flotilla, as it was known, had stopped transporting spies by that time in the war because it had become very dangerous. But somehow a nurse, the landowner's daughter, no less, who worked at Hamilton Manor, talked him into making this one last trip. But unbeknownst to him she was helping a Nazi escape with her too. He suspected nothing because the woman was a local, he'd known her all her life. She'd dressed the Nazi in civilian clothes too. But halfway across the English Channel he began to think that something was up. The traitors came clean then and the Nazi held John up at gunpoint before he hit him over the head with the gun, afterwards sailing to France and leaving him unconscious on his boat. He was lucky he came around before it ran ashore.'

Sophie struggled to take in what he was saying and felt for the first time the guilt and shame her family had perhaps experienced over the years.

'How can I find out more about this?' she enquired.

'I'm sure his grandson would love to tell the tale. You'll meet Barney – we joke it's short for Barnacle because he lives on his boat – down the street. He's always in the Blue Anchor at lunchtime – end of the bar. You can't miss him. If you want to know the whole story, you should catch him there this afternoon. Trust me, he'll be there. Probably on about his third pint by now.'

He chuckled then, and she made her way out of the museum, wondering if she was doing all of this in vain. What if, instead of clearing Vivienne's name, she found evidence to incriminate her?

When Sophie arrived at the Blue Anchor, ten minutes later, the smell of hops, the damp outside and fresh salted fish greeted her. Sophie realised straight away she was the only woman in the room, as all the heads swivelled to acknowledge her as she stepped through the glass door with the word 'BAR' engraved on it.

The bartender was drying a glass and nodded to her as she approached him. 'Can I help you, love?' he asked in a dry monotone.

'Uh, a gin and tonic,' she replied, not wishing to give away her real reason for being there. Walking into a rural pub and announcing you want to talk about the Nazis wasn't exactly an easy conversation starter.

She peered down the row of men who were hugging the bar. Woollen skullcaps and thick jumpers, plus thick knee-length boots, hinted at their likely occupation in the fishing business.

When the bartender arrived back with her drink, she drew her head closer and asked him quietly, 'Is there somebody here called Barney?'

He nodded to the end of the bar where a short man was nursing half a pint of ale and chatting to the person next to him. Feeling on her back foot as the only woman in the place, Sophie grabbed her drink and took her courage in her hands. She moved to the end of the bar where Barney had just said something raucous, and three of the men next to him burst out laughing.

She waited till the laughter died down before she smiled graciously, and asked, 'Excuse me, are you Barney?'

He swivelled on his stool and looked her up and down. 'Who's asking?' he snapped, his eyes full of suspicion.

She imagined she looked extremely out of place, with her south-eastern accent and designer clothes that would've been very common on the London streets but felt unusual here.

'My name's Sophie.' She hesitated from telling him her last name. She was beginning to realise that it was possible that some people here might remember the negative connection to her family, and if Vivienne had indeed assaulted this man's grandfather, it might not be in her best interests to let on right away who she was. 'Someone from the museum told me I could find you here. I have an interest in a story that you may know about.'

'Story?' he asked as the other lads looked on. She could tell by their animated nudging and nodding that it wasn't very often a young woman approached Barney in the bar. 'Why don't you pull up a stool? I've got thousands. Which one would you like?'

She did as he urged, awkwardly perching on the edge of the bar stool as she took a sip of her drink. She decided to tell him a white lie. 'I'm down from London doing research on the work of the fishermen during World War Two.'

He sat back on his stool and eyed her with interest. 'Research?'

'Yes.'

'What kind of research?' he asked warily.

'I've been doing some work at the Imperial War Museum. A lot of photographs have turned up from World War Two and we were just interested in how the fishermen in this area contributed to the war effort.' Her declaration came out in a jumble of words and she knew her face flushed. Nevertheless, he seemed to buy her lie.

'Well, we were a big part of the war effort. My grandfather, John, used to sail his boat over to the north of France, taking all manner of people. He was even in the D-Day landings. He saw some stuff all right.'

'Tell me about him,' she encouraged.

His face lit up. She'd obviously struck on the tale that he invariably wanted to tell, because he settled into a comfortable storytelling rhythm. He reaffirmed what the museum owner had told her, about the way the boats were used to mingle with the French fishing boats. But then he brought up the story involving Vivienne.

'What can you tell me about that?' she enquired. 'It sounds terrifying.'

'It *was* terrifying for my grandad, John. He had to have three stitches in his head, and he always had vertigo after that. That Nazi hit him so hard, cracked his skull good, he did, struck him from behind. Didn't get a chance even to defend himself. Fortunately, once he came round he had the whereabouts to get himself back to England, but he was very nearly caught.'

'The Nazi was alone?' she enquired carefully.

'No, he went with a local girl. She turned up on the beach with him. My great-grandfather had previously taken her over before, for SOE was what was rumoured. It's a spy network, you know, spies that went in from London and such. That's what my grandfather did, he said, though no one told him what the people he was transporting were doing. But he said she was dressed in French civilian clothes and had a large suitcase, that probably had a radio or something in it. Her name was Vivienne Hamilton, from up at Hamilton Manor. Apparently she had a reputation even before the war as being reckless. The sort that thinks the rules don't apply to her and that she can fight the war any way she wants. God knows why those London folks sent her.

'Well, a year later when she had come back to work at the house, the fisherman had stopped taking spies in because it was getting too dangerous, but somehow she talked my grandad into it. Then she sneaked her Nazi lover out of the hospital – they say the door was left open in the library – and knocked out a guard.' He grimaced with disgust. 'Her family and the hospital staff didn't want to believe that she'd done such a thing. But why would she knock out a guard from behind if she wasn't part of the plot, if what she was doing was innocent? Surely they both would have been in cahoots, right?

'Anyway, she knocked out a guard in the house, smuggled out this Nazi, and went down to the water's edge, where my grandfather often stayed on his boat, ready to go out early fishing.

'She talked John into having them aboard the boat, and because she'd dressed the Nazi in civilian clothes, he suspected nothing right away. But as they started to sail across, apparently my grandfather started to suspect something. He could hear them talking in a different language, not English, between themselves, and why would they hide that?

'First, he thought maybe he was a Frenchman she was smuggling back to Paris, but then he confronted them, and Vivienne told him she was protecting the man because they were both in the Nazi Party. By this time the Kraut had changed into his uniform. As the sun was coming up, Grandad John turned round and got the shock of his life, seeing a Nazi in full uniform there on his boat.

'My grandad tried to talk this Vivienne out of whatever she was doing, he'd known her since she was a young girl. But she kept repeating this was what she wanted to do. He asked her, 'Is he holding you as a hostage?' Then she shook her head, saluted, and shouted, 'Heil Hitler!' And he knew she wouldn't have done that if she'd been a hostage. She was a bad 'un all right. Somehow the Nazi had corrupted her and managed to turn her to the other side.'

Barney stopped and folded his arms. 'Good job she didn't come back alive. She'd have probably come to an unfortunate accident over here. Or spent the rest of her life in jail. But I mean, why did she have to knock out my grandfather? She could've escaped; he could've got back here unharmed. Didn't have to knock him out, did they?' Barney paused, shook his head, and slurped at his pint. 'Anyway, there're a lot of good stories as well. That's the only one with a bad 'un in it.'

Sophie felt sick. It was one thing to suspect that Vivienne had become a Nazi, but to hear about her saluting and striking a man… Surely this did point to the fact she was either being manipulated or had converted to Nazism. One thing was for sure, this was fairly compelling evidence. If Sophie had still been practising law, Barney was not someone she would have relished cross-questioning. The one bright spot was she could now be pretty sure that at least at the beginning of the war Vivienne appeared to have been working for the right side.

Sophie pondered all of this as she sipped her drink, zoning out Barney who seemed to want to tell her another ten stories. She listened politely and nodded at the right times, but her mind was far away, trying to figure this all out. Surely, SOE would have put Vivienne through her paces to make sure she was trustworthy;

something major had to have happened for her story to have taken such a dark and disastrous turn.

Sophie managed to slip away after about another twenty minutes, claiming she needed to get home. But Barney could've gone on for much longer.

'Let me know if you need any more stories for your research. I'm here most days between midday and two.'

She nodded, and he must've cracked a joke about her as she left, because the bar dissolved into echoes of laughter behind her as she closed the door. She was pretty sure it was something crude and didn't want to know what it was. As she strode home she thought about her great-aunt again and she wondered about what kind of a person she was. Even with what was pointing to a tragic end, Vivienne must have been confident and self-assured, not like Sophie, who had somehow lost herself along the way. Maybe as she uncovered more of this story she would find out where that audaciousness came from, what it was that drove Vivienne, and what motivated her to do such daring – and dangerous – things.

Chapter 15

1943

As Vivi continued living in Paris she felt such a mixture of emotions, but mostly she swallowed down her feeling of being terrified and reminded herself she was doing this for England. Her country and the Allies were counting on her to do her job. In a way she was no different to the thousands of young men who marched off every day to do battle. She just wished she felt more sure of herself, more brave. She now saw all her bravado and rebellious ways of her youth through the lens of a harsh reality. And who she had been now seemed so vapid and translucent in the face of the courage she had seen in the French people every day. But nevertheless she kept moving forward, doing the best she could. Some days it felt exciting. Vivi remembered standing next to a German officer on a bus one day, her jacket padded with false ration cards, with her heart trying to thump its way out of her chest. But when he had nodded in her direction before exiting the bus, she had felt exhilarated because he hadn't suspected a thing, and she had felt the win. She was a spy and she had just defeated the enemy in her own small way.

Her work for F-section kept her busy as a courier and a wireless operator. The only feeling of normality for her was in returning home in the evening to the family she lived with who treated her with great affection.

Mr Renoir, Pascal, was a scholarly type. He read a lot and kept up on all that was happening in the war via any newspapers Vivi could obtain through the underground. His wife, Florence – or Maman as they all called her – was ever practical and modest, and she cooked the most wonderful meals even from the war rations. She insisted that her family assemble for dinner each evening despite the fact that food was scarce. Their conversation lingered late into the night, and Vivi became truly attached to the family in an extremely short amount of time.

It was there, one evening, she learned about why they'd joined the Resistance. The whole family and Vivi had been enjoying a delightful dinner, on the finest blue china, and they'd had candles lit, not because they craved the ambiance, but because the Nazis restricted the electricity throughout the day. They had been chatting about the war, when suddenly Florence became wistful.

'This war is very personal to us, you see, because as well as Yvette we also had another child. A son who has passed away… Patrice.' Silence fell around the table as the Renoirs stared into their soup, lost in their memory of him.

Vivi found the courage to ask them, 'Tell me about your son.'

Florence smiled, and there was a gentle reverence for his name upon her hostess's lips. 'Patrice was a wonderful boy. Strong-willed, and with intense feelings about this war. He was too young to fight in the Great War, so when we faced this atrocity a second time, he couldn't wait to sign up to fight for his country, to free France from the Germans.'

Florence crept silently from the table and picked up a photo in a silver frame from a drawer in a sideboard – obviously placed there, apparently still too painful to be out on display. She passed it to Vivi, and she stared at the picture of the brave young man with defiant eyes. A younger version of his father stood in his uniform, captured, as Pascal added his thoughts to the conversation.

'Taken the day before he went off to fight this war. He would have been twenty-four now,' Pascal said. 'Twenty-four years old. He died at twenty-two, right before his twenty-third birthday.' He shook his head, as if trying to loosen that thought from it. 'That's no age to die.'

Yvette looked sombre. 'I wish I was old enough to be able to fight in the war.'

Her mother scowled at her. 'Yvette, you are all we have left. Do not speak of such things. It will be over one day, and you will have a husband and children, and we'll put this time behind us. But until then, we'll do all that we can for the Resistance to bring about the end. We are more than grateful for what you are doing, Claudette, and even though we know you will be with us such a short time, we hope you feel as though you're a part of the family.'

'I do,' responded Vivi. 'I do feel a part of your family! I've grown to love all of you so much.'

Yvette perked up. 'It has been wonderful to have a sister of my very own. I need to learn to speak good English because after this war is over, I plan to travel, and one day I will go into fashion and become a fashion designer, and maybe I'll travel to London and Rome,' she said with great excitement.

Her mother tsk-tsked her. 'You, my dear, will pick up the dishes and help me wash up. These flights of fancies of yours are nothing more than that.'

'I will just be grateful to get books again,' said Pascal, wistfully. 'So much of the paper is used for other things now, and books are scarce. Claudette, if you come across any books, I would appreciate you bringing me one or two.'

Vivi smiled. 'I will look, but with my pupils, who knows? Do you like children's stories?'

He chuckled. 'At this point, I'll take anything.'

As they all made their way into the kitchen, and everyone pitched in to clear up and do the dishes, Vivi thought again how this felt so familiar, such a traditional lifestyle in such a changing world. Eating, talking, dreams and the desire for books… such simple things, and yet it was hard to know if any of these future dreams would be possible.

The only thing she feared now more than the Nazis taking her away was them hurting this family. The Renoirs had been so kind to her. The thought of it tormented her in her sleep. And so often at night, Vivi lay awake, thinking on this. So much of the preparation she'd gone through before she came had not equipped her for the emotional turmoil she would feel being in France with real people. Vivi felt she could tackle someone with a knife, but could she endure the wound to her heart if anything happened to these wonderful new friends?

She shuddered with the thought. She could not let them down. Yvette had to be a fashion designer and Mr Renoir would have his books.

Chapter 16

Present day

On the way back to the manor Sophie had another thought: what about the man Vivienne had eloped with, the Nazi? He had to have a family too. Maybe there was a way of tracking down Vivienne through him, maybe they had even had a family together. When Sophie got home, she asked her auntie Jean if she could look around in the attic in case there was anything that was left about the hospital.

'Good luck with all that dusty stuff,' Jean stated, screwing up her nose. 'I don't know why we even keep it. I'm sure I will get rid of all of it, after Dad... Well, it would upset him right now though, so it's all somewhere in boxes up there,' she said, shaking her head, as though that would get rid of all the controversy around it.

Sophie made her way up to the enormous attic and looked around in dismay – old pieces of furniture, curtains, bedding, ugly works of art. There wasn't anything in here that looked worth saving. After about an hour of searching, she did find a box. On the side of it, it said 'hospital records'. Sifting through it, right at the bottom, she found a book with the word 'admissions' printed on the front. This would be a good place to start.

Each line on the pages would have the name of a soldier, his date of birth, his serial number, what he had been admitted with, and his final outcome. As Sophie looked through, she was astonished at how many patients had come to the hospital during the war and was sad to see many had died there. Turning the pages, she finally came upon the name of the person she thought she might be looking for and a chill ran through her body as she read it. In one of the columns were the words, 'German POW'. She ran her finger along the line and read the name of the man that her great-aunt had apparently fallen in love. It was an interesting entry with a name she couldn't read having been crossed out and the name *Marcus Vonstein* put in its place. There was another German patient that arrived after Vonstein, but he was very young, just twenty. Too young to have reached such a high rank in high command as the man Vivienne had left with, according to the newspaper article Sophie had read. She quickly scanned through the rest of the book but these POWs were the only ones entered in the ledger during the relevant 1942 to '43 timeframe.

Vonstein had been admitted with a broken leg, multiple cuts and a head wound, nothing too serious to impair his escape with the help of a capable nurse by his side. But this information could be valuable. She scribbled it down.

As she continued to look through the attic she uncovered a box marked only with the letter 'V' and her heart jumped. Could this be V for Vivienne? Sophie dragged it in front of the dusty circular window at the far end of the attic and started to unpack it. There were some old clothes mostly, jumpers and skirts. She scrutinised them, trying to age them, but she wasn't sure. There were some childhood mementos and at the bottom a stack of books. Looking through them she noted they were mainly children's books and they were musty, with a lot of the pages stuck together, but one stood out from the rest. It wasn't well-worn like the others, in fact it looked as if it had only ever been opened to the one page. Sophie glanced at the front – it was a poetry book by famous English poets. Handwritten inside the cover was a verse of a poem called 'Remember' by Christina Rossetti. Sophie read it.

Remember me when I am gone away,
Gone far away into the silent land;
When you can no more hold me by the hand,
Nor I half turn to go yet turning stay.
Remember me when no more day by day
You tell me of our future that you plann'd:
Only remember me; you understand

Did Vivienne write it? she wondered. Sophie opened the book
to the page with the corner turned down. It was a poem by Lord
Byron, 'She Walks in Beauty'. Sophie smiled – it had been one
of her favourites at school. She started to read it then she noticed
something. Standing up and getting closer to the window she
stared at the words. It was faint, but under some of the words
was a pencil mark. Sophie's heart started to race. Could this be
the poem Vivienne had memorised? She opened the front of the
book. It had been published in 1943, so it had been brand new
during the war and it was the only poetry book in the box. Vivienne
must have bought it just to learn her code. Sophie quickly rushed
to her bedroom to find the copy of the coded message she had
photographed at the records building. Then sitting down at the
desk in her bedroom with a pen and paper Sophie attempted to
decode the message using different words in the poem, but no
matter what she did nothing made any sense. She felt deflated. It
was so difficult without knowing which words to use.

Sophie got up and stretched, and as she did so she knocked
the book of poetry from the desk and it fell to the floor, its pages
splayed out. Bending down to pick it up, something caught her
attention under the book's dust jacket, which had been knocked
askew in the fall. Just under the flap she could see something else
was written. Removing the cover she scrutinised the faint pencil
marks. It was a list of more code words in their groups of five,
written out over and over again. Then two lines in English then

more lines of code. It looked as if Vivienne had been practising her coding right there under the flap of the book. The long list of letters still didn't make any sense but Sophie moved closer to the window to read the lines in English. The first said *Café Liaison*, and the second mentioned a dog, it just said *Terrier*. Sophie quickly went onto her phone and looked up Café Liaison and it didn't take her long to discover there was a café by that name situated in Le Diben in Brittany close to the place the Helford Flotilla went occasionally to drop off SOE operatives. She felt a thrill, almost as if she was a spy herself; this café may have been her great-aunt's place of contact. It also confirmed her hunch that the Byron poem was the code Vivienne had used. Or at least the first layer.

Sophie made a decision – she definitely needed to go to France, to where Vivienne had been an agent. Maybe there would be more clues there.

She placed the book in her pile of research and she also added Vonstein's name to her information from the admissions book she had found. Then she did a Google search, but it turned up too many people with the same surname. Getting another idea, she typed the name into Ancestry.com – she had an account for her work. Sometimes it was useful to know more about the people who may have lived in whichever building the trust was working for.

She searched. There were still many Vonsteins. Sophie pared it down by his date of birth by the information in the admission books – he would have been thirty-four in 1944. She looked for Vonsteins of that age, and came up with four, and added a copy of their names into her Google doc. Two families appeared to live in Germany, according to the local census, one family had moved to the Netherlands, and the other was living in Paris. It occurred to her that asking them about their past might be difficult. Sophie couldn't imagine that a family of Nazis felt any better than her own family when it came to their experiences during the war, but hopefully, she would get emails back, maybe some more information.

Two Marcus Vonsteins had died during the war. Sophie sent messages to relatives of both men, informing them who she was and what she was doing and hoped that they could help.

After closing her laptop, she went down to have dinner with her family, and enjoyed the warmth of being with them. It made her miss her mother so badly. Her auntie Jean had made a wonderful beef stew, and she felt as if she were putting on weight just being here.

It had been the right decision to come to Cornwall. If she'd been in London alone, she'd have felt unbearable sadness about the split with Matt, but instead, being around people who were welcoming and kind reminded her of what family life was about, and that there were other parts of her life she could embrace to help her feel safe and secure. Since Emily's and her mother's death, there was only her gran who lived in London, and she had forgotten how much she loved Cornwall. It was so reminiscent of every childhood summer holiday.

'How is your research going?' Jamie asked as he heaped a serving of Jean's treacle sponge onto his spoon. 'Did you find out more about our war skeletons?'

Sophie paused, not sure she wanted to tell them about the conversation with Barney. It only confirmed what everybody believed. Jean added a pot of tea to the table and joined them both, interested to hear what Sophie had to say.

Playing for time, Sophie scooped up a spoonful of the pudding that had been practically forced onto her, and at once wondered why she had held back. It was warm, sweet and moist, with custard of the perfect consistency. The ideal comfort food.

'I found some records in the attic that might help me find out more,' she stated circumspectly.

'Such as?' Jean asked, pouring them all a cup of tea.

'Well, I found the name of the German officer Vivienne may have left with.'

Her auntie blew out air. 'Why would you want to know about him?' she asked defiantly. 'If it wasn't for him, she never would have gone. I mean, finding out about a relative is one thing but are you sure you want to go down the path of looking into the past of a Nazi?'

'If there is a chance to clear Vivienne of what potentially comes down to treason, I think I need to find out more about the reason why she left, and he is the key to that.'

Jamie sipped his tea. 'Do you think it's possible that she had a *good* motive for breaking a Nazi out of the hospital?'

'I think there might just be more to the story than first meets the eye. At one time, Vivienne must have been a good person. She went through the rigorous training of becoming an SOE operative to help with the war effort. Surely they would have known if something wasn't right? They would have tested her on every level.'

'You're forgetting the power of love,' reminded Jean wistfully. 'That can make even rational people do crazy things.'

'I know how it all looks, and what everyone believes,' continued Sophie, 'but I keep coming back to her trip up to London in 1944 – and if she was there on war business – and asking myself: why would she do that if she was planning on becoming a traitor? It's all so intriguing.'

'Well,' said Jean, getting up and collecting all the dishes, 'I just hope it doesn't all end in tears. What if you find out she was involved in Nazi atrocities? She could have killed people, who knows? I just hope for your sake, Sophie, continuing looking for answers here doesn't end up making the whole sorry tale even worse.'

'So, what now?' asked Jamie, genuinely interested.

'I think I need to go to Paris. There may be more war records and information about the Resistance, and I need to be where Vivienne was. Also, there is a chance some of Marcus Vonstein's relatives live there.'

Jean looked up from the suds she was amassing in her washing-up bowl. 'Please be careful with them. If their grandfather was a Nazi...'

Sophie felt exasperated. 'I doubt they are too. And anyway, I am not Vivienne, Auntie Jean. This is a completely different time.'

'But the past has a way of repeating itself,' Jean stated solemnly. 'I would just hate for you to get hurt.'

Jamie smiled. 'Mum, you are the voice of gloom and doom.' He gripped Sophie's hand. 'I think you should go, even if it turns out everything is what it originally seems. If fate went to all this trouble to open this door, you should at least walk through it.'

Sophie nodded, grateful for his support. She thought about Emily, and how visiting her grave brought her so much solace. Maybe finding Vivienne's would do the same for this unfinished story somehow, and at least Great-Uncle Tom would know where his sister was buried.

But she also couldn't help feeling there was something larger for her waiting on the other side of this story, as if this were a bigger part of her own destiny too.

Chapter 17

1943

For four weeks, Vivi's life continued to fall into a comfortable rhythm. Each week she explored the city, read to children, carried documents and delivered messages. Three times a week she successfully communicated intelligence back and forth between France and SOE in England.

Vivi was ever meticulous about her procedure, never leaving the antenna outside to be detected and shutting down her wireless after fifteen minutes so there was less chance of the enemy detecting her broadcasts. She also took alternative routes whenever she visited her Resistance cell, which she would do twice a week to communicate instructions from London and receive any of their new requests in return.

As the days of the war forged ahead, Vivi wondered how long she would be in France, but that question was settled faster for her than she'd expected.

The last time she would stay under the Renoirs' roof was on a bleak night. Paris had been enduring an onslaught of a bombing campaign from the Allied forces, and it was on the third of those nights that the air-raid siren had sounded right in the middle of her broadcast. She cut it short to get to the shelter, when a substantial bomb came down near to the house, shaking the residence and throwing her to the floor. The walls of her bedroom crumbled in around her, and dirt and debris covered her bed and the wireless.

Her ears rang with the noise, and when the brick dust cleared, she heard someone screaming from somewhere else in the house and recognised it was Yvette. Her first instinct was to find her. Jumping to her feet, she raced through the building calling to her, 'Yvette, where are you? Yvette!'

Monsieur and Madame Renoir were out visiting family and had planned to stay the night so as not to have to rush back for the curfew, so the two girls were home alone. Yvette continued to cry out in agony as Vivi stumbled through the debris towards her frantic screams, finally finding her pinned under the immense table in the front room.

Pulling the table off her, and lifting Yvette into her arms – she was as light as a feather, Vivi carried her, both of them covered in brick dust and dirt, down into the cellar, where she tended to Yvette's wounds.

The raid lasted for what felt like an eternity, and as the all-clear sounded, she knew she needed to go out and find someone to check over her young friend, who was in a great deal of pain. Venturing into the street, she was overwhelmed by the devastation that greeted her. The acrid smell of burning buildings rose above the city like a cloud, hanging heavy and choking its residents, with nothing to comfort them but the clanging bells of ambulances and fire engines as they scrambled to their destinations.

After more than an hour, Vivi gave up. It was impossible to get anyone; so many people were injured and in a far more critical state than Yvette. It was only when she started the long walk back to the house, that she remembered her wireless. Had she retrieved the antenna after she'd finished her broadcast? She had signed off, but was it still dangling there?

Vivi raced back through the city, stopping abruptly when she rounded the corner of the Renoirs' road as her worst fears met her. Being marched out of the house by Nazis were Monsieur and Madame Renoir, who had evidently rushed home after the raid.

These people who had taken such good care of her! Behind them, in a soldier's arms, was her wireless.

She retreated into the shadows, turned around and ran. Should she turn herself in, tell the Germans it was her fault? That the family she lived with knew nothing of her activities? But her choking fear alongside the trauma of the attack muddled her thoughts. So instead she ran till she could no longer go on, hot breath racing through her lungs, her heart breaking. Eventually, she collapsed onto a chair at a table of a closed pavement café to gather herself.

She would have to go to the safe house.

She grappled to rake through her memories until, eventually, she remembered the name she needed. Boulogne. The house was in Boulogne Street.

Numb and overwhelmed, she forced her feet across town. Arriving at the right street, Vivi shuddered with the bitter cold and fear, but stopped abruptly when she sighted the number she had memorised. All the Resistance houses she'd encountered since she'd arrived so far had been inconspicuous, brown shabby doors down dark alleyways. However, this one was elaborate. It had a large oak door, painted vivid crimson with a light on over the top.

Exhausted, she knocked. Recalling the name, she muttered it to herself – 'Madame Mazella'. That was the person she needed to identify.

Nothing could have prepared her for the character who flung open the door with force. Standing to meet her was a girl heavily made-up and wearing a low-cut dress with the majority of her cleavage visible.

Vivi stifled her reaction.

'Yes?' enquired the woman, frowning at Vivi as she looked her up and down.

'Madame Mazella?' Vivi enquired in a hushed tone.

'She's inside,' the woman snapped.

As Vivi stepped in, it was as if she'd entered a different world. Outside was the war and madness; in here was sheer decadence. The hallway was lavishly decorated, a thick, colourful Turkish carpet, red and gold walls and heavy velvet curtains. The air was dense with the smell of stale tobacco and cheap perfume. From the hallway, a door was opened, revealing a parlour. A woman giggled, and a man passed by her, looking her up and down before he stepped outside beaming. Vivi felt thoroughly confused, this was not what she had expected. An older woman arrived, also in thick make-up with shiny red lips. Her hair was piled on top of her head, a crayoned beauty spot drawn on one cheek.

'What do you want?' she demanded.

'Someone told me to come here.' Vivi coughed, her throat dry from the smoke and dust in the streets.

'Who?' she growled.

Vivi leaned forward, fighting the scent of cheap perfume that threatened to overpower her as she confided, 'The Terrier.'

The lips of Madame Mazella curled in the corners as she croaked out, 'We have not seen him for a while. I'm presuming you are in trouble.' Her voice was low and gravelly with the recognition of Terrier's name and the effect of the cigarettes she obviously smoked.

Vivi nodded her head.

'Come with me,' Madame Mazella instructed and, turning away, made her way up a remarkably elaborate staircase as another girl wearing nothing but her underwear came tripping down the stairs holding the hand of a man who looked drunk.

It was only then that Vivi realised what this was. She was in a brothel. Oh, good God, Terrier had sent her to a bordello? This would have been highly amusing to her if it wasn't for the fact she was in such a desperate state. Vivi followed behind the madam, and as they passed room after room, she could hear people in the throes of passion.

Vivi tried to orientate herself. All her training had not prepared her for this.

'You can have Marie's room. She is not well, so will not be here today.'

Madame Mazella unlocked a door and pushed it open. The smell of more cheap perfume, stale cigarette smoke and whisky greeted Vivi's nostrils. She stepped into the room, afraid someone would be having sex right there in front of them. But as the madam put the light on, the room was empty apart from the large double bed that dominated the room.

'You will be safe in here, but we don't serve breakfast,' the older woman quipped with a curl of her lip. 'You can stay here until someone comes for you.' She then shut the door and locked it before Vivi could say anything.

Exhausted, she sat on the edge of the bed, wondering what to do next. She searched the room and found a half bottle of Scotch and a packet of cigarettes. Unscrewing the top she swigged straight from the bottle. She was so thirsty, but she also needed to calm her shaking limbs and fast-beating heart. It wasn't until she finished her second cigarette that her breath started to slow and then the weight of all that had happened started to sink in. At first Vivi tried to sleep on the top of the cover, not sure it was clean enough to climb inside, but the sounds all around the house were very distracting and she was so on edge she kept waking with a jolt, her body prepared for combat.

Then at one point, in the early hours of the morning, someone hammered on her door.

'Marie, it is me, Marceau. I am here, my flower, my pet. Are you in there for me? Marie, don't be mad. Open the door.'

She sat bolt upright, trying to figure out what to do. If she answered him, she was worried that when he saw that his usual girl wasn't there, he'd come in after her and she didn't want to draw attention to herself or have to tackle someone in a brothel. Vivi waited, breathing quietly in the darkness, as he continued to hammer on the door.

Eventually, he left, and she walked to the window and pulled aside a threadbare purple velvet curtain with gold tassels, heavy with dust. Paris was still alight with fire and in the distance there was the hum of bombs dropping. She felt sick, Yvette was injured and the family that had taken care of her were gone. What would happen to them all now? More than anything, there was guilt. It was because she'd left the antenna on display that they were even being arrested. She had been so stupid and foolish. They had trained her, but nothing had prepared her for how it would feel to cost people their lives. Vivi was crippled by the pain and the sting of regret.

Lying down, she must have fallen asleep then, because the next thing she knew was somebody else beating on the door. Vivi looked towards the window. Even through the thin, dusty, greying net curtains she could see the sun was high. It must be late morning already; she must have slept straight through.

The person hammered at the door again.

'Go away!' she shouted. 'Marie is not here.'

Suddenly she heard a key in the door. Someone was coming in. Vivi thought through her training. She hadn't been expecting to use it in a brothel, but she was skilled in hand-to-hand combat. She looked around the room for anything she could use as a weapon, but there was nothing but a chamber pot. Picking it up, Vivi swung it up over her head. The door opened, and she held it high. And then, to her relief, she saw a familiar face.

'Very nice, how much do you charge?' Terrier smiled as he looked around the bedroom.

Vivi dropped the pot, relieved, and sank onto the bed.

Behind Terrier, the madam shook her head saying, 'Please get her out of here quickly. We need this room back, and we don't want trouble with the Nazis.'

But Vivi was shaking violently with the adrenalin coursing through her body. Terrier sat next to her on the bed. 'Claudette, listen. We have to go, do you understand? We have to get you out, now.'

His voice filtered through as he laid his hand on her shoulder. Vivi nodded and barely remembered the trip out of the brothel and back to the train, where Terrier resumed his regular deception, linking her arm, giving the impression they were a couple to people around them. She tried to keep her head down as they scuttled through the streets. All she felt was regret.

But once they were in the carriage alone, he looked kindly at her.

'It's my fault,' she spluttered out. 'I should have retrieved the aerial. Now that poor family… what will happen to them?'

Terrier turned and stared out of the window. 'It is war. It is a hard time. Though it was unfortunate you drew them to the cell.'

'What?' she snapped, staring at him, incredulously. 'Someone uncovered the network?'

He eyed her warily. 'We assumed it was you. One of the houses was raided last night.'

She shook her head. 'I told the household nothing. I wanted to protect them.' Then she remembered something. 'Yvette followed me one day to a Resistance meeting. Do you think she told them?'

He lit a cigarette and handed one to her. Vivi took it, her hand shaking, but as she drew in smoke, it calmed her. Terrier was silent. He didn't have to say anything more. Vivi sat there with her grief, not only with the thought of the family being tortured, or even murdered, but all the members of that cell. All their lives were now weighing down her conscience. Vivi felt young and ridiculous. What had made her think she could do this? Thinking it would be an adventure, that she'd be brave, that she'd change the world. And because of her foolishness, her ridiculous bravado, they were now all dead or on their way to prison. She sat back in her seat and felt numb.

'We have to get you out in case anybody else has tracked you.'

She realised with a shock he was also concerned for himself. Yvette's family knew of him, even though they didn't know where he was from. Vivi hoped that would spare him. On the return trip to Anne-Marie's, Terrier was silent, with just the rattle of the carriages on the track to comfort her. And when they got her out two days later by another boat, she felt nothing but grief and regret. Vivi had failed. She had not been careful, and now people were dead.

Chapter 18

On arriving back in England, Vivi stayed for a short period at the manor with her family before being summoned to London to report to SOE. The guilt and shock she'd felt on returning to Britain had subsided into a latent depression that made her feel sick to the pit of her stomach. She was plagued with visions of the family who she'd put in harm's way and the cell of brave Resistance fighters who had now been captured. Vivi couldn't even think about whether her mistake had caused any of this and her outlook was bleak.

Her father had been tentatively positive when she had arrived home, clearly quietly thrilled she might finally be settling down. The manor her family lived in had many rooms and beautiful gardens, and it had already been fully converted into a military hospital, with young men arriving while she had been gone.

'It'll be handy having you here, Vivi, particularly because you speak so many languages. I think it'd be better for you to be a nurse than whatever else you were… doing.' He'd said this over his newspaper, after breakfast the day she'd arrived home. He had punctuated his thoughts by nodding his head slowly, as if acknowledging the fact that he knew what she'd been doing was secret. Then added, 'This is a much more acceptable occupation.'

Vivi had agreed, at least in that moment, to help out where she could. After all, she knew, even after all the training she'd been through, she had failed at her mission and that it was probable that her time as a spy was now over.

A few days later, Vivi was travelling on the train to London. As she passed through major cities, the marks of the war were everywhere. Bombed-out buildings, barbed-wire fences and posters in every station reminding people of the cost of talking about the enemy. 'Loose Talk Costs Lives' they warned her. So do wirelesses and antennae being left out, she thought to herself with a sinking feeling of guilt.

On arrival in London, Vivi made her way quickly to Baker Street, to where she had an appointment with her handler in the afternoon. As she walked through the streets with her gas mask over her arm, Vivi felt sick to see the destruction the ongoing bombing campaigns were doing to this beloved city. At the office, Vera Atkins, the woman who took care of all the girls in SOE and who had been her original recruitment officer, eyed her with sympathy.

'Would you like a cup of tea?' she'd asked her. Vivi had nodded her head; she could tell the woman had wanted to say more. 'You know, we're all trying our best, Vivi. Sometimes things don't go right. That doesn't mean that we're not all trying.'

Vivi nodded again and looked at her shoes. Bad news obviously travelled fast.

Going in to meet with her handler, she noticed it wasn't Jepson, the head of the division, who she had been expecting. This couldn't be a good sign. If he'd had another mission for her, surely she would have been ushered into his office. Instead she was met by a serious-looking man who looked up at her through a dark fringe and dark, heavy glasses. As he moved over to the filing cabinet to pull out her file, she noticed he had a marked limp, probably from the First World War, or maybe early action in this one.

'Vivienne,' he said, returning to his desk and looking down at her file. 'Why don't you tell me what happened?'

Vivi sat back. The last thing she wanted to do was relive the horrors of what had been her life over the last week under the intense gaze of her new handler. She knew she would have to tell him everything that had happened. She started at the beginning, about the work that she'd been doing and the successful broadcasts she'd been part of. It was easy to talk about that. She felt proud of her work, but her voice started to crack as she talked about the family she'd been living with and assigned to, and the night of the bombing itself.

The man wrote some notes in the file as she talked. She couldn't manage to explain about what she'd done with the wireless. He looked up at her.

'Why don't you start at the beginning of the evening? Bombs can be a pretty nerve-wracking thing. Believe me, I know,' he said, tapping his leg.

Vivi shuddered as she remembered the horrific experience but then slowly went on to outline the incident from the beginning.

'So, it was your antenna that was still outside as the explosion happened?' he clarified.

She nodded her head. 'I signed off,' she added, trying to reassure him that she'd been following procedure. 'But then, the young girl in the house was screaming and in a great deal of pain. In my need to get to her and help her, I forgot to retrieve the aerial.' Her voice petered off.

'What did you do then?'

She explained how she'd run, looking for someone to help Yvette. How she'd come back to the house and seen the family being arrested. 'I then went to the safe house, as I had been instructed. Then I came home,' she stated flatly, fighting back the emotion.

The man waited for a second, then wrote something in his file, stamped it, and closed it shut.

'Vivi, the country is very grateful for your service, but your actions in France give us concern that you might not be of the correct...' He searched for the right words that would be the least offensive. '... calibre for missions that put you under such intense stress.' He put down his pen and spoke in a quiet, informed way.

'The fact of the matter is we feel you may be too emotional for the job, allowing the people around you to affect you in such a way that you don't complete your tasks. Agents need to be detached, keep their eye on the prize, not let sentiment sway them in any way, never losing sight of the ultimate goal of serving the country and winning this war. You did your best, no doubt, but when other people's lives are at stake we have to be very conscientious about our operatives.'

She nodded. 'I know I did things wrong, but I also know I am capable of doing much better of being exactly what you need, I know deep inside me there is the exact person you are talking about, if only you would give me another chance.'

He looked at her with great sympathy. 'Vivienne, it's a war. We're all being tested to our utmost ends. Do not feel any shame for what you did. Braver men have done worse. But I'm afraid we can't put you out in the field again.'

She nodded, already having suspected that was probably going to be the case.

'We just can't trust…' He didn't finish his sentence, simply adding, 'There is just too much at stake, you understand.'

'Of course,' she replied. Blowing her nose and rolling back her shoulders, she jutted out her chin as if she was ready to take on the world. She got to her feet and thrust forward her hand. The young man nodded, and shook it.

As she walked to the door he said quietly, 'Good luck, Vivienne, and thank you for your service.'

She didn't look back, moved right past Vera Atkins' desk without even acknowledging her. She felt so embarrassed, so ridiculous. Why had she thought she was good enough for this?

On the train home, Vivi felt the sense of loss start to sink in. For the year, training, preparing for her mission to France, had been all that had possessed her, that had given her a sense of purpose. And now, she had nothing, and she felt useless.

A WAAF came into her carriage in her uniform and sat down next to her. Vivi tried not to show the tears streaming down her face, but the woman noticed straight away.

'You all right, dearie?' she asked sympathetically.

Vivi nodded, turning her face away to look out the window.

The woman tapped her hand. 'It's a hard war. Did you lose somebody?'

Vivi nodded.

'Were you close?'

She nodded again, thinking of the family in France, and all the people in her underground cell. The weight of the pain was too much.

The woman squeezed her hand. 'Chin up, dear, make them proud.'

Vivi thought about those words. Would she ever get the chance to do that again?

On arriving back at the manor, another ambulance of soldiers was being brought in. There was already a patient in her bedroom so Vivi had had to move into a box room that had not been slept in for a while.

On arriving at the entrance, the matron who was taking care of all the admissions nodded at Vivi. 'Oh good, another pair of willing hands, I hope. We are desperate to train more nurses. Please tell me that is why you are here?'

Vivi drew in a breath and explained who she was, but that she would indeed be happy to help. She was issued with a nurse's uniform and taken through some basic first-aid skills.

'Your job will be to help make them comfortable while they're here,' the matron informed her. 'We're very understaffed. And you can also feed them, do minor duties, bed baths and such. No actual medical duties unless you want to be trained. Though that can also be arranged as well.'

Vivi nodded. 'Whatever you need. I am happy to be trained.'

Matron nodded her approval.

Making her way into the main hospital ward, she was surprised. She hadn't ventured too far into the manor since she'd got back from France, being in such a dazed and emotional state. Instead, she'd chosen to hide herself away in her room or her father's study, or walking the garden, for the past week.

The large room that used to be the ballroom was now full of hospital beds. White, metal-framed beds jammed together on both sides of the space. In the middle was a nurses' station, cabinets of drugs, and all manner of medical equipment. She introduced herself to the ward sister, who smiled at her and started right away to give her simple jobs.

Vivi was working with another nurse called Marion. She had dark-brown curly hair and lively eyes. She was petite and wiry, but strong, with a great sense of humour.

'Come on, I'll put you through your paces,' she encouraged.

Vivi found she was automatically attracted to her bubbly personality as they changed beds together, and she listened to Marion, who seemed to know exactly the right thing to say to soldiers in so much pain.

'A lot of it's their minds,' she confessed to Vivi. 'They've been through a lot of trauma. You need to read to them, or talk to them, or just listen to them. Write a letter to their sweethearts for them. Try and offer them some hope. That's the best you can do. Some of them like me to read to them from the Bible. It makes them feel calm. But on the whole, you just do whatever you need to do.'

Day by day, month by month, Vivi got better at what she was doing, and increasingly more equipped for the basic medical procedures that were needed on a daily basis. Soon she had been nursing for almost a year and could take out stitches, administer injections, and perform a number of other medical procedures. As the staff became fewer and the patients greater, her duties increased. The interaction helped her, stopped her thinking about what she'd done. But when she had time to consider it, in her heart she felt as if she'd failed. All she really wanted to do was the undercover work. It had been so rewarding. Vivi had felt skilled for that work, from the languages she could speak, to her stealth and determination. Even though she'd had moments of being terrified, there was just something inside her that had told her it was what she was really *meant* to do. There was no need for her armed-combat training in the hospital wards.

The hardest times were the nights. Vivi found it difficult to sleep. The estate backed onto the beach, and even though they were under the blackout, sometimes she would slip out of the manor. And even though a lot of the sand had barbed-wired fences and was planted with mines, she would walk along the seashore, looking out at the water over the fence, and it calmed her. Her thoughts always returned to France and the family she had left behind.

It was one night like this when she saw it. She'd been on one of her late-night walks, out after midnight. It had been a full, bright moon as she'd crept along the beach, when, all at once, above her in the air, there was a sharp flash of light and then the sound of a plane coming down, its engines obviously in trouble. She could see it silhouetted against the moon, but once it hit the water, it seemed to disappear from her view. It was out about a mile. She knew she should let someone know straight away. She couldn't tell if the plane was German or English.

She rushed home to the manor and called the local police station and coastguard to report her sighting.

'Vivienne Hamilton, how did you see that from the manor window? I hope you weren't out on the beach, that would be dangerous,' reminded the local constable, who she'd known all of her life.

'It was a very clear night,' she lied.

He didn't sound convinced by her excuse, but nevertheless, the police arrived promptly. Grabbing her binoculars, she crept out to watch the recovery mission.

Boats bobbed out on the water, the frantic glare of torchlight searching as the men called out to one another. Occasionally they would find debris that they hauled up onto their boats. All at once, one shouted urgently to another, and she saw a light that was trained out onto a particular spot on the water, where there seemed to be something floating in it. Focusing her field binoculars where they had centred their attention, there indeed was something in the water, limp and dark. The rescue crew leaned over and heaved the dripping mass up the side of the tiny fishing boat. Vivi drew in breath, because even though she couldn't tell for sure, it looked as if it might be a body.

Chapter 19

Vivi had barely returned from the beach and was in the kitchen making herself a hot drink before returning to bed when the door was flung open and there stood Marion, who'd been assigned to night duties.

'Thank goodness,' she gasped. 'Vivi, we need your help. The local authorities have brought in someone who was in the water!'

Vivi was surprised. If it was the same person she had just seen pulled out, she had thought he was dead. Following her friend, Vivi quickly grabbed her nurse's apron from the uniform closet. She pulled her hair back into a bun and adjusted her nurse's cap as she walked to the observation room.

She was amazed to find it bustling. Whenever patients came in, they were assessed in an area that in a former time had been the butler's pantry, before being taken to the ward. Normally at this time of night there would just be a doctor and a nurse or two, but Vivi was surprised to see the tiny room was filled with people. Three policemen, two members of the Home Guard, two doctors who had started working on the patient, and another nurse.

'Oh good, they've found you, Vivi,' commented one of the doctors. 'We know you speak good French, is that correct? We have reason to believe by the papers in this man's pockets that he may be from France.' The doctor pointed to soaked documents drying on a table next to him.

Vivi looked down at the patient and something stirred within her, as though she'd known him or had seen him before but she couldn't recollect where. His body was still limp as they started to remove his clothing so they could see the extent of his injuries. She noticed his body was strong and athletic, his leg looked broken, and there was a severe cut to his forehead which one of the doctors was already attending. His damp blond hair was layered across it and his brow was lightly spattered with his own blood.

Vivi was mesmerised, caught by the angelic expression on his face that made him appear as though he were trapped somewhere between this and the next world. He had a strong chin and his face had a boyish quality to it even though it was grey and his breathing was shallow.

He was French, Vivi thought with a jolt, and again her mind returned to Paris. Part of her wanted to run from the room and never speak that language again and she started to tremble, but part of her was also captivated by this person.

When she didn't answer the doctor, he turned to her again. 'Is that correct, Vivi? You speak French?'

Vivi quickly nodded as she was jarred back into the present moment.

'We might need you here just in case we can get him conscious.'

'I'm amazed he survived in the water,' she whispered as she continued to help the other nurse take off the rest of his sodden clothes.

'Yes, fortunately someone called us,' stated the local constable. He eyed her with the acknowledgement that she'd been the one who made the call but he obviously didn't want to get her into trouble with the Home Guard about being out at the beach.

'But I don't understand why there was a French plane this far over, all the way over here in Cornwall?' she commented, trying to make sense of it.

'I know, it's a little bit of a mystery,' the constable continued as he stared down at information he had written in a small notebook. 'But the plane hasn't yet been recovered. It must have hit the water at such a speed that it broke up. We believe this man was a passenger. So we're out looking for the pilot and any debris now.'

The man mumbled in his sleep as she started to remove his boots and straight away Vivi could see why. He also had a deep wound to the leg that was broken. She mentioned it to one of the doctors, and he came to assist her.

They continued to work through the night, and as soon as the patient was stabilised, his wounds were sewn up. Unconscious, he was taken to a quiet room in the house, away from the main ward, one that was kept set aside for infectious diseases and which would now act as the man's hospital room until he was conscious, so he could be observed.

Stripping back the stark white sheets and grey woollen army blankets, together she and Marion placed him into the bed. Once they had him settled, Vivi looked around. This was a cheery room and had been her playroom as a child. How odd to think that patients now stayed in here. Again, she studied the man's face, and though it was Marion's job to monitor him through the night, she felt a pull again, something she couldn't explain, a desire to be close to him. Vivi shook the thought from her mind. She was tired and he was French, that was all. His presence just brought up so many conflicting emotions for her.

Vivi finally fell into bed about three o'clock, but was unable to sleep and instead lay staring at the ceiling, remembering once more what had happened to her in Paris. Would she ever feel all right about it? As the memory of Yvette's laughing eyes swam before her, she still felt such anger towards the enemy that had stolen people she cared about from her. And it was hard to think that the home she had been a part of was not full of the people she loved. Monsieur Renoir sitting in the corner of his room poring over a book she had managed to find him, and from the kitchen, the sounds and smells of Maman creating something magical out of their rations. Tears stung her eyes again as she felt so much sadness for them all.

Vivi barely slept that night and was awoken with a jolt the next morning with someone banging on her door. As she peered at her clock she realised she'd slept in through the start of her shift. Bleary-eyed, grabbing her dressing gown, she opened the door. It was the matron.

'Oh good, you're up, Vivi.'

'I was working in the middle of the night.'

The matron stopped her with a raised hand. 'I know all about it. There's no need for you to explain. We didn't expect you on the ward this morning, but we do need you, nevertheless, as our French patient is starting to stir. Can you get dressed as quickly as possible and go to his room, see if you can get any more information from him?'

Vivi nodded. Feeling exhausted, she closed the door and made her way into the bathroom to get ready. Putting on her uniform, she contemplated what it'd be like to have someone here from France. Maybe it would help her make amends somehow?

Arriving at the room, she moved inside, and it took a moment for her eyes to adjust to the darkness, though even from the doorway she could see his own were closed, his breathing was laboured and his blond hair was draped across his pillow. His chest was bandaged, as was the wound on his head, and the broken leg had been set. As she approached his bed, he groaned and very slowly he opened his eyes. Vivi caught her breath, noticing they were of the deepest blue as he attempted to focus on her.

'My name is Vivienne Hamilton, Vivi,' she said in French, placing a hand on his arm to reassure him. 'I speak French and will be here to attend to you.'

Slowly, he nodded.

'Your plane came down in the water, but it wasn't recovered. Was anyone else with you, can you remember?'

He looked at her blankly for a moment, then shook his head. She wasn't sure if he was saying there was no one else or that he didn't recall.

He opened his mouth and whispered one word, 'Où?'

'You are in a hospital in Cornwall, England and are safe here. Now, I need to examine you.'

He nodded again, his eyes following her as she approached the bed to look at his chart to review her morning duties. Moving about the room, she drew out her stethoscope. As she gingerly pulled aside his hospital pyjamas, she noticed once again that his chest was firm and muscular. As he watched her intently, and she drew close to him to listen to his heart, she had that feeling again, that pull that drew her to him as if she knew him or had always known him. Vivi tried to shake off the odd sensation so she could do her job.

Placing the stethoscope on his chest, she noted his heartbeat was a little weak, but the rhythm was good. As she moved over to get her blood-pressure gauge, his voice reached out to her.

'Mademoiselle?' His tone was deep and measured.

'Vivi,' she reminded him.

'Vivi,' he corrected himself, then with what seemed like a great deal of effort, he whispered, 'Merci.'

'It's my job,' she informed him, trying to sound businesslike. But for some reason, at the sound of his voice, her heart was pounding and she was starting to feel hot. Maybe the nursery needed a little ventilation, she mused.

Walking to open a small window, she took a deep breath. Then, she took medication that had been prescribed for him from the bottle, something for the pain she was sure he was in, even though he seemed very calm.

Pouring a glass of water, she held it out, but he just looked at it as if even lifting his hand would exhaust him. So gently she placed the tablet on his tongue as he watched her intently before swallowing it down with the sip of water she offered him. Then his eyes fluttered closed again.

Chapter 20

Over the next few days, Vivi continued to nurse the Frenchman, and as he grew stronger, he told her his name was François. Though he never said as much, she wondered if he was French Resistance, though the fact he had been flying to England was scant evidence. Even if he was, she knew he couldn't talk about what he was doing in detail, but she desperately wanted to know if he had heard any more about the family that she'd been living with when she'd been in Paris.

One evening, Vivi got the answer she had been hoping for. She had been assigned to the night shift and as she had been checking on François he started mumbling in his sleep and she heard clearly the words *quarante-huit* and then the word 'Prosper'. Prosper was the name of the leader of her network. Her heart skipped a beat, her instincts had been right – this was a French Resistance fighter. It all made sense to her. And though she knew she should probably be cautious, Vivi found she desperately wanted to connect with someone to see if there was any news from her fallen cell.

The next day Vivi had finished giving him some soup, and he was sitting upright in bed, watching her, as he usually did, as she continued performing her medical duties. His eyes revealed nothing as he listened to her chattering to him in French.

'I know you probably can't talk about it if you are, but you said something in your sleep last night about… *Prosper.*'

His face showed nothing. Convincing her even more he was an agent.

'I'm sure many patients say ridiculous things in their sleep, why are you interested?'

She took her heart in her hands. She knew being impulsive was one of her weaknesses, but her need to know about the Renoirs was keeping her awake at night. She was desperate for any information.

'I have some interest in that word,' she said carefully.

He just nodded without saying anything as she changed his bandages. She didn't want to give anything else away and she felt a great sense of disappointment at his silence.

Over that week as his strength started to grow, she looked forward to visiting François. Was it their possible shared experiences or the fact he was so attractive? She wasn't completely sure, but she knew attending to him was the highlight of her day.

One afternoon, Vivi brought him a book she'd found in the family library that was written in his native French.

'I thought you might like something to read,' she informed him as she handed it to him.

He thanked her, though his expression, as always, appeared cautious, as though he didn't totally trust Vivi. She remembered from her own training with SOE that you were always taught to hedge towards caution when dealing with anyone. You could never be sure that the person you were talking to was actually who they said they were. But as the days went on, he seemed to be feeling more confident around her and started to open up to her.

One day, she decided to find out for sure if he in fact was an agent. As she wheeled him out into the garden, she used a phrase that she had been taught to identify herself as an agent.

'I have noticed it is hard to get daily newspapers on Sundays,' she said, holding her breath.

He looked up at her, searching her face before whispering back, 'But books are of course still available.'

It was the correct response to her code and her heart leapt as she knew at once he had to be an agent.

When she had been undercover she wasn't really supposed to talk about her work in France, but what could it matter now? And maybe he would have information about the Renoirs. Maybe, when he was well and continued on his mission he could let her know if they were safe.

'I was a member of Prosper Network,' he informed her in quiet tones. 'Do you know of it?'

'Of course.'

He went on to talk about the cell she remembered. Her heart gladdened with his knowledge of the people and of the organisation she'd been a part of and surely if he knew so much he could be trusted. Vivi wouldn't give out anything classified, places or agents, but she was so desperate to make a connection.

'I was also working in Paris,' she informed him in a whisper. 'I was a wireless operator for a while before there was...' She stopped to collect herself. 'A tragedy.'

He nodded, observing her closely. 'You are very fortunate that you made it out alive. I know the cost to the operatives has been...' He faltered too, choosing his words carefully. 'The cost of life there has been high in F-section.'

She nodded, relieved to finally talk to someone else about it. Since his arrival she had grown to really like this man, and once this door was open, he too appeared to need to unburden himself.

Vivi talked about her time in France before the war, and he spoke about his family in the Alsace region and how he'd grown up on a farm. As he spoke about the vineyards that his family still owned and the love he had for it all, it affirmed to her once again why they were fighting this war – to protect people like François.

'Why did you join the Resistance?' she asked him one evening, as she was reapplying his bandages.

He looked desolate. 'My brother,' he whispered. 'My brother was killed. He was the one. The one who was supposed to take over the vineyard. He was taller, smarter, brighter than me. He was the most obvious choice, and he loved working alongside my father. But he was killed by a German soldier over the price of our wine, just slaughtered there in front of my mother. I wasn't there,' he continued sadly. 'But I will not rest until these animals are defeated.'

He became agitated as he spoke, shifting his weight in the bed, trying to find a comfortable position.

'My father and sister have been devastated ever since and my mother has barely spoken. If Marcel had gone off to war and been granted a hero's death, that would have been one thing, but to be killed in his own vineyard over a ridiculous dispute... I will never get over the senselessness of it all. I left my family then and journeyed to Paris to see what I could do. Since then I have joined Prosper and I've been working undercover.'

As she nursed him they often talked about the people they knew in Prosper and the people that she missed. So many, he had informed her, had gone missing or were killed. She found herself being drawn to his gentle and easy spirit, though he seemed agitated, clearly wanting to get back into the fight.

One day she decided to ask him for the help she so desperately needed. 'There was a family I lived with, and the day I left Paris I didn't have time to check on them. I have great concerns for their safety. Is there any way when you go back you can check for me?'

'Write their names down,' he told her. 'I will memorise them then I can check for you and get back to you with their well-being.'

She hesitated for only a moment, studying his face for any sign of distrust, but his blue eyes conveyed nothing but a desire to help. Quickly, she wrote their names and the address.

'How long do you think it will be before I can leave?' he asked. 'I need to get back. There is important war work to do.'

'Soon.' She smiled. 'We have to wait for your leg to set properly and you still have a few injuries that we are taking care of. We need to watch for infection. I understand your desire, but we need to make sure that you're in one piece before you go back to work.'

'Is there any news of my aircraft?' he asked cautiously.

Vivi shook her head. 'There wasn't ever any wreckage recovered. And the pilot has not been found.'

He nodded his head, but Vivi noted there was something more. Something more than him just asking. She could see it in the intensity of his expression and wondered what it could be.

Chapter 21

As François started to get well, Vivi was able to take him out onto the grounds of the manor more often, and as the weather began to turn warmer, she would wheel him out to the spring garden where tulips and daffodils were starting to push through the dark, frozen ground. If it was warm enough, they would sit out there and talk away from the confinement of the hospital. Their conversations became more fluid, more intimate. As every day passed, Vivi found her attraction to him growing. His easy laugh and manner, the long lashes and his piercing blue eyes that with one look could twist her stomach into knots.

One bright spring day, she had wheeled him out and they sat in their favourite spot. It was chilly and she had covered him with a blanket, even though a weak winter's sun was trying its best to warm up the cold earth.

'I am so grateful to you, Vivi,' he said, his gaze meeting hers. 'Not only for your nursing, but for your companionship. This war has not given me many moments to pause, where I have just been able to live. There has been so much to do for as long as I can remember. I have either been preparing for a mission, on a mission, or recovering from one. It has been such a long time since I was just able to be myself with someone else.' His eyes found hers with intensity as he added, 'Someone I'm starting to fall in love with.'

He slipped his hand on top of hers. She felt a jolt of electricity through her body. She had wanted to hear those words from him and touch him for over a week but had been holding back, examining the feelings she had. Vivi had never been really in love before. She'd had a number of dalliances but nothing with the strength of feeling of this attraction. If this was anything like the beginning of it, she couldn't believe the attraction she felt just looking at him, being with him, with him holding her hand. It felt like something was complete in her, created by whatever this was between them.

Vivi shook the tears from her eyes, experiencing a mixture of joy and the sadness that constantly loomed over her. 'You wouldn't say that if you really knew me,' she stated flatly.

He looked at her, startled. 'What do you mean?'

'I'm woefully headstrong. I jump in with both feet before I think anything through, and I have a…' She paused. 'A past I'm not proud of.'

He lifted her hand gently to his lips and kissed it. 'All of the qualities that I love so much about you. Many people would have been cautious with a foreigner. You have made me feel so welcome and cared for.'

'I've done terrible things,' she blurted out before she could stop herself. 'People died,' she said. 'People died because of me, because of my lack of thought, and I have to live with that every single day. I'm not sure I want to burden anybody else with that pain.'

He gently took hold of her shoulders so she would be facing him and, placing a finger under her chin, he raised it so her eyes met his.

'Vivi, we all have to do things we regret in this war.' He swallowed. 'Deceive people that we love, say things and be things that we never in our life imagined that we'd have to be. But you have to remember that we are doing it for a greater good. We are just small cogs spinning inside a huge wheel. But every one of us is important. Sometimes we make mistakes. Because we are human. That is all you did, Vivi. You made a mistake.'

'People are dead,' she sputtered out.

'You don't know that for sure. Your French family may still be alive.'

She shook her head. 'I just have a terrible gut feeling. I think that Yvette would have written back if they were all right. I wrote to them a while back under a different name, and I've heard nothing from them. What I would do to go back and put these things right.'

She started to sob.

He pulled her into his arms then, and Vivi allowed him to hold her. As hard as it was to talk about these things, his empathy and the care that she saw in his eyes made it all right somehow. It was as though he understood.

'I, too,' he whispered into her ear, 'have done terrible things that I regret. But if I just focus on that, I will never be of any use to anyone. I will never be able to put things right by making this war end. That is what drives me every day – the end of this war so we can go back to living our lives. Vivi, please, I want you to think on these things.'

As he held her, she felt complete, wanting to stay there next to him for the rest of her life. But Vivi knew she had to hold back, keep back everything she was feeling. She was his nurse, and she was also afraid to let anybody else in. She didn't want anybody else to get hurt, especially someone she had such strong feelings for.

Feeling foolish for crying in front of him, she pulled away and took out her handkerchief, blew her nose and wiped her eyes.

'I should get you in before it gets too cold,' she informed him as he watched her intently. She looked down at him, and as if it were the most natural thing in the world, he pulled her down and kissed her gently on the lips. Just a friendly kiss that said, 'We're in this together and I understand.' But it felt so incredible to Vivi. The things she'd known with her heart in her life to this point had been a mere shadow of the feeling she had now. As he pulled away, she looked into his eyes. She wanted to stay there for the rest of her life, there in the garden. Then something else suddenly hit her. Soon he would be going back to fight, and she would lose him to the war. The pain of losing him started to grip hold of her heart in a way she'd never known.

Vivi stood and started to wheel him back to the ward.

'You're a good nurse.'

'As you can see, I am not a good nurse. I'm not supposed to kiss the patients.'

'It is a great help for healing,' he joked with her. 'I'm beginning to feel better already.'

She smiled as she pushed the chair. As they headed to the ward, both her heart and her mind were in distress. So many feelings were coursing through her body, emotions she didn't seem to have any control over. Immense joy mingled with the sadness of the impending loss. She felt overwhelmed with all of it.

Back in François's room, Vivi helped him into his bed, and he squeezed her hand one more time before she left him to get on with her duties. The feeling of that touch lingered in her memory, and as she worked the rest of the afternoon, she would periodically look down at her hand and would remember his touch, wondering again where this would lead.

Chapter 22

One morning, a couple of weeks after François had arrived, Vivi heard a commotion in the great hall, and when she went to find out what was being said, Marion told her something had been washed up on the beach, part of an aeroplane. As Vivi was finishing her shift for the night, she decided to walk down to the beach to watch the recovery effort. She hoped it might be her patient's missing plane and would love to find something for François, something she could give him back of his personal belongings.

PC Tassker, the local constable, was there, along with the Home Guard and a small group of locals, all watching as the debris was gathered. Part of the fuselage had washed ashore, as had some of the cargo, a jacket and mission equipment, and finally a case was dragged up the beach. This created quite a stir amongst the onlookers. Tassker stepped forward.

'Come on, everybody,' he said in his official voice. 'This is war business. I can't have you all lingering around here. We have to wait until someone from the War Office comes down to look at all this.'

Everyone started protesting.

'It won't hurt just to take a peek inside,' stated Vivi, eyeing the suitcase with anticipation. 'I have a patient in the hospital, and he lost everything when his plane came down. If this wreckage is from that plane, then there may be important documents, pictures of his loved ones. You could at least take a peek.'

PC Tassker looked around nervously. The Home Guard were occupied close to the water, inspecting some more of the fuselage that was being brought up the beach.

'You'll be the death of me, Vivienne Hamilton,' he said, blowing out air.

'Come on, Henry,' she implored. 'Just a quick look?'

The policeman carefully snapped open the clasps and threw back the lid, and they both stood back in shock. Instead of civilian clothes, as she'd expected, and personal items, the first thing to greet them was a German army uniform. By the stripes and the flags on the pocket, she knew instantly that this belonged to a member of high command. Vivi was confused and disappointed. This case wasn't from François's crash, but obviously another plane, maybe shot down by their own forces.

'Now we've gone and done it, Vivienne,' spluttered Tassker with great concern. 'Look at the state of that. That's a Nazi uniform. What's a Nazi's uniform doing on a plane all the way over on this coast?'

Vivi shook her head, trying to make sense of it herself, then she had a thought. 'The man I've been nursing was from France. It can't be his. Or maybe it was something to do with the work he was doing,' she offered.

'We should probably just close it up again and say nothing,' PC Tassker said, sounding desperate.

Vivi shook her head. 'I need to know what this is, Henry.' She knelt down and started to rustle through the clothes and then she found some paperwork in a sealed container, that had amazingly mostly survived seawater damage. The uniform did indeed belong to a member of high command. She opened it up, and to her horror, there was the picture of her patient and below it the name, Major Marcus Vonstein.

She shook her head in disbelief and tried to make sense of this. Surely this was wrong. Why did François have German paperwork if he was undercover for the French Resistance? Then a fear-inducing thought struck her, as she remembered every single word that she'd told him about the Prosper Network.

She didn't even wait for Henry to close the suitcase. She marched right back to the house, her heart beating hard in her chest, and straight to François's room, flinging open the door. Her patient was sleeping. She didn't wake him gently.

Slamming the door behind her she snapped in German, 'Major Vonstein, I presume.'

Instantly his eyes opened and he looked concerned.

'You have found my suitcase,' he said quietly, answering her back in German.

She looked into his eyes and she tried to read him. But he was blank and it took everything within Vivi's control not to grab her bandage scissors and stab him with them. He had deceived her. Instead, she approached his bed, her body shaking with anger.

'You used me. You used me to find out information.'

He shook his head vehemently.

But before she could say anything else, the door opened again and in came PC Tassker with the Military Police who were always present at the hospital. Vivi translated for them all.

'We have reason to believe that you're a member of the high command of the German army and, in that respect, we must take you into custody.'

François's eyes did not leave Vivi's and she saw the desperation in them as he answered.

'As you can see, gentlemen,' he said pointing to his leg, 'I am unable to resist your request.'

One of the military policemen continued, 'You shall now be guarded, and as soon as you are well enough, you will be transported to a prison that we have locally for enemies of the Allies.'

The patient nodded.

They walked over and handcuffed him to the bed.

Vonstein shook his head in disbelief. 'That is unnecessary. My leg is broken.' He then shouted after Vivi as she started to leave, 'Miss Hamilton, I want to thank you. I am grateful for all your care.'

Vivi did not look back. She had too many feelings going on inside her shaking body. Mainly anger and frustration, but she also felt so foolish she was beside herself. As she rushed from the room all she could think about was what she had said to him, and the people she might have put in danger, yet again.

The next day, an officer arrived from the local regiment, ahead of the members of the intelligence services who would arrive from London in a few days to interrogate the prisoner. Vivi was summoned to the matron's office to meet with them.

PC Tassker introduced him to Vivi. 'This is Vivienne Hamilton. Her family owns this manor. You can trust her. She also speaks fluent German.'

The field officer eyed her quizzically. 'And why is that, young lady? Why do you speak German?'

She looked between the two of them and the matron. She knew that she wasn't supposed to really speak about SOE, especially after what had just happened with Vonstein. But what was the harm now?

'I lived in Europe for some time. And I have, in the past, done war work. That can be checked upon. I'd rather not talk openly about it, but I have been trusted by the government in the past.'

The man nodded, understanding that Vivi was protecting the work that she'd done, and he seemed satisfied that she would be a good translator for them.

'You understand, Miss Hamilton, that we have to be careful? If there was any chance that you were working for the enemy, you could translate things to the prisoner that could be of consequence. Matron tells me you and the prisoner were quite close.'

Vivi flushed, speaking rapidly to cover her embarrassment. 'That was before I knew who he really was. You should have no worries of me treating him any different than any other Nazi, now I know who he really is.' The picture of him kissing her swam into her thoughts and she shuddered with the memory. How could she have been so foolish? She continued to reassure the officer. 'Of course, I'm happy to provide a transcript of the things we talked about, if you wish.'

The authorities went with Vivi to interrogate Marcus though he gave nothing but his serial number, name and rank. The whole time his eyes never left her face but she found a spot above his head to ask him the questions, fighting her anger mixed with tears.

After the meeting they all reconvened in Matron's office.

'We had an idea that he'd be awkward. It's pretty much what we expected,' the field officer informed the matron. 'However, we've caught wind of something we would like to track. Afraid I can't give you any details. We have a feeling this man may have been a part of something the enemy was cooking up, and we'd like to find out what it is. With your permission, Matron, we'd like to bring in another German soldier. The hope is, as they talk freely with one another, he will disclose some secrets of where he's from and why he is here. We will set up a listening device in the room so that we can track everything that is said. In the meantime, Vivi, if you can continue to win him over, you can try and find out anything that you can.'

Vivi nodded with great reluctance.

After he left them, Vivi felt sick. She hadn't realised how much she had started to feel for François… *Marcus*, she reminded herself, with great bitterness. François did not exist! Brushing away tears, she made a decision she would use all the skills she had learned with SOE to find out everything she could. She would not let this Nazi get under her skin.

In the afternoon, as she leaned in to wrap the bandage around his back, his eyes met hers for a minute. 'I'm sorry I had to lie to you,' he whispered to her in French, and there he was again, her François. He made her tremble; it was such an easy act he could slip into, and she fought back her feelings. When she didn't answer him, he gently touched her arm. 'I hated doing it, please believe me, but we are at war. We do what we have to do.'

She stared at him with disdain. 'You didn't need to prey on my hurt and pain just to get information.'

He genuinely looked remorseful. But she pulled her arm away from him before he could say any more.

Vivi held herself back from slapping him. Not just for his deceit, but for the feelings that were still brimming inside her. She wanted to hurt him for putting them there.

Vivi continued to wind his bandage around his chest and he looked at her with surprise. 'Are you trying to cut off my circulation? Maybe kill one body part at a time?'

He was being light with her, but she was having none of it. She finished her work and turned and left the room without giving him a backward glance.

Moving downstairs, the matron beckoned her into her office again.

'I've just heard from the authorities. The government is sending us another captive in the next day or so. He's en route. They'll put them in the room together, and hopefully our prisoner will open up to him, and we will learn more.' She went on to explain the situation. As luck would have it, a German reconnaissance mission had been shot down in the North Sea, and three men had been taken prisoner. Two were on the way to jail, but one needed medical attention. They would equip the room with listening equipment when Vonstein was taken out for a procedure. The purpose was to try to get Vonstein to relax and chat and then they could glean more information about the enemy.

Vivi nodded and started to leave the room.

'Vivi.'

She turned.

'Thank you for doing this. I know how difficult it must be. But we can make a difference, here in this little hospital, if we find out information that can help our boys.'

Vivi nodded and reminded herself, once again, this was why she was doing this: for the good of the country, for all the people that she'd lost. Maybe she could put things right, even in a small way.

Chapter 23

The day after she visited the museum in Helford, Sophie decided to book passage on a private boat trip over to France. They ran from the harbour on bank holidays and other occasional weekends so locals could have a few days on the continent and buy cheap wine.

'Are you sure you want to do this?' her auntie Jean asked as they sat eating dinner the evening before. 'Wouldn't you rather stay here in Cornwall, relax a little longer?'

She shook her head. 'I need something to keep me busy. I have things I'm...' she paused to find the right words, '...dealing with in London, and with everything I have been through in the past year I feel as if I need to be doing something more to keep my mind active.'

Jean nodded with knowing, apparently not wanting to ask for any clarification. Since Emily's and her mother's death, many people had responded this way when she displayed any kind of emotion. The nodding, the squeezing of her hand, some even quickly changing the subject. No one really knew how to deal with this kind of tragedy. It was too raw and unfair and words just didn't seem to be enough.

Sophie turned her mind to what she was there to do. Through her research, she had managed to gather a lot more information about the route the Secret Service had taken from Cornwall through France to Paris, via the Helford Flotilla – a group of fishing boats that sailed right from the village – and she was eager to investigate further.

She arrived at the dock early in the morning. There was a brisk chill at the water's edge, though her group of fellow passengers were in good spirits. Finding a seat close to a window, her mind drifted as the captain of the vessel droned out safety instructions in a strong Cornish accent. Seagulls bobbed and weaved in the surf looking for their breakfast. It was hard for her to imagine what this port would have been like in wartime.

Was what she was doing futile? she wondered. The lawyer in her reminded her there were always so many ways to see a story. But it was hard facts that told the truth, and they were something glaringly missing in Vivienne's story. Yes, she had gone with the Nazi, but why? Until she uncovered more facts that would help her understand Vivienne's reasons, she would not be able to settle.

It was a long trip, and as the boat finally approached the small port of Le Diben in Brittany, Sophie shuddered. How strange to think that her great-aunt had known a similar view nearly seventy years before.

As Sophie stepped onto the quay, the seaside town was quiet in early spring, mainly closed for the season, though the cafés, restaurants and gift shops were all open. Sophie had wanted to take Vivienne's exact journey to Paris. The spies' course had also been outlined in the museum in Helford and she knew one of the coffee shops, the one written in her aunt's poetry book, acted as a port of call for visiting spies, connecting them with their handlers and ensuring their safe onward trip. Maybe it would be a good place to start?

The café Sophie had read about was called the Liaison, and it was still open. Walking down the cobbled streets she found it and stepped inside. In contrast to the otherwise sleepy port town, it had a lively atmosphere. Modern art pieces were illuminated by spotlights and loud jazz music was playing. At the counter, a coffee machine was steaming with life as patrons sat along the bar, chatting to the baristas. The smell of fresh coffee and warm pastry reached out to greet her; apple and custard tarts, cheese and ham filled baguettes, and chocolate croissants. Her mouth watered as she made her way to the counter.

In her broken high-school French she ordered a coffee and one of the flaky pastries that was calling to her from a glass counter below the bar.

'You are English, no?' the jovial young man behind the gleaming coffee machine asked as she ordered.

Sophie nodded, knowing for sure what had given her away – languages had never been her strength.

'You are here for a holiday this early in the year?' he questioned, raising his eyebrows.

'No.' She shook her head. 'I'm here to do a little research.'

'Research? In this little fishing town?'

She smiled. 'I'm actually on my way to Paris. I'm hoping to follow the trail of a relative during World War Two.'

'The spy network. You are following the trail of the spy network.' He smiled with knowing. 'Our café was very famous during that time, did you know?'

'That I have heard,' she said. 'I googled you.'

He laughed. 'Here, let me show you. We have a special place dedicated to the people that did this.'

He wiped his hands on a bar towel and led her to a wall of photographs. A banner above it said 'World War Two Heroes' and there was a scattering of black-and-white shots of people taken in the café.

He pointed to a photo of a stout man with a balding head, holding a tray of pastries in front of him, a cigarette balanced on the corner of his mouth, with a petrified-looking woman by his side.

'This is my great-great-uncle Pierre. He ran this café. He worked for the Resistance.'

Sophie nodded, amazed that someone so ordinary-looking could be a local hero.

'They never caught him. They never knew what we used the café for during that time.'

Sophie scanned the photos quickly, looking for Vivienne, but she was disappointed to see there was no one as striking as her great-aunt, with her platinum-blonde hair and pretty heart-shaped face.

The barista pointed out other characters, telling her different stories of bravery. 'This one,' he said, pointing to a short man with glasses, 'killed a Nazi by sabotaging his car. This woman slept with Nazis to get information. This woman confronted and killed a Nazi in an alley in a town close by and was unfortunately hung for it, and this man slowly poisoned the food of German officers, giving them terrible stomach problems.' Sophie was amazed as he continued, 'They had to be very careful, because sometimes the enemy would come pretending to be undercover. That happened once with a beautiful female English spy who turned out to have secretly joined the Nazi Party.'

Sophie shuddered inside. He had to be talking about Vivienne with her blonde hair and green eyes, but she tried not to show any connection. 'Do you know much about that story?' she asked, working to keep her tone even.

'Only that she was a traitor. A beautiful blonde, just like you,' he joked, flirting openly with her. Sophie felt her cheeks flush, not only with the compliment but also with the truth of the comparison. 'The story is that she came here earlier in the war pretending to work for the British. But she was obviously a double agent because she was spotted at the train station later in the war with a German officer.'

He pointed at a picture of a handsome young man with a heavy dark moustache and dark eyes, rocking back on a chair in the café, a cigarette in his hand. 'This man was called the Terrier. He used to transport many of the spies to Paris.'

Sophie sucked in breath at the mention of his name, and thought about the word in the poetry book.

'Did he meet the woman who defected?' she asked quietly.

'Maybe, I don't know.'

She looked at the curling black-and-white photo. The Terrier looked so unassuming and relaxed, as if he were on holiday in the south of France, not working for the underground.

'What happened to him?'

'I think he was betrayed. It was a hard time,' the barista added, flatly.

Sophie continued to browse the photographs. The people looked so ordinary. Underneath them were written their names and all they did during the war. It suddenly struck her how courageous people could be.

The young guy smiled at her as a new customer walked into the café. 'I have to go and serve, but feel free to stay.' He saluted her. 'Vive la France.' And off he went, being drawn into happy chatter with a new customer.

She sat down at the table in front of the photo wall, slowly drinking her coffee and pulling off pieces of the delectably warm croissant to pop into her mouth as she stared at the photos, thinking about the Terrier. How had he been caught? Had her aunt Vivienne known him? Or had she been the one who had turned him in?

She couldn't think like this. It was too awful.

After her coffee, she made her way to the little bed and breakfast she had booked for the evening. It was a sweet farmhouse located on the outskirts of the village and the woman that ran it insisted Sophie join her and her family for dinner, though she didn't understand a lot of the conversation, which was mainly conducted in French. After dinner Sophie went for a walk along the coastline. The wind had picked up since she had arrived and it roared past her ears, whipping her hair about her face. As she watched the angry waves crashing forth onto the beach and spraying frothy white foam onto the rocks, she wondered what it had felt like to suddenly be in another country before the internet and mobile phones. Vivienne must have felt so isolated with just the other French Resistance spies to guide her.

After her walk, Sophie was exhausted, and so had an early night, falling asleep thinking about isolation and loneliness and what it really meant.

In the morning she opened the curtains to a brand new day and felt a sense of hope. If she was really honest with herself, Matt wasn't the right person for her – well, not any more, not as the person she was now. Over the last year her grief had changed her. Before, it had been all about the chase, the money, the status. But death had made her see what really mattered. Family mattered, genuine love mattered, and the need to change this world for the better, to have a sense of purpose. Had Vivienne ever felt the same?

After a breakfast of buttery rolls and creamy goat's cheese from her host's flock, Sophie said goodbye and found the bus station. Looking at the timetable, she noted she could get to a city called Morlaix, and that the bus left soon. From there she knew she could catch a train to Paris.

The trip through the French countryside relaxed her as the bus trundled past what she guessed were mainly holiday cottages, whitewashed and gleaming whenever a glint of morning sun broke through the heavy grey clouds. Some were obviously second homes with expensive cars parked in the driveways. That had always been Matt's dream, a holiday home abroad. His words echoed in her head – 'I'm in love with her.' They twisted in her stomach. She thought about Vivienne. Is that what the German had done? Deceived her? Pretended he had really loved her to get what he wanted? She realised that's why she needed a good conclusion for Vivienne's story. She desperately needed someone to have a happy ending, even if it wasn't herself.

As the bus pulled into the town of Morlaix, Sophie was charmed by it. Lots of cream- and lemon-painted buildings with rows upon rows of ornate, framed mullioned windows. Overshadowing it all was a splendid stone viaduct. She found the train station and was soon on her way to Paris. As she pulled in at Gare du Nord, Sophie's spirits were lifted by the energy of the city. Many tourists and people were humming around the train station, even though it was so early in the year. She had reserved an Airbnb before she'd left Cornwall the previous morning and made her way to the little flat in the Sacré-Cœur region. Walking through the streets, she was enchanted. Art, music and beauty were all the hallmarks of the City of Lights, and she was happy to enjoy this break away.

Once she settled into her apartment at the top of a black-and-white building with a spiral staircase and a balcony overlooking a square, she noted the abundance of outdoor cafés and, feeling very European, went down to have some lunch right on the street. Taking her laptop with her, she decided she could do research while she was there.

Finding the perfect place with red-and-white-striped awnings and white wrought-iron tables, she placed herself in a corner of the cosy pavement coffee shop, ordering a cheese and tomato baguette. A thrill ran through her as she flipped open her laptop. She loved researching and she needed to locate the war museum, which had an exhibition of Resistance fighters. Now she was here, she needed to get as much information about the agents and their work during the war as she could.

First, though, she toggled through her emails to see if the people that she'd found and messaged on Ancestry.com had replied. There were messages from two of the relatives of different Marcus Vonsteins. Both insisted they did not have a relative who'd been in the Nazi Party nor who had been in England during the war. The third Marcus Vonstein she had found had fought for the Allies, which only left one relative, an Alex Vonstein, who seemed to live in Paris. She re-checked her inbox. He had not messaged her back, but she wondered, as she was already here, maybe she could locate him and ask him herself.

He came up straight away when she searched for him on Google, and fortunately he had a business not far from where she was. Alex appeared to be an artist. There was a picture of him with his arms crossed, outside his shop, his name depicted on the green awnings. She looked closely at the photograph, wondering if he looked like Marcus. He had broad shoulders, blond hair and blue eyes. His smile was warm and inviting, and he had a schoolboy quality to his demeanour, as though he had just run into the frame from playing a game of rugby.

After finishing her lunch she typed in the address of the shop on her phone and set off in that direction. If he wasn't the relative she was looking for, then at least she could cross him off her list.

Walking through the streets, it was a very pleasant day. Some late-afternoon sun came out to greet her, and though it was weak and it was still seasonally cold, it was a welcome sight. Arriving at the shop, Sophie pushed through the door, and a bell tinkled above her as she went inside. The smell of burned coffee and acrylic paint met her. Through crackling speakers, loud music was playing. It had a haphazard, frantic energy about it. This was obviously the shop of a working artist.

On the way in, she browsed his paintings, mainly modern-art pieces, depictions of Paris. Walking to the counter, she waited patiently for a while, but no one came. Sophie could hear someone whistling in the back, so she called out, 'Excusez-moi.' Nothing. So she shouted again. Suddenly, the whistling stopped, and the face of Alex Vonstein appeared. He was tall, maybe six foot, had grown a beard since the photo on the website, and across one of his cheeks there was a fleck of red paint.

'Forgive me,' he said in French. 'I was so busy setting this canvas I didn't hear the bell.' He wiped his hands on his apron, which was tatty around his waist and covered in paint, she guessed, from previous projects. 'Are you looking to buy something?' he continued.

Sophie understood the gist of what he was saying, but his French was too fast for her, so she hoped he would understand English.

'I'm from the UK and I was looking for you to ask you a question. Do you speak English?'

'Of course, we are all taught to speak English as children. How do you do?' he said jokingly, putting his hand out. 'Very nice to meet you. Would you like a cup of tea?'

She smiled at his impishness.

'I know this is an odd question, but I'm doing some research about the war.'

His face looked curious. 'The war?'

'World War Two. My name is Sophie Hamilton. I had an aunt who came to Paris during that time, and may have worked for… the Nazi Party.'

He folded his arms. Was he being defensive? She wasn't sure, but she continued.

'Apparently she came across here with a Marcus Vonstein and with your name…'

He sucked in a breath and his face clouded. She'd obviously hit on a nerve, because his friendly demeanour became very antagonistic.

'I got your email. I take it you are talking of my great-uncle Marcus. He caused my family much heartache. My mother has borne the burden of what that man did for all of her life; it was hard being the relative of a Nazi.'

She nodded. 'I understand. My family too had a difficult time, but I can't escape the feeling that there is more to the story.'

'What more could there be? The man was a Nazi and I'm guessing that your aunt was Vivienne. My family learned about her. The two of them were like the Bonnie and Clyde of their time. I don't know what else you would need to know from me.'

'I understand that's what everyone believes, but there are still many gaps in the story.' She went on to tell him about the photograph that she'd seen at the Imperial War Museum, and he became a little less guarded and more relaxed as he listened to her.

Finally he shook his head. 'That might work for your aunt, but there's no photograph at the Imperial War Museum of my Nazi relative. Trust me.'

She nodded. 'Would you be willing to talk to me in more detail?'

He studied her for a second, then shook his head. 'I know nothing more than what I've told you.' He leaned forward across his counter, his tone softening. 'This is a beautiful place, Sophie, even this early in the year. You should not be worried about dead people. Why don't you enjoy our lovely city instead? Maybe buy yourself a piece of art.' A lightness in his spirit had returned as he pointed at a particularly large prominent piece. 'You won't regret it,' he advised her.

She shook her head. 'I have to go. If you change your mind, I wanted to let you know that I'm going to have dinner somewhere around here tonight. In fact, is there anywhere you'd recommend?'

'What is your budget?'

'Modest.'

'Then you should go to Claire's. It is just down the street here. You'll get a nice glass of wine and something warm to eat, but it won't blow your budget.'

'I'll be there at seven o'clock if you change your mind. I would love your help,' she added with a smile.

He shook his head. 'Not that I wouldn't enjoy the company of such an attractive woman' – she blushed – 'but there is no way for my mother's sake I would want to drag up the past again.'

Chapter 24

It was just as she started her dinner that evening that Sophie spotted Alex entering the restaurant. He approached her, an apologetic look on his face.

'I was wondering,' he enquired, 'if I might be able to join you?'

She smiled. 'Of course.'

'I'm so sorry about the way I treated you this morning,' he said as he pulled up a chair. 'You really took me by surprise. The war is such a painful history for my family. It's something my mother talked about ceaselessly when I was a child, *her* excruciatingly sad childhood. You see, one of her uncles was murdered, the other became a Nazi, and her mother's fiancé – my grandfather – never came home from the war, which left her with the shame of being brought up as an illegitimate child.

'But after you left, I realised that none of this was your fault and that, in fact, you were probably living under the same curse that I was. It also struck me that if, for some reason, your great-aunt had indeed been working for the British, that there was a very slim chance that my great-uncle was also working for the Allies too, so I thought I should at least entertain the thought.'

A waitress came over, and he ordered some dinner. Sophie watched him as he chatted comfortably with her. Under different circumstances, Claire's would have been a marvellous place for a romantic evening. It was a tiny bistro, with black awnings that were decorated with gold detailing and signage. Marking its territory on the Parisian pavement were low black railings and flower boxes filled with a fresh-smelling evergreen shrub. Inside, candles illuminated elegant white walls with large artistic black-and-white photos of Paris. On the tables, antique wine bottles, with cream-coloured wax melted down them, and in the corner someone was playing the accordion.

As she watched Alex, Sophie admired the ease and self-confidence he exuded, and coupled with his blond hair and lively blue eyes, she realised, with a little embarrassment, he was also very attractive to her. He finished giving his order, and when Alex looked across at her, Sophie blushed, feeling a little self-conscious about the direction her thoughts had been heading. She hadn't been out with a man for the first time since Matt, three years before, and though this wasn't anything like a first date, she still felt a little awkward.

She needn't have worried about what she should talk about though, because Alex didn't seem to be burdened in the same way. He was happy to tell her all about his life in Paris and she listened to him as she watched him alternate between removing mussels from their shells from a moules marinière, with dipping crusty chunks of warm French bread into his bowl. As he chatted Sophie enjoyed the intoxicating aroma of garlic and parsley, captured in a white wine broth, that swirled between them. Sophie loved her dinner as well. The crispy pan-fried chicken breast served over polenta and braised endive with a rosemary-gorgonzola sauce was warming and delicious.

All at once he stopped talking and looked over at her with deep intent. His eyes flickered ice blue in the reflection of the candlelight.

'What about you, Sophie, tell me about yourself.'

As she looked across at him, wearing such a sincere expression on his face, she felt she could have told him anything and he would have understood, even about Emily. She didn't know if it was the wine she had drunk three glasses of, the atmosphere, or the look in his eyes, but all at once she wanted to tell him. Not because she needed his sympathy, God knew she'd known enough of that over the last year, but because she wanted to be honest with him and share with him why putting all the pieces of her life back together was so important. Taking a deep sip of her wine, she started the story that was so familiar but never easy for her.

'I lost my mother and my daughter last year. My daughter… she was sixteen months old.'

Sophie looked across the table at Alex to gauge his reaction and sensed the kindness that he had to offer her. An assurance of safety, a genuine concern for her pain. It had been a long time since someone had looked at her like that, as if what she had to say really mattered. He didn't change the subject as so many did, he just poured her another glass of wine saying gently, 'Tell me about your daughter.'

Sophie took a deep breath and took another large swig of her drink before she cleared her throat and started the story.

'I was a lawyer. I worked in London, and I loved what I did. It's what pushed me to get out of bed in the morning and to stay up late into the night. I loved getting justice for people who deserved it and who wouldn't have had a chance without my help. I felt as if I really changed lives.

'When I found out I was pregnant with Emily, I was shocked – she wasn't planned, and my boyfriend at the time, her father, was concerned about how it would change our lives. He too was very career-driven. But I assured him I was a modern woman, that I could do it all. I would still be a lawyer and would hire a childminder. My mum had offered to take care of her a couple of days a week too.

'But from the minute Emily was born, I was captivated, I had no idea that my heart was capable of so much love. I couldn't even watch the news without the mama bear in me rearing up and wanting to protect her from all the evil in the world. She was all wide-eyed innocence and unconditional love. So, leaving her to go back to work was so much harder than I had ever imagined. It nearly killed me that first week. I think I cried on the train every day after I handed over my precious bundle to the person who might hear her first word or witness her first step. At the time I knew many women who had children and careers, and I wondered how they made that emotional adjustment so easily. But as time went on I got more used to it, it was never easy, and the guilt was always there just under the surface, but I assured myself it was best for both of us. I needed something more than just 'Mummy and me' classes, and she needed to learn to be with other people.'

Sophie took another sip of her wine; this was always the easy part of telling her story, the before. The next part would be much more challenging. She swallowed her wine and took the temperature of their conversation. Was there judgement in his eyes? Would he be able to handle what she had to tell him about herself? But Alex's eyes continued to reflect his compassion.

Sophie felt the hoarseness creep into her tone, the quiver in her voice, the now-familiar tremble of her hand as she held her glass close to her chest to help collect her strength somehow. It all conveyed the rawness of emotion that still hovered so close beneath the surface.

'On the morning of her death, I had a first meeting with a very important client, so I was very distracted. My mother arrived to take care of her, as she had since she was small. Emily adored her grandma, but that morning she was clingy and fussy and didn't want to go to her. I assured my mum she was teething and asked if she would be willing to take her later in the afternoon to her swimming class. Selfishly, I'd wanted my daughter worn out so that when I got home, I could put her straight to bed, so I could stay up late to finish the work that I knew I would have after the meeting. As I got ready to leave, Emily clung even tighter to me, her little chubby arms locked around my neck so tightly as she screamed, tears running down her reddened cheeks as she begged me to stay.'

Sophie started to weep openly as she continued, the memory still so hard to recount.

'Eventually, still screaming, I managed to unpeel her from me and kissed her gently on her little downy head, saying, "Mummy'll be home soon. You'll see Mummy soon." I handed her to my mother as she continued to wail. Mum just shooed me out the door. And grabbing my bag I didn't even look back, I walked out to my car, and all I could hear as I walked down the path was her little tiny voice screaming, "Mummy! Mummy! Please, Mummy!"'

Alex reached forward and grabbed her hand, but still didn't turn away from her pain, he just offered his strength, and she was grateful for that.

Pulling out a tissue and blowing her nose, Sophie continued, 'Why didn't I turn around? Why didn't I go back? Why didn't I!? It was as if she knew, and I didn't listen. It was as if she knew she would never see me again.'

Sophie's trembling hand lifted the wine to her lips. She could finish it now; the worst was over. The terrible guilt was always the worst part of her story.

'My mother drove to the swimming baths, but she never reached them. On the way there, a truck driver looking at his phone because he was lost and trying to read a map, looked down too long and missed the light and ploughed right into my mum's car. They said it was instantaneous, that both of them were taken quickly, but I think that's something they just say so you won't worry about it.' Her voice cracked again as the emotion got the better of her. 'For months afterwards, all I would hear was Emily's little voice screaming, "Mummy! Mummy! Please, Mummy!' in my head, and I will never get over that. I will never ever be the same person I was before because of that one moment, that terrible memory.

'And the weird thing is, when people talk about grief, they talk about it like it's an illness, as if you have the flu, as if one day you'll just feel better if you wait long enough. What I've realised is I'm never going to feel better. This is just an emptiness I'll live with for the rest of my life. And I've come to accept that. It's a shadow that's always with me and always will be.

'What I don't know is how to go on living, how to move forward from hearing her voice echoing in my head. How do I find something, a reason to live, a reason to keep doing this? I don't mean I feel suicidal, though I've had my moments there too. What I mean is, all the joy, all the light in my life, has gone, and the fear of never knowing that light again is my deepest nightmare. My mother was my best friend, and my darling girl was the joy of my life. I wish I could find my way out of the darkness so I could feel happiness again, feel anything again. I can't even imagine what that would be like.'

Alex squeezed her hand. 'Oh, Sophie, I do not know what to say. You have suffered more than I can imagine. I have no words of wisdom for you. I've never lived through something like that. But I want you to know that you have my friendship if you want it.'

Swallowing down the rest of her wine, Sophie nodded, grateful he didn't try to pacify her with trite suggestions for how to deal with her grief. There was no patting of the hand with the classic, 'it will get better in time' statement. Or worse still, 'You weren't to know, you can't feel bad about that.'

'So, until I find the key to the end of this pain,' she added, blowing her nose again, 'I will keep putting one foot in front of the other and breathing in and out and hope that somehow my life will make sense again one day.'

'This is why finding out about your aunt is so important to you,' Alex stated.

'She looked a lot like my mum does... did. And even though the truck driver was prosecuted, I can't shake the feeling that it wasn't really justice, because it didn't help bring back what I lost. And I think there's a part of me that feels that if I can get to the truth for my aunt, whose name no one has even tried to clear, I can maybe bring back one person to my family. I do know the truth will probably just be what everyone already believes, but I just can't let this rest until I know for sure, till I have real evidence. It's the least I can do for her memory, she can't fight for herself any more.'

Alex nodded and offered her an understanding smile.

Sophie was glad she had told him, it had been a long time since somebody had heard the story for the first time, and she had needed to say it. And though she wasn't totally sure why she'd told him, practically a stranger, it felt good, cathartic, somehow.

As they started their dessert, poached pears in a crème de cassis sauce, she moved on and broached the subject of their shared history, filling him in with everything she knew. Sophie told him of the story that she'd followed and reluctantly told him about some of the other things she'd uncovered, including what the fishermen had told her in Cornwall, realising that if they were going to work together on anything, it was only fair that she was honest.

He listened intently and echoed the thoughts that she had, the fact Vivienne had been a spy early on in the war was encouraging and the fact she was at SOE's building signing in with her undercover name right before her elopement was also interesting. Until they could prove she had been in Baker Street that day for any other reason, there was still hope.

When she told him about the poem and the message that had been sent under the Sparrow code name right before the D-Day landings he stopped eating and said, 'Assuming by then she and my great-uncle were working together, maybe there is something in the message that would help us understand what was going on.'

'That is partly why I have come. I have the first layer of the code, and I'm reading a book about code breaking, but I still haven't figured it all out yet. I just keep thinking about how far I have come and it's like she's helping me from the other side.'

She smiled ruefully, to hint she was just being playful. But he seemed to take it seriously.

'There is so much we don't know, and it is a miracle the way you came across that picture. If you hadn't have done that you may never have known about your aunt. Let's hope someone is helping us,' Alex said, raising a toast of thanks towards the ceiling with a grin.

As they finished eating, Alex offered to walk her back to her apartment. They strolled along the Seine and the night was clear and the sky was filled with stars. In the background the Eiffel Tower was ablaze with a cream glow and the river was illuminated with shimmering pools of white light cast forth from elegant black lamp-posts dotted along the way. On the river, boats were moored for the night and only rocked when river restaurants steamed past them with their own pools of pink and red lights that brightened circular tables of dinner guests. In the tourist areas every kind of street performer was out working, from young men playing enthusiastic renditions of Beatles' songs on battered guitars, to fire eaters and jugglers. They walked away from the Seine and towards the Moulin Rouge, its façade aglow with its festoon of lights and magnificent windmill.

All at once, Alex turned to her. 'It's amazing to think your great-aunt and my great-uncle could've walked along this very same street together, isn't it?'

She shivered with the thought and wondered what it must have been like to have been a couple in World War Two. For Sophie, she couldn't easily let go of the image of the two of them in German uniforms walking the town. But there was also the conflicting thought that inside those dreadful uniforms there were two people, ordinary people who just happened to be working for a despicable enemy. What had driven them down such a dark path?

As Alex walked her to her apartment he turned to her. 'If you want, I think we should get together tomorrow. I have the day off. We could maybe start with my family records. They are all locked away in a safe that I have access to.'

She nodded and took his hand when he offered it. It was soft and warm, and as he leaned in to kiss her gently on both cheeks, she wasn't sure if she imagined it, but it appeared that he lingered just a little longer than he had when he had greeted her.

The following morning, Alex arrived for her bright and early. The chill of the past couple of days had been washed away by an early-morning rain, and the streets of Paris smelled fresh and new as they bustled into life.

'My family lives in an apartment on the outskirts of the city,' he informed her as he led her out to his tiny car that was parked on the side of the road. 'We have many family records back there. I think it would be a good place to start. My mother is away for a few days, so we won't need to burden her with what we are doing.'

On the way, he stopped at a little patisserie, and they went in to get breakfast before they started their journey. Once again, Sophie was drawn in by the scent of fresh bread, croissants and French pastries. Alex ordered a couple of glossy apple tarts for them, and with paper cups of dark steaming coffee, they headed out the door.

'It is very un-French,' he stated seriously, 'not to stop and eat properly, but I believe we have a lot we need to accomplish, and I thought that you'd want to get out to the house as soon as possible.'

She nodded as she drank her coffee and devoured the flaky, buttery pastry and for a moment wished she lived in Europe.

On the way, he filled her in about his family. His stepsister, Dominique, lived in the south of France, while he and his mother had stayed in the north. He preferred to have a little apartment in town, close to his work. His mother's apartment was located in a beautiful old stone chateau that had been converted into individual dwellings. Sophie was amazed at the beauty of it. Perfectly manicured gardens, a large circular pond with a fountain, and tight box hedges all framed the handsome grey-stone mansion. It was set high up on a hill, with a stunning view of the underlying countryside.

Making their way up the elegant staircase to the individual numbered flats, he produced some keys from his pocket and escorted her inside. Leaving her in the front room, he went upstairs to retrieve the documents he'd talked about.

Sophie walked towards the black wrought-iron balcony that looked out across the magnificent gardens and pushed open the patio door. After taking two deep breaths of fresh air, she turned and took in the tasteful furniture. The room had high ceilings and mirrors that reflected the graceful architecture. A beautiful chandelier hung in the centre of the ceiling, its multitude of crystal teardrops glistening and bouncing prisms of rainbow sunlight around the room. She started to stroll towards the walls and noted a couple of pictures mixed in with other modern-art pieces with Alex's name on the bottom. Everything in the room was highly polished, a mixture of wood and glass. It was exquisite.

Alex arrived back after a short time with a large box that he placed on a table and unlocked with an ornate key. As he flipped open the lid, the musty smell of ancient documents filled Sophie's nostrils. Alex started to sift through the papers and set apart everything to do with Marcus's side of his family. He located his great-uncle's birth certificate, and Sophie looked it over. She thought once again how young he would have been during the war, in his thirties.

Alex riffled through a few more of the files and pulled out a couple of black-and-white photos of Marcus, and Sophie realised Alex had the same fair hair and piercing eyes. Their build was very different. But it was obvious they were related.

'We look a little alike, you see,' he stated then, reading her mind. 'My grandmother, Amy, lost her fiancé during the war, though she was already pregnant with my mother, and my mother never married either, or rather, not until I had already grown up. Which is why I am a Vonstein. She found love with my stepfather, who owned a cheese factory and did very well for himself, and she was glad to finally change her name.'

Sophie was drawn to a photo of Marcus standing in a vineyard with a man of similar build and two young women, one fair, one with dark hair, her head thrown back, caught in the midst of laughter with a young child gathered in her arms. She turned over the photo and on the back were the words 'Marcus, Amy, Marcel, Essie and Amélie' scribbled in pencil.

Alex caught what she was looking at. 'That is Marcus, with his sister Amy, my grandmother, his brother Marcel and sister-in-law Essie. Before they were killed.'

Sophie stared at the picture of the young child in her mother's arms, about the same age as Emily when she died.

Sophie froze. 'Killed?'

Alex nodded his head thoughtfully. 'During the war. Marcus's sister-in-law was Jewish.'

A sob caught in Sophie's throat. 'The baby too?'

Alex's eyes met hers and it was if he didn't want to answer, understanding the personal impact for her. But she already knew what he'd say.

Sophie put down the photograph and stared at the young child again, so innocent, so happy, and the wave of grief that was always just under the surface found its way to her throat. She swallowed it down.

Searching through more of the documents, Alex eventually came across Marcus's death certificate. It stated that he had died on June the tenth, four days after the Normandy landings, and Sophie wondered if Vivienne had still been with him at that time. They'd never recovered a death certificate for her. It was as if she just disappeared.

Sophie stared at the picture of Marcus and his family smiling in the vineyard, and suddenly he seemed very human, a real person, so different from what she had imagined.

Chapter 25

1944

Vivi didn't sleep at all after discovering her patient's real identity. Going over and over in her mind all the things she'd told Vonstein, she wondered: *How had she been so foolish?* She was trained to be guarded with her words no matter what, and here she was, offering all the facts about the Resistance that he'd wanted. Her only hope was that he would spend the rest of the war as a detainee of His Majesty's government and never get back to France.

But still she kicked herself and, worst of all – though she was loath to even admit this – she still felt attracted to him. Just the day before he'd leant forward and touched her hand and still she'd felt a thrill race through her body. Now she despised herself for feeling anything for this man who had been undercover as a German spy. One thing she was sure about: he was very good at his job. She hadn't suspected in the slightest that his cover story wasn't real or that he was not French Resistance. He must have been well equipped for his mission with the intelligence he'd had.

When Vivi arrived at her duty that morning, she knew that this was the day that they were planning to start monitoring Vonstein. After they prepared the room with listening equipment, they wheeled in the new young patient and they placed him next to Vonstein. He, too, was shackled to the bed. The British officers who brought him in didn't speak German very well, so Vivi translated for them all.

'We have someone to keep you company. One of your expatriates came down in the North Sea and will also be a guest of our government for the rest of the war. I believe his name is Herman Schmidt.'

Vonstein nodded and eyed the other man distrustfully, though by the next day, it was as though they were the best of friends. They talked about their life before the war in Germany, the food they were both missing, and the type of schnapps they found they both had an affinity for. On the second day, Vonstein asked more about Schmidt's mission. He explained what he was doing and that his commander, a Fredrik Eichel, had also been arrested and was in jail.

'Once I am well enough, I will have to join him there.' He lowered his voice to a whisper. 'There was one other of my group that escaped. As far as I know, they didn't find him, and from the things we saw and photographed, he has some very interesting things to tell them about where the real invasion shall be coming from and it will not be where our army thinks it will be.'

Vonstein made some positive noises, then Herman changed the subject, asking about a place in Germany that they both knew.

That evening, Vivi was working the night shift again when there was a call put out, and medical staff raced to the Germans' room. The new patient had been sleeping when he had awoken to see Vonstein was unconscious, frothing at the mouth, blood gushing down his chin. The doctors were busy saving the life of an incoming patient, and vowed to be there as soon as they could. In the meantime they determined he would need to be isolated in case it was contagious.

The guards assisted Vivi as they moved Vonstein, still unconscious, into a smaller room. So many of the rooms were now occupied with soldiers that there were only a few to choose from, and this was no more than a cupboard they used to use for extra linens, but it was a secure room. As the guards went back to check on the original room and the other nurse on duty left to get the doctors, Vivi tidied up the mess around her. But as she turned her back for a second, she felt an arm around her waist, and Vonstein's hand came over her mouth.

'Please don't move and don't scream, Vivi,' Vonstein whispered in French. 'I don't have long, and I need to talk to you alone.'

Vivi was frozen in terror, her mind racing. He must have faked his illness, maybe bitten his own tongue. And with him being apparently unconscious, they had removed his handcuffs to transfer him. She sucked in a breath, trying desperately to remember her training, but he had hold of her in an extremely tight grip. She could scarcely breathe.

Suddenly, he switched to speaking English in her ear. 'Listen to me, Vivi. This is really, really important. I don't have long. I am honestly working for SOE as well. I have secretly defected from the German army, but my plane came down when I was travelling back into Paris undercover, to rendezvous with my French Resistance team before I continue my critical work with the Germans. I have to get back directly. If I am missed much longer, it will become evident there was a complication, and they will ask questions. The guards are talking about eventually moving me to jail, but I have a job to do and I have just received some very important news about a fugitive who has information that I have to intercept and deal with.'

Vivi flinched at the realisation of what that could mean exactly.

He continued, 'Please, Vivi. I know it's an enormous step for you to trust me. Think about how you felt about me in the first week. That is who I really am. Not this act I have to put on.'

She could hardly breathe as she was listening to him, every kind of emotion overwhelming her.

'I know it is hard to trust me, but I'm going to ask you to do something. There is one operative in London who knows exactly who I am and about my deep cover. I need you to go to Baker Street. Not just to prove to you who I am, but to also let them know what happened to me. I had expected my commander to find me by now, as I have not checked in, and as I said, he is the one person who knows what I'm doing undercover within the German intelligence. You need to locate him and speak to him in person, to tell him where I am. Do you understand? Since one of the French Resistance circuits was uncovered, we believe there is a mole in SOE and many agents have been killed and captured, so I couldn't just call him or send a message, it is all far too dangerous right now and my work is imperative to the war effort. It has taken me a long time to make the Nazis trust me, and I'm under clear orders never to break cover. I would go myself if it was possible, but I am trapped here. You are my only hope and now the time has become critical. I was hoping if they believed I was French Resistance I would have been released from here once my body had healed, so I could go to London myself about this. Then I would never have had to tell you any of this so we could keep the real work I was doing a secret. But right now I have no other alternative than to trust you with this information.

'Come back later and I will give you all the details. My only hope, Vivi, is the fact you too were SOE and know how important our work is, so you might feel compelled to help me.'

Vivi realised she would be able to find out as soon as she went to SOE in London and called his bluff if indeed he was a Nazi. But what if this was some sort of elaborate plan to somehow keep him out of jail?

Abruptly, there was a rattling at the door. Vonstein let go of Vivi and hopped back into bed. She remained frozen for a moment, not knowing what to do, but when she turned, she noticed he had put his hand back into the handcuffs and locked them. Why wouldn't he have just used her as a hostage to get away? In her gut, Vivi had a feeling this man was good, but could she trust it like before? She thought about how her fear had let her down in Paris, and how that whole family had suffered because of it.

As the doctor came into the room, he asked Vivi for an update, and in a shaky voice, she told him about Vonstein's medical episode. He examined the patient as the last words Vonstein had said echoed in her mind.

Vivi left the room as the doctor asked her to get specific equipment and her whole body was shaking. She didn't know who to trust, but she still had to work. And she had to admit, he intrigued her. As the doctor finished his rounds, around three o'clock in the morning, she slipped back into Vonstein's room. His eyes flashed open.

'Shut the door behind you,' he hissed in French.

She came to the side of his bed, but not close enough where he could grab her again.

'How do I know you're telling the truth?'

'You don't,' he said. 'Which is why I need you to go to London. I need you to trust me. Vivi, you're the only person who can, and you need to go to London before they transfer me to prison. I have prolonged this as long as I could, but I have to get back to my work in Europe.'

'Your leg is still mending. You cannot go back yet anyway.'

'I'm afraid I have to. The work I have to do is too valuable. Ask for the Rook. When you go into his office, tell him, that I, the Hawk, my code name, am here. And give him the word "fortitude". This will make sense to him. Vivi, understand this is of the utmost secrecy. You cannot share this with anybody else but the Rook. No one. There are concerns about a mole over there, which is why virtually no one knows about my mission. So tell no one else. Do you understand? Not even your boyfriend, or your husband.'

'You're fortunate I have neither,' she informed him with a smirk.

A look of relief washed across his face for a moment. How odd, she thought. He'd been so detached with her since she had assumed he was a German, and yet for a moment, he looked like a man. Not an agent, or a patient, but just a man.

'Vivi, you need to go tomorrow. Can you do that before they talk about transferring me?'

She stood at a distance with her arms folded. 'First, you have to tell me everything and I mean everything!'

He nodded. 'I know.'

'Is your name Marcus Vonstein, or François?'

He smiled. 'Both. I am Marcus François Vonstein. The unfortunate pairing of a German father and a French mother. Which is why I also speak both languages.'

'Why didn't you tell me the truth?'

'I was under orders never to reveal my real German identity unless it became absolutely necessary and' – his eyes met hers intensely – 'it became absolutely necessary.'

'Why should I trust you?'

He lay back on his pillow and seemed thoughtful, before whispering, 'Because I have everything to lose and nothing to gain by what I am about to tell you. I am Major Vonstein of the German Army. I joined the army when I was young – before Herr Hitler took over – and I was proud to serve my country. But this war has been horrific, and I also started to see things happening that I knew weren't right. At first I turned a blind eye, but the rumours started to surface of what was being done in our name, and I was sickened by it, especially the treatment of the Jewish people.'

Vivi was frustrated. 'So all that you told me about your family was a lie, the vineyard, your brother...'

Marcus slowly shook his head. 'Not all of it. The story was true except why my brother died.' His voice started to crack and it took him a minute before he could compose himself.

Vivi sensed his raw emotion and determined either he was an incredible liar or what he was telling her was true.

He got lost in his reminiscence. 'My sister Amy is older, but my brother and I were just a year apart, grew up together on the winery and it was the best possible life for two boys who had no God-given sense and plenty of ways to find trouble. Fresh air, good food and a mother and father who adored us. We were closer than twins, fought defiantly for each other and against one another when we felt passionately enough about a topic. Marcel really was the bravest and strongest, the best of the best. Everybody loved him. He was the first to help a stranger or a neighbour and had a quiet confidence that I secretly envied. A way of sharing the best of himself in such a way, you thought it was your own.

'As we grew into manhood it became obvious that his heart belonged to the farm. The dark rich earth, the growing, the satisfaction of producing the best wine in the region became his passion. He fell in love with the smell of the grapes as they ripened on the vine, the new greening branches in the spring, the pruning and the harvest. Once he set his heart in this direction there was never a morning that he wasn't up checking the fields at dawn. The farm was all he cared about and my father was ecstatic to share his knowledge and love with his younger son. But as he started spending more and more time with my father, the ground started to shift between us and we stopped being together all the time, and I was lost without him. I tried to find my footing, my place in my family, but there was no purpose for me any more. I felt isolated and as if I no longer fitted. So I went to find camaraderie somewhere else, somewhere where the ground would be strong, where things wouldn't change, where I would have friends for life – so I joined the army. I wanted to make my country and my family proud. And at first it was good, and when he first rose to power, Hitler seemed great for our country. We had been pummelled by the First World War and our spirit as a nation was broken, the treaty that was placed on us so hard to rise above. As we barrelled into another war I was all for it at first, we wanted back our honour, our respect, ourselves. My family were concerned. They didn't see how killing more people would help. But I was conceited and arrogant...' Marcus started to break down, his voice trailing off to a whisper.

'What happened to your brother? To your family?' Vivi asked gently.

He turned his face from her, the tears starting to well in his eyes, and instinctively she grabbed his hand. Even if he was a German,

the enemy, she recognised pain when she saw it. It reflected her
own that she carried in her body like shrapnel.

He pushed through his anguish. 'My brother was put in charge
of the vineyard and when I would come home on leave, things felt
more balanced in our lives. We had found our places in the world
and we could return to the relationship we had known in our youth.
Then along came Essie.' He smiled as he remembered her. 'Beautiful, warm, wonderful Essie. One of the kindest people I have ever
known, with eyes that could see right into your soul, and a love that
gathered everyone. She brought our family into her glow and though
I had thought we were close before she came, she made us a family.
Of course my brother fell in love with her, and they married as our
army were advancing into Russia. When Amélie was born almost
nine months to the day of their wedding, everything seemed once
again to be working out for him. And I went on blindly following the
Führer. I wasn't really tracking what was happening at home. We were
busy, you know, taking over countries and stripping people of their
homelands.' Marcus spat out the last of his words with real disgust.

Vivi's question came out in a whisper, 'What happened to Essie
and Amélie?'

Tears streamed down his face unabashed. 'Amélie grew into a
lovely child, with blonde hair and blue eyes like her father, but
there was something Essie had not told us: she was Jewish.'

His last statement hung in the air, poignant and heavy, and
Vivi started to tear up – she knew the end to this story. So many
Jews were going missing, presumed dead. Hitler had been hunting
them down since the beginning of the war.

'The Gestapo found out about her and they never even gave her
a chance to defend herself. Essie and Amélie were shot and killed
trying to escape the farm, and my brother too, trying to protect
them. They were all slaughtered.'

Vivi sat down on the end of the bed, all of her anger and fight
leaving her body. She pulled Marcus into her arms and let him

sob there. Once he was recovered, he looked up at her, his eyes red and pleading as he pulled her damp cheek next to his so he could whisper in her ear.

'This is why I have to do this, Vivi. I can't let them down. I have to do it for my family. For an innocent child and the brother I will never see again.'

'But how did you end up over here?'

'After this happened I wanted revenge, and the best kind I could think of was not to defect but to turn on them. To my dying day I will be fighting against this regime to get Hitler out. I made contact through a mutual friend with someone who also was unhappy with the way our leaders were conducting themselves and I was put in touch with SOE. I have been working with them for six months now. I was here to brief them and deliver some highly sensitive information and was flying back when the plane I was on experienced engine trouble and we had to land in the sea. I remember nothing else until I opened my eyes and saw your beautiful face.'

Vivi nodded her head slowly as he finished his story. 'I will go to London. Not because I totally trust you, yet, but because I need to know for myself what is going on here.' She suddenly felt great relief. If he was who he maintained he was, then all the things she had said about the Resistance were of no consequence. He already would have known about these things.

'I shouldn't have told you the things about the Resistance,' she whispered regretfully.

'Vivi, we're all human, desiring connection, even in the craziness of this world we find ourselves in. I do not hold that against you. It is lonely, our life. It is normal to take any kind of kindness, whenever we can.'

She listened to his words and recognised the look of resolve on his face. She didn't know why she did it. It was impulsive. But she came forward and kissed him gently on the lips as he looked up at her with hope.

'If you are who you say you are, then thank you for being brave. I know how hard that can be.'

He smiled. 'I'm counting on you, Vivi, and I am trusting you. I know you are the right person. And one last thing... All I said about my feelings for you was true, none of that was a lie.'

She smiled, though still felt wary. Everything about this was so hard.

Making her way out of his room, she nodded to the guard who was waiting there and went back to make her arrangements. She would leave on the 7 a.m. train. That way she could be back in Cornwall by the late evening. She was nervous, but she felt a sense of excitement. At last, maybe she could be of service to her country again.

Chapter 26

The next day, Vivi left for the train early in the morning. She informed her family and the sister on duty at the hospital that she had a sick friend in a distant town who she needed to visit and would be gone for the day. Before she left, she pinned on her family's brooch, hoping it would bring her luck. Leaving the hospital, no one seemed to be suspicious of her intentions, and she slipped away unnoticed.

All the way to London, she thought about the discussion she'd had with Vonstein the night before, trying to anticipate every angle he could be employing. If he were working in the underground for the Reich, then surely he would use all of his tactics to get himself out of the hospital, because once he was in prison, it would be a lot harder to escape.

Vivi couldn't be sure he wasn't deceiving her, and yet, once again, there was that gut instinct that he was telling her the truth. Besides, she reassured herself, if SOE trusted him, then why shouldn't she? Vivi determined that the thing that would sway her one way or the other was when she got to talk to his commander. Surely he would put her mind at rest.

Vonstein had further advised her that the Rook's real name was Captain Meade and she should only use his code name as a last resort if she needed to convince them to let her in there.

As she arrived in London, she was shocked at the devastation the ongoing bombing campaigns had inflicted on the city. Everywhere, buildings were blackened, others hollowed out from where they had burned almost to the ground, while beautiful landmarks had been damaged beyond recognition or destroyed altogether. It drove her to be more determined to do what she could to bring this war to an end.

Walking from Paddington station, she made her way swiftly to Baker Street. Over the last few years, it appeared it had also endured a massive bombing offensive, and she found herself astonished at the way the bombs must have fallen, that one house could be hit and around it the whole area, even the street, could be left intact. One site on her route still bore the marks of what looked like a massive bomb landing close to SOE on the crossroads of York Street and Baker Street, clearly causing wide structural damage. As she strode into the Baker Street offices of SOE, which were unscathed, the place right next door was nothing but rubble.

She made her way down the corridor and opened a door into the office that Vonstein had directed her to. She was greeted by a rather severe-looking secretary, who eyed her suspiciously over the top of her glasses.

Vivi stepped forward, her voice trembling. She remembered how she had felt at the last SOE meeting the year before she had been to, right before they'd stamped her unfit for duty. How devastated she'd been. She couldn't let this mission fail.

'I would like to speak to Captain Meade, please.'

A curious expression crossed the secretary's face. 'Captain Meade?' she echoed.

'Yes. I need to speak to him, right away.'

'Please take a seat and wait here,' the secretary responded, and striding out from behind her desk, she tapped on the door of an office a few feet away. The woman went in, and Vivi could hear muffled voices as the secretary talked to someone inside.

Vivi sat down on the chair the woman had offered. The door opened again, surprisingly quickly, and a man looked out warily towards her. Then he murmured something to the secretary, and she nodded and went back to her desk.

'I'm afraid it will be impossible to see Captain Meade today. You should make another appointment with someone else.'

'You don't understand,' she replied. 'My name is Vivienne Hamilton. I work for SOE,' she lied, 'and it is imperative that I see Captain Meade today.'

The woman looked with concern at her.

'I have some urgent information he needs to hear.' She leaned forward and whispered under her breath, 'I need to speak to the Rook.'

The woman's eyes grew large and she returned to the same office and knocked on the door. After another hushed conversation inside, the man strode out into the hallway and came to greet Vivi. He shook her hand.

'Please come with me, Miss Hamilton,' he encouraged and ushered her into his office.

'I have some critical intelligence I need to communicate to you,' she whispered as she closed the door.

'Please sit down.' He offered her a chair and, sitting back behind his desk, eyed her intently. 'What do you know about Captain Meade?'

She quickly looked at the name on the desk and realised this wasn't the right person. 'I must not have been explicit. I'm not sharing the information with anyone but the Rook himself. I have classified information that I can only share with him.'

'You can share it with me,' he stated with a doleful smile.

All at once the secretary returned and dropped a file on his desk, which he looked at briefly before nodding at her. The secretary left the room.

Vivi watched him. He looked trustworthy, but after the last few weeks, she had learned to be extremely wary about her conversations. Vonstein had been explicit Whatever his mission, it was of the utmost secrecy.

'I don't mean to be disrespectful, sir, but I've been given precise instructions to only speak to one person.'

Confusion crossed the man's face, which softened to irritation. 'I'm afraid that is impossible.'

'I can't tell anybody else,' she stated, pressing the point.

'I'm not trying to be difficult,' he responded, 'but, you see, the Rook is no longer with us.'

Vivi was confused. 'He is somewhere else in London?'

The man blew out air and strolled over to the window and then shook his head. 'When I say "he is no longer with us", I mean in this world. I'm afraid Captain Meade was killed a couple of weeks ago.'

Vivi sat back in shock. 'How did he die?'

'Unfortunately, a wall collapsed on him during a recent bombing.' He walked back to his desk and pushed the file his secretary had brought in towards her. 'You were SOE, the Sparrow, that's true, before you were asked to leave. So you can see, I am a little concerned about trusting you with any further details.'

Vivi was astounded.

Reading her expression, he smiled. 'Don't look so surprised that I know of you,' he added, shaking his head. 'You are very striking and not easy to forget. Your file came across my desk a few weeks ago. I just happened to remember your face.'

The information I have is vital.'

'And you can share it with me,' he repeated, moving back to his seat.

Vivi's throat became dry. She desperately didn't want to make another mistake, and she'd learned that it was better to remain silent than to say something that she could never take back. It had been a risk trusting Vonstein, but she had made him a promise, and she intended to keep it.

Vivi shook her head. 'I thank you for your time, but I need to go.'

His eyes narrowed at her for a moment and then he clasped his hands. 'If you change your mind, please come back. You can trust us here.'

She stood up and shook his hand, but Vivi no longer trusted anyone. Her frustration bubbled up. The frustration of not knowing who to trust. How to help the situation. She felt powerless.

Vivi made her way out of the office and out the main door. For a second she paused in the doorway and looked out across London. From the top of the steps she had a perfect view of Baker Street, and looking down to the road, she felt a new boldness. Vivi wasn't certain what would happen next, but she knew somehow she would do the right thing and felt good about trusting her gut. Vivi was going to use all of her wits from now on, even with Vonstein. Though she also couldn't avoid the fact that something in her trusted him, something intangible she couldn't put into words, but she was going to let that guide her. She knew one thing, that he cared for her, and she was choosing to trust that love.

When Vivi arrived back in Cornwall that evening, she informed Vonstein of what she had found out, and saw just how devastating it was for him.

'I have such important work to do. I have to leave somehow,' he said, with utter discouragement in his tone. When he looked at her, she could see the desperation in his eyes. 'Vivi, I know how hard it must be for you to trust me, but I need your help for one more thing. You need to somehow get me on a boat back to France. I know I am asking a lot of you, and I can only imagine how conflicted you must be feeling, but people's lives and the success of the upcoming Allied invasions depend on me being back in place in Paris.'

He reached out and took her hand, and she tried to fight the thrill that ran through her body. She needed to think straight.

'How far would you get with your injuries? You still need a nurse for your leg at least for another few weeks. Who will take care of you over there?' she asked, wanting to make him wait until she had worked out who he really was. Her gut was telling her he was Resistance but her training was reminding her not to trust anyone.

'If you can get me onto a boat, I will take care of myself once I get to France. The… Party will look after me. They will be very impressed I escaped the British – it will actually help me curry favour. Please, Vivi, there is no one else I can trust. Once you have me on the boat, you can come back here and say I forced you to do the things you did. That way you will be blameless. But I have to get back to Paris.'

After she left him that night, Vivi tossed and turned, trying to decide what to do. If he was the enemy, it would make her a traitor, but what if he was telling her the truth?

At three o'clock in the morning, she made her decision. There was really only one way to be sure he was who he said he was, and that was for Vivi to go with him. In his weakened state, she would have the upper hand. Furthermore, if it became clear he was not really undercover, she could expose him to operatives still working in Paris and maybe he could be stopped. But if he was telling the truth, she may have a chance to help her country once more and put right some of what she had done wrong.

Chapter 27

They set the escape plan for the following evening, going through all the details carefully. Vivi had alerted the same fisherman from before that she needed to go back to France. He was a little reluctant at first, as it had become more and more dangerous and the Helford Flotilla had not been dropping agents in France for a while. But Vivi used all of her persuasive charm and eventually Mr Thompson agreed to take her. The only thing Marcus didn't know was that she would be travelling with him. Vivi decided she would tell him at the last minute. That way he had less time to protest.

She left the fisherman, and a thousand thoughts and feelings assaulted her as she moved around the harbour, looking across at the beach, teary-eyed. She had a sinking feeling. Vivi knew how dangerous this mission was, and if that wasn't hard enough, the fact she could not tell anyone what she was planning to do made her feel isolated and alone.

Making her way back to the manor, she knew she couldn't tell her brothers or sister, or her father either. But she would find a way to let them know her intentions were good, and hoped that they would think the best of her.

Vivi swiped away tears with her hand and fixed a smile on her face to greet her brother, Tom, who raced up the beach to meet her, telling her he was off fishing with his small bamboo rod. She had a plan that would, hopefully, help them understand who she was even though she knew how her actions would be perceived.

'Tom, I have a little gift for you. When you come back from fishing, I'd like to give it to you.'

He nodded with enthusiasm.

She was on the evening shift, so she spent the day preparing the clues she would leave for her family. Clues that she was still the Vivi they knew and trusted. Unfortunately, her older sister now lived in Canada and Vivi realised with a real ache she may never see her again. This was devastating to her, but she kept reminding herself it was probably a good thing, as Caroline was the one person who would have been able to see through her deception.

Once she finished painting a picture for Tom, she pulled down the well-worn copy of the book she intended as a clue for John. Hopefully he would remember her favourite story. Then, she wrapped all the gifts, including the family brooch for her sister, and, after writing the letter they would receive after she was gone, she walked to the post office and posted it. Her task completed, she felt the true weight of what she was doing. For her father, Vivi copied the poem 'Remember' by Christina Rossetti into the front of her poetry book, and turned down the corner on the page where she had been practising her code. She was afraid to leave him a note in case he read it and, thinking she was being reckless, told the authorities and somehow managed to stop them. She hoped that once she was gone he would see the book and understand she was working for SOE again.

Before her hospital shift started, Vivi called both John and Tom into the library.

She handed John his gift.

'It's not Christmas,' he said. 'Why are you giving us presents?'

'Can't a sister give her brothers gifts for no reason?' she asked, ruffling his hair as he smiled at the book in his hands.

'Golly, can I have this? It's your favourite, you don't want to keep it? You once said you'd never give it to me, ever!' he said, turning it over in his hands and running his fingers down the delicate gold-leafed pages.

'I changed my mind,' Vivi answered, trying to keep her voice light. 'Do you remember my favourite story, John?'

He half-nodded, as all his attention was focused on flicking through the pages. 'The one about the swallows,' he muttered, staring at a beautiful inked drawing of one of the characters.

Vivi fought her tears. This was harder than she would ever have thought.

She gulped them down before saying, 'That's right. Remember, when you read it, to think about me. And this is for you, Tom,' she added, handing him his gift.

He opened it up. It was the picture she had painted that afternoon of sparrows on a branch. She knew he liked birdwatching, but she hoped that when this was over, if it didn't end well, that SOE would inform her family of her death and tell them her code name, and then he would understand the significance of the picture.

'You're the best sister in the world,' he said, flinging his arms around Vivi's neck.

Vivi was surprised at his show of emotion. She tried not to allow the tears to fall, quickly swiping them from her eyes. Vivi didn't want her brothers to know just how important this moment truly was. She hoped she would come home but nothing was guaranteed.

Tom turned the painting over and read the date. She knew it would be important to him one day, because after today this date would be sealed in his memory as maybe the last time he'd seen his sister. Because, if things went wrong and she was unable to get back, she knew there was a chance she could be perceived as a traitor.

After giving both her brothers a huge hug, which they both squirmed out of, she went to spend a little time with her father. He'd been in the office keeping out of the way of all the household activity since it'd become a hospital, and she often found him there reading or just staring out of the window. He was at his desk writing a letter when she walked in.

'Oh, Vivienne. How's your day going?'

She swallowed back the pain, keeping her voice even. 'Well, thank you, Father.' It was important that she kept anything from her tone. She wanted a moment to remember him and be close to him.

He looked up and indicated the letter on his desk. 'I was writing a letter to someone I was in the Army with, encouraging him. It looks as though his son is to be sent out. This is such a hard time for us as parents. The Great War was hard enough, and now we're seeing so many young boys being sent to the front once again. It is worrying. In some ways, I'm glad you're a girl, Vivienne. You'll never have to fight as we did.'

She swallowed again. If only he knew.

'I am glad that all that business in France is over. But I worried about you when you were gone. You know my feelings on this. I don't think we should involve women in war work.'

She sat down in front of his desk and took his hand. 'Sometimes, Father, they need us for the reason you talked about. We can slip unsuspected and silently in and out of worlds where the enemy feels the same way and dismisses us as just women. What better disguise do we have than being female?'

He shook his head and sat back on his chair. 'But it's a hard life, Vivienne. I've been in a war. I know. You're making life-and-death decisions, not only for yourself, but for other people. I'm not sure you would have the aptitude for it. You're quite a reckless person, my dear.'

She was taken aback with the brutal truth of what he was saying, especially with the overwhelming guilt she felt. But if anything, instead of deterring her, he made her more focused to get it right this time. He was trying to be kind, trying to hold onto her for himself. After losing her mother, he had become clingier. But she also had her own journey and had to prove, not only to her family but also to herself, that she was capable of doing the right thing.

'We all must do what we must do, Father,' she stated defiantly.

He looked up quizzically, as though he sensed something else behind her statement.

Vivi continued, 'I wanted you to know how much I love you and admire you.'

He seemed surprised at her confession. They weren't a family for flowery language. In fact, this was the first time she'd ever told her father she loved him, and it appeared to unsettle him.

He responded by squeezing her arm. 'You're a good girl, Vivienne. Don't tell anybody else I said that.'

She knew that was his way of saying he loved her too. She then got up quickly and left, first slipping her poetry book onto the corner of his desk. Vivi didn't want him to see the tears that had started streaming down her face, and she needed to prepare for her mission.

At the beginning of her shift, Vivi and Marcus went over the plan. Since his health incident, he was still in the side room, which wasn't bugged, so they could speak freely. At seven o'clock she would bring his food, and the equipment he would need for the mission would be smuggled in on the tray. She had managed to get hold of a gun, her father's old weapon that she'd found in his office drawer, and she'd been amazed to note it was still loaded. Also, a knife to pick the handcuffs that still kept him locked to the bed.

Marcus wasn't terribly strong yet, but at least he was walking around. Vivi knew the hardest part would be getting him across to France. Once they were in occupied land, he could move freely in his German uniform with her by his side.

Earlier that day she'd taken items from his suitcase that was being kept in Matron's office. Once she gave him his food, with the things he would need, she would return at ten o'clock, the time she normally would check on him. Then would come the hardest part. She would go into the room and Marcus should be ready. At that point, once she exited the door, he would knock out the guard. If there was any resistance, she too had the skill to subdue the soldier. She would then remove the soldier's sidearm in case she needed it as well. Vivi had also managed to smuggle out Marcus's

French Resistance clothes and she hid them out of sight on the grounds. He would wear them on the trip over, only changing into his uniform once they got close to France. This would stop the fisherman from being suspicious when they boarded the boat.

At seven o'clock she brought in the food, and Marcus watched her as she hid the gun and the knife under his pillow. He seemed heartsick as he watched her.

'You're very brave, Vivi. I know how much this is costing you.'

She nodded, unable to speak.

He continued, 'But if something goes wrong, you will be giving up your honour.'

She shook her head. 'But if everything goes to plan, I can be sure the right people know the work you've done.'

He looked bleak. 'But there's also a chance they won't find out. I want to make sure you'll be able to live with that.'

She thought about her siblings and her father. Yes, it was hard. Harder than she ever thought it could be. But she also thought about the troops, the young men and women fighting so hard to win their freedom. Marcus still had a tremendous job ahead of him, and she could help him.

'I'm not worried about it. I'm a firm believer that the truth always comes out in the end. I don't know how but I just know that things are going to turn out all right.'

He nodded at her, and she left the room, noticing the guard barely turned to acknowledge her, which was good.

By nine thirty that night, she had prepared everything else she needed. Buried in the bushes in the garden were her things. She would tell Marcus of her plan to go with him once they got to the boat. She walked around the house one last time, her heart breaking, but she knew she had to do this.

Going up to Marcus's room at ten o'clock, she acknowledged the guard, who already looked half asleep. Going in, she helped Marcus out of bed, as he had already picked the lock of his handcuffs. When he had his balance, he nodded to her and she opened the door. The guard didn't even turn around, and Marcus hit him heavily and he groaned as he crumpled to the floor. Vivi felt a twinge of regret, but after checking he was just unconscious, beckoned Marcus out.

Checking the passageway, which was empty, the two of them pulled the man into the room and onto the bed, where Marcus shackled his hands. They also tied something around his mouth so he couldn't cry out. It would be at least three hours before someone else came to check on Marcus. Hopefully it gave them enough time to get away.

Making their way southward down the corridor, Marcus limped and breathed heavily as he leaned on her arm. He was obviously in some pain but shook his head dismissively when she asked about it.

Just as they got on the downstairs landing, Tom's door opened, and he came out into the hallway, standing in his blue-and-white-striped pyjamas, his well-loved bear folded under his arm, and stared at them. His eyes screwed up as he noticed Marcus, as if he was trying to figure out who he was.

'Tom,' Vivi whispered in a reassuring tone, ushering him back into his room. 'What are you doing out of bed?'

'What are *you* doing, Vivienne? Why are you walking around with one of the sick soldiers?'

'I have some important work I need to do, but, Tom, you need to go back to sleep.'

She put him in bed and kissed him on his head, whispering into his hair, 'Don't forget who I am, Tom. Don't ever forget.'

Then she rushed from the room, hoping that he would alert no one else to what he'd seen as they moved stealthily down the rest of the corridor.

Chapter 28

Marcus and Vivi made their way to the back of the house, through the family quarters. This was not guarded, and she knew they had less chance of being stopped. Vivi opened the patio doors in the library, which she had unlocked the hour before, and they slipped out into the garden.

Though he was in some pain from his injuries, Marcus managed to keep up, and she could hear him breathing heavily as he followed her. Vivi cursed the fact that there was a full moon and hoped that no one would see them leave. When they reached the bushes, he changed into his French Resistance clothes she had stashed there, and she pulled out her hidden bag of belongings too. Marcus, whose full concentration was on staying upright while he dressed, took a minute to register what she was doing.

'What is that?' he hissed through the darkness, eyeing her bag, for a moment appearing suspicious of her.

'My things. I'm coming with you.'

He stopped dressing abruptly, a look of real concern on his face. Taking her gently by the shoulders, he pulled her close, so even in the darkness she could see the tenderness in his eyes.

'No, Vivi, I can't let you risk everything. You need to stay here and eventually put the record straight. You can tell people I held a gun to your head. Otherwise, what will people think of what you have done? I can't let you do that.'

Vivi steeled herself and spoke her mind. 'You need a nurse. You will never make it on your own. Your wounds are healing, but you need someone to take care of you, and as you're leaving for Europe, I will be coming, too.'

He looked crestfallen. 'You cannot come with me. It would be too hard for me to be in the field with you. I would be an easy target for anyone who wished to harm you. I could not, I will not, endanger the woman I love.'

Vivi caught her breath. It had been implied up till now, she had even whispered her feelings to herself, but this was the first time he had declared his love for her.

It was if he realised it too and pulled her closer, holding her desperately. He kissed her passionately then, and even in the chaotic moment of their escape, the world around her melted for just a moment as she felt she belonged right there in his arms.

When he pulled away, she was breathless. 'It's no good arguing with me. Anyone will tell you I am headstrong, and once I make up my mind, no one can change it. Besides, you can't get on the boat unless I am with you. The fisherman wouldn't trust someone he'd never met.'

All the fight seemed to leave Marcus then, and it was as if he realised he was caught. He could return to the hospital, where he would be taken to jail and his cover might be blown, or move forward and get on the boat with her. Reluctantly, he nodded and they took off towards the beach.

'Just until I am well, then you must return.' He spoke to her sternly, and she nodded, knowing in her heart of hearts she would never be able to leave him. But that was another day's battle.

As they left the estate grounds, Vivi looked back one last time to her home, and her heart was heavy. She feared she would never see it again, and as she glanced up towards the upper-floor windows for a second, she swore she saw Tom's face at the window, watching her. Vivi hoped more than anything it was her imagination. She didn't want his last memory of her to be her escaping with this prisoner.

Out along the beach path, Vivi helped Marcus down the wet sand to the dock. The old fisherman was already there, smoking his pipe, seated on the stern of his boat, looking out across the moonlit bay. As they approached, he eyed the two of them suspiciously.

'All right, Vivi. What's all this about?'

'We need to get across to France, just like last time.'

'And who is this?'

'This is one of the other operatives from SOE,' she stated. 'He's coming with me this time.'

The older man didn't seem very convinced but nevertheless let them onto his boat.

This was such a different trip across the water for Vivi than before. She had thought she had been nervous as a wireless operator. But now, with a spy who would be undercover with the Nazis by her side, her fear grew, as she wasn't sure what would happen when they got to Brittany.

The captain, John, didn't speak to her much this time around. Every now and then he would look across at her accusatorially, and Vivi would try to smile her reassurance.

As they got closer to France, Marcus changed into his Nazi uniform, as they had decided that would make it easier for them to move through the country. As he placed his peaked cap on his head, for a second Vivi felt regret. Seeing him in the clothes of the enemy was so shocking, and it was as if his whole demeanour changed. Gone was the man she had come to know, and morphed in his place was Major Vonstein of the Third Reich, and for a moment she was fearful of him. Now he would have to play a role and she had to hope she had not made the biggest mistake of her life.

The fisherman didn't see Marcus changing, as he was preoccupied guiding the boat into position towards the beach. When he finally did look back, the shock on his face was palpable.

'What's this all about, Vivienne?' he spat out, looking with great contempt at her. 'Who is this man!?' And as though the penny dropped, he stared at Vivienne. 'Please tell me this isn't the prisoner they pulled out of the water a few weeks ago? Everyone in the village was talking about it.'

Vivi knew that for the deception to be complete, she could not tell him of their plan. This had to look convincing. All at once, Marcus pulled out her father's pistol and, pointing it at John, slipped back into his heavily accented English, with a clipped German manner.

'You will do as we tell you. Fräulein Hamilton has seen sense and has joined the Third Reich and will take her place by my side, representing the greatest country on Earth.'

'Don't do this, Vivienne,' Mr Thompson implored her. 'You would bring such shame to your family. And your poor mother, God rest her soul... she would be heartbroken if she was still alive.'

Vivi forced out the words, hoping he couldn't tell that her heart felt as if it was pounding out of her chest. 'I've made my mind up, John. I am disillusioned with Britain and everything it represents. The Führer and his vision for our world are what I want to be part of now, and you and nobody else can stop me. Heil Hitler!' she said, raising her right arm.

John seemed incensed and reached forward for his wireless, but Marcus cocked the barrel of his gun. 'I wouldn't do that if I were you. It could be very unfortunate if you do.'

Vivi looked over at Marcus. Surely he wouldn't shoot him. This was a man she'd known all of her life. Though she knew there'd be difficult decisions they had to make along the way, she did not want to see people harmed for no good reason.

Marcus must have sensed her discomfort. 'I do not want to shoot you in front of the Fräulein, so I suggest you step back from your wireless, sir.'

John hesitated but finally stepped away.

'I want you to pull straight into the beach, where we will get off.'

The captain did as he was told and pulled the boat alongside the beach. It was still dark, and there was no one to catch the ropes this time around. As Vivi prepared to jump up onto the beach, Marcus turned around and pistol-whipped John across the head, and he slumped to the ground.

'Did you have to do that?' hissed Vivi.

'We have to give ourselves some time.'

Vivi nodded, checked that John was still alive, wanting more than anything to take the time to bind the wound that had opened up on his forehead but knowing that time was of the essence.

They travelled through the quiet streets of Le Diben where she'd landed before, and she thought about the last time she'd been here. It felt like yesterday, but being by the side of a Nazi was haunting. They made their way to a German post, where Marcus introduced himself, showed them papers and explained the plane he had been travelling on had engine trouble and had to make an emergency landing in Brittany before taking off to return for repairs, and he needed to get to Paris as soon as possible. The Nazis in this sleepy little town were taken off guard at seeing such a high-ranking officer in their midst, and Marcus was formidable in his role.

They didn't even question his story or ask about Vivi. Instead they lent him the only car in the village to drive to Morlaix, where they would be able to get a train. As they set off in the car they both sighed with relief. Because of Marcus's injuries, Vivi had to drive; fortunately she had learned that as part of her training. As she gripped the steering wheel and wove the car down the country roads, Marcus reached forward and squeezed her hand.

'You are amazing.' He smiled at her. 'Not long now.'

Back at the train station again, Vivi bought tickets for Paris. In his uniform, Marcus was very much the Nazi, and she had to keep reminding herself that he really was working undercover for the British. He was so good at the part he played. Even the way he spoke to her, in his abrupt German, sounding every bit in control. As they were waiting to board the train, someone caught her eye.

She turned. Someone was watching her intently, and she sucked in breath when she realised who it was. Hunched in the shadows was Terrier, leaning on a post, smoking a cigarette on the platform, obviously waiting for another operative. Making eye contact with Vivi, he walked towards her.

'Look who flew back. No one told me you were coming,' he said, obviously glad to see her.

'I would stop and talk, but I have things I have to do,' she blurted out, aware of the flush that was creeping across her cheeks.

Suddenly, Vonstein was beside her and Terrier stepped back in shock. She knew she had to do what she had to do, even though this would be hard.

'I'm leaving for Paris. I am now with the Nazi Party,' she stated harshly.

The shock on Terrier's face was visible and he backed off, not waiting to hear any more, blending into the crowd as he was so good at doing. But Vivi sensed he was still staring at her from somewhere inconspicuous on the platform. As she boarded the train and made her way into the carriage, it broke her heart to sit there looking out for him, to know that all of these people may have thought so poorly of her. But Vivi reminded herself that it was for the greater good. If her faith in Marcus was right, it would be a matter of weeks, and then once this mission was finished, she could come back, and she and Terrier and Anne-Marie could laugh about it, and she could explain how she'd been undercover. But right now the pain in people's faces as she appeared to have deceived them was a lot harder than she'd anticipated.

Once they were in the carriage, and confirmed they were alone, they slid the door shut, and the train moved away. Vivi felt the weight of what she was doing. Why did she constantly jump into things without thinking them through? She looked at Marcus. What if he really was a Nazi? She hadn't thought about that for some time, but suddenly it struck her once more. He could be a double agent. He could say all these things just so he could get back into Paris. Marcus looked down at her then with great compassion.

'You're doing really well, Vivi,' he whispered to her in English. 'I know this is hard for you.' There was such a gentleness in his tone and such care for her. He took her hand then and kissed it, gently. 'Thank you, brave warrior. I am so grateful to you, and so will Mr Churchill be when I tell him. You have trusted me and now I think you deserve the same. You know already I have to go back undercover as a Nazi. But the reason the timing is imperative is because the Allies have a large planned offensive coming up and my job is to thwart Hitler's efforts to get accurate information. I have been careful to progress my career to a place where I can do this. It is dangerous work and if I am found out, I will be executed, but if I don't do it thousands of people could die. This war has to end and Hitler is a madman who must be stopped. I just hope I can help speed it up.'

She nodded, understanding the gravity of what he had to do.

When guards came on the train to check her papers this time, it was very different being with Marcus. When one emboldened inspector asked to see her papers, Marcus reprimanded him so harshly for demanding something from his assistant that the poor man couldn't apologise enough. Though it was clear getting false papers for her had to be a priority, Vivi actually felt sorry for the guard, knowing the authorities on and off the train weren't the Gestapo, just local law-enforcement officers, strong-armed into working for the Germans, and people who cared little for who was who.

As the train moved on through France towards Paris, Marcus told her about his childhood, and stories of him and Marcel. She saw the sadness behind his eyes, but also the relief to be doing this for them. He continued to tell her about his life as they wove through the countryside, only becoming stiff and Nazi-like whenever somebody walked down the corridor and looked in.

They made a plan. If she was to remain, she would become his secretary. That way he could keep her safe. 'As soon as we get to Paris,' he told her, 'I will get in touch with a contact I can rely on to get you false papers.'

On arriving at the station, Marcus took her straight to his apartment. Once he unlocked the door and they walked in, he sank into a chair, obviously exhausted, not only from being in a great deal of pain from his wounds, but also from the pretence they had been keeping up. Vivi quickly took care of him, changing his bandages and getting him into bed.

It was only at this point that Vivi broke down. All the stress and pressure and the lying overcoming her, welling up inside her, and she started to sob, letting go of all the fear and regret she'd held so tightly inside.

'Why don't you lie down for a while?' he suggested with deep concern in his tone as he pulled back the blankets. 'Get an hour's sleep. We have a lot ahead of us. You'll need all your strength.'

Taking her hand, he pulled her towards him and kissed her gently on the lips. The exhilaration of that feeling startled her, and for the first time, she felt aware that she was alone with this man in his apartment, in his bedroom. Even with the overwhelming surge of regret and emotion, it was exciting as he pulled her into bed next to him and enfolded her in his arms.

Nestled safely against him, she could hardly keep her eyes open but as she drifted off to sleep all she could see were the faces of the people that had worked with her in Paris, all coming back like ghosts.

Chapter 29

Present day

The day after their visit to Alex's family's apartment, they visited La Musée de la Libération de Paris, and Sophie was heartbroken to see so many photographs of the faces of people who had sacrificed their lives during World War Two, many of them young, some only surviving a few weeks working undercover for the French Resistance because it was so dangerous. Sophie kept hoping she would see Vivienne's name there somewhere, maybe under an obscure plaque, somehow hidden, undiscovered, identifying her as one of the war heroes, or perhaps giving clues to the message she still hadn't decoded. But Vivienne wasn't there. They walked around the exhibition listening to the audio of extraordinary stories. She was starting to build up a good idea of what Vivienne had done for France and was amazed to find out that the wireless operators, the kind Vivienne had been, only had a life expectancy of six weeks.

There was a little about the Germans too, information about the occupation. Sophie enquired about where to go if she wanted to research the war records of a German commanding officer who had been there during World War Two. The docent gave her more references to check on the internet, assuring her that the Germans had kept meticulous records. 'We don't keep that kind of information here. We are celebrating what the French did during the war in the Resistance,' he informed her.

After they left the museum, Alex was full of all the stories they had read about as they walked again along the Seine. It had rained earlier in the day, but now the whole city was alive with a clean, fresh smell as the sun played peek-a-boo with the clouds. Sophie looked around, and was reminded that Paris was a delightful city. But as Alex chatted by her side, she couldn't help feeling a sense of sadness as she gathered her coat around her. She and Matt had come here a couple of years before and walked this very path. It had been the summer then, so the weather had been much more accommodating and it had been a good weekend for them. They'd enjoyed themselves. Now she was alone, again.

When they got to Alex's gallery he ducked inside to check his messages with the young woman he had left in charge. She followed him in as his assistant pointed to a picture she had evidently just sold for him and he nodded, nonchalantly. But when Sophie looked at the price she was taken aback – it was almost a year's wages in her research job. She looked over at Alex, realising for the first time he was potentially much more wealthy than she had assumed. There was nothing of the starving artist about the price of that piece.

He seemed occupied with an intense conversation he was having with the young woman, so excusing herself, after arranging to meet Alex later for dinner, Sophie made her way back to her rental apartment.

As Sophie arrived at the restaurant a couple of hours later she noted it was a mild enough evening that she was able to sit outside, and she enjoyed watching people interact, listening to the hum of the distant traffic, and inhaling all the great food smells wafting out from the restaurant's kitchen.

'I'm sorry I'm late,' Alex said, arriving thirty minutes after she'd got there, finding Sophie snuggled deep inside her coat and on her second glass of wine. 'A customer kept me late at the shop, and I wanted to get something for you I had in my apartment. I remembered it today, after you left. I had almost completely forgotten about it.

'As I told you, it was very hard for my mother, knowing her uncle had done the terrible things he had done, so she never wanted to see any reminders of him. But in spite of that, she kept some pieces. And I remembered I still had some of his things from earlier in the war.'

He sat down and ordered a glass of wine, then handed her a cigar box, no bigger than six inches square. She opened it and removed the contents. It was full of German medals Marcus had won during the war and papers commemorating the work he'd done for the Reich, which chilled her. Sophie held the spiky metals in her hand, including the Iron Cross, wondering what atrocity he'd committed to gain that particular favour with his commanding officers. There were also his enlistment papers and the letter sent to his family about his death. She looked at it and screwed up her eyes.

'Interesting,' she mused. 'I wonder if Vivienne and Marcus were still together. This letter suggests he died outside Paris. Why weren't they in Paris? Do you think Vivienne died with him or somewhere else? This is a little unusual. We need to dig deeper.'

Alex sipped his wine and stared intently at her.

'After you left yesterday, I thought about that photo in the museum and, if there was any chance that Marcus had been working for the British undercover in any way, how much it would help my mother. She still feels the disgrace. I could not tell her I was looking into this. But I'd like to continue pursuing it with you if you would be agreeable,' he suggested.

Sophie sat back and looked into his blue eyes. He was so good-looking, tall, and with such an easy manner. She'd instantly liked him, but also was becoming wary of how fast this was all moving, she needed to set some boundaries to protect her own heart.

'It would be nice to have your help, but it would be just business,' she finally responded.

He looked astonished. 'I hadn't thought of anything else.'

She smiled as he looked so put out by her comment. 'You are French,' she joked.

Understanding her insinuation, he chuckled. 'Do not believe everything you hear about the French. We also like our sleep. But I think this would be challenging for you to do alone, particularly as your knowledge of my language is not the greatest. I also speak German fluently, like a lot of people from Alsace. I was encouraged to learn it even after my mother decided to come to live in Paris.'

Sophie thought of her family and the languages Vivienne's generation had learned. 'Okay.' She smiled. 'I would love your help.'

After they finished a wonderful dinner of steak, with the lightest, crispiest fries she had ever had in her life, and then had slogged through a rich, dark slice of chocolate cake, they took a stroll. Alex showed her the area of Paris where many of the Resistance operators who they had learned about earlier at the museum had lived. There was even a brothel that had been a safe house and had been turned into a little museum. Sophie stood outside the ornate crimson door down a dark passageway and wondered about the secrets those rooms had kept. They looked at other buildings, too, some marked proudly with a plaque stating their function during the war and Sophie wondered if Vivi had been housed in any of them. The stories in the museum about the agents were harrowing. She couldn't imagine what it must have been like.

After Alex walked her home, she made him a coffee and they looked up on the internet the new information the museum staff had told her about. It appeared there were further German war records housed in a building in Berlin.

'We could fly or it's about eight hours by train,' Alex suggested.

Sophie grinned. Clearly Alex was becoming as obsessed as she was. She suggested they opt for the train journey, as she felt the need of time to collect her thoughts before she had to face whatever was waiting for her in Berlin. Something in her gut told her she would find answers, good or bad, in Germany and she was suddenly afraid this story might not end well. Also, she found she shamelessly wanted to spend longer with Alex and this would extend their time together.

'We can go tomorrow if you like,' he suggested. 'I'll sort tickets and meet you at the train station at nine. And maybe you can sort the hotel?'

Sophie nodded nervously, but there was also an excitement in her stomach, a thrill from the idea of going away with him, even though she had been clear about what this was. She reminded herself they would have separate beds in separate rooms, and she was grateful because she wasn't totally sure she could trust herself with him.

'You don't need to be at your gallery?' she asked.

'Oh, it can last a few days without me. I'll close it up. It's a glorified art studio, really. I don't sell that many paintings, maybe two or three a month if I'm lucky.'

She smiled, totting up in her mind how much that would bring him in if all the pictures were of a similar price to the one she had noticed today.

Once he'd finished his coffee, Sophie walked him to the door and he kissed her on both cheeks. She felt a little spark. But she pushed the feelings away, telling herself she was still raw after the break-up with Matt, a little needy for any kind of affection. Sophie watched Alex walk down the quaint circular staircase and disappear out into the Parisian evening and felt such warm feelings towards him.

That night, Sophie had a vivid dream of the bombs dropping on France and woke up sweating. She could only imagine what it had been like for Vivienne and the other people of the Resistance. She got up and booked two rooms in a hotel for her and Alex in Berlin, then enjoyed fresh coffee on her balcony, watching the streets of Paris come to life, before she had to leave to meet Alex at the train station.

He was waiting for her with a cup of coffee and a warm croissant.

'Did you eat?'

She shook her head, laughing.

'I had the feeling that you would be preoccupied,' he responded, handing her the drink and the pastry. She took them gratefully.

They decided they would get the nine-thirty train, which would take them all the way to Berlin.

As they travelled from Paris, they talked the entire time, for the whole eight hours. But she still didn't tell him about Matt. She told him about everything else – he already knew about Emily, but she talked about her work, her home, her cat. Just not, 'oh and by the way, I just got dumped'. Not, she realised, because she was hurting, so much as she found she simply didn't want to talk about her ex. He was her past, he would always be Emily's dad, but he had been right – their relationship hadn't been going anywhere. He'd done it the wrong way, but he'd done them both a favour in the long-term.

Alex, on the other hand, didn't seem to have any trouble talking about his personal life. He also had a cat, and had just finished with a girlfriend, three months before. 'And she broke my heart,' he said, placing his hand on his chest. 'But she went to a better man, so what can I say?'

They arrived late in the afternoon. Sophie mused how each city had its own smell. Berlin's was damp and clinical. Around her, people chattered in many different languages, none of which she understood, and suddenly she was so grateful that Alex was with her.

'Let's get a taxi,' she suggested.

They made their way outside and Alex gave the taxi driver the name of the place where they were staying. On arrival, she was glad to see that the hotel was a hive of activity and there were quite a few people buzzing about. She hadn't wanted anything too intimate, and having lots of people around could stop things becoming too intense between the two of them.

Depositing their bags in their rooms, they went down to have dinner. Alex interpreted the menu. 'I hope you like sausages,' he mused as he translated. 'They have ten different types right here.'

Sophie shook her head. 'Do they have a salad?'

'They do, but I hope you want it with sauerkraut because it all seems to come that way.'

After the food arrived, Sophie recapped everything she knew. He listened attentively.

'It's so odd that she went back to France though. I mean, if SOE threw her out, why would she come back to work for them? I know you want the best outcome for your family, but the fact is, it all points to her being a spy for the Germans, a traitor,' he said.

She agreed but said, 'I still need to see it for myself to believe it.'

They decided they needed to get an early start, so he walked her back to her room, kissing her politely on both cheeks and squeezing her hand before disappearing into his room.

That night, as she went to sleep, she thought again about her great-aunt. Had she fallen in love with Marcus? If he was half as lovely as his great-nephew she was beginning to understand the attraction. And what did that love mean when there was a war and they were on opposite sides? How could she follow her heart, and also do the right thing?

Chapter 30

1944

The morning after they had arrived back in Paris, Marcus left Vivi in the apartment while he went to make contact with his cell. He had also wired his German office the evening before to let them know he had returned, saying he had sustained some injuries in a bombing raid, which was why he was back later than expected. Though Vivi had been heartened to see that his wounds were repairing well, his leg was still a constant bother to him, and he had to rest often after he walked on it.

Vivi waited all day for him to return, unable to leave the apartment without papers and his Nazi protection. When Marcus finally arrived back, she was in the kitchen making herself a drink.

'How did it go?' she asked, greeting him and quickly helping him down into a chair.

He exhaled loudly. 'It went well. I don't think anyone suspects anything. They have all been so busy, they were just glad I had finally returned. I have also made contact with the other members of the cell here, a person I can trust, and tomorrow they will get you your papers.'

She looked into his blue eyes. He looked tired and worn with the stress of it all.

'How are you feeling? How's your leg?'

'It is healing.' He smiled as she gave him a cup of coffee. 'I have an excellent nurse,' he added.

That evening, he appeared awkward as they approached the bedroom. 'Please, you take the bed,' he insisted. 'I can sleep on the sofa.'

But she took his hand and gently led him into the bedroom.

'There have been so few moments of joy during this war. I think when we have the opportunity to share some love that we should take it,' she said, reaching up to undo the buttons of his uniform.

He gently took hold of her wrists and pulled her hands away. 'I know I have had to hold you at arm's length, but you have no idea how difficult it was for me, the times I held back from kissing you. One particular morning in Cornwall, when you first found out who I really was, I watched you as you changed my bandages. It took all of my strength not to pull you into my arms and make love to you right there. It was the hardest thing I have ever done. When you thought I was your enemy, when you would leave the room, the agony in just knowing how much I'd hurt you, how I had lost your trust, kept me awake most nights. Now, having your forgiveness and your companionship is more than I could ever have hoped for.'

Vivi pulled him towards her then and felt the sheer bliss of safety and completeness as his body enveloped hers. And in response to the desire coursing through her body like electricity she started to tremble, the attraction overwhelming her. Looking up into his concerned blue eyes, she gently stroked the scar on his forehead that was healing well. She laced her hands through his hair, and he closed his eyes in response, and when she gently stroked the back of his neck, he shivered and opening his eyes he looked down on her with so much love.

'We have both been through a difficult time,' she whispered, studying his face, his strong jaw, his full lips, getting lost in the deep blue of his eyes that drew her in with their intensity of emotion. As she gently ran her fingers down his face, he teased out a breath, and she felt his heart starting to race in his chest beneath her breast, his lips so close to hers. 'I think we deserve some happiness now, don't you?'

She pulled him towards her then and kissed him passionately on the lips and he responded by pressing her in so tightly against his body, he almost lifted her off her feet and snatched away her breath. It was as if now, with permission to love her, he could unleash all the passion he had been holding back for so long; the passion he had kept so carefully in check so he could fulfil his mission. He lifted her gently into his arms and placed her on the bed. As a shaft of moonlight found its way through a chink in the curtains, illuminating his face for a second, she saw tears in his eyes.

'Are you sure, Vivi?' he whispered, his voice hoarse with the emotion and his breath coming thick and fast now with his desire. 'I wanted to marry you before we… I wanted all of this to be done the right way.'

She smiled up at him, thinking what a charming but impossible dream that was. They were undercover spies in one of the most dangerous places on earth. If they made it through another day alive it would be a miracle.

'After the war,' she assured him as she started to unbutton his uniform. 'We can think about all that after this war is ended and we have won.'

It felt surreal as her hands ran down the grey woollen cloth of his tunic, with the black-and-silver Iron Cross he'd won for bravery reminding her he had belonged to the Third Reich before her, that he still did. She removed the clothes of the enemy to reveal the man she loved inside. Before they knew it, they were undressed and urgently seeking one another, finally able to satisfy the hunger that burned like a raging fire through both of them. Their lovemaking felt all the more exquisite because they could get lost in their pleasure, when so much of their time was preoccupied by their fear and anguish. They made love for hours that first night, indulging in the pure bliss of one another as the weight of the world around them disappeared.

Once she had her new papers, Vivi's way of life became even more intense than when she was in France with SOE. She'd gone from the relative ease of living in Cornwall again to being in league with a spy, working for and being in love with a man the world saw as a Nazi. Becoming Marcus's secretary, she wore the Nazi uniform, and each day as she walked through the streets of Paris and approached the building where her enemy waited for her she wondered if that day would be her last, if one misstep would change everything. The only high point for her was she got a chance to see Marcus in his work, every day, and she was in awe, not only of Marcus as a human being, a simple man she was in love with, but at his skill at fooling the Reich and maintaining his calm, calculating demeanour in every situation. Driven by his desire to defeat Hitler, he was meticulous in his deception.

One of his jobs for the Germans was to examine and correlate all the information coming in about the Allies' movements and brief his commanders. But instead of doing that he would carefully change documents to advance the Allies' cause. It was a nail-biting roller coaster for her on a daily basis. Also, knowing that back home she was probably being perceived as a traitor broke her heart, especially when she thought of her father and her siblings. The one thing that propelled her forward was the thought of the people she had already let down, who had probably been arrested or, indeed, worse. The brave people she had met who had inspired her. She wanted no more needless deaths because of her. She owed them all her life and service and she believed bringing down the Nazis from within was their greatest hope.

As well as working with Marcus, she tried desperately to find out what had happened to the Renoirs, but even via Marcus's high-level Resistance contacts, there was no news of her friends.

Some of those early nights, when Marcus was sleeping deeply, she would sob into her pillow, heavy with the guilt. Yvette with her curious eyes and mane of blonde hair, her perfect life as a fashion designer ahead of her, or Monsieur Renoir with his hunched figure and contemplative nature, both fiercely protected by the fiery presence of Maman. She had to do this for them. What was the price of her reputation in comparison to the risks other people had taken to keep her alive?

With her false papers now in order, and with Marcus's recommendation, it had been easier to slide into a job with the Reich than she'd foreseen. At his office, and with her excellent linguistic skills, it had been easy for Vivi to move into the position of his assistant. Her cover story was that she had been working for the Third Reich from the beginning of the war, even pretending to be a wireless operator for a time to get intelligence on the Parisian underground. Marcus would brandish about her story to other officers and brag about her earlier 'betrayal' of SOE groups in France as if it were a tremendous gain for the Third Reich, explaining away the reason she wasn't still there pretending to work for the British as due to the fact she'd come under suspicion. The higher in command seemed to accept the story, even showing admiration about the fact such a beautiful woman shared Marcus's office, obviously a perk for a man who had such a distinguished standing in the Nazi Party.

There was only one officer who seemed distrustful of her; he was one of Marcus's peers, Captain Von Klaus, a squirrel of a man with beady eyes that pierced her with his gaze. They had been at a party when she'd been introduced to him, and he'd taken an automatic dislike to her.

'You're German?' he spat out with a great deal of disbelief in his tone.

Vivi nodded. The cover story she and Marcus had come up with was that she'd been born in Berlin, a place she had stayed many times with her mother during her European trips before the war.

'How did you meet her, Major Vonstein?' he demanded, glaring at her sceptically as Marcus sidled up to Vivi's side. With great irritation, Von Klaus swung around and addressed Marcus. 'We have to be vigilant, Major Vonstein. Do you know everything about this woman?' he said in an accusatory way.

'I can assure you,' Vivi spat back before Marcus could even answer him, 'I am most trustworthy. I am here for the Third Reich, and the Führer. I even worked as one of our mighty leader's secretaries in an office in Berlin, and if the Führer trusts me, I hope you would see fit to do the same.'

The officer was taken aback. Hitler's name carried a tremendous deal of weight, and no one wished to do anything that would make him look foolish.

He grunted and finished his drink. 'Well, I hope that you turn out to be all that you appear to be,' he declared, strutting away briskly.

Marcus gave her a sideward glance. They didn't speak about it until later that evening when they got home. After he had taken off his uniform, she drew close to him as he stared out the window across the Parisian night sky, awash with a million stars.

'Do you think he'll be a problem?' she enquired.

'I'm not sure.'

She noted the anguish in his eyes. 'What is it, Marcus?'

He searched her face. 'Vivi, when we left Cornwall, all I could think about was getting back here so I could continue the work of SOE. And now I wonder, with my British contact being dead and being so deep undercover, is what I do worth it? And then I look at you and realise I've brought you into this, and I feel terrible. I am just not sure how this will turn out, and I am responsible.'

She turned him to look at her. 'Listen to me, Marcus. This was my choice. I, too, have ideals I'm serving – my conscience, the higher good – and I owe many people in my life. I recognise the danger, and honestly...' She paused, weighing her words before she admitted, 'I never expected to return home to Cornwall. And if I did, imagine how I would be perceived. I'm not here officially undercover, I'm not even here with SOE, but I know what we're doing is right. We have a higher purpose. People may never know what we've done or why we're doing it. That doesn't mean that we aren't supposed to do it.'

He smiled. 'How did you become so wise?'

She laughed, slipping her arms around his waist. 'I don't feel very wise. I feel small – an insignificant piece of something so much bigger. But I want to do my best. I want to do the right thing for my country. Meeting you and falling in love was a wonderful benefit I could have never foreseen.'

He turned to her and tenderly kissed her. 'You know, my greatest fear is that you'll be taken from me, tortured or worse, and I won't be able to do the right thing at the right time.'

She pulled away. 'Marcus, you can never think like that. I could never be happy if I knew you'd done the wrong thing to save me and help the Germans win this war. We have to stay strong for one another.'

He nodded, and then took her in his arms, holding her as though he never wanted to let her go. When they made love that night it was tender, as if he wanted to appreciate every part of her, not just her body, but that he desired to be joined with her on a much deeper level.

Chapter 31

Within a matter of weeks, Vivi appeared to win over the Germans' trust, all except Captain Von Klaus, who continued to eye her warily whenever she came into contact with him. However, her cover story was established and believed, and Vivi continued working as Marcus's assistant as, day by day, he recovered.

The first time she put on her German uniform was surreal and she had stood looking at herself in the mirror, tears streaming down her face, knowing at this point there was no going back. The office they worked in was a long, sprawling building with a vast network of staff working with them. Marcus had an office on the second floor.

The information came in all different forms, but mostly wireless transmissions that had been intercepted by the people in the listening room. Those messages were always coded, and the staff would copy them down precisely as they were received. They would then hand those off to the decoders, who would do their best to figure out the information using captured code books and then pass the messages back to Marcus's office.

The Germans also got intelligence from reconnaissance missions. The pilots took photographs of land-transportation movements, Allied ships' whereabouts, air bases and the number of planes, and any amassing of the forces in particular areas that could alert them to upcoming attacks.

The last way they would acquire information was through Allied agents who were captured in the field. After they were interrogated, any new intelligence would be verified against other information Marcus had received from alternative sources.

To do her job as his assistant, Vivi was allowed to move freely between all the offices, so often went down to visit the girls in the listening pool or speak to the officers' wives and even the children that sometimes came to the office to visit their parents. She became popular, with her friendly outward demeanour and the desire to help in any way she could, often taking extra work from colleagues. Vivi quickly earned a reputation within the office as being not only industrious, but capable of doing whatever needed to be done. And the fact she also spoke good French boded well for her within the office; she found other members of the Gestapo would rely on her to decipher messages or correspondence that came in.

Lastly, she would aid Marcus in sorting through documentation and writing the reports he would present to the Reich. As a spy, his most essential job was to deceive them. As the information from the Allies filtered through the network, he intercepted it, changed it, and offered it to high command as the truth.

'We have to be extremely careful, Vivi,' he'd informed her. 'We have to let some of the true information through, and some we can manipulate. We cannot bring any suspicion to this office.'

As Marcus's secretary, she also attended the high-level meetings to take notes. She was there one morning as he presented his findings to the group.

'It appears the offensive we have feared may be considered over the next few months,' Marcus stated as he stood in front of a desk of ten of his peers. They met every week in an underground bunker that was dimly lit and smelled of mildew. An experience Vivi did not enjoy, but it was secure, and the higher members in the Reich insisted on caution to keep them all safe. In the dingy room, they assembled around a circular mahogany table, officers of the highest calibre from all the departments.

As he spoke, Marcus handed out a picture of an operative who had been killed. Vivi made sure to avert her eyes.

'This man managed to give us information that the Allies will indeed attack, and though he wasn't clear about the target destination, everything I am receiving continues to point to an assault in the Calais area.'

'How can we be sure this is not subterfuge?' stated Von Klaus as he rocked back in his chair.

Marcus continued, 'To be fair, sir, we can't. But I think we have to go with the best available information we have as it comes in. My task, as you know, is to coordinate and gather all that information. So, please, anything you get, bring to me, and then we'll continue to have these weekly meetings, where we can see any pattern emerging, so we can defeat this enemy and their pathetic network of underground spies. It should not be hard; they are only a group of women and Frenchmen.'

There was a ripple of arrogant laughter around the table as Marcus gave up the floor for another senior official, who wanted to update them on what was happening on other fronts.

During the meetings, Vivi purposely kept her head down and proceeded to take notes of everything that was said. At the end, it was her responsibility to make copies for everybody. And she made sure they all got them in good time. Her role, she decided, was to make herself invaluable, yet keep a low profile. No one knew about her and Marcus's affair. They kept that very quiet, travelling home separately and leaving home at different times. The evening was the only time they could relax. And for those moments, those few hours a day, they lived for being like any other loving couple.

Every day her love for him grew. Not only did she love the strength she saw in him, but also his kindness and gentleness. For a man who had lived his whole adult life as a soldier she was amazed at his depth of compassion and caring for her. He adored her, and his love for her was immense and he showed that love however and whenever it was possible.

She generally tried not to think about where this affair would go. She feared they'd both be captured and killed, but she pushed those thoughts from her mind. At night she lay in his arms and for the briefest of moments all she had to be was herself and to love him.

Deceiving the Germans in their office seemed to work more smoothly than she'd expected. No one appeared to suspect either Vivi or Marcus. Vivi was amazed how easy it was to lie as long as she was convinced of it herself, even though it was a balancing act to know what intelligence to let filter through.

However, a few weeks into their mission, Von Klaus informed them he had requested their office receive a visit from high command.

'Is there something you are unhappy with, Captain Von Klaus, that I should be aware of?' Marcus enquired with obvious irritation.

Von Klaus walked over to the adjoining door that belonged to Vivi's office and closed it. Vivi quickly moved to the door and pressed her ear to it to hear the muffled conversation.

'I met with Field Marshal Rommel on my last visit to the north, and he has some interesting theories about the possibility of an upcoming assault. I think it wouldn't do any harm to have his opinion on this matter. So, I believe he will be sending someone to work with us, to help you with your assessments of the situation.'

Marcus sounded agitated as he responded. 'It is, of course, kind of Field Marshal Rommel to assist us in this matter, but I am surprised he has the manpower to extend to us when we have been having such a high success rate here on our own. Do you have concerns about my work I should know about?'

Vivi noted Marcus's last remark was framed as a question, but it sounded accusatory.

Von Klaus responded, matching Marcus's inflection. 'I think, with something as important as a potential invasion, it doesn't hurt to have all the expertise that is available to us. I'm sure you are doing' – he paused as she heard him open Marcus's office door – 'your best.' His last comment sounded derogatory. But before Marcus had a chance to respond, she heard Von Klaus salute with a 'Heil Hitler' and leave the room, closing the door behind him. His footsteps echoing down the passageway.

Rommel's officer, Major Weissman, stalked into the briefing room a few days later, just before the weekly meeting, and Vivi watched him with extreme concern. He was a bulky man, somehow squeezed into his uniform, with red pouch-like cheeks and black pins for eyes. He paced nervously around the room, observing everyone, giving off an air of disdain, appearing not to be impressed with anything he saw.

The meeting started as it generally did, with each of the officers giving an account of how their departments were working. There had been some issues with getting the artillery they needed and the Resistance had been a constant annoyance to them as it blew up train depots and lines, thwarting their ability to get what they needed dispatched throughout the country. As each of them spoke, Major Weissman studied them carefully, as if weighing up whether he trusted what they had to say or not.

Finally, it was Marcus's turn to speak, and he updated them on his efforts. 'We have seen some increased activity with the anticipation of a significant offensive from the Allies,' he informed them, passing out some statistics Vivi had created for him.

Weissman shifted in his seat. 'Do you have any information of where the presumed attack could take place?'

'I do,' responded Marcus, not flinching with any intimidation. He passed out further information. 'At this point, with all of our resources, our reconnaissance, and where we feel that the Resistance is focused, our best intelligence suggests it will be Calais that would be the prime location for the enemy to attack.'

The Major groaned and drummed his fingers on the table to show Marcus had not persuaded him.

'Major Weissman,' Marcus enquired, 'do you have other information we should know about?'

The major stood, swaggering to the front of the room. Marcus seated himself as Vivi sat poised. She had a bad feeling about this new officer. Until now their lies had been working well, but the fact that high command was taking more of an interest in the data they were collecting concerned her.

'They have sent me from headquarters because Field Marshal Rommel has a theory that the presumed attack from Calais may be no more than a ruse from the British to have us amass our forces in the wrong place. He is becoming more and more convinced that an attack via Normandy would be more obvious.'

Vivi sat frozen in her chair, not letting her gaze meet Marcus's. She did not want to give away anything she was thinking as she remembered the quiet conversation they had had just the night before over dinner in their flat.

Marcus had informed her of the details of a ploy that the Allies were working on to help convince the high command the attack was heading to Calais, not Normandy, which was the plan. All the way along the Thames Estuary, the British had made fake boats and ships created by an illusionist so that when photographs were taken from the German aeroplanes, they would give the impression of a unit assembling to sail. From that location, Calais would have been the shortest route; the trip from Normandy would come out of the south coast and would take an extra ten hours. The hope was that this ruse would fool the Germans into believing that the Allies wouldn't do anything that dangerous.

Weissman finished his assessment, and Marcus stood to respond. His commander-in-chief stared at him through a furrowed brow.

'Have you picked up anything along these lines, Major Vonstein? What would be your assessment of the situation?'

Marcus projected his own air of arrogance. 'I am grateful for the major's input and for Field Marshal Rommel's assessment of the situation. But I have to be clear: The information we have gathered does not reinforce this in the least. Everything we have supports the opposite.' He handed out the photographs he had brought with him, showing the pictures not only of the Thames and the amassing armada there, but also Scotland, where fake encampments had been created to give the misconception of an army gathering there too.

'Why would the Allies spend such considerable time converging their troops to this point in Scotland?' Marcus continued. 'If anything they will come in through Norway, that is the expected route from Scotland. There is no way they would travel all the way down to Normandy; it is just too far and too dangerous. All of the agents we have captured have informed us along these same lines.'

The major harrumphed.

'It may be that this is such a closely guarded secret they are not even informing their own agents,' continued another member of the party at the table. 'We are doing remarkably well with enemy spies in Paris. We have been very successful, as you know, at infiltrating them and have captured many of whom they call the Prosper Network. None of them seemed to be convinced – even with a little persuasion from us – that the attack is to come from London to anywhere other than the Calais area.'

Vivi shuddered inwardly at the word 'persuasion' and tried not to focus on exactly what that meant to her former cell.

The debate continued, and even though Weissman seemed to remain suspicious, the other commanding officers seemed pleased with the information Marcus presented.

After the meeting was over, Major Weissman strode over to talk to Marcus. 'My commanding officer has informed me he would prefer me to work more closely with you, so you should send us any information you get through as we continue to observe this situation. I should let you know that Field Marshal Rommel is still convinced by some activity we have seen in the Resistance and with a heightened amount of sabotage in Normandy that the attack will take place in that area. If you come across any information that would support that, we expect your help, Major Vonstein.'

Marcus nodded. 'Anything that comes in I will keep you informed about, straight away.'

After he left, and finally, when Marcus and Vivi could speak alone back at their apartment, she voiced her fears over supper.

'Yes, it is a concern,' responded Marcus. 'But we have to stay convinced of what we believe. We have to stay strong, Vivi.'

'They will never break me,' she responded sternly. And she had meant it at the time, but she had no idea how much her resolve would be tested.

Chapter 32

Vivi continue to remain strong until one day something happened that would shake her to the core. She had been at the offices of a different branch, delivering the information that Field Marshal Rommel's major had requested. She had several photographs from a reconnaissance mission, and the latest details of where the so-called enemy forces were assembling. As she was leaving the building, she saw them dragging in a prisoner and it sickened her to see. When he turned his face towards her, she recognised him immediately. Terrier. His eyes were blackened and his face bruised, but it was definitely him. She caught his eye, and the look of bewilderment was clear on his face.

Rushing back to her office, Vivi signalled to Marcus they needed to talk straight away. Leaving the offices, where he was constantly concerned there were bugs and someone may be listening in, they went for a walk until they were alone. She told him what she had seen, and his face revealed considerable concern.

'This is unfortunate, Vivi. He has seen you and knows who you are and what you were doing in SOE. It means if they interrogate him he could let your identity slip, and it could ruin everything we're doing here. I'm afraid there is only one course of action.'

'But you tell people about my past, use it as a victory.'

'But he actually knows the truth and with Weissman being so particular…'

Vivi stared at him, struggling to understand what he was suggesting to her. Did he mean they had to help Terrier escape? But by the look of weighty concern on his face, she knew it could only mean one thing. 'You would murder him?'

He responded softly to her, recognising how painful this would be for her to hear. 'We may have to sacrifice him, Vivi. This is too big a mission, too broad for just one life.'

'But Terrier helped me, took care of me. I was nearly caught by the Germans, and he helped me. I would never betray him. When I saw him at the train station I told him I had defected.'

'I'm sorry, Vivi,' he said, shaking his head. 'He still knows more about you than is safe. I will take care of it myself and I will do it... kindly.'

'No,' she spat at him. 'Please don't do this. There must be another way.'

When they got home, they fought for hours, Vivi trying to convince him this wasn't for the good of the country but just to save her. He agreed that part of his motive was that, but also he felt her work was of the upmost importance and that if she was exposed, it could put a spotlight on their department at a very crucial time in their work. Eventually, as she sobbed into his shoulder later, she understood with a grieving heart that Marcus was right. She cursed herself for the fact that Terrier had seen her. What she could have done to prevent it, she did not know, but the thought that someone else's blood would be on her hands was just too hard for her to deal with.

She cried herself to sleep that night, loathing everything about this war; her fears overwhelming her. What if at the right moment she couldn't be as strong as Marcus needed her to be? She wasn't afraid of interrogation, but she wasn't looking forward to it either. Vivi was much more fearful of letting someone else down. She couldn't go through the pain of that again; it was just too hard for her.

*

The next day, when Marcus arrived at the place they were holding Terrier, he had already been killed by another officer. Marcus told Vivi that evening as they sat side by side.

Vivi found herself, for the first time in a long time, livid with Marcus. As he tried to calm her down, she asked him over and over, why hadn't he stopped it the day before? Why had he waited? And how could he have even contemplated killing her friend? They argued until finally she pulled herself onto the sofa and cried herself to sleep again. Even though he had tried to comfort her or reason with her, Vivi hadn't been open to hearing any of it. She was so overwhelmed with the grief and the loss of her friend.

As she went to sleep, her mind was filled with free-flowing pictures of her brief but intense time with Terrier, the way he had saved her on the train, and rescued her from the brothel. The night he had danced with her in Anne-Marie's kitchen until they were breathless in a last moment of frivolous fun and joy, there with those two friends she would never get to go on a picnic with.

She woke with a start in the middle of the night, the weight of her sadness forcing her from sleep. With the apartment dark and quiet, and with the lights off, from the sofa she could see out through the patio doors onto the balcony, where in the distance she could just make out the Eiffel Tower, a solid, dark shadow against the moonlit night.

When she'd trained with SOE, they had told her about the loss of life and how they would have to deal with it, but nothing had prepared her for the pain every time she lost someone close to her. Even though she'd only known Terrier for a short time, the fact he'd taken such good care of her, saved her from being caught on several occasions... She'd felt a fierce loyalty towards him, and now Vivi felt like she'd let him down.

Was this guilt ever going to go away? Would she ever not feel guilty for these lives and people around her? For the first time since she had arrived, she contemplated going back to Cornwall and reclaiming a simpler life. It was respectable to be a nurse; there was no shame being in Britain, staying there to patch up the boys. Why did she feel she had to be so heroic?

Then Vivi thought about Marcus. She could never imagine leaving him, and she knew he was stronger with her by his side. As angry as she was with him right now, somewhere deep inside her, Vivi knew what he'd said was right. But she hated it. She hated him for it. Right then, at that moment, she knew she couldn't go back to England, but she didn't want to face going forward, even though she knew she had to.

Chapter 33

Present day

Sophie had to face going forward to whatever might be waiting for her in her great-aunt's files in Berlin, and she was glad to have Alex by her side to support her. It had been so much harder than she had expected. Sophie could barely vocalise why Vivienne being innocent had become so important to her, but it was, and she needed this to work out okay when so much in her life had not. Something about being in Germany made it all seem so much more real, with the war history so close by and the clipped brusque language being spoken all around her. And, even though they had only just become friends, she felt a connection and a kinship with Alex because of their shared family history. Whatever Vivienne and Marcus had been to one another, they had had a connection that linked her and Alex.

Sophie had discovered that the Germans did indeed keep meticulous records, but nothing had prepared her for the Deutsche Dienststelle of Military Federal Archives where the German army's personnel records were kept. There was a vast wealth of the history of all that had taken place during the war; today's German people believing that transparency and accuracy was a crucial part of their recovery from their feelings of historical guilt.

The serious young man who had greeted them at the desk seemed used to dealing with relatives from all over the world who wanted to put records straight, and treated them both with extreme respect and attention.

She offered him the details of her great-aunt Vivienne, and Alex gave his uncle's serial number and name. They had a lot of the records and files online now, on their website, but the man reassured them that it wasn't uncommon for people to want to see the evidence for themselves.

Taking them to another room, a library of documents and files, he searched for the numbers and names, pulling out the appropriate files and placing them on the table for Sophie and Alex to look through.

'And here are the records of what your great-aunt did during that time,' he declared, speaking to Sophie in English. 'And where she worked for the Reich.'

Sophie started to shake as she looked through the files. She read correspondence written by Vivienne, day-to-day functions of her department during the war and the official letters she had written. It was surreal to read her aunt's written words in a German document.

The files were decidedly plain and ordinary. Sophie didn't know what she'd expected. Something more like a movie, she supposed, full of intrigue and innuendo. But everything she read was so matter-of-fact, different intelligence gathered and placed in a brief for people to read. More than ever, Vivienne started to feel real. Not just a phantom in a photograph at the Imperial War Museum, but a real human being.

Across the table, Sophie noticed Alex appeared frozen, his attention captured by something he was staring at and she came across to see what it was. He had opened the pages to Marcus's war records, and the first thing on the top was a picture of Marcus in his full Nazi uniform. Once again, the resemblance shocked her. Alex looked so much like Marcus, it made her shudder. In the picture, Marcus was stood with notable senior members of the Third Reich, and seeing them all together with an inscription that stated the photo was taken after an important meeting with high command was chilling.

'It's still hard to believe,' he murmured to Sophie, 'that this is real. I know my family have told me about it my whole life, but seeing it like this really brings it all home.'

Sophie nodded, placing a reassuring hand on his shoulder before returning to look through Vivienne's files. There was a photograph of Vivienne, too. She was staring right at the camera, standing with her arms folded, looking up as if someone had just asked her a question, her chin at that undeniable Hamilton angle. And by her side was Marcus. His expression was serious, as though he was engaged in something important and they had interrupted him to take the photograph.

It was haunting, seeing them together, and as she took in her great-aunt's pose, it struck her how relaxed she seemed. This didn't look like a woman who had been taken to Paris under duress. If anything, this looked like a woman who was happy, content, in love, even, and she realised again that after all of this, the conclusion could point to that very first version of the story her family had always believed was true. That Vivienne had, in fact, worked for SOE and had been discharged because of her incapability, then had fallen in love with this Nazi and had smuggled him out of England, back to Paris, where they both could do the Führer's bidding.

Sophie hated how every scrap of evidence seemed to lead her back to that conclusion. Even if Vivienne had been at SOE that day in London, it could have been for something underhanded, part of her plot to smuggle the Nazi out of the hospital. Why had she assumed something different?

Alex must have sensed her thoughts because unconsciously he took her hand and squeezed it. 'It's hard to take it all in, isn't it, Sophie?'

She nodded.

All at once, Alex sucked in a breath.

'What is it?' Sophie asked.

He shook his head, unable to speak. He pushed the sheet of paper over to Sophie. She picked it up and started to read. It outlined how Marcus had died. Apparently he'd abandoned his post in Paris, three days after the D-Day landings, and had been shot in an alleyway by a young woman. 'He couldn't even be a hero for the Germans,' said Alex, shaking his head. 'He ran away like a rat leaving a sinking ship.'

Sophie reread the words 'shot by a young woman'. Could it have been Vivienne? Did something go horribly wrong between them? Did she finally find her patriotism?

Sophie also shook her head. 'I'm so sorry, Alex.'

At the bottom of the report about his death was a list of what had been gathered on his person, his uniform, and his personal effects. A ridiculous list of unimportant things, nothing that hinted at the person he was or why he had done what he had done. It was so final and chilling.

Sophie quickly looked to the end of Vivienne's file, but there was nothing about her death. No death certificate or details of how she had died.

On the way out, the young man shook his head when she asked about that and told her that even today they were recovering records, that she should leave her email address and they would contact her if anything else came up.

She thanked him, closing the file, and they both left their details.

After they left the Federal Archives building they sat side by side in the taxi, both lost in their own thoughts. It had been a shocking and raw experience. Seeing things in black and white was very different to hearing stories. Pictures of Vivienne in her uniform with her Nazi lover and her distinctive handwriting in official files. The chance of her really being undercover for SOE was slipping out of sight.

They'd both taken photographs of what they had seen, and when they got back to the hotel and were drinking coffee, Sophie swiped through all the photos, trying to come to terms with the facts. It just overwhelmed her. Tears started to stream down her face. This was so much harder than she'd expected. Sophie hadn't even known her great-aunt, but the sadness of what had happened, coupled with her grief, that now always seemed to lie just below the surface, was too much for her.

Alex took her in his arms then and held her tightly, apparently feeling the same pain. All at once, his lips were upon hers, and she felt this deep need to be close to him. Only Alex could understand exactly how she was feeling.

The kiss shocked her, not because it was unexpected, but by the way it made her feel. It felt right, not awkward like a first kiss, but as if she'd been kissing Alex for years. When eventually, breathlessly, she pulled away, she knew she wanted more, wanted to be even closer to him, to feel safe, even if it was for a moment. Sophie suddenly felt very far from home, and Alex was the only touchstone of comfort she had. She wasn't sure if it was being away from all she knew or whether it was the pain and the hurt of what she was finding out.

Soon they were back in her hotel room and he stood in her doorway apologising.

'I'm sorry, Sophie. I didn't mean to kiss you like that.'

'Me neither, but I'm not sorry.'

She pulled him inside the room and closed the door. Everything inside her ached to be loved. As Sophie kissed him again, she realised that she and Matt had not been this close for months. Even after Emily, he had been around but not really *there* for her. She'd never been a one-night stand kind of person and couldn't even remember the last time she'd slept with someone she wasn't in love with, but somehow, in this tiny hotel in Berlin, it just felt right.

Sophie started to kiss him more intensely. He responded in kind, obviously hungry for closeness too. And before they knew it, they were naked on her bed, making love. The first time was fast and urgent, as if they needed to work out all the hurt and pain of what they had discovered through their bodies. But the second time was slower, gentle, more thoughtful, and as she looked up into his hypnotic blue eyes, it felt right, soulful and meaningful. When they were both spent, she lay in his arms, her eyes closed, enjoying the closeness of him.

'I didn't mean to do that,' Alex whispered as he gently kissed her neck.

'Neither did I,' said Sophie, laughing. 'But it feels good, doesn't it?'

They both laughed then. And she allowed herself to enjoy the moment. She wasn't sure if it meant anything, and she didn't care. Sophie just wanted to continue feeling safe and warm in his arms.

After they'd showered and he'd gone back to his room, they met later for dinner and didn't talk about it. It was as if they both wanted to preserve the preciousness of the experience without analysing it or trying to work out what it all meant. But there was something she needed to say, to tell him, because if this was going to be something, Sophie needed him to know she wasn't ready for a relationship.

He was talking about the last time he had been in Berlin when suddenly she blurted it out.

'I just broke up with my boyfriend and I wanted you to know that. I'm really raw, Alex. What we just had was lovely, but I have to be honest with you. I'm not sure I have it in me for anything more at this moment in my life. I'm still really smarting from that last relationship.'

He held her hand and she shook her head in response and he seemed to sense she didn't want to say anything further. He stroked his thumb across the back of her hand in gentle reassurance.

'Take all the time with us that you need. And if this is supposed to be anything more, it will happen in its own way, in the right place and time. Until then, I think we should just enjoy what it is right now. But I must tell you, Sophie, you're the most amazing woman I've met in a long time. I feel so free with you, more myself than I've felt with anyone. You are so easy to be with.'

She smiled then and covered his hand. 'I feel the same way.'

If only her heart was free, she thought. If only she still wasn't in so much pain, wasn't grieving Emily and now the end of her relationship. Since Emily's death she hadn't wanted to open her heart again, though something inside her told her someone like Alex would be the perfect person to explore that experience with at the right time. She just wasn't ready for anything more right now.

Just then, her phone chimed with an email. She scrolled down. It was from the desk clerk of the archives office they had visited that day. He claimed he had a message for her. She called him straight back, and he spoke in the same hushed tone as before.

'I have something that might interest you. After you left, I was putting away the files and entering them into our database when something came up. There is a woman who now lives in Berlin who has put a note on these files about those specific war offices, saying that she was there during that time and is open to being contacted. I believe she may still be alive. Would you like her address and phone number?'

Sophie was surprised. 'Yes, I would!'

'It seems her father was part of the same office you enquired about, and that she may have met or had some time with either of your relatives. She is very elderly, so I wouldn't expect much. But I thought you might want to know.'

Sophie wrote down the phone number and told Alex what the clerk had said. She called the number straight away. It was early evening, seven o'clock, and a woman answered the phone. She didn't seem to be able to speak English, so Sophie handed the phone across to Alex.

He spoke with the woman briefly, then wrote down something on a napkin. When he hung up the phone, he told Sophie what they had said.

'The woman I spoke to is the granddaughter of the woman in the file, Elsa Strauss, who worked in the offices with Marcus and

Sophie when she was a girl. Elsa would visit her father there, who also worked for the Germans. She – Elsa – has agreed to see both of us. We can go over at ten tomorrow morning if we want to speak to her, but we need to know that she is very ill, in the final stages of cancer. So, she's frail, but, according to her granddaughter, her memory is intact, and she is eager to talk to us, while she still can.'

Chapter 34

1944

After that one night, they never spoke about Terrier, and slowly Vivi opened up her heart again to Marcus. She couldn't understand why this had been the only way, and as much as she wanted to take time to process all that was happening, there was also so much pressure at work, and the constant fear of being detected, that they had to trust one another.

In the evenings, when they were together, were the most magical moments of all. Vivi didn't know if it was the intensity of not knowing if she would live or die, but the feelings she had for Marcus obsessed her. All she ever wanted was to be in his arms, holding him, listening to him tell her how much he loved her. Occasionally, she would recall how she'd heard about spies who were capable of turning agents by pretending to be in love with them, but nevertheless, she couldn't accept this was Marcus. The way he looked at her couldn't be contrived, could it? He showed her such tenderness and love.

On the nights when the bombing was relentless, they would often move into the tiny shelter under their apartment, where they would whisper between themselves about things that had transpired during their day. A near call with some intelligence they had falsified or a new account that the Allies were doing badly were both things concerning enough to keep them awake. Then on those evenings, after the all-clear, they would be too restless to sleep and they would move out onto their little terrace balcony, where they would sit with great sadness, observing the night skies of Paris alight with buildings on fire and the sounds of voices calling desperately to one another in the dark.

Other nights the skies were quiet, and when it was hot, they would also go out on the balcony. On those nights, because of the mandatory blackout, the moon and the stars would be tremendous. They would stare into the sky as Marcus would point out the various stars and patterns, and in return she would tell him stories she knew, all manner of tales she could remember from memory. Her favourite was called 'The Call of the Swallows' from the book she'd given to John.

Even with all the heartbreak around them, they felt so much joy just being together. Vivi had posted a letter to her family the day she left, that wouldn't have been delivered until after she had gone. Other than that one letter, and without the capacity to connect with anyone in their families because of the work they were doing, they sometimes felt like they were the only spies in the world.

'One day, all of this will be over,' Marcus told her as they were stretched out on a blanket one night, listening to artillery guns in the distance. 'One day, ordinary life will happen again.' He took her hand in his and kissed it. 'And you and I will wander through the streets of Paris as husband and wife, with our three adorable children, and it will be as if all of this was a dream.'

'Are you proposing to me, again, Marcus?' she asked, smiling, half-joking herself.

He grinned back, looking directly into her eyes. 'Would you marry me if I asked you this time?'

'Not right at the moment,' she responded coyly. 'But I appreciate the sentiment, and it is a beautiful dream to have.' She lay back in his arms to consider it.

'So maybe I will ask you again soon. You know that I love you, and when all this madness is over, I crave a genuinely simple life.'

'You wouldn't carry on working for the British government?'

'No, I think I'll become a stockbroker, or an accountant, something simple.'

She studied him with a curious expression. 'I can't imagine you as a stockbroker.'

'And what about you? What will you be?'

'I don't know, a pilot, or a lion trainer perhaps? That'd impress my little brothers.'

He gathered her close in his arms. 'And if anyone could do it, you could. You're definitely one of a kind, Vivi, my sweet, brave girl. Sometimes I feel terrible that I've taken you from your family.'

'You didn't take me. I left. I had to come. There are more ghosts to appease than you would know. So, I have to do your work with you. I have many reasons for that, and you were just one of them.'

'Just one? I don't know if I should be flattered or offended,' he added with a smile.

'I crave the end of the war, though. But that part of it worries me, Marcus – that we won't get out of this alive. The day we got on that fishing boat, I had a premonition that would be my last time on British soil. As I watched the shoreline disappearing, I just knew I would never see it again. I can't think too much about it. We have too much to preoccupy us, and I try not to consider it, because I must make my family proud. I know this is the place where I can be the greatest help to the war effort, even if no one knows what I am doing. But the whole situation is so sad. My only joy is that I have you by my side.'

'I feel the same way,' he whispered into her hair. 'My biggest fear,' he added, 'is that I will have to choose between your life and the work, and honestly, I'm not positive I could sacrifice you, my darling. I've already sacrificed a lot for this work, and it's already cost me so much. It would not be worth anything without you. I know it is wrong, and I imagine it goes against everything we've been trained for. But, that's how I feel. I am strong because of you. You have encouraged me to become this person.'

Vivi shook her head. 'I don't want to hear you say this. We have a job to do, Marcus, and if for any reason you had that choice, you would need to make the right one. Winning the war is more important than my life. So many people's future depends upon us.'

Chapter 35

A couple of months had passed and Vivi and Marcus's work was proceeding effectively, their biggest concern being Rommel's Major Weissman, who often asked for further updates. Apart from that, they had a system well established. The intelligence would come in and be handed over to the decoders, Vivi would pick up their findings and bring them to the office, Marcus would then change the intelligence marginally, and then Vivi would produce fake records about what was transpiring. They were scrupulous not to change too much, just a few miles off a suspected raid or a parachute drop, sufficient enough to keep the German army from suspecting anything.

One morning there was a knock at Marcus's door and a staff member announced that Major Weissman was demanding to see Marcus straight away.

Marcus frowned. Vivi was at his desk taking notes in shorthand and glanced at him. 'Was he expected here today?'

Marcus shook his head.

The major strode into the office.

'Major Weissman.'

'Major Vonstein, Vivienne.' He spoke dismissively, peering at her and giving the impression he wished her to leave.

She left for her office, leaving her door slightly ajar. It needn't have mattered, as Weissman was loud.

'It has come to my attention, Major Vonstein, that more than a few mistakes are coming through this office. Rommel has placed me in charge of collating all the intelligence, and out of all the offices, yours has a high rate of getting facts wrong. Now, how do you justify that?'

Vivi heard Marcus stand and stride towards his adversary. 'I am glad to see you, Major Weissman. I am aware of these issues, and I have been looking into it myself. It appears some of the staff were using older decoding books, and I am about to put that right. I appreciate your thoroughness with this matter, and with both of us working on this, I'm positive we'll get to the bottom of it.'

She heard Weissman exhale. He was evidently frustrated, but also had planned to lay the blame with Marcus, but then had been met with a less-than-hostile reception.

'Field Marshal Rommel has instructed me to put these areas right. We cannot have any department make needless mistakes. There are a lot of resources that are wasted when we get the wrong report.'

'Of course, Major, I agree. We'll get to the bottom of it between the two of us,' Marcus stated.

'I would like to increase my monthly visits to weekly and insist on being at the meeting here tomorrow so I can evaluate all the information you get through your office myself.'

'You feel this is necessary?' Marcus stressed. 'Surely Field Marshal Rommel would have more important work for you than this mere administration job.'

'I would be glad to help. These are Herr Rommel's orders.'

Marcus stayed silent for a moment, then said, 'There has been an acceleration over the last few months, and it has stretched our listening pool to their limits. If it is possible, I would prefer a few more members of staff to help them down there. This may alleviate some of the strain.'

Weissman must have agreed, because she heard him proceed towards the door and leave. As soon as she heard the door close, she went in to see Marcus.

'What have we received over the last week?' he asked her in a whisper.

She informed him of the directives they'd had and how she had adjusted them.

'Change as many back as you safely can. Maybe allow two or three, the most significant, to go through with fake information. We have to give the dog a bone, but we don't have to give away the farm.'

At the meeting the following day, Marcus made his presentation and Major Weissman listened but was unconvinced. 'I plan to make a tour myself today and meet with your staff, if that is all right with you, Major,' he stated abruptly.

Marcus nodded.

His commander looked at him. 'This will not hinder your work for us, Marcus?'

He shook his head. 'I am willing to do whatever needs to be done to make sure the correct information is received and translated.'

'Then instead of travelling to a different office I would like to remain here indefinitely,' added Weissman. 'Help keep things on track.'

Vivi was staring down at her notebook and did not look up. She was writing the minutes of the meeting and dared not imagine what this might mean. Until now, they'd done a fair job of thwarting a lot of the enemy's campaign, and the Resistance had managed to get messages through. Without even looking at him, she knew this was a concern for Marcus as well. They couldn't allow all of them through, just the ones they'd thought were most significant. But now that Operation Fortitude, the code name for the upcoming invasion, was in full swing, it was an absolutely crucial time. The more secrecy they could create, the more impactful the offensive would be when the Allies finally showed their hand.

After that meeting, Major Weissman became an irritant. Each day he would arrive at the office and watch everybody working.

He would go through files, read through things and listen to the translations.

It was on the third day that Vivi happened to be down receiving a message from a decoder when she overheard a conversation the major was having with a translator.

'This code you translated that said "maximum effort, Calais", do you recall it?'

'I don't remember it, sir. There are so many. It could have been any of those.'

'It was so specific, do you remember this one?'

'I remember maybe "maximum effort". I don't remember noticing the word "Calais". Let me look in my records.'

Vivi recognised it straight away. They had changed it, added the word 'Calais' to keep the Germans from suspecting the real place of the landings. She tried not to show her concern as she smiled and chatted to members of the pool and then gradually made her way out of the room and back to Marcus's office.

Vivi hurried down the corridor, and once behind the closed door, she had to catch her breath. He stood up from his desk with concern.

She rushed to his side and whispered in his ear. 'They found out about "maximum effort" and that you added the word "Calais". He is down there now talking to a member of the pool.'

Marcus nodded. 'That gives me a little time to be ready.'

He didn't get long though, because within a few minutes, Major Weissman was knocking at his door.

'Major Vonstein, do you have a moment?'

Vivi exited to her room and left her door ajar again, but this time Weissman must have noticed it and came over and closed it loudly behind him, which meant Vivi had to walk to the door and listen with her ear pressed against it.

'I have something extremely urgent to report to you. I think we have a problem here in your office.'

'Then tell me, Major Weissman, so we can put this right.'

'Do you remember getting this code?' Vivi assumed he handed him the piece of paper.

Marcus responded, 'I have to be honest with you, sir, we get many through the office, hundreds. Is there a problem with this?'

'Yes, there is a problem. Your coder did not put in the word "Calais", but somebody else did.'

'That's a very serious accusation. What are you implying?'

'I'm implying someone in this office is trying to sabotage our efforts, to create a distraction. I'm implying, sir, that you have members of the Resistance working here in your building.'

'That is a very harsh claim and a very serious one. I am shocked to hear such a thing, but I am grateful that you brought this to my attention. I shall look into it immediately.'

'I think you should do more than that. I want to continue to offer my services. I will review everything from the decoders. Everything that is decoded, I would like to see. Then we have two of us watching out for the mole.' He sounded suspicious, as though he didn't trust Marcus, either. His tone grew quieter. 'Your secretary, sir, what do you know of her? I had a conversation with Commander Von Klaus yesterday, and he voiced some concerns about her.'

'Vivi? She has an impeccable war record. She convinced the British she was working for them even though she is German, and executed an incredible campaign, and she has been nothing but stellar.'

'I notice the two of you are… close,' Weissman continued warily. 'It's dangerous to be close in these days. I suggest you find a different woman to meet your needs. People that we work with could be compromised. We don't always see what is right in front of us.'

'I can assure you, Major Weissman, you can trust my assistant. I myself would trust her with my life. But I will listen to your caution and be aware myself. Thank you for your advice.'

'I'll be downstairs. Everything that comes in I will look at and, hopefully, we will root out the person who is doing this. This is a very serious situation, you understand.'

'I do, and I thank you for your help, sir.'

Vivi heard Weissman walk out of the room. She cracked her own door to make sure he'd gone all the way down the hallway before she slipped back into the side room and into Marcus's office.

'Major Weissman, I fear, will make things exceedingly difficult for us,' he whispered into her ear.

Vivi nodded. 'With the push right now, with so many issues with the Resistance, they are working so hard. What do you plan to do?'

'I plan to step back a little, let a lot of the correct information through, though we have to protect the advancement no matter what. That cannot be compromised. If people have to be sacrificed to that end, then that is how it will be.' He looked despondent.

Three days later, they found themselves in an impossible situation.

It was 5 June 1944, and early in the morning. Marcus and Vivi had both arrived at work when a pilot came to their office. This meant it was something important. German pilots went out routinely to collect intelligence and take photographs of the Allies' movements. He informed them in hushed tones that he had spotted and taken pictures of ships setting sail from the south of England, many ships, and it had concerned him. He had taken the films straight down to the lab, and they had developed them, quickly.

'I thought I should bring this photograph up myself, sir. It seemed particularly important.'

'You were right to do so,' responded Marcus. 'Please leave this with me.'

The pilot hesitated before continuing, 'Major Weissman asked me to report to him as well.'

'Leave the major to me. I will report promptly to him. This needs to be kept under the utmost secrecy, do you understand?' The pilot nodded. 'No one outside this room should know what you have in here. Please instruct the people in developing to keep this to themselves. There is a chance that we have somebody from the Resistance working here.'

'Not me, sir. I am loyal to Hitler. Heil Hitler!' he saluted, and Marcus nodded.

The pilot left the room.

Vivi came in. She could see that his face was pale. 'What is it?'

'It may have started, but these photographs could demonstrate they may be heading to Normandy, and we have to keep this secret for the next twenty-four hours. It will take a while for them to amass, get all the troops across, and it is up to us to ensure no one alerts the Germans to what is going on. They have a huge army waiting to be deployed, to whatever coast they feel will be the one where the British are to land. I have to find a way to hide this for twenty-four hours, Vivi.' He paced the room anxiously. 'If we destroy it, then there is a trail right back to this office and that could end our work prematurely. But if it is misplaced, we may look more incompetent than traitorous.'

'Give it to me,' she suggested. 'I will slip it in with some files in my office, then if Major Weissman hears anything and searches your office, he won't find them.' Vivi took the photograph from him and placed them within a file marked with a different title. She recognised it would only be a matter of time before things would be known, but maybe that was all the Allies would need, a short amount of time.

Vivi hoped with all of her heart that this offensive would be the beginning of the end of the war. That she and Marcus would soon be able to escape, that they could finally be free. But in the meantime she needed a little insurance. Vivi had been thinking about this for a while. She knew it was dangerous but now things were so desperate, she had to have a backup plan to get her and Marcus out of the country fast. But in order to do it Vivi would have to risk her cover. If anyone found out what she was doing and reported back to the Germans what was going on it would be certain death for her and maybe even for Marcus. But there was one place she felt she may have a chance, a place where discretion was of the upmost importance.

Leaving the office, Vivi rushed through the streets of Paris, sweat trickling down behind her ears and gathering under the collar of her German uniform. At every turn, she was aware of heightened energy. On what seemed like every corner, the people of Paris were whispering in huddled groups. She hoped it was the news she and Marcus had been waiting to hear, but feared the enemy might still gain the upper hand.

Vivi barely had time to check over her shoulder as she raced down the darkened alley, her footsteps beating out an echoed rhythm that fought against a cracked water pipe that gushed out a beat of its own. Arriving at the door of the address she had memorised, Vivi stopped to catch her breath and wipe at the beads of perspiration that had collected under her cap. Gulping back hot sticky air that burned her lungs, she gathered herself, trying to clear her mind and remember everything she had been taught; it felt like an eternity since her training.

Her racing heart began to return to normal as Vivi momentarily considered her life and the man she loved. She had to do this. For him and for the cause they both believed in. Tears brimmed in her eyes as Vivi remembered the night before when they'd lain in one another's arms, a full moon streaming through the window, casting its shadow across their bed, when she'd thought, just for that moment, even amidst all the madness, that somehow her life was perfect.

But in the last twelve hours, all of that had been put in jeopardy. Now Vivi had to focus on what was right. But would she be strong enough to do what she had to do? The betrayal was so hard, but the one thing that kept her alive every day was the knowledge that she was doing all this for love, the noblest reason of all.

So there was one last thing she had to do. One thing that could make the difference between who won this war, and who lost.

Summoning up the courage she needed, Vivi knocked on the door.

It was Madame Mazella who opened it herself and seeing who it was, she offered a crooked smile.

'Well, look who it is, I thought you left a long time ago. Did you change sides?' she snarled, taking in Vivi's uniform as she looked her up and down.

Vivi shook her head vehemently. 'I'm undercover,' she hissed in reply.

The madam folded her arms under her vast bosom, most of which was on display. 'What do you want?'

Vivi spoke quickly. 'Can I come in? I have something very important that I need your help with.'

The madam pursed her bright-red lips together, which distorted the pencil-marked mole on her cheek into a thin black line and then, shrugging, signalled her in with a jerk of her head.

Leading Vivi into her office, the older woman closed the door, trapping outside the usual scent of cheap perfume and stale tobacco that permeated the rest of the house. Vivi looked around in astonishment. Every surface of her tiny dark room was piled with clutter. Clothes, boxes, feathers and odd trinkets that were bizarre in nature. In the corner a stuffed parrot missing its tail feathers hung in a gilded cage, that had a red feather boa coiled around the chain. On the other side a large wooden elephant sprouted what looked like real ivory tusks. In the centre, hats of all description were piled up almost to the ceiling, alongside a dusty pile of sheet music that was stacked up on an old piano that seemed to be missing most of its keys. The only place to actually sit was a very worn, purple velvet chaise longue that was placed under a cracked window, that itself was being kept open by an elaborately decorated Japanese fan.

Madame Mazella seemed unaware of how her oddity of a room was disorientating and in such contrast to the stark grey world of the war outside. Lighting a cigarette, the madam blew out smoke before she spoke.

'Are you in trouble again?'

'Yes. I need to find a wireless operator. Do you know where there is one?'

'I might,' she said nonchalantly, picking something from her teeth and sucking her tongue against the gap it had created. 'You know a lot of agents have been going missing, and it doesn't look good. It is rumoured even that rascal Terrier is gone.'

Vivi's heart stung with the mention of his name, and she felt the pain again of the loss of that friendship. 'I know,' she murmured. 'I was surprised you were even still here.'

Madame Mazella started a croaky laugh that rolled around her chest and bounced her heaving bosom. 'Where would I go?' she said, shrugging her shoulders.

'I thought, maybe they would raid you.'

The older woman continued to laugh until tears appeared in the corners of her eyes. 'They wouldn't close us down, we are too valuable to their men. Besides, I have some, shall we say, "friends" in high places who wouldn't want certain stories getting back to their wives in Berlin.'

The madam raised her eyebrows, and appeared to see the desperation in Vivi's eyes before moving to a desk.

'Look, I do know of a wireless operator that might be able to help you.' She pulled out a piece of paper, wrote down an address, and handed the paper to Vivi, who memorised the address and then tore up the note.

As Vivi got up to leave, she surprised herself by hugging the older woman. The madam chuckled again.

'Thank you for all you are doing, Madame Mazella. You too are fighting this war.'

A wry smile crossed the older woman's lips. 'I don't think I will be getting a medal for my work though, do you?' she said with a twinkle in her eye.

Vivi bid the madam goodbye and could still hear her chuckling as she closed the door and raced off to the address she had memorised.

Chapter 36

Unfortunately for Marcus and Vivi, they didn't get to fool Major Weissman for very long. The next day, the person who had developed the photographs happened to mention to the major the information that had been uncovered the day before.

Weissman had realised that he had not been informed and, with great concern, marched his way into Marcus's office. This time he did not even care that Vivi was in the room.

'Major Vonstein, I have something that I'm very concerned about. Field Marshal Rommel is telling me activities have increased all over the coast. We are almost certain that an attack from the Allies is upon us. I heard that yesterday you received critical information I have not heard about.'

'Critical information, Major Weissmann?'

'Apparently there were photographs taken of the Allies in the water, heading towards us. Do you have those photographs?'

Vivi looked at Marcus.

'I can't recall seeing anything,' he said, trying to play for time.

'I was concerned that would be your answer. So I think it is only right that we search your office, and if you care about the Reich, you won't care about the intrusion.'

'Of course not,' snapped back Marcus. 'I have nothing to hide. I want to get to the bottom of this as much as you do.'

Major Weissman signalled to the men he had brought with him, and four guards came in and started rifling through Marcus's office and scattering files.

Marcus sat coolly on the edge of his desk.

'If you need any help, to know where things are or where they need to go back to,' he spat out, the sarcasm undeniable in his tone, 'I can be of much more help to you than just this bombastic display.'

Major Weissman ignored him, marching up and down the office, tapping his hands behind his back.

The searchers found and pulled out copies of photographs that were filed away of different reconnaissance flights that had been captured on film and splayed them out on the desk for Weissman to see, but the one from the day before was not there.

All at once, the pilot entered the room and saluted, summoned by Weissman himself.

He swivelled and glowered at the young man.

'Captain, tell me what you did yesterday.'

'I did a reconnaissance mission to take photographs of the enemy aircrafts and ships.'

'And what did you do with those photographs?'

'I had them developed downstairs as instructed, Major.'

'And then?'

'I brought them here to this officer.'

'And I had them sent on to your commander,' said Marcus defensively. 'Did you not receive them?'

'I did not sir.'

'Who did you send with the photographs?'

'I was commissioned to do that,' stated Vivi, a slight tremor in her voice.

All eyes turned to her, and Marcus looked at her with great concern.

'Search her office,' snapped Weissman.

The soldiers ran in and started to pull her room apart. It didn't take them long to find the photographs in the budget file. She cursed herself, maybe she should have destroyed them, though she had feared that their absence would raise more suspicion. She had just hoped to delay them for a few days to the give the Allies a chance.

'Did you hide them in this file?' demanded the Major, barrelling over to her.

Vivi came up to her full height, refusing to be intimidated by the bear of a man. 'It was a mistake, sir.'

'Arrest her,' snapped Major Weissman to the guards as he looked at the pictures.

Weissman stared at her, the anger burning in his eyes, as a guard handcuffed her and led her away to a cell.

Hours later, Vivi was seated in an interrogation room. Weissman swaggered about the space, asking her questions over and over again. After a while he ordered Vonstein to join them. Marcus looked distraught. He was caught between wanting to serve his country and saving the woman he loved. Weissman bore down on her again.

'Are you working for the enemy?'

Vivienne denied it over and over again, prepared to die for her cause.

Weissman lifted his hand and struck her across the face.

She looked across at Marcus, signalling to him with her eyes that she was prepared to take the fall and for him not to react. His fists were balled and she could see it was taking all of his effort not to blow his cover and defend her. Vivi knew it was the only way. There was still much to do. If the Allies had set sail, Marcus would need to be at his post to give them as much time as possible, as much chance to complete their mission.

'I strongly disagree with this,' growled Marcus.

'You disagree with the fact she works for the Resistance, or that I am dealing with a crime, sir? It appears, Major Vonstein, you have bad taste in women. Or are you working with her?'

Marcus responded with disgust. 'How dare you accuse me of what you imply? I have nothing to do with what has happened.'

Weissman swung around and confronted Vivi again. 'Then we will have to get more persuasive in our tactics.' He balled up his fist.

Vivienne looked at Marcus and could tell it was going to be too much for him. She spoke up.

'I worked alone. I used Major Vonstein. I saw that he had an attraction to me. I pretended I had an attraction to him and used him to do what I needed to do.' And switching to her native British, after speaking German for so long, she smiled and said, 'Long live the King.'

Pulling back his hand, Weissman slapped Vivi across the face. The force of it was so brutal Vivi thought she would die, and it took her a moment to catch her breath and regain her equilibrium. As she reeled back, she could see it took all of Marcus's strength not to react.

He strode forward. 'No more. She has confessed,' he shouted. 'She is obviously a traitor. What is this achieving?'

A sadistic smirk came over Weissman's face and he said to Vivi, 'I suppose we could torture you. But if you've managed to get yourself into such deep cover, you're obviously very smart, and we don't have a lot of time. I am very busy right now because of this new information and I do not have time to interrogate you. So I think we shall just execute you. It will be tidier that way. You are a traitor to us, and you shall pay that price.'

'I object,' shouted Marcus. 'She's just a foolish girl. Maybe she changed a few notes, but we are still winning the war. I think we should hold her in a cell until we can decide what we need to do with her.'

Weissman spun on his heels and jeered at Marcus, 'I'm sure that is precisely what you think we should do. It is unfortunate. You obviously have feelings for this woman. But I would like to know where your loyalties lie. Are they with the Führer or… this spy?'

'I object to that grave insinuation. I have a spotless war record. I have done nothing but work tirelessly for the Reich to bring about the victories in this war.'

Major Weissman nodded his head. 'I have reviewed your record. This lapse in judgement seems to be a momentary slip. It is fortunate that I found out now, but how can we be sure that you have not been working with this traitor?'

'I can assure you I have not.'

'I'm afraid assurance is not good enough. You need to prove yourself once again to the Reich. So at ten tomorrow morning you shall be the one to execute her, out here in the square.'

Vivi felt the air disappear from her body. Up until this point, she had been ready to die. She'd known the day she'd got on the boat pretending to be a Nazi that if she got caught she would have to die as one. But now, if Marcus was ordered to kill her, she didn't think he could do it. And if he didn't do it, they would kill him. The only hope was for him to take her life to show his loyalty.

Weissman continued, 'So you have a choice: the Reich or this girl. You show us your loyalty, and we will believe you. She has been a traitor. She has hidden important information and no doubt altered messages. A most unfortunate choice of secretaries, sir. Take her back to her cell,' he snapped, 'and you shall prepare for her execution tomorrow morning.'

Marcus looked devasted. For the first time since they'd started working together, she feared that he would not do the right thing. And instead of just her life, many lives could be lost. He was such a high-ranking officer and his intelligence was imperative, especially once the offensive was in progress. Passing on false information and diverting the enemy away from the chosen beaches could make the difference for the Allied forces between a successful invasion and a mass slaughter.

They dragged Vivi back to her cell. That's where he came to secretly visit her, two hours later. As the door closed behind Marcus, Vivi ran to him and put her arms around him and held him tightly.

'Marcus. Marcus.' She said his name over and over again. His whole body folded into hers.

When he looked up, there were tears in his eyes. 'I didn't know this would be so hard. When I was trained, they told me not to let my heart become softened by a woman. And look at me.' The tears were streaming down his face.

She kissed him, passionately, until they both were spent and he pushed her gently back.

'I have a plan, Vivi, for us to get away. It is going to be difficult. He wants me to shoot you outside in the courtyard, and he will probably watch. But I will make sure the side gate is unlocked. I'm sure there'll be other soldiers. When I raise the gun to shoot you, I will turn and shoot them instead, and we will have a chance of escape.'

'And what then?' she said. 'What about the work that we've done? And where would we go? Marcus, you're not thinking clearly. We knew the danger when we came on this mission.'

'Why did you say it? Why did you say it was you? I could've taken the blame.'

'You need to finish the work that we are compelled to do. Don't you see, my love? If you don't finish this work, if you don't do what you're meant to do, many lives could be lost, not just mine.'

'But how will I live without you? How will I go on?' Marcus started to sob.

She took his face gently in her hands, and kissed away his tears.

'You will go on, Marcus, because you are the strongest, bravest person I have ever known. You have already sacrificed so much. This is such an important time. If the Allies are here you are needed more than ever. Your diversionary tactics may be all that stand between the Allies and a slaughter. If you walked away now, everything you have worked so hard to achieve could all be in vain. We are two tiny people in this vast and crazy war, with no idea of what effect we are having, but I do know this is important. Your ability to continue to work is paramount and has the potential to save thousands of lives and help end this madness. You would have killed Terrier. And only now do I truly see why that needed to be. So, you will kill me tomorrow and then you will continue to do the work you're meant to do. I have just one thing to ask you.'

He pulled her in again, held her so closely she could barely breathe. 'Anything,' he whispered in her ear.

'Please, after this is over, go back to England and make sure my family know I was not a traitor. I do not want them to live with that black mark against their name. It has been the hardest thing for me, knowing how they must feel about me. Would you do that for me, Marcus? I need you to stay alive to do this—'

He interrupted her. 'You'll be able to tell them yourself. My plan will work.'

'What if they get hold of you and torture you too?'

'They won't do that. Besides, I always have my suicide pill.' He had removed it from his tooth and had placed it in his breast pocket, where he tapped it.

She was shocked. 'Why do you have that ready?'

'Because if for some reason you die, I will not live. I will die with you.'

'Marcus, you have to be brave.'

'I cannot be without you by my side.' He clung onto her, wrenching sobs making his chest heave.

'You can't do this, Marcus…'

There was a knock at the door, and a guard opened it.

'Major Vonstein, someone is coming. It is rumoured to be Major Weissman himself to check on the prisoner.'

Marcus kissed her one last time, his tears dripping down his face and soaking hers. Then, gently brushing his hand down her cheek and looking deep into her eyes he was gone.

While Vivi was alone in her cell, she sat and thought. She thought about all that they had achieved and how she'd never known Marcus not to be strong. One thing Vivi knew for sure as she lay there was that she was going to die tomorrow and she could not let

Marcus take his life. She was surprised how calm she felt about it, as if she had always known this would be her fate. There was still so much to do. And everything they had done for the Resistance would be revealed, and would be worthless, if Marcus didn't do his job. But she knew she was the only one thinking straight. So Vivi came up with a plan of her own.

Chapter 37

The next morning, Weissman came to see her bright and early. 'It's the sixth of June 1944, my dear. Not many of us know the day we'll die, but you do, and then we will see if your boyfriend is who he says he is. I look forward to attending your execution,' he added coldly.

He left her then, and Vivi's whole body shook with the cold and the fear. She would never see England again. She would never see her family again. She would never play with Tom, read books with John, or laugh with her sister. This was it. She was going to die. But more than anything, she couldn't bear the thought of being anywhere – even Heaven – without Marcus.

Vivi's thoughts drifted to when she'd been at school and a teacher admonished her because of her spelling, informing her she would never do anything of any significance in life. While this wasn't exactly what she'd planned, Vivi hoped that her modest part in the war effort would save lives.

Terrier's smiling face swam into her memory, and tears filled her eyes as she thought of his words, 'I want to go out in a blaze of glory. I would rather live a short but exciting life than die of boredom in obscurity.' Is that what she was choosing? To die in a blaze of glory? It sounded so much grander in word than the reality of this cold dark cell where she would spend her final hours. Vivi was pretty sure there would be no monument erected in her honour as Terrier had suggested for himself. No one but God and Marcus knew what she was doing, and things had happened so fast she had been unable to follow up on the wireless transmission she had sent to England. She thought of Anne-Marie, wherever she was, probably in hiding, mourning the death of her brother. She thought of the Renoirs in Paris and how they had given her a place to live and a family. Where were they now?

Vivi was convinced of what she needed to do. She needed to die to pay the price of so many people who had been killed because of her. She may not have always been courageous, but she could be now.

Suddenly her thoughts returned to that time on the boat when Mr Thompson had turned to her and told her she would find the courage when she needed it. She knew more than ever she needed it now, and she hoped with all of her heart that she could go through with it so that Marcus could finish the work they'd started. One thing she knew: no matter what transpired, she would die today.

When they came for her that morning, her whole body was shaking, betraying her relentless inner courage, but she was ready. It amazed her she'd survived this long. Many operators barely lasted weeks. If she were still with SOE, she'd probably have been dead by now, anyway. At least this way she could help the Allies, by keeping Marcus's cover. As they marched her to the square, there was considerable commotion around her, and she overheard two of the soldiers talking to another as they positioned her in front of a wall. They were saying there was a substantial advance on the Normandy beaches taking place. Vivi felt relief. It had started. The Allies had made it to France.

Marcus needed to stay alive even more now, to continue the confusion that needed to take place so the invasion would be successful. Vivi felt a sense of pride. She had put her country first. She had done the right thing for Britain. She found those feelings of patriotism washing away the dread that was throbbing through her body.

When Marcus arrived he looked terrible, as if he hadn't slept all night. Two other soldiers flanked him and also Weissman. Vivi knew the Germans always executed people with more than one person armed, just in case one of them lost their nerve.

Marcus walked to the centre of the courtyard. She saw him stealthily touch his breast pocket – the suicide pill. He had meant what he said. If for some reason it went wrong, and they killed her, he would take his own life. Vivi knew the capsule had to be cracked between his teeth to release the cyanide.

He strode up to her, the two guards by his side. It appeared by their scrutiny that Weissman had told the others to maintain a good eye on him. As he looked to her, he signalled with his eyes to the gate at the end of the square, informing her that his plan was in place. She nodded, going along with what he was suggesting, but she had her own plan now.

'Do you have any last words?' he said loudly so Weissman could hear him. The major stood to the side of the square watching the proceedings.

'I am sorry, Major Vonstein, for deceiving you and making you believe that I loved you.'

Behind Marcus, Weissman sniffed, as though he was confirming he had been right all along.

Marcus looked confused, and then seemed to realise that she was playing a part for the soldiers.

'Yes. It was most regrettable. Fortunately, I didn't believe your lie, so there is no harm done. You have betrayed the Reich, and you must pay the price for that. Do you have any last requests?'

'Just one,' she said, and seizing hold of him, she pulled him in close, kissing him fully on the mouth, and with the skills she had learned in her training, picked his pocket. Quickly, she placed the capsule in her mouth and bit down hard.

Marcus stepped back in panic, realising instantly what she had done. He looked bewildered, as if he was trying to figure out what she was doing and how this was part of their plan.

She continued, 'I understand, Herr Vonstein, that you need to kill me, to execute me for my crimes. But I want you to know...' she lowered her voice and looked right at Marcus, 'I regret nothing,' she whispered tenderly. Then, for everyone's ears, 'I die for my king and country, and I am proud of the work I performed here.'

Vivi tried not to gag as she swallowed down the burning liquid. The taste was putrid as it permeated and burned, searing its way through her body. She stared at him, wanting his face to be the last thing she would see.

He must have seen the agony on her face, by the look of horror upon him, but then his face registered with the utter desperation she would die. She was forcing him to continue the work, not giving him a choice. Vivi saw it in his face, saw the recognition of what she'd done.

As the excruciating pain racked through her body, it took her breath away, and, in agony, she shouted out to him, her last words in French. 'Remember the swallows!' And she hoped he knew what she was trying to say to him and that he would remember her favourite story.

He looked at her with shock then, appearing to realise her plan that if he didn't shoot her, she would die an agonising death and it would be clear she'd committed suicide by the cyanide tablet and there would be questions. It left him with no alternative. She watched his hand shake as he lifted the barrel of the gun and pointed it at her, the anguish palpable on his face, but her eyes showed him only love. She didn't even feel the pain from the bullet that slammed into her skull, as she crumpled to the ground and her world became black.

Chapter 38

Present day

The following morning Sophie and Alex were ushered into a parlour. It was like stepping back in time, an age gone by. Elsa Strauss was obviously a woman of wealth; gilded pictures and heavy furniture, dark and imposing, anchored the room. A young woman who introduced herself as Chloe, Miss Strauss's granddaughter, came through to speak to them.

'Oma can see you now. I will warn you, she gets tired quickly, but she has been eager to speak to you since she knew you were coming.'

Alex and Sophie went into the bedroom. Inside the four-poster bed, the tiny figure of a woman seemed almost out of place in all of this grandeur. She wore a white lace cap, and her eyes were closed. In hushed reverence, they approached the side of the bed. Chloe nodded to them and touched her grandmother's arm.

'Oma, they are here.'

Feather-like, the older lady's eyelashes fluttered on her cheeks before her eyes slowly opened, and she took a minute to focus on her ceiling and then each of their faces.

As they drew closer to the bed, Sophie could hear that the elderly woman's breathing was raspy and rattled through her lungs as though any one of the breaths could be her last. Chloe brought in two chairs so they could sit by her side. Alex looked across at Sophie apprehensively.

'This is Sophie Hamilton,' continued Chloe, in case she needed to refresh her grandmother's recollection. 'And Alex Vonstein.'

The woman stared at Sophie with great tenderness and then, flicking her eyes towards Alex, she shook her head. 'You two should not be together. It is not right. History mustn't repeat itself.'

Sophie glanced at Alex, who shook his head at Sophie with dismissal.

Sophie drew closer to the bed so she could hear her clearly. 'Miss Strauss, do you know why we are here?'

The woman's eyes were closed again, as if the pain of seeing them together had overwhelmed her. When she finally opened them, they were watery and thoughtful. 'You are Vivi's great-niece.' She stated more than asked the question. She stretched an arthritic hand towards Sophie, and the younger woman took it in hers.

'You knew my great-aunt? She went by Vivi?'

Miss Strauss nodded. 'Vivi, she was such a spirited person, but too beautiful for her own good.' She then flicked her eyes back at Alex. 'It was most regrettable,' she whispered, with disgust.

'Can you tell us about what she did during the war?'

Miss Strauss nodded. 'It is a long story, but I will tell you as much as I can until I become tired. It is one I've wanted to unburden myself of for a long time.'

She lay back on her pillow and took in a heavy breath.

'I met Vivi in 1944, and the first time I saw her I knew this was a woman I needed to pay attention to. She commanded the room when she walked into it. Vivi was not simply a beauty but…' She wet her dry lips with her tongue and reflected on the right word. 'Hypnotic. She drew you in, and you trusted her, which is why it was unfortunate she was so deceived.'

Sophie felt her stomach lurch, and she reached for Alex's hand.

The woman's eyes rolled back in her head, and she moved from speaking English to speaking a mixture of German, even some French, it naturally being too strenuous for her to have to continue translating.

Alex started translating her words for Sophie.

'She was the light of the office. I was a mere young girl at the time. I would visit my father who worked there, and I would see Vivi in the office, and she was luminous. She made everyone feel important.' She rolled her eyes towards Sophie. 'You look a lot like her,' the elderly woman declared, staring intently at Sophie for such a long time it was almost uncomfortable. Sophie nodded, fighting back the tears that were brimming just below the surface.

'I never liked the Nazi Party. I thought they were ridiculous, but a ten-year-old girl doesn't have many choices. So I put up with their goose-stepping, ridiculous rules and devotion to Hitler, who was just a crazy man in my eyes. But Vivi knew how to love. Yes, she loved. She loved that officer, Marcus Vonstein. Oh, they weren't out in the open about it, but everyone could tell by the way she looked at him. Which is why it is so sad that she was so deceived.'

'What do you mean "deceived"?' whispered Sophie, hoarsely.

'By Vonstein. He lured her in.'

Sophie suddenly felt uncomfortable holding Alex's hand, and she looked across at him briefly. He was intent upon the woman's face, listening carefully to her words so he could translate, but she suddenly thought about her own heart. Had she opened it up to Alex too quickly? Then she shook the thought from her mind. This wasn't Marcus; this was Alex. This man had shown her more care in the last few days than she'd felt from Matt for years. She reminded herself she was becoming so swept up by the story she wasn't sure what was fact and what was fiction.

The older woman coughed, and Chloe brought her a glass of water and assisted her while she sipped at it, birdlike.

'Such a long time ago,' she continued after recovering, closing her eyes again.

'I can tell she's getting tired,' Chloe said.

Sophie became anxious. 'I need to ask her something else. Miss Strauss, do you think you can answer one more question?'

Marcus translated.

The old woman's eyes flashed open again, as if she was forcing herself to remain in this present moment. Slowly, she nodded her head. 'What else do you need to know, my dear?'

'I... I just need to know how Vivienne died.'

The question was weighted and heavy in the air, and the woman stared at Sophie as though pondering whether she should tell her.

'You do not know?'

Sophie shook her head. 'We have no war records. All we know is that she was a Nazi.'

The woman hinted at a smile. 'I can tell you many things, and it was a crazy time, but I don't think she was a Nazi. I think she was in love with the wrong person. And she was executed.'

'Executed?' asked Sophie, swallowing down the word.

The old woman shook her head slightly. 'It was *his* fault. Vivi wasn't evil like so many of the rest of them.'

'Can you tell me anything about her last days?'

The woman nodded her head. 'It is not a happy story. I was young, but that meant I could slip in and out of rooms like a ghost without people really being aware of my presence. I overheard my father talking about it, just bits and pieces, but I have built up my own version of what happened. My theory is that Vonstein... Marcus... had somehow seduced her into coming to work for him. The day before the D-Day landings, he received some information, that he carelessly misplaced, that the much-awaited attack was about to take place in Normandy. The high command was furious with him because of the error. Until that point, they had believed that the strike would take place in Calais. There was a hideous row, which even I heard from my father's office, and eventually, Marcus blamed Vivienne for the mistake. They were so furious they demanded that she be executed.' The old woman hesitated. 'Her execution took place the following morning. They marched her out into the courtyard.'

'And they shot her?' whispered Sophie, her voice trembling.

The woman spoke again in German, and Alex heard the words, but he didn't seem to be capable of translating them.

Sophie looked over at him. 'What happened, Alex? What did she say?'

The elderly woman repeated the words, but Alex's mouth just stayed dropped open. He coughed and then swallowed. 'She said she was murdered at the hand of my great-uncle, that he alone murdered her.'

Sophie stared at Alex. His face was ashen. She glanced back at the woman. Surely there was a mistake. Surely, even though Marcus used Vivi terribly, he wouldn't have killed her? Sophie realised then she'd been hanging onto a hope, a hope he'd loved her, genuinely loved her, and hadn't been using her. But now, with these particular words, all hope of that had been ripped from her.

'How can you be sure?' asked Sophie.

The woman's speech became faltering. 'I was there. I was there as her body slumped to the ground. I wasn't meant to be. I'd heard there was an execution, and oh, how I loved Vivi. I had some childhood notion of stopping it, but when I got to the courtyard where it was to take place, the horror and the weight of it froze me, so that all I could do was hide and watch.

'They issued the orders, Vonstein lifted his gun, and, to be fair, he hesitated for a second. Then she shouted out to him some words in French. I remember them as it was such a strange thing to say – "Souvenez-vous des hirondelles" and he raised his weapon and put two shots into her head, and she collapsed to the floor and was dead.

'He was not a good sort, your great-uncle, I'm afraid, young man. His office tried with all of his might the next day to thwart the plans of the landings to cripple the wireless network across Germany and France and would've succeeded. But somehow the plan went wrong. A day or two later he too was killed, fleeing Paris, I believe. Good riddance. I'm sorry to say, but it was a good thing.' She coughed again, and Chloe signalled them it was time to leave.

Chapter 39

After their visit to Frau Strauss, Sophie and Alex were quiet, alone with their thoughts, and travelled back to the hotel in silence. On exiting the taxi, they stood on the street, neither sure what to do. Finally, Alex asked if she wanted to go for a cup of coffee and she nodded. They made their way into a coffee shop on the corner and ordered drinks and were halfway through drinking before one of them spoke. It was Sophie.

'I'd like to visit my great-aunt's grave. Do you think there is a way we can find out where she's buried?'

'I'm sure with the war records, it shouldn't be too difficult. We can go there in a while if you want.' He studied her as if he was trying to weigh her up. 'Sophie, you've barely spoken. Are you okay?'

She nodded. She didn't want to tell him Frau Strauss's words had put a wedge in her heart, and now she was finding it hard to connect with him. She knew he wasn't Marcus, but still, their sad history made it almost impossible for her to feel warmth towards him.

'What do you think about what we heard today, Alex?' she enquired.

He peered into his coffee cup before speaking gently. 'To be honest with you I am amazed that Vivienne fell for him. If only we could tell exactly what transpired between them.'

Sophie closed her eyes and tried to recall everything that the woman had said to her. She'd been so shocked by the admission of the execution that she had missed a lot of what had been said around those words. Now, she tried to remember the exact conversation.

'What did she say about Vivienne? She said something in French. Do you remember what those words were?'

Alex also seemed to be trying to retrieve the memory. 'Remember the swallows? That's what I think she said. "Souvenez-vous des hirondelles",' he reiterated the words in French.

'What could that mean? Do you think she was signalling something to him? It's an odd thing to say right before you die. Surely you would plead for your life? It sounds so out of place. Do you think for even a second she was challenging him to kill her? I know it sounds preposterous, but maybe it was a signal between them?' Sophie speculated.

'But "remember the swallows"? What could it mean?'

'I have no idea.'

He reached forward to touch her hand and instinctively she drew it away.

'Sophie? What's wrong?'

'I need time to come to terms with this. Things are happening too quickly.'

'Do you mean what we're finding out about Vivienne and Marcus, or between us?'

She glanced out of the window, trying to avoid his question.

'Sophie, are you having any regrets about what has happened between us?'

'I don't know, Alex. I have to be honest with you, I'm struggling with all this new emotion. It's a lot to take in, and I'm exhausted. I didn't sleep well last night, you know, realising we would see Frau Strauss today. I think I need to take a step back. Things have happened incredibly quickly between us.'

He took time to respond to her. 'It has not exactly been the most edifying day for my family, either. Bad enough that my great-uncle was a Nazi. Now I know that he murdered women in cold blood, it's hardly going to help my cause very much. I was so hoping to take good news to my mother, something positive.'

'I think I'm going to lie down for a while,' Sophie decided, finishing her coffee and making her way to the hotel. She was grateful they hadn't got a room together so she could gather her thoughts. She tried to use the analytical part of her brain to pull all the pieces together and create a different conclusion, but everything pointed to one thing: Marcus had killed Vivienne. But why, if Vivienne was really a Nazi? Just because she made a mistake?

Meanwhile, Sophie knew she wasn't being totally fair to Alex, but she needed time to think about all this, so she texted him to say she would eat in her room that night, and after a light dinner, she fell asleep in her clothes at around nine o'clock.

She woke up in the middle of the night freezing and changed into her pyjamas, then crawled under the cool sheets. Why had she stopped feeling anything for Alex? Her heart felt numb and cold. Was she being cowardly? Or was she looking for a way out, fearful because of what had happened with Matt, not wanting to move on from her grief?

Sophie tried to keep things in perspective. She would visit Vivienne's grave out of respect tomorrow, and then go home to London. Had she only been away for a little more than a week? It felt like her real life was an eternity away. She closed her eyes, thinking of her flat and her cat, and it brought back feelings of warmth to her. That's what she would do. She would go home and file Alex away as a holiday romance. A fling. A need to move on after Matt. Hopefully it wouldn't hurt him too much. She had so much going on inside her, she couldn't possibly contemplate a relationship right now. These thoughts settled her as she went to sleep.

The next morning Sophie felt clearer than she had for days. She dressed and texted Alex to ask him to meet her downstairs for breakfast. When he came down and met her twenty minutes later, it was apparent he had just got out of the shower. He smelled fresh, his blond hair damp and tousled, his blue eyes showing concern.

'How did you sleep?'

'Like a log,' she stated. 'Yesterday was so hard. I guess my body just needed a good rest.'

Alex sat down, and she noticed he didn't reach for her hand or hug her or even offer the customary kiss on both cheeks. He was being careful, probably allowing her to dictate their interaction. He had obviously given some thought to their relationship after what she'd told him the day before.

'Sophie, I want you to know, I understood what you said yesterday, and I think we both have a lot of emotions going on right now. I think you're correct that we must slow down and take things gradually, and I think you are right that we shouldn't pursue something between us at the moment. We both need time. But let's at least finish everything we're doing here,' he continued, 'and see where we are after that.'

Sophie nodded as a waitress approached the table and took his order. When her eggs arrived, she found that she wasn't hungry and pushed them around her plate.

'So, do we need to go back to the records place to locate the graves?' she asked.

He nodded as he scooped a spoonful of his boiled egg. If anything, he seemed more relieved by their clarifying conversation than she did.

They finished their breakfast and made their way in the taxi. On the journey, they made casual conversation about Germany and the weather and the hotel they were staying in. Sophie wondered, at that moment, if it was over. She despised the way her heart felt conflicted. She wasn't sure she wanted this. But she couldn't believe that just over a week ago she'd still thought she was in love with Matt. These feelings that had come upon her so quickly had overwhelmed her, while also reminding her that there were other people out there, people who she might be able to feel something for again one day.

Sophie looked across at Alex, who was staring out of the other window, and enjoyed being with him. It was not just the attraction she'd had, but how comfortable she felt around him. He was so warm, so attentive, so different to Matt.

They arrived at the records office and it didn't take long for them to track down the cemeteries where both Vivienne and Marcus were buried. With a shudder, they realised it was the same one in Normandy.

Later that morning they flew straight to Normandy and hired a car to drive to the cemetery. Years before, all the German soldiers had been moved from the many graves that they had been placed in around France during the war years to this location for ease of visitors looking for their relatives.

Sophie bought flowers on the way from the airport, and when they arrived, her whole body shook with the experience. She had not considered how much all of this would affect her, her mind going back to burying her mother and her darling daughter such a short time before. Seeing her struggling, Alex put a reassuring arm around her, and she allowed him to comfort her as they found their way down the gravel path to the rows and rows of white crosses that stretched in long lines as far as her eye could see. Someone had given them a number at the gate, and they had to count along the rows until they found the correct one.

When they got there, she moved to stand in front of the tiny cross. It seemed so simple and plain. With tears running down her cheeks, she stared out at all the crosses and thought about all the stories of people's lives that lay beneath them. With her hand still trembling, she laid the flowers on Vivienne's grave.

'Dear Vivienne, I don't know all of your story, but I'm sorry for how you died.'

She thought again about the phrase 'remember the swallows'. What could it have meant?

After they visited Vivienne's grave, they also found Marcus's cross, and they stood before it. She felt overwhelmed as tears continued to slide down her cheeks. Tears for the great-aunt she had never known, and tears for a war that had created both monsters and heroes at the same time.

'I feel guilty,' said Alex, looking down at the cross. 'I have done nothing wrong, and yet I feel guilty. I don't know how to put this right.'

She reached out and took his hand in her own. 'If nothing else good comes out of this, at least we will have met each other.' He looked at her hopefully. 'As friends,' she reiterated.

As they departed the cemetery, they were both thoughtful. They travelled to their hotel in silence, and when they arrived, they talked about the next step.

'We can get a flight back to Paris in the morning if you wish,' he suggested.

She nodded. 'I think tomorrow would be good. But I will fly straight back home to England.'

Sophie had already decided not to say anything to her family about what she had found out; it was better they not know the truth. That, in all likelihood, everyone had been right. Sophie had not been able to prove Vivi hadn't been a Nazi and now she knew that, even worse, she had been executed at the hands of the man who she had loved, and who had deceived her.

A man who looked so like the man standing in front of Sophie right now.

Chapter 40

The next morning both she and Alex took early flights, he to Paris, she to London. She would pick up her car in Cornwall at a later date, knowing she would have to go down and tell her family what she had found out sooner rather than later. She decided to spare them Vivi's painful death at the hand of the Nazi she loved, who had betrayed her.

As they rode in the taxi to the airport, Sophie felt lonelier than ever. It'd been hard enough when she and Matt had finished, but the alienation between her and Alex echoed because it was the reverberation of a relationship unfulfilled and tinged with so much regret. He, too, seemed thoughtful.

Her flight was leaving first, at 8 a.m., and he helped with her baggage and to check in. When they arrived at passport control, she turned to say goodbye. Sophie had decided to give him a quick hug and then to turn and get on her plane, but instead she was caught by his expression, which was communicating a profound longing and sadness.

'Look, Sophie, I know things have been extremely challenging for us both, but I want you to know something. I am not Marcus Vonstein, I am *Alex* Vonstein. I don't know what this is between us, if it is anything yet, but I will tell you one thing: it feels as if something remarkable is possible. Something we shouldn't just walk away from without giving it more thought. And I'm leaving the door open, Sophie, because I don't give away my heart easily. I'm not a serial dater. I don't have the energy for trying people on like shoes, or swiping on Tinder. But this just doesn't feel like that. This feels like something extraordinary, like the world conspired for us to be together. I know that sounds crazy.' He smiled. 'But think about how we even met. I really like you, Sophie, and I feel like this could be something, if we could think about the two of us, and let go of the past. If you and I had just met here, in a café, I think you'd be coming back to Paris with me right now.'

His words struck her heart. There was a genuineness to him that she could sense, something she'd never really felt from Matt. To push through the pain, she took him in her arms and hugged him, and for a moment everything within her wanted to stay there. But she quickly pulled away.

He leaned forward and brushed her lips with a gentle kiss. 'If you just need time, Sophie, you know where I will be.'

She nodded and, clutching her bag, hurried off through security.

Just before she turned towards her gate, she got a glimpse of him one last time. He stood there, his hands in his pockets, watching her, an intense expression on his face, and she was captivated.

Sophie swallowed the tears that were swelling, making her throat ache, handed over her boarding pass and withdrew into the departure lounge. On her way home, she thought about his words. Sophie wished her emotions weren't such a jumble. So much had happened in such a short amount of time. She couldn't fathom what was real or not real any more. She'd lost track of all space and time and wasn't sure how she felt about anything.

Sophie scrolled through her phone to review any messages, trying to get herself back into work mode. She would return to her job the next day.

When she arrived at her flat and opened the door, her past greeted her. It was as though time had stopped. Scattered across her room were her belongings, looking discarded and unloved – a couple of bags, a scarf, a jumper, her shoes – cast off haphazardly before she'd left. Her bed, unmade, her wardrobe doors open where she'd grabbed a few things and not even bothered to clear up behind her.

Needing some love and comfort, she went around to her neighbour's to retrieve her cat, who looked decidedly bigger than when she'd left him.

'Oh, he's a good boy,' her neighbour commented. 'You can always leave him with me, Sophie. Such a good boy.' The neighbour patted his head as William purred contentedly, looking almost regretfully at Sophie, who he knew would not feed him in the way he'd obviously become used to. Though, when they got back to the flat, he showed his affection by putting his paws on her chest and purring in her face.

After a short cuddle with the cat, Sophie went around the rooms, getting rid of everything that reminded her of Matt. She shoved it all into a black plastic bag. She wasn't sure what she would do with the numerous gifts, photos and the sweatshirt of his that she'd slept in so many times, but she knew she didn't want to see them right now. When she was done, she stuffed the bag in her wardrobe – she'd deal with that on a different day – as she reminisced about Alex. At least he'd given her one thing. He'd shown her that love after Matt was at least imaginable.

Sophie didn't sleep well again that night. She had nightmares, with Alex and Vivienne and Matt all talking to her and frantically trying to tell her things. When she woke up the next day, she was sweating. Getting ready for work, she was glad that today there would be familiarity. After days of emotional turmoil, the thought of a quiet day in the office sounded wonderful.

On arriving there, Jonathan looked up at her with relief.

'Thank God, Sophie. I can't find anything in this office without you.' Looking around his desk scattered with papers and files, she knew what her day would entail: helping her boss figure out everything that had happened since she been gone and filing it accordingly. Sophie was extremely grateful for the distraction.

Thankful for the stability of this wonderful job, she smiled broadly. 'I'm so happy to be home.'

'Well, I didn't think you'd be so enthusiastic about all the work I'd have here, but if this is how going on holiday affects you, you should go more often.' He smiled at her.

Sophie went into her office. There were already piles of files and a number of unopened letters on her desk. She surmised she would need to spend the morning opening them and responding. It wasn't till just before lunchtime that Sophie pressed the button on her answering machine and took notes. She heard a familiar voice in amongst them.

'Hello, Sophie. Testing, one, two, three. Oh, I do hate these machines.' It was her gran, and the sound of her voice made her smile. 'It was lovely to see you, dear. I just wanted to let you know. Come by any time. You don't have to wait for a special occasion. I'm always here, apart from Thursdays when I go to bingo or Mondays when I take Mrs James her groceries. Housebound, you know, love. We all take it in turns around here.'

Sophie was grateful for the ease and familiarity of her grandmother's life, though was a little frustrated that her gran had called her work number instead of her mobile.

The message continued. 'Oh, yes, and by the way, I found that letter. You know you asked me about Villainous Vivienne? Well, I found it. Not sure if it's anything you are interested in. It doesn't say much. Should probably throw it out,' she muttered, evidently talking to herself. 'Anyway, let me know. If I don't hear back from you, I'll just get rid of it. Don't need any more rubbish hanging about the house. Haven't got a clue what I've got in half these drawers,' she rambled on. 'Okay, well, have a nice day, dear. Don't forget to call your gran.'

Sophie pounced on the phone and dialled quickly.

Bessy didn't answer right away, and when she finally did, on the last ring, she was panting. 'Hello.'

'Gran, it's me.'

'Me?'

'Sophie.'

'Oh, hello, love. You just caught me. I was getting the washing in. I think it's going to rain, love. You haven't got your washing out today, have you?'

Sophie cut her off. 'Gran, I was ringing about the letter.'

'The letter?' Gran seemed confused on the other end. 'What letter, dear?'

'Grandad's sister's letter. Remember? From Vivienne during the war?'

'Oh, that letter. I think I've thrown it away. I didn't hear from you. Hang on, let me have a look around.' There was a clang as she put the phone down on her telephone table, and the sound of her shuffling down the hallway.

Sophie clung to her phone, hoping that her grandma had not been thorough.

A few minutes later, the receiver was picked back up. 'That's a funny story, you know, Sophie. I was going to throw it out, and then I got a call from the woman down the road here. Her cat got out, and it worried her, and we all went out to look for it.'

Sophie held her breath, hoping Gran would get to the point.

'Anyway, we didn't find it. It came back on its own two days later. Stupid thing. Well, during that time, I put that letter in a bag by the door to take out to the rubbish and forgot all about it. It's here, dear. Did you still want to see it?'

'Yes, please, Gran, don't throw it out. I'm coming over in the next hour.'

'Oh, okay. Are you sure you want to come all this way? There's not much in it. I read through it.'

'Please, Gran, I need to see it.'

'All right, love. If you're insistent. It will be lovely to see you. I think I'll bake some scones. See you in a bit, then, Sophie.' Her gran put down the phone.

Grabbing her coat and bag and leaving right away, she started to piece together in her mind everything she'd learned. Vivienne had gone out to France with SOE and had been on a failed mission. Somehow she had met Marcus at the hospital and nursed him, and together they'd gone to France. She did something unfathomable and the man who was supposed to love her had killed her for it. But that he'd killed her at all still raised a question mark. Sophie hadn't been able to find that out, and she knew this was clinging to a sliver of hope. Though surely, if there were something in the letter that proved Vivienne's innocence, the rumours would have been quashed years before.

Getting the train over to her grandmother's, she felt the stress of the last few weeks and desperately wanted to finalise this mystery. On arriving at her gran's flat, she tried not to appear too eager as Bessy talked about the weather and her washing. She already had her ironing board set up in her kitchen, and the smell of the freshly baked scones wafted from a plate on the table.

'Sit yourself down. I'll make a cup of tea,' Bessy said. 'You get going on one of those scones.'

'Gran, I'd love to, but I don't have long.'

'Yes, dear, of course. I should make you a ham sandwich.'

'Gran, the letter!' she said, trying not to sound frantic. 'You have the letter?'

'Oh, yes, of course. Let me go get it.'

Bessy went into a hallway closet and rustled through a plastic bag with rubbish in it, and as she searched, she mused about it. 'I shouldn't get your hopes up too high, love. There's not much in there. I don't think it's going to change anything you already know. Not even sure why your grandad kept it. But for some reason he would never let me throw it out. I think he had some sort of latent childhood hope that, even years later, she would turn up and put everything right. Funny what we hold onto… Here it is!' she suddenly announced.

She pulled out a handwritten letter in her aunt's scrawl and placed it on the table in front of Sophie, then busied herself around the kitchen, making her granddaughter a sandwich.

Eagerly, Sophie picked up the yellowing envelope with the faded script and pulled out an aged sheet of paper. It was dated the day before Vivi had left England with Marcus.

> *Dearest John and darling Tom,*
>
> *I hope this letter finds you well. And by now, I will no longer be there. I cannot tell you everything I am doing, but I want you to know that I love you both so very much. There are things right now that are bigger than all of us, and I need the two of you to be brave and courageous and help Daddy in the hospital there. Many people there need help and are sick, and I won't be there, as I have to do something important right now.*
>
> *I hope you will take special care of the gifts that I gave you. I chose them especially for you both. They're very important to me.*
>
> *Tom, I painted that for you because I know you love birds. But the sparrow also has a very significant meaning for me. I hope you will take care of it and whenever you look at it, you will think of me and always, always believe the best of me.*
>
> *And John, darling, I know you are still young, but I know you love to read so much, so that was why I left you our favourite book, the one I have read to you so many times. You remember my favourite story in there, don't you? The one that makes me cry and you always tease me about? 'The Call of the Swallows.' I want you to read that and think of*

me. Think of all the times that I would snuggle up in bed next to you and we would giggle and read together. Think about what the story means, the deeper meaning, and think of me when you read it.

I know that you are probably confused right now. But know deep down in my heart that I love you both and will never forget the most amazing brothers that anyone could have.

And darlings, I want you to know something. What I'm doing today, I believe, is for a higher good. I may be making the worst mistake of my life, but I feel compelled to do it. I have done many things I am not proud of, but not what I do today. What I do now is so the right side can win this war, and I know in my heart who that should be, even though many may perceive my actions as wrong. But I need to give you all a chance to grow up and get married and have children and grandchildren and nothing is as important than giving us a hope for tomorrow. And if I die doing it, at least you can be assured it will be in the pursuit of what I thought was right.

Much love now and for always. And be good for Dad.

And fingers crossed and God willing, we'll all be together soon.

And I hope you always remember me as a person with a <u>heart</u> whose love is <u>innocent</u>!

Much love

Vivi xxx

As she stared at the letter Sophie noticed two words were underlined, 'heart' and 'innocent', and she recognised them straight away as being from 'She Walks in Beauty' by Lord Byron, the poem underlined in Vivi's book. Maybe Vivi was sending them a message in case she needed them to know how she was planning to code future messages?

Sophie couldn't help but draw in a gasp as she read the words. Her gran turned with concern. 'Is everything all right, Sophie?'

Sophie nodded, quickly pulled out her phone with the coded message and started to use the two words that were underlined as the key to the cipher. It took her about an hour but finally she hit on the right combination and sat back and read her great-aunt's message for the first time.

> *Back in the field hawk restored to his nest net is closing need immediate extraction for hawk and sparrow invasion deception successful coming home.*

Sophie held her breath as she read her aunt's words. This proved she was really working for the Resistance, because there was no other logical reason for her to message England for an emergency extraction unless she was back undercover. Hawk and Sparrow had to be Vivienne and Marcus and the date on the message right before the D-Day landings and mentioning the 'invasion deception' suggested she was talking about the invasion of Normandy.

Tears of relief rolled down Sophie's cheeks, Vivienne had been a hero, she had died for her country. Sophie started to sob as she read the last two words of the message again. Because, after seventy-five years, Vivienne still wasn't home.

Gran came over to check on her as Sophie explained what it all meant and she shook her head with disbelief. The two of them sat there in a reverent silence for the woman who had died so long ago but whose bravery had never been recognised.

Suddenly Sophie remembered something else.

'"The Call of the Swallows".'

'Sorry, dear?'

'The story in the book that was given to Grandpa was called "The Call of the Swallows".'

'Oh. Yes, I think it was. Odd kind of book, as I recall. Your grandfather had it for ages, knocking about, but oh, I got rid of it years ago, Sophie. Some sort of Arabian Nights-type tale.'

'Can you remember what the story was about?'

'I can't, love. It's not one story. It was lots of stories. Fables and short stories about princesses and kings and toads. You know, the usual fairy tales.'

Sophie was only half-listening, as she was scrolling through her phone, looking on Amazon for the book, but it was clearly long out of print.

She sighed, then jumped up and kissed her gran on the cheek. 'I've got to go, Gran.'

Bessy looked shocked. 'What about your sandwich and scone?'

'Sorry, Gran, it's my first day back, and I have already been gone a long time.'

'I'll put them in a bag for you.' She grabbed a bread bag, complete with breadcrumbs still in the bottom, and shoved a buttered scone and the sandwich into it. She also pulled out a packet of crisps and handed them to her granddaughter as she followed her down the hallway. 'Promise me you'll eat it all.'

'Yes, Gran. Whatever you say.'

'I'll be feeling those hips when you come around again. Make sure there's something on them.'

Sophie couldn't help but smile.

Making her way hastily back to the Tube, Sophie felt light. This letter was the key to the whole story. Vivienne had been telling the children something relating to the story about the swallows. But what was it? It was so important she'd shouted it out at her execution. Maybe she'd wanted to remind Marcus of the same story.

Sophie knew more than anything she needed to find that book, and she knew exactly where to go for it.

Chapter 41

On her way home from work that night, Sophie stopped off at her favourite second-hand bookshop, squeezed down an alley from a modern shopping high street. Arcadia was a cavern housing every kind of book. It was a place she loved to come to escape. Old-fashioned bevelled windows hinted at its roots as a pharmacy years before, with two stone steps and a small wooden door that even she had to stoop to get inside.

But once she was there, she was greeted with everything that gave her joy. Rows and rows of books from floor to ceiling on dark mahogany shelves and even more stacked on the floor in careful piles. And the bookshop owner, a Mr Kersley, was living his dream. He'd retired from academia ten years before, and now it was his greatest joy to bring the classics back to the masses. You wouldn't be able to find the latest edition of a top-selling paperback, but if you needed to understand Greek mythology or the structures of Rome's hierarchy during the twelfth century, then this was your place.

It was kept as silent as a library, which Sophie loved, with a number of haphazard but comfortable chairs placed throughout the shop for patrons to enjoy with a cup of coffee that Mr Kersley's wife, Beryl, liked to prepare for her customers. Sophie was a regular.

'Hi there, Sophie,' called out Beryl as Sophie stepped down into the shop. 'Would you like your usual?'

'That would be wonderful,' responded Sophie as she allowed the ambiance of the ancient books and the world below their covers to welcome her in. The smell of coffee, leather and oak embraced her as always.

Mr Kersley always wore a shirt and a woollen cardigan, but each day a different-coloured bow tie. He looked up from his heavyset glasses that were a throwback to Michael Caine in the 1970s, and his smile did nothing to move the heavy wrinkles on his brow. He took off his glasses and beamed.

'Well, if it isn't my favourite city lawyer. Are you looking for more books about the Blitz? I've got an interesting stack in about the Houses of Parliament, and not just about the Guy Fawkes plot to blow it up, but something much more fun. Are you game?'

Sophie smiled. 'I might be. Though I'm actually on the lookout for something completely different.'

'Ah,' he said, walking from behind his counter to meet her. 'Pray tell?'

'Well, it's a book that's out of print, I believe.'

'That's not a problem for us.'

'I think it's a story about fables. A relative of mine owned it during the war, so I'm guessing it was written a while before that. But there's one story, the story the book is named after, I think it may be called "The Call of the Swallows".'

He knitted his heavy brow and chewed on the corner of his spectacles as he contemplated the name. '"Call of the Swallows",' he said deliberately. 'I have a recollection of a book with that name. Give me a moment.'

He went back to his desk and looked through the shop's inventory on his computer.

'Yes, yes, I think this is it. You're right, it's one of the stories within the book of the same name. It's a set of Aesop-style tales, Greek mythology, Roman stories, fables, et cetera. It says we have one copy. Let me see if I can find it for you.'

He made his way down through the maze of shelves as the smell of freshly brewed coffee and the sound of Beryl humming to herself comforted Sophie. He took out a small stepladder in the section that said 'Greek Stories' and pulled down a dusty cover from a top shelf.

'I'm afraid it's not in great condition, Sophie, which is probably why I haven't sold it. These are the kind of books I try to weed out. Fortunately, it managed to miss my overhaul of last winter, but you're welcome to have it for half price if you're interested in it.'

He handed it down to her. It was a heavy book with a leather-bound cover that smelled musty with age. Some of the pages had a little water damage, and she half-expected moths to fly out as she opened up the book. But they were crisp and as thin as those of a Bible, and also gilded. She quickly went to the front and ran her fingers down the contents. The name of the story was indeed 'The Call of the Swallows'. It appeared to be the author's signature story. She thanked Mr Kersley and made her way to a corner chair, where Beryl placed a coffee cup on a coaster, and she settled down to read the story.

It was set out in an allegory format, not unlike *Arabian Nights* or *Aesop's Fables*. This one centring on the beginning of the world. It told the story of a magical interpretation of how the world was formed. A love story between a prince and princess from different kingdoms – one of the light, one of the dark, neither of whom were able to live in one another's world. But then the prince became so obsessed with his love for the princess that he was prepared to let his kingdom die just to be with her. So she sacrificed herself for the good of the whole world and everyone else in it.

Chapter 42

As Sophie closed the book, the final piece of the puzzle fell into place, and she knew at last what it all meant. Vivienne hadn't died at the hands of her lover. She had taken her own life somehow, had sacrificed it for her country and to protect whatever she and Vonstein were doing. She had taken the fall. That's why she'd reminded Marcus of the name of the story at the moment of her death.

She pondered Vivienne's story on those terms. What if he hadn't wanted to execute her? What if she'd forced his hand somehow, reminding him of her sacrifice? Though Sophie didn't know all the pieces of the puzzle from so long ago, she knew one thing: her great-aunt had not been a victim, nor a sacrifice after a casual affair. The coded meaning was clear: she had been doing work for her country. Vivienne had never quit being a spy.

Sophie took the book to the front of the shop.

'Did you want to take that old thing?' asked Mr Kersley with a sniff.

'I do. It's the last piece to a puzzle that is extremely important to me.'

He smiled, looking pleased. 'Well, in that case, I'll even wrap it for you.' He took out some brown paper and covered the book then taped it and handed it to her. 'That will be five pounds, Sophie.'

She handed him the money and placed the book in her bag, thinking how this one small purchase for such a paltry amount of money had the potential to change the story of her family's history.

And that of another person's family too. A person who was on her mind. Alex.

Sophie had been so hard on him when she'd left, so harsh with him, and he hadn't deserved that. Taking it out on him because she was starting to have real feelings for him and she despised herself for that. She had driven him away because she didn't want her heart to get hurt again.

But now Sophie wanted to share all this news with him. She texted him straight away, telling him she thought that she'd found some more answers to the story. She noted then, with sadness, that he read it but didn't respond. Maybe she'd blown it with him. The thought made her feel miserable, because even though they were just at the beginning of something, it had felt sincere and loving.

Sophie decided the next day she would go to the National Archives and present them with the information that she had and see if they had anything there that would help bring about a conclusion.

She made an appointment with a Mr Scullin, and when she arrived armed with all of her material, she felt like a schoolgirl summoned to the headmaster's office. He was a man of little levity and listened as she plunged into her story. He was impressed when she showed him the decoded message and his eyebrows only quirked once, when she mentioned her findings in 'The Call of the Swallows'. He took notes as she explained Frau Strauss's claims.

'Was there someone with you to witness her story?' he asked, looking down at his paper.

'Yes, Alex Vonstein, Marcus's great-nephew, and Frau Strauss's granddaughter, Chloe, were both there.'

'If she is able, we'd want a written confirmation from Miss Strauss of what she witnessed to be able to look at this case. And if you can give me contact details for the other two, that would be very helpful.'

Sophie realised then it wasn't as straightforward as presenting the facts. They had to look into this and confirm them for themselves.

She must have looked disheartened, because as she put her hand out to say goodbye, he shook it saying, 'I'm sure it'll all work out. There were many loose ends left dangling at the end of the war, stories like yours that are still coming out. The MOD is very open to making sure people get the recognition they deserve for what they did. Let us look into all the facts we have on our side and we'll be in touch.'

Sophie felt a little heartened by his words, but still, it was frustrating that it would take even longer. She wanted the record put straight so she could go back to Cornwall. This was the journey she was most looking forward to. Tom needed to know what his sister had done, that she hadn't been the person they had all suspected.

Travelling home, Sophie felt a little deflated and wished more than anything she could talk to Alex. Looking at her phone, she noted he had still not texted back. With this kind of information, if they'd been in France, maybe they would have opened a bottle of wine and celebrated.

With a sudden awareness she realised she really missed him.

Chapter 43

Sophie received a call from the National Archives two weeks later. 'We have some extremely exciting news for you. We are planning on bringing all of our members together so you can share what you have. We will present what we know, and then we can attempt to put some of these records straight. It appears that we have evidence that backs up your claim about your great-aunt Vivienne. Could you come in here on Wednesday at 4 p.m. and present what you know about her story? It doesn't have to be particularly long, but just tell us everything you know.'

'Yes, of course,' Sophie answered with a new sense of excitement.

As she turned off her phone, she thought of Alex. He'd replied to her text eventually but they hadn't spoken since she'd left France, and she found she was still missing him terribly. In that brief time he had been such a great friend to her, and this had been their story to pursue, not just hers. She shared her good news with him, texting him about her appointment straight away. He texted her back saying it was incredible and thanked her for telling him, though adding that perhaps he wouldn't share anything with his mother until there was something he could show her in writing.

A week later, Sophie made her way to the National Archives, into a spacious office with tables and desks filled with people – amateur historians, and other World War Two archivists –with notepads and phones poised to record. The man who had organised the event came to the front of the room and introduced her. There was great excitement as she presented her facts and they listened attentively, taking notes.

Then they turned out the lights so they could show a short film featuring some clips all about SOE work. It also highlighted the story of the betrayal of F-section, otherwise known as the Physician Network. There was still a mystery about how the network had been exposed. Many people believed one of the operatives in France, a man called Henri Déricourt, had acted as a double agent; the other rumour was that the British government sacrificed their agents to protect the Normandy landings. Lucky to have escaped alive, Vivienne Hamilton had evidently been there, working under her code name, Sparrow, when many operatives had been captured and eighty killed.

Sophie sucked in a breath. Thinking again about the picture Vivienne had painted for her uncle Tom.

The man at the front pulled up some photographs. 'It appears that Vivienne had escaped from France and SOE at the very time that the cell was being uncovered by someone working for the Germans who was betraying those in the Physician Network. Many of the agents undercover, like Vivienne, took the blame for what was happening, wondering if somehow it was their own incompetence, a wireless discovered, or their coding being inadequate that had caused the fall of the cell, when all the time it was someone else who was sabotaging the network.'

Sophie wondered if her aunt had felt responsible for her cell being discovered.

When he was finished, he sat down and one of the archivists got up. 'The reason we have requested this gathering is that we have found material that may corroborate Miss Hamilton's story that we would like to present. It appears that there was a spy working for the British government, known as Hawk. His real name is in the file as the initials MV. He rose to high up in the Nazi command and joined our spy network in 1943. But his only handler, the

Rook, was killed, and then Hawk went missing, presumed to be dead. However, it appears even though he was radio silent with London because of his concerns about leaks, he'd continued his work, right up until the D-Day landings. Though records seem to suggest that he then disappeared, and never came back to Britain to claim the honours he was due.

'But with Sophie Hamilton's help, we were able to confirm Vivienne visited SOE and it was documented she had asked to see 'the Rook'. This links these two stories and suggests the MV on the record is the same Marcus Vonstein who was shot down in Cornwall and made an escape with Vivienne. The fact that Vivienne didn't tell SOE Marcus was still alive suggests she was already working with Marcus and that he had probably instructed her not to talk to anyone but the Rook. It was most unfortunate that the handler was killed, so it appears that Marcus had to take matters into his own hands. Vivienne Hamilton gave him the means of escape. With her formal training with SOE, it seems she was able to assist him to get back to Paris to finish the task he'd started. The only unknown is how Vivienne actually died. Though Miss Hamilton spoke to an eyewitness who believes she was executed, Miss Hamilton has offered a further suggestion, that unfortunately we cannot confirm, that somehow her aunt took her own life, maybe even by allowing Major Vonstein to kill her.'

Sophie felt the sting of that theory again. Maybe Marcus had no choice and somehow Vivienne had persuaded him for the good of the work they were doing. But still it felt so cowardly and cruel. And she once again wondered if he had ever really loved her.

Suddenly, a voice called from the back of the room and she recognised it instantly. Alex strode to the front.

Sophie's heart started to pound as he came forward, and she realised even though they had been apart none of the feeling she had for him had diminished.

His eyes flicked towards Sophie as he smiled. 'I wonder if I can speak to that and offer a possible alternative ending to this story. I am Alex Vonstein, a relation of Marcus's. I have been thinking about the coded message and 'The Call of the Swallows' ever since Sophie told me about it because I really believe Marcus and Vivienne were in love. And I could never imagine taking the life of the woman I loved no matter what someone had commanded me to do.'

His eyes met Sophie's again and the sincerity in them made her blush as he continued.

'After Sophie contacted me, I went over and over all the information we had gathered and something struck me as I reread the death report about my uncle. I'd read other similar reports and unless the death had been documented as self-inflicted, there was usually a cyanide pill recovered from a tooth in a slain officer's body. But in Marcus's case, it was noted as missing. We also know he was shot in Morlaix. Not captured by the Allies. So if he had already been shot, why would he take the pill then? Would he really choose to add to an already agonising death for himself? After I read this, I called Frau Strauss once more, and asked if there had been any physical contact at Vivienne's execution. And she said she remembered Vivienne grabbing him and kissing him. She hadn't wanted to tell Sophie when we met with her and confirm that even at the end her great-aunt had been so needy for the Nazi officer's love. She didn't see how hurting Sophie would help anything.

'But I don't think that is what Vivienne was doing. I think there's a chance that his capsule was in reach and she took it from him. That she may have actually killed herself. That is about the only reason I could see to shoot the woman he loved, if it was to in some way be kind to her. And because he loved her, he couldn't see her in the absolute agony she must have been in, and so instead took her life with a bullet.'

Tears sprang to Sophie's eyes – it all made sense now. That had to be why Vivi had shouted the name of the story at him, she knew he wouldn't have the ability to do what he needed to do so she had done it for him.

Alex continued, 'Without Vivienne, Marcus would have undoubtedly been revealed, and this would have uncovered a spy who was absolutely crucial to the war effort. And knowing the strength, determination and personal bravery of her great-niece in her own life it doesn't surprise me that Vivienne would do this.'

There was a hushed reverence around the room as every person weighed what Vivienne might have done for her country. Then slowly the archivists moved together to confer with each other and then one came over to speak to her.

'We're all of the same mind. We're going to take all the information you've gathered, plus the information we've collected, and we will put a presentation to the National Archives so that the war records can be altered to try to get your relatives the recognition they deserve. They may even receive medals, posthumously.' He smiled. 'For their services.'

Sophie nodded, her eyes still filled with tears. 'That's incredible, but to clear their names will be more important to our families than any medal could be. Thank you for taking the time to listen to me.'

At the end of the presentation, when the lights went back on, Alex had returned to his seat at the back of the room.

Nervously, she approached him. She found herself feeling coy, her heart trying to beat itself out of her chest.

'Thank you so much for coming.'

'I had to. Besides, I had another reason,' he said, a smile crossing his face. 'I had a very special friend here that I missed and I wanted to check on.'

Sophie realised how much she'd missed him in just two weeks and, hugging him, she enjoyed how it felt to be close to him again.

'Well, this should finally make my mother happy,' he declared as she released him. 'I have you to thank for this, Sophie.'

At the exit of the building, he turned to her.

'I don't have to leave right away…' He left his declaration open-ended, she assumed not wanting to put any pressure on her.

She smiled. 'Well, you treated me in Paris, I should at least take you for dinner.'

After they had a very pleasant meal and she walked him to his hotel, she realised how special this was, this feeling of being accepted for who she was. He wasn't enamoured with Sophie the high-powered lawyer, and didn't seem at all interested in how successful her career had been. He couldn't share in her heartbreak over Emily, but he understood her and he had shown he cared and wanted to listen. And he seemed to simply enjoy being with her.

When he leaned forward and touched her lips with a gentle kiss, she didn't pull back. It was okay. It was okay to move on from Matt, open up a space in her heart after the death of her daughter and mother, even if this turned out not to be something long-term, at least it felt good for now. For the first time, in a long time, Sophie felt safe.

On the way home, Sophie knew there was something she needed to do. And once she arrived, she went straight into the nursery and quietly closed the door behind her. Flicking on the light, she turned and drew in a long slow breath. She hadn't been in here with the light on in so long.

Walking across the room, she sat on the chair next to Emily's cot, her hand brushing the cotton of the soft pink sheets, Tigger smiling up at her from the duvet. As Sophie looked around, tears started to well. But this time, instead of going straight to her guilt and pain, Sophie forced herself to dwell on the good memories, allowing them to filter through her darkness. She studied everything in the room. In the corner was Emily's favourite stuffed toy. A giraffe she had called 'Gaf', her childlike way of saying its name. He had gone everywhere with her, except on that last day, and she had slept every night with her tiny fingers caught up in his golden mane, spiralling her hands through the golden tufts to ease herself into sleep. Gaf now sat on the toybox, diligently, as if waiting for his playmate's return. On the bookshelf over her bed, Emily's baby books were piled up high, on the top, the creased pages of *The Hungry Caterpillar* revealed how many times Sophie had read that story to her. In the wardrobe, along with Emily's other clothes, the favourite pink sweater Alice had knitted for her to grow into, which had sat untouched and unworn for over a year. Sophie sighed.

'Darling, Emmy,' she whispered out into the quiet, still room. 'I'm here to say goodbye.' Her voice started to crack as the tears began, but she pushed forward. She needed to do this. 'Not to you, sweetheart, you will always be forever my girl, and there won't be a day that goes by that you won't be a part of my heart. But Emily, I have to move on from this pain. And though it breaks my heart, I also know if I don't take this step, I could be sitting in this nursery for the rest of my life. I know you are in the arms of your grandmother who loves you so much. I know now, my sweet girl, that you didn't come into my life with all your wonderfulness just to leave me with all this sadness. And I'm going to try, darling. I'm honestly going to try every day to only think about all the fun we had together.

'Mum, I miss you so much.' Sophie's voice started to crack again. 'So many things have happened that I have wanted to tell you about. And there are so many things I forgot to ask you about because I thought you would be here for so much longer. I love you, Mum. I always will.'

Sophie paused, and then continued, 'Aunt Vivienne, I thought my job was going to be finding out if your reputation was deserved. But instead, your acts of courage have reached from the past and into my life and restored my hope. I now have a reason every day to fight my way out of the darkness. Because if I don't, then everything you did, everything my mother and daughter were to me, becomes meaningless. I believe now that I didn't find you, but that you found me, to remind me of what was truly important.

Which is to live the life I have every day, even with the pain. I don't know when I will see the light again, or how it will feel to be in the presence of that light after all this grief, but at least now I do have a reason to look for it. Because I have a choice to live, when you didn't. I want to thank you. Thank you for your sacrifice and for showing me so clearly what bravery looks like.'

Sophie's voice started to fade with the intense emotion as she closed her eyes and imagined all three of them together in the room with her. Her mother so wise and loving, her great-aunt so daring and strong, and her darling daughter, so perfect and joyful – all taken way too soon, but all of them there to encourage her forward.

Wiping away her tears, Sophie opened her eyes, and her heart felt lighter and warmer somehow, and while she was still feeling emboldened by her aunt's acts of bravery, she reached into a cupboard and pulled out a box, and with tears still streaming freely down her cheeks, she began to pack away Emily's things.

Chapter 44

Now that the knowledge of what Vivienne had really done during the war was out in the open, there was one last place she needed to go: back to Cornwall to set the record straight for her uncle Tom.

The morning after their dinner, Sophie called Alex at his hotel and asked if he wanted to join her on her trip. He was delighted, and they travelled together in a hire car so she could drive her own back. On the way she realised, with surprise, she'd never taken Matt down to Cornwall. Even though their holidays often coincided she had never thought to invite him. But somehow, being with Alex, everything felt easy. He seemed to sense that she needed to take it gradually and didn't force anything. He appeared to simply like being around her and she enjoyed being around him. They talked about art and music and her favourite architecture and what he was considering painting, and she wasn't sure where this relationship was going but she liked how she felt around him.

Sophie had mentioned to her auntie Jean that she'd be arriving in Cornwall with a friend, but she hadn't elaborated any more on what she was coming about, so when she arrived in her auntie's kitchen with Alex, eyebrows were slightly raised.

'And this is Alex,' said Sophie, introducing him.

Auntie Jean greeted him suspiciously, clearly remembering how recently Sophie and Matt's relationship had finally crumbled.

'Alex and I have been working together on our joint family history.'

Jean stared at them. 'Are you speaking about Vivienne's story?'

'Yes, and his full name is Alex Vonstein. The man she disappeared with… this is his great-nephew.'

Jean stared at him again as though she didn't trust him. Like she was looking at the ghosts of the past coming forward to haunt the present. She stepped away from him distrustfully, and instinctively turned to put the kettle on.

'We have new information, Auntie Jean, and I wanted to share it with you.'

Her aunt seemed to need to prepare herself for whatever she was going to hear. 'Well, let's wait till your cousin gets home. He's been out in the fields this afternoon checking on the sheep, but when he gets back, we'll make a nice dinner. Then you can tell us all about… this news.'

After eating an excellent dinner of lamb and roast potatoes, they settled themselves in the front room. Sophie started at the beginning of the story, informing them about the work that Vivienne had done for SOE. She showed them the war records she'd gathered. Her auntie Jean just looked at it in dismay and shook her head, struggling to take everything in.

Alex then continued the story, informing them that his great-uncle had also been working for SOE.

'He was a Nazi,' stated Jean, briskly.

'He was deep undercover. He'd been back here receiving a briefing about the undercover work he would be doing for the D-Day landings, and his plane went down on the way back to France. We believe he was under a strict mandate to not break his cover for anyone, and it appeared only one person in SOE knew what he was doing. Unfortunately, the operative who knew about his case was killed. What we've deduced is that he must have told Vivienne of his plan because he needed her help. She'd made her way to London to find his SOE handler, but when she realised that he was dead, she felt she couldn't divulge the secret to anyone else. The photographer took this picture, the one that was in the war museum, as Vivienne was leaving that meeting. We have records of her being in the building under her code name, Sparrow.'

'Her code name was Sparrow?' Jean asked.

'Yes, that was the name she worked under in SOE'

Jean furrowed her brows again. 'You know she left Dad a picture of sparrows she'd painted?'

'Yes, I saw it. I think she was trying to tell him her code name, like a secret message that she wasn't evil, that she had a plan she was following. But she couldn't tell anyone the whole story. It was all top secret.'

'Well, blow me down,' said Jean as she sat down hard in her chair, staring at all the photographs that Sophie had taken at the records office and the decoded message. 'So all this time, all this suffering my family went through, and she was serving her country. I can hardly believe it.'

Suddenly there was a rattling at the door. They all turned around, and there was Uncle Tom. 'You're talking about Vivienne, aren't you?'

Jean jumped to her feet, speaking rapidly. 'Hello, Dad. I thought you'd gone up to have a nap.'

He continued without listening to what she had to say. He stared at Sophie, repeating himself. 'You're talking about Vivienne, aren't you?'

Sophie stood up. 'Yes, Uncle Tom. She was working for the Special Operations Executive undercover and the Germans—'

Tom interrupted her as he saw Alex in the room. He balled his fists, and the fury was unmistakable in his tone.

'Him, she went with him.' He pointed his finger at Alex in accusation.

Sophie realised the confusion. 'No, Uncle Tom. This is Alex Vonstein. This is his great-nephew.'

'Don't listen to him. He took her from here, from her home.' Tom's agitation escalated as he hopped from foot to foot. 'Why did you take her? Why did you take my sister away from me?'

Alex rose to his feet and Jean went to the side of her dad.

'Dad, this isn't the same man. This is a relative of his, and you've got to calm down. Vivienne was good. They were both working for the British.'

Finally, Jean managed to get Tom to sit down. It appeared it was all extremely confusing for him with his long-term memory being so much stronger than his short-term. But he continued with his animosity towards Alex. 'I saw you from the bedroom window. I saw you take her and I knew then I would never see her again.'

'She had a greater purpose, Uncle,' said Sophie, gently touching his arm. 'She had to do something that nobody else could do. There was no alternative way to get him out. He was being guarded and he helped save the lives of many men during the D-Day landings. He and Vivienne, they confused the enemy. That's why they had to stay undercover.'

Tom closed his eyes, trying to take it all in as Sophie continued to tell the story. She didn't tell them about the execution, thinking it might be too difficult to hear, but she told her aunt how the words in the coded message and the storybook, 'The Call of the Swallows', had filled in the missing parts for her.

Suddenly, Tom's eyes opened wide. 'I remember that story. She gave it to John before she left. She told him to read that story.' Suddenly, the relief showed on his face, as if the penny had finally dropped. 'She was doing the same. She was doing the same as the princess in that story, wasn't she? I knew she couldn't have been bad, no matter what people said about her with all those dreadful rumours.'

'No, she wasn't,' said Sophie. 'And we're able to put the record straight now. I had a meeting yesterday with the National Archives, submitted all the facts to them. They also had information for us, and if everything works out correctly, they will put the war records straight, and they will honour Vivienne as a spy who laid down her life for her country. You may even get a medal.'

Tom looked at Sophie, his voice cracking. 'Where is she?'

Sophie spoke softly, taking a gentle hold of his wrinkled hand. 'Her grave is in Normandy, just outside. Alex and I visited her there and left flowers.'

'I want to send some.'

'Yes, we will do that,' said Jean, stroking his hand.

Tears were in the corners of his eyes as he spoke with real conviction. 'I always knew, Jean. I always knew she was good. Now I know for sure it's true. I cannot tell you how happy I am to know the truth.'

'Let's get you back to bed, Dad. I think that's enough excitement for one day,' said Jean as she helped her dad up.

Then, all at once, it was as if a wall came down and he appeared to forget the conversation. He looked around the room a little bewildered, saying, 'I can't remember why I came down, but a nap sounds good.' He then grinned at his daughter and patted her hand, 'Ah, look, Alice is here.'

'This is Sophie, Alice's daughter. Remember, your great-niece?' Jean corrected him.

'Ah,' he stated flatly, as though the realisation of his dementia had hit him once again. 'Of course, hello, Sophie. I guess this is your young man?'

Alex nodded, not wanting to add any more confusion, and Jean led him from the room.

Once they'd left, Sophie's cousin Jamie spoke. 'This is so unbelievable. You did such an exceptional job putting all these pieces together. I will go down in the morning to the museum and give them the photocopies of this evidence. I think it's a story that needs to be told, don't you?'

After they had coffee, Sophie led Alex around the estate and showed him the route Marcus and Vivienne would have taken through the side bushes down to the water. As the sun started to set, they stood on the beach where, seventy-five years before,

Vivienne and Marcus had stepped into a fishing boat to pursue a cause bigger than themselves.

'You can't imagine,' said Alex softly, 'what it must have been like to have the choices they had back then.'

Sophie shook her head, and gently he took her hand and she let him. She wasn't sure what this was with Alex, but she wasn't going to hold back. She was going to let it become what it would become.

They stood on the edge of the beach as the sun was setting over the water, and hungry seagulls circled overhead, dropping shells on the stones to crack open for their dinner. Out on the water, a couple of fishing boats were coming in with their evening catch, bobbing on the waves, the brass on their hulls glistening, reflected in the last rays of the day. As the wind whipped up, Sophie closed her eyes and imagined her aunt Vivienne standing on the bow of a fishing boat with Marcus, the man she loved, by her side, heading away across the water to her destiny.

Epilogue

6 June 1944

Marcus stood over the body of the love of his life, struggling to come to terms with what had transpired. Staring at the blood seeping from the wound in her head, mingled with the smell of cordite in his nostrils, it took every bit of his strength to stop himself from retching. There was only one thought that now gripped him, that dominated him: that there was no time to mourn. It had cost Vivi everything to do what she had just done, and now he had to do the right thing. He owed it to her. If he collapsed or broke down, her death would have been in vain.

But it nevertheless took every inch of his strength to turn and walk away from her, to not throw himself on top of her and gather her into his arms and hold her one last time while there was still warmth in her body.

As two guards carried her away, he knew with a vengeance what he needed to do.

Returning to his office, it was clear from the intelligence coming in that the Allies were on French soil and the landings in Normandy were in progress. Marcus became hyper-focused, continually pushing Vivi's face from his thoughts when it goaded and tormented him, threatening to take him down into the darkest place of guilt and grief. Unlike his mind, Marcus's heart was shut down; it was paralysed. But he used his detached emotional condition to throw himself into his work, fearlessly disrupting as many of the German responses as possible, and now he was reckless. He didn't care if he got caught. All he wanted to do was honour Vivi's memory by saving as many of the Allied soldiers as he could.

He didn't leave the office for three days, only sleeping for ten minutes at a time when he collapsed across his desk with exhaustion. Then, on the third day, he returned home briefly to shower and that's when he had found it. Slipped under the door of the apartment, a letter from someone he didn't know addressed to 'Claudette'. When he opened it he broke down. How he wished she could have read it. One of the members of the underground cell must have delivered it. After creating false papers for her they were the only ones that knew about Vivi's past identity. He allowed the tears to slip freely down his cheeks as he read the impeccable handwriting.

> *Dearest Claudette,*
>
> *I cannot tell you how often I have thought about you since we were jailed that night in Paris, and hoped with all of my heart that you made it out of France safely. When my family and I were arrested we were separated and didn't know for a time if any of us had survived. I will not lie to you, our time with the Germans was not a pleasant one, but hope kept me alive, in the most desperate of times. Hope of seeing my family again and also the fact that knowing you were out there doing what you were called to do. I knew France had a chance with you on their side.*
>
> *We were released unexpectedly, ahead of what appears to be the Germans preparing for evacuation. I want you to know we are all well, if not a little thinner and a little scarred by our experience, but we are in good health. Yvette has even talked about planning her life as a designer now the Germans are leaving France. We found out after we were released many of the underground from the cell you worked for had been captured, something must have gone terribly wrong. I just hope you made it out.*

We all send you our love and thanks, we will never be able to pay the debt this has cost you, but know we are eternally grateful and hope one day to see you again. Yvette will leave this letter at the door of one of the cells she knew of and we hope a kind person will be able to pass it on.
Much love,
Pascal Renoir

After he wept for a while, Marcus knew what he had to do – he had sacrificed enough, it had cost him everything. Returning to work he went straight down to where he knew they were holding Vivienne's body, no one having the time to bury the corpse of a traitor. Reverently, he entered the cold, darkened room. And when he finally saw her there, he let himself howl, holding her frigid hands, kissing her wax-like cheeks, tears streaming down his face as he told her again and again how much he loved her and how he would tell her family how brave she was. He gave her the letter, placing it in her stiffened fingers.

'They made it, my love, your family. They made it, you can sleep easy now.'

Drying his tears, he rushed back to his office and removed all the files of Vivi he could locate, trying to hide her work for the Nazis. He also changed her burial instructions so she might rest where other soldiers were, and so she would get proper burial rites, and in all the chaos he hoped that no one would check on it.

Placing all the other documents into a briefcase, he made his way out into the chaotic streets of Paris.

He headed for Brittany. It took over a day to get there. It was pandemonium everywhere, but he didn't care. His duty was done. All he could think of now was reaching her family. He owed that one last thing to Vivi.

Finally reaching Morlaix, he sought to commandeer a car to get him to the coast, but no one wanted to help him, everyone standing up to him, emboldened by the attack. Marcus could have forced them, held a gun to someone's head, but he was tired of this war and no longer wanted to play this role.

Eventually, someone informed him a person wanted to help him at the other end of town. He was halfway there, walking through an alley, when he heard someone call his name. He turned and peered through the darkness.

'Marcus Vonstein,' the woman spat out again with sheer animosity, the outrage and hatred clear in her tone. Marcus couldn't see her face. What he could sense was the pistol that was pointing right at him.

'Who are you?' he demanded.

'Never mind who I am. Let me tell you who my brother was. You maybe knew him as the Terrier. He was brave and fun-loving and a patriot, and you were part of the group that murdered him. When someone informed me you were looking for a car, I knew I would be murdering a Nazi today.'

Marcus placed his hands in the air. 'You don't understand. I have something I need to do. I'm undercover for SOE. I'm not a Nazi.'

'Of course you aren't,' she scoffed, laughing sarcastically. 'You're all running like rats caught in a trap. Where's all your bullying and bravado now?'

'You don't understand,' he implored, opening up his briefcase and removing the file he had on Vivienne. 'Please read this. Please, before you shoot. I have some crucial evidence I need to get to England. I have to put the record straight.'

'I don't want to hear your lies,' she spat. 'I know you murdered my brother and I know you'll say anything so that I don't kill you.'

Without hesitation, Anne-Marie lifted the gun and fired three bullets straight into Marcus's body; one hit him in the shoulder, one in the leg and one in his stomach. The pain ripped through his body, and his legs buckled, slamming him into the ground in absolute agony.

He struggled desperately to hold on to Vivienne's documents, her life, her work, her bravery, and crushed in his hand her photograph pinned to the top of her file. The proof of all she'd done. Desperately he tried to hold onto it all. He had to get it to England, to her family. Marcus started to black out; the pain was now so intense he thought he might be sick. As he heard the echoed footsteps of the woman leaving the alley, the life started to leave his body and his fingers began to fail him.

All at once, a wind whipped its way down the street, towards him, the walls of the passage creating a wind tunnel that ripped the documents from his hands. Marcus watched helplessly as the file emptied into the wind, creating a paper trail of Vivienne's patriotism that swirled, twirled, danced above his head, taunting and teasing him until finally a second blast took it all up and out of his sight as it separated onto a thousand different journeys. Marcus felt desolate. It was all she had asked of him, and he couldn't even do that one thing for her. That stung more than the pain tearing through his body.

As he watched the last piece spiral away, the only thing that consoled him was knowing, even though he was in agony, that in a few moments it would be over and he would once again be reunited with his love, and they would be together again forever. He closed his eyes, listening to his breath that now came in ragged spurts, the smell of his own blood filling his nostrils. Sweat soaked his face and hands as the pain in his body became insufferable.

To sooth himself, Marcus closed his eyes and pictured her face, her laugh, her eyes reflected in the moon from the balcony on the nights when there were no raids. Nights where she'd told him stories of swallows and bravery, where they had imagined a world where they could be together, forever, where there was no war, no evil, no sacrifice. In his mind's eye he glanced down from the balcony onto the street. There he could see two people sauntering through the streets of Paris, on a perfect spring day, a couple madly in love, hand in hand, finally being able to enjoy the end of a very long war.

A Letter from Suzanne

Dear reader,

I want to say a huge thank you for choosing to read *When We Were Brave*. If you did enjoy it and want to keep up to date with all my latest releases, just sign up at the following link. Your email address will never be shared and you can unsubscribe at any time.

www.bookouture.com/suzanne-kelman

If you loved *When We Were Brave* I would also be very grateful if you could write a review. It's great to hear what you think, and it makes such a difference helping new readers to discover one of my books for the first time.

I love hearing from my readers directly too – you can get in touch on my Facebook page, through Twitter, Goodreads or my website.

You can read on to learn a little more about the true story that inspired this novel, as well as the complete 'Call of the Swallows' story.

Thanks,
Suzanne Kelman

 suzkelman

 @suzkelman

 www.suzannekelmanauthor.com

The Inspiration for
When We Were Brave

While doing Resistance research for my previous book, *A View Across the Rooftops*, I came across an astounding story that stopped me in my tracks. It outlined how, in 1943, a Resistance cell called Physician or Prosper Network in the French section of SOE was infiltrated by the Germans. This resulted in hundreds of Resistance fighters being rounded up by the Gestapo, with eighty of them losing their lives, many of them dying in concentration camps.

One of the theories for this was that a mole or a double agent compromised the network. This concept was difficult enough to contemplate. But there was also another theory that the British government had sacrificed the spies to save the location of the D-Day landings. That theory, that is unproven, is that knowing one of the agents was compromised, the British government willingly sent falsified information to deceive the enemy. Whether that theory is true or not, it made me realise just how important preserving the site of the invasion was and how crucial that was for the success of that campaign.

As I started to do some more digging, I began to uncover all of the incredible deceptions that were created to preserve the location of the D-Day landings. Codenamed Operation Fortitude, the deceptions were elaborate, from the illusionist commissioned to create fake ships in the Thames to the staged army encampments set up in Scotland. All were devised as a ruse to fool the enemy pilots taking photographs on reconnaissance missions who were reporting on the Allies' activities.

On reading all of this, I felt compelled to write a story from the point of view of one of those young spies in the Prosper Network who would have been undercover during that time in the midst of people being rounded up. There must have been a lot of confusion, a lot of guilt and a lack of understanding of why everything was going so wrong. Alongside the historical backdrop of the war in Europe, I also wanted to create a contemporary character living through her own pain and guilt. I desired to try to find a way for the heroics of the past to reach forward into her life, encouraging her through her own personal trauma, and this is where the story, *When We Were Brave*, originated.

As I started to breathe life into it, I have pondered many times what kind of person became a spy and what we can learn from the devotion and bravery of what is still called the greatest generation. I also wondered about the many heroic people who worked within the Resistance whose stories, for whatever reason, have not been recognised. How their quiet determination worked to ensure the Allies invasion was successful.

I hope that when you finish this story, you will take some time to consider not only the brave men who raced on to the beaches of Normandy that day in June 1944, many of them to their death, but also the many people who sacrificed their lives in a quiet way, not unlike the eighty spies of Prosper, in the pursuit of our freedom. I also hope it gives you, as it did me, a new appreciation for the real cost of that freedom and the chance it gave us to have an ongoing hope for our future.

Acknowledgements

Whenever I'm in the midst of writing a book, particularly in the latter stages, clothes go unwashed, food goes uncooked, and let's not talk about the bathroom. I'm so grateful to have two men in my life who truly support the work I do.

To my husband Matthew, the light of my life, who sat by my side as my historian, as together we tried to fathom out the coding of World War Two spies, and who answered questions like, 'Was there a bomb we can use in the Paris area in late spring 1943?' I am so grateful for your patience, kindness and incredible knowledge of this era. Thank you, darling, as always, you are my rock and supporter, and every day with you is fun even when we are knee-deep in British espionage.

Also, to the other man in my life, my wonderful son Christopher, who on the third straight day of sandwiches for dinner, quietly did all the washing, without me even knowing till I pressed send on my manuscript.

To my amazing friends who are closer to me than family. They love me for who I am, support me no matter what and are always there for me.

Firstly, to my best friend, Melinda Mack, who not only turns up to all my readings but also supports me emotionally when I'm hitting those heavy deadline days. Thank you for always being there to reach out to, and for just messaging me and asking if you can swing by and drop off a latte. You are indeed a special friend, and I'm so grateful for you in my life.

Also to Kim Weatherall, Shauna Buchet, Eric Mulholland and K.J. Waters. All of you are so special to me, and I'm so grateful for the light and love you bring to me every day. I am indeed fortunate in this world.

To my personal working team, my agent Andrea Hurst and my editor Audrey Mackaman. I so appreciate you both.

Lastly, but not least, I want to thank my amazing Bookouture team. You are a fantastic publisher, and I feel so grateful to be doing what I love with an incredibly supportive and visionary team as yourselves. To my excellent editor, Isobel Akenhead, thank you for always encouraging me to the edge, supporting me to find the depth that is possible, and then making my words sound beautiful as well. I am genuinely in awe of your ability and feel very privileged to have you as my editor.

Also, to Oliver Rhodes, Peta Nightingale, Alexandra Holmes, Lauren Finger, Kim Nash and Noelle Holten, thank you all for your support.

And to you the reader, thank you for coming on this journey with me in this shared act of storytelling, the dance between the writer and the reader. I appreciate every one of you, and I am thankful every day.

The Call of the Swallows

In a time gone by, before the world as we know it was properly formed, when it was just an echo of all it would become, it was still malleable to new ideas with the promise of hope.

Nothing was set in stone. No jagged rocks had formed the mountains. No salty sea surrounded the land. Flowers and fauna were barely whispers on the winds, and the streams were just beginning their circle of life.

At the dawning of time, the birds and the beasts in their infancy trod the dark earth in a brand-new world, which time and age had not yet eroded.

At this awakening there were two separate spheres of the world. The top was the land of darkness and was ruled by King Jerakar with an iron fist. He ruled over the forgotten things of the universe, the horned and tailed creatures, the unspeakables, the goblins and the elves, all of the night creatures, and all those who slithered or crawled.

At the southern end, another king ruled, who was of a completely different nature. He ruled with love and kindness, beauty and poetry. In this land of light there lived the water sprites and the fairy people, the dragons and the unicorns, all the gentle creatures of fur and feather. All these beings flocked to live in that southern half, drawn into the brightness by the magic of King Wassur.

Both kingdoms had great fear of the other, so separating the two worlds was a forbidden forest that no one dared enter, and for many years the two worlds lived in harmony as long as the twain did not meet, as long as no one crossed over into the other land.

As time came to pass, the King of the South had a daughter, Apheria, who grew to be the most beautiful woman in the southern world. She had long tresses of golden hair that cascaded down her back to her feet, eyes of the brightest blue, and skin as white as alabaster.

As she became of marriageable age, King Wassur of the South had concerns that someone would take advantage of such a beautiful young woman, so to keep her safe, he hid her deep away in a magical glade, on the edge of the forbidden forest. Safely tucked away until the king could find a suitable suitor for her. But Apheria became bored of the glade and was of an adventurous spirit. She knew she should obey her father, but something deeper inside called to her.

In the midst of the day she would hear the songs of her favourite birds, the swallows, their tiny voices on the wind like a cascade of miniature bells. *Apheria, come, come out to the fields, to the woods, to the streams.* When she heard this call, she would make her way out to the very edges of the forest so she could smell the earth, run her hands through the cool water, and see the sky beyond the canopy of trees. She would lie in the grass and look up at the clouds and make wishes. Apheria would also collect flowers and ferns, stone and bark to decorate her glade.

One day, she found herself being drawn farther and farther away from the glade until she was closer to the edge of the forbidden forest than she'd ever been before, a hairsbreadth from the world of the North. Apheria knew it was dangerous to be so close to the darkened world that lived above her, but having never seen it before, she was drawn by the inky blackness, mesmerised by the fullness of the moon and the scent of the night blossom that ran along that border to entice her.

What she did not realise was that King Jerakar of the North had a son, who was the same age as Apheria. His name was Josiah, and he had been heartsick for a wife for a long time. That very night he was out by himself, walking with the knowledge that in the whole of his dark kingdom there was no one for him to love.

But by the light of the moon he saw Apheria picking blossoms along the edge of the forest. And as he watched her, bathed in moonlight as she tripped along the border of the middle kingdom, he fell in love instantly.

For twenty-one days and twenty-one nights, he wooed her, bringing all manner of gifts from the darkness that she had not seen before to delight her. He played music to her, told her stories, and slowly, she, too, fell in love.

One day, word came from King Wassur of the South that he had a potential husband for his daughter. Apheria became heartsick and so Josiah came up with a plan. He kidnapped her from her world and drew her into his own to be his wife. She was thrilled to marry the man she loved, but the darkness of the world overwhelmed her. She was a creature of the light, a creature of the day. For on the south end, the sun was always high and it was always summer, whereas on the north end, it was always dark and it was winter.

Day after day, Apheria's inner light started to wane, her bright eyes became dim, and she became depressed, as she missed the light of the sun. So Prince Josiah came up with another plan. Taking a lasso, he harnessed the sun from the south and pulled it to the north and the kingdom was filled with light. And as it warmed the world, Apheria started to come to life again. But the creatures of the northern land were night creatures, of the cold and the dark, and they couldn't tolerate the heat of the sun, and all in that land began to dry up and die under its relentless heat.

In the Southern Kingdom, the creatures of the light also suffered. Eventually, the swallows that lived in the Southern Kingdom couldn't tolerate the cold and darkness and flew to follow the sun to the north.

When the swallows arrived, they called to Apheria, and she was so happy to see the birds she adored from her land. But when they reported to Apheria that her father's kingdom was suffering without the sun to keep it warm, her heart was broken. Without the heat of the sun, they told her, the crops were failing and the beings of her kingdom were dying.

She realised that neither kingdom could live as the other, so she begged her husband to release the sun so both kingdoms could survive. And with the sun she sent the swallows to send messages of love to her family and the creatures of the South.

However, day after day in the land of the darkness, Apheria became ill, growing sicker and sicker, so sick that even being in the middle of the earth in the forbidden forest was not enough to rouse her. She needed the full light of her kingdom to survive.

Prince Josiah, so in love with her and heartsick from her illness, decided to bring back the sun and cared nothing of the cost to his own land, caring only for her, and willing to bear anything in order to make her well.

But when Apheria heard of his plan, she realised that his love for her had caused a kind of madness in him, an overwhelming desire to be with her at the cost of them all. And she decided with a heavy heart they could never be together. For the greater good of their world she knew she would have to be the brave one.

As Josiah set back out to harness the sun, Apheria pressed into her breast a silver dagger, knowing she had to die to save both kingdoms. And as she died in his arms, he realised she had sacrificed herself to save them all and his heart was broken.

After Apheria died, King Wassur and the King Jerakar were united in their grief, the King of the South with the loss of his daughter and the King of the North with the sadness in his son. And in honour of Apheria's sacrifice, each decided to grieve her for six months of every year. So, for six months of the year the sun would remain in the South and both kingdoms would flourish, but for the other six months of the year the sun would be harnessed and brought to the North, so both kingdoms could suffer and grieve.

And in order to never forget what she had done, the swallows were commissioned to follow the sun on its journey, and they would call out to each kingdom in turn the story of Apheria's bravery and the sacrifice she had made for their world.

Made in the USA
Coppell, TX
21 July 2020

31425056R10187